The Far Bank

THE OLTRARNO PASSAGES
BOOK TWO

MICHAEL MANOSCA

Visit the author's website at www.michaelmanosca.com

The Far Bank

The Oltrarno Passages - Book 2

ISBN:

978-1-969915-17-8 (paperback)

978-1-969915-18-5 (electronic)

978-1-969915-16-1 (hardcover)

Library of Congress Control Number: 2026912242

First Edition.

Los Angeles, California, United States of America

"To course o'er better waters now hoists sail
the little bark of my wit,
leaving behind her a sea so cruel."

— Dante Alighieri, *Purgatorio* (14th century, Florentine)

"PEPPERO-THINGIES ARE THE BEST PART."

The Fore Street Deli was a go-to for Kieran and Pat — three, sometimes four times a week, the only exception being if they caught a Friday shift. Then it was Sal's on Cumberland. Pat had once threatened to file a union grievance when dispatch tried to send them across town at eleven forty-five on a Friday. She hadn't been serious. Probably.

Their last run had been a simple transport from an elementary school — a kid who'd decided he was the next great high-wire walker and tried to cross *on top of* the swing set. He learned a short lesson from Isaac Newton, found out exactly how gravity worked, and had the broken arm to prove it.

Kieran had seen the little tough guy trying not to cry in front of his friends, all of whom had gathered around in that wide-eyed ring kids made when something went wrong and nobody knew what to do about it. Some older lady — the principal, he assumed — was already talking a mile a minute to Pat by the time they'd wheeled the stretcher across the playground. Pat was better at that part. Paperwork. Principals. Insurance company bullshit. Kieran preferred to help people, not document them.

He'd knelt down and positioned himself between the boy and the crowd, blocking the view. Couldn't have been more than ten, but he was fighting the tears like his reputation depended on it — which, at that age, it did. Kieran had seen enough of this in the couple of years since he'd started the job. He'd wanted to be a psychologist. Or a psychiatrist — he could never remember which one needed the extra degree. But there wasn't enough money, and he was itching to get out into the world. So right after high school, he'd started his EMT training and worked his way toward his paramedic certification. In those few years, he'd dealt with enough broken bones from falls, and the occasional acrobatic ambition on playground equipment to know that the injury was usually less frightening than the audience.

"Hang in there, buddy," he'd said, kneeling close enough that the boy could focus on his face instead of the thirty kids staring. The boy was frightened — Kieran could see it in the way his chin kept quivering even as he set his jaw against it. "Hey. Why did the skeleton go to the doctor alone?" The boy looked at him, tears suspended, and shook his head. "Because he had *no body* to go with him."

Kieran gave him the look — eyebrows up, waiting. The boy groaned, but the giggle came anyway, and that half-second of distraction was all Kieran needed to stabilize the arm and get him ready for transport to Maine Medical. Pat handled the school nurse, the principal, the concerned parent who arrived with her coat inside out. Kieran wanted to make sure the little daredevil wasn't too scared on the way over. In the ambulance, the boy had asked if his arm would be bionic after they fixed it. Kieran told him absolutely, but only if he ate his vegetables. The boy said that was a pretty steep price. Kieran agreed. They shook on it — left-handed.

"Pepperoncini?" Pat asked, like he was a dumbass.

"Yeah. Those things. They're the best." Kieran wasn't looking up from the counter where Liz — the manager, the usual server, and the only person in Portland who understood the architectural complexity of his sandwich — was building his monstrosity. "More, please."

"You're such a little boy," Pat laughed.

He didn't argue. He liked what he liked.

This was standard operating procedure. Pat would stand at the counter studying the board like she'd never seen it before, squinting up at the specials as though the menu might have transformed overnight into something entirely new. It never did. Kieran knew what he wanted before they'd even said the word *lunch.* Pat wouldn't bother asking where to go when she drove — she'd just pull into the lot and climb out of the ambulance.

"Hold up!" she'd yell, every single time. "I'm gettin' too old and fat to keep up with your carrot top."

"You're not even thirty!"

"Yeah, well. I keep this up and I'll be fifty before I know it."

It was a game. They both knew their parts, and the routine had calcified into something neither of them would dream of altering. It had started the day Kieran was assigned to work with her — she'd looked him up and down with an expression that suggested she'd been hoping for someone taller, or at least someone who could reach the top shelf without standing on the bumper. He wasn't one to assume, but he suspected she was a lesbian. Steel-toed boots even on days off. Put a black leather jacket on her and she'd fit right in with a biker gang. And while she wasn't tall — though he wasn't about to say so — she looked like she could kick your ass without putting down her coffee.

Kieran watched her deliberate over the menu board. He knew what would happen. She'd fuss and change her ingredients five times before Liz behind the counter would simply wrap whatever she'd assembled and slide it across without comment. Kieran was sure she'd seen it all before. Liz had to have been making sandwiches for people who couldn't make up their minds since long before Kieran was born.

He wasn't any taller than Pat, actually. Probably an inch shorter without his boots, though he'd never admit it and she'd never ask, because some questions were better left between a man and his shoe inserts. He could hold his own.

Growing up the middle son in an Irish Catholic house, you learned to take a hit. Sean — older, broader, built like a Patriots lineman though he wound up working as one for the electric company — had played hard and expected Kieran to keep up. Kieran may not have won many of those, but he'd made Sean earn it. Danny, his little brother, was already taller than him and had more confidence than Sean and Kieran put together — but he was the one who came down the hall at night to talk about the things neither of them trusted with anyone else. Their father, Patrick, had long since stopped coming home.

Inside, though, Kieran knew he was a teddy bear. He loved making people smile, especially when life turned to shit. Which it always did. At least in his line of work. He'd ended up in a job that delivered on that truth with consistency. Nobody ever called an ambulance just to say hello.

"You gonna stand there and stare off into space like a dumbass, or do I need to check your blood sugar?" Pat said as she passed him to claim their usual table by the window — the one with the wobbly leg that she'd been complaining about for six months and Liz had been ignoring for seven.

"Just imagining a world without your wit."

"It'd be a sad, sad day." She slid a handful of napkins across the table.

"I only need one, Jeez."

"You say that every time. And every time you end up with goop on your chin."

"It's not goop. It's the peppero-thingees juice."

"It's goop, Callahan."

This was another of their routines — the napkin game. Pat always won. She'd already pulled at least a dozen from the dispenser, the same dispenser she restocked herself once when Liz was in the back and didn't notice. Kieran had made the mistake of riding in Pat's personal car exactly twice. Both times he'd had to excavate the passenger seat from under a geological layer of napkins, receipts, empty coffee cups, and what appeared to be an entire season's worth of Dunkin' Donuts wrappers. He still didn't understand how she fit inside it.

Kieran savoring his peppero-thingees, Pat already second-guessing the changes she'd ordered — when their radios squawked.

"Medic 4, Medic 4 — priority one, 27-Delta, active shooter, injuries reported, 314 Forest Avenue, Glickman Library, USM Portland campus. Stage for police clearance. Tac-2."

The deli went quiet for half a second — just Liz looking up from the counter, her hand frozen mid-wipe — before Kieran was already reaching for his jacket.

"Medic 4, copy. En route." He looked at Pat. "Jesus. What happened?"

Pat was already moving, sandwich abandoned, her face shifted into something Kieran rarely saw. She never looked concerned — not outwardly, not in front of him. She'd told him once that the day she let him see her worried was the day he should worry. But this was an active shooter. 27-Delta. Injuries reported at a university library on a Thursday afternoon.

Something bad had happened.

Pat drove them up Forest Avenue as several other units converged from both directions. Police must have swarmed the scene the moment the call came through — the university library was surrounded by a sea of strobing red and blue, cruisers angled across the road, yellow tape already going up. A cop waved them off Forest, around to Bedford, and up the narrow service path that led to the building's side entrance.

Kieran felt the shift happen — the thing his training had drilled into him until it became automatic. The deli, the sandwich, the napkins, the kid on the swing set — all of it dropped away. His vision narrowed. His breathing slowed. Everything that wasn't the job stopped mattering.

"Medic 4, on scene," Pat radioed.

They grabbed the jump bag and followed a pair of officers through the entrance and into an elevator. Pat was talking to their escort — a young cop who'd been on scene early enough to know more than the dispatch had given them. His voice was controlled, professional, but his hands were shaking. Kieran noticed. He always noticed hands.

He'd been to plenty of bad calls before. Car crashes on the highway with traffic screaming past at seventy. A house fire where he'd worked on a man they'd pulled from the building while the crews were still fighting the blaze behind them, embers drifting down like snow. But this was different. SWAT was here. Helicopters above. Officers in tactical gear clearing rooms on a floor he could hear through the elevator walls — the sound of a building being taken apart room by room.

He set it aside. All of it. That was the training. Not courage — just focus. The ability to make the world small enough to hold.

The elevator opened and they followed the officer around a corner. Bookshelves. Study tables. Chairs overturned. And a young man on the floor in front of a table near the railing, lying on his back in a way that suggested he'd been standing when it happened — surprised, maybe. Turning toward something he'd seen or heard.

"We just found him while we were sweeping the building," an officer said.

Kieran was already kneeling. Breathing? Yes — shallow, labored. Conscious? His eyes were open, looking up, struggling to focus. Young — mid-twenties, maybe. Close to Kieran's own age. That registered somewhere and was immediately filed away.

"We're here. Can you speak?" Kieran asked as Pat knelt on the other side and began cutting the man's shirt, exposing his chest.

Kieran's eyes moved fast. Two wounds. One on the upper chest, just left of center — the skin around it already pulling with each breath. The other lower, in the abdomen, bleeding freely.

"We're going to roll you carefully," he said. His gloved hands worked alongside Pat's to check for exit wounds. The man moaned — a sound Kieran heard as a good sign, because it meant he was still present enough to feel pain. They eased him back.

"Open pneumo — I need a chest seal." He said it fast, already reaching into the bag. He tore the package, peeled the Halo seal, and placed it over the upper wound, pressing the edges flat. The sucking sound — that wet, rhythmic pull of air through a hole that shouldn't exist — changed. Sealed.

Pat placed the leads and clipped the pulse ox onto the man's finger. "He's tachy — one-forty and climbing."

Kieran pulled the QuikClot gauze from the bag and leaned in to pack the abdominal wound. His hands worked steadily — apply, press, hold. But his other hand, the one not packed with gauze, found the man's without deciding to. It just happened. The way it sometimes did.

He looked directly into the man's eyes. "Stay awake for me, okay? I'm right here."

The man's fingers tightened slightly around his. He tried to speak — his lips moved, formed something that might have been a word or might have been nothing — but Kieran needed him focused, not talking.

"Just hang in there. Stay with me."

Pat began positioning the backboard. They moved him onto the cot — smooth, practiced motion. Straps were quickly tightened before rolling him to the elevator and out to the rig, past officers who stepped aside without being asked, past the yellow tape, past the growing crowd on the sidewalk that Kieran didn't look at.

Pat helped Kieran secure the cot in the back.

"I need a second line," Kieran said as Pat prepared the TXA drip. He placed the O2 mask over the man's face and found his eyes again — still there, still looking, though the focus was drifting. "Just breathe. Stay with me." The man was hovering somewhere at the edge, and Kieran could feel him slipping.

Pat jumped up front and pulled out. The siren opened up above them.

"Pressure's low, but he's compensating," Kieran called through the partition, his fingers on the man's wrist, feeling the pulse — fast, thready, but present.

"Medic 4 to Cumberland Comm — en route Maine Med, one priority one, adult male, GSW, packaged. ETA seven minutes."

"Medic 4, copy. Maine Med advised."

Kieran took the man's hand again. He didn't have to. No training manual mentioned it. But somewhere in his first year, on a call he couldn't even remember the details of anymore, he'd learned that a hand was the last thing people let go of.

"Stay with me," he said.

The man squeezed back. But the grip was going weak.

"Don't close your eyes."

The man's eyes were dimming — that slow retreat Kieran had seen before, the light pulling back rather than going out.

"What's our ETA?" he called up to Pat.

"Five."

Five minutes. Kieran held the hand. Watched the face. Counted the breaths.

Maine Medical came into view through the back window. Pat pulled the rig to a stop and Kieran began prepping for transfer — disconnecting the monitor leads from their mounts, adjusting the O2 line for mobility. The back doors swung open and Pat was already pulling the cot while Kieran came around to meet her, falling into step on the other side.

The moment they came through the automatic doors, the trauma team was moving toward them. He began his report, his voice level and precise — the voice that didn't sound like his:

"Adult male, approximate mid-twenties, two GSWs — one upper left chest, one lower abdomen. Open pneumo on the chest, sealed with a Halo. Abdominal wound packed with QuikClot, pressure held in transport. Tachy at one-forty on scene, current rate one-twenty-eight. Pressure low — eighty over fifty, compensating. Two large-bore IVs, TXA running, O2 via non-rebreather. GCS was fourteen on scene, down to twelve in transport. He's been conscious throughout — responsiveness declining last two minutes."

At the trauma bay, the team leader called out: "On my count — one, two, three." The team lifted him across in one motion, and the man was theirs.

"We've got him."

Kieran looked once more at the man's eyes. They were barely open now, the lids heavy, the irises moving slowly like someone trying to find a face in a crowd. Then a nurse stepped between them, and the curtain began to close, and Kieran felt Pat's hand on his arm.

"Cot's clear."

Kieran nodded and turned away. He pulled his gloves off — the snap of latex, the sudden cool air on his skin — and followed Pat back down the corridor toward the ambulance bay. His hands were steady. They always were, during. It was after that they sometimes weren't.

As he passed an officer standing near the intake desk — one of the cops who'd followed the ambulance in — Kieran noticed he was holding a book bag, a set of headphones, and an iPhone. Personal effects. The things a person carried into a library on an ordinary Thursday afternoon, expecting to carry them back out again.

Just as Kieran walked past, the screen lit up. A message.

From Eli.

Chapter Two

THE WEATHER HAD BEEN unpredictable lately. Seventies not two days ago — one of those false springs that tricked everyone into leaving their jackets in the car — and then a freeze warning with a chance of snow issued last night, because Maine had apparently decided that April was just winter with better marketing. Eli looked out from his desk on the second floor of the office building, down at his white Volvo sitting in the lot below, and felt something close to prepared.

He still couldn't quite believe he owned it. A 2023 XC60, white, immaculate. Graham had signed the title over as if giving someone a Volvo were simply the practical thing to do. Which, knowing Graham, it was. Eli had argued. Graham had waited for him to finish arguing and then handed him the keys.

Better than sitting at that bus stop in the snow tonight. Which reminded him — he needed to stop and pick up something for dinner on the way home. They were almost out of everything, and the idea of Niles braving the chaos of a grocery store was enough to make him smile. Niles, who was currently perfecting a humanoid robot in the corner of their living room — a machine that could theoretically walk, gesture, and respond to voice commands — but couldn't navigate the chips and crackers aisle at Hannaford.

So Niles. He smiled again.

His corporate messaging app pinged. Reception.

He wondered if he had a package downstairs. He couldn't remember where his last Amazon order was being shipped — the apartment or the office. He'd started having things delivered to work because the front door of the building didn't lock properly and someone on the second floor had lost three packages in November. Derek blamed the UPS driver. Claire blamed the building. Eli blamed the lock, which had been broken since before he moved in and would be broken long after he moved out.

Eli, you have a visitor.

Visitor. That was odd. In the three years he'd worked here, he couldn't remember having a visitor. Niles had never come by. Graham had picked him up out front a few times, but he'd always texted from the car. Nobody visited.

On my way, he typed, and got up from his desk. He walked through the sea of cubicles and office plants — the plants were Sandra's project; she'd declared the office "spiritually dead" in January and had been waging a one-woman campaign of ferns and succulents ever since — and took the stairs instead of waiting for the elevator, which had been moving at a speed that suggested it, too, was spiritually dead.

As he walked down into the lobby, he saw Graham.

Standing by the front desk. Still in his coat. Holding his hat in both hands, the way he did when he didn't know what to do with them. Looking at Eli with eyes that didn't move.

Eli paused on the second-to-last step.

He'd known Graham long enough to read him. Could read him across a noisy restaurant, across a crowded room, across the front seat of a car in the dark. Something terrible had happened. And Graham had driven here to tell him in person.

Eli took the final two steps. He watched his own feet on the stairs — the industrial carpet, the scuff marks from a thousand shoes — and then he reached the ground floor and looked up and found Graham's eyes again. The small tear in the corner of his left eye. Frozen there, half-formed.

Niles.

Eli hadn't bothered putting his hearing aids in for two days. Why bother, he thought. There was nothing to say, so no reason to try and hear it.

He looked up from the sofa to see Claire waving at him from the kitchen doorway. He pointed to his ears — the universal gesture — and she nodded with the expression of someone navigating a room full of things that might shatter. She disappeared and came back with a scrap of paper, kneeling beside the couch to hand it to him.

> I'm heading out tonight to Justin's. Text me if you need anything.

He nodded. A small wave was all she got. He hadn't had the heart to tell her or Derek what had happened when Graham brought him home Thursday. Everything was a blur. His car was still parked at the office. Had he even eaten? He couldn't remember. It didn't matter.

Derek and Claire must have found out from the news — it had been everywhere, the kind of story that led every broadcast and filled every feed for days before the cycle moved on to something else. Eli hadn't turned on the TV. Hadn't bothered to shower. He couldn't. Not yet. All of Niles's things were still in the bathroom — his shampoo on the shower shelf, his razor on the edge of the sink, the particular way he folded his towel into thirds because he'd read somewhere that it dried more efficiently that way. Still in the bedroom, too. His textbooks stacked on the nightstand. His engineering notes in a neat pile on the desk. The charger cord plugged into the wall, still waiting.

Eli had taken his own pillow and fallen onto the sofa Thursday night. Not crying. Not sobbing the loss of someone he had never expected to find. No great reflection on the cruelty of the universe or the unfairness of a world that would take Niles Ashworth from it. Just.

Nothing.

Derek and Claire moved around the apartment like they might break something. Tiptoeing past the sofa, speaking in low voices he couldn't hear even when he was wearing his aids. He didn't care. Sometimes being deaf helped. Took away his having to deal with the rest of it — the platitudes, the well-meaning questions that had no good answers. No *sorry for your loss.* No *anything I can do.* No *he's in a better place.*

His pocket buzzed and he pulled out his phone. There were more unread messages than he'd normally leave — Eli usually responded within minutes. He hated the sight of notification badges piling up. But what was he going to do — copy and paste *thanks for reaching out* to everyone? *I'll be okay* over and over again?

He scrolled through them. A couple from Graham — gentle, unhurried, expecting nothing back. One from Anthony, short and practical, saying he was available if Eli needed anything at all and to call at any hour. Even Michael, all the way out in Nashville, had sent something — and that one surprised him, because Michael was eighteen and barely knew Niles, but the message was simple and direct and didn't try to fix anything.

But Eli opened the one from Levi.

LEVI

I know what it's like to feel alone but not this way

I wish I was older and knew better what to say

I love you. 🩶

Eli read it twice. His eyes pressed shut. His jaw tightened. He threw the phone back onto the sofa and turned toward the window — but something caught his eye. In the far corner by the bookcase, half-hidden behind a stack of textbooks Niles had been meaning to return: the robot. The half-finished humanoid project, the one Niles had been most excited about. Wires trailing from one shoulder. A servo motor exposed in the chest cavity. One hand completed, the other still skeletal — just the aluminum frame, the fingers articulated but unfinished, reaching for something it would never hold.

Niles could barely respond if you asked how he was feeling. Could sit through an entire dinner with people and contribute maybe six words, all of them carefully chosen and none of them revealing. But ask about that robot and he'd talk your ear off. He'd light up — genuinely, visibly — and explain the servo calibration, the weight distribution problems, the breakthrough he'd had with the ankle joints. He'd talk for twenty minutes without pausing and then stop, suddenly self-conscious, and say, "Sorry. I'm doing it again." And Eli would say, "Don't stop." And mean it.

Eli wanted to cry. Wanted it badly. Wanted to do what they did in the movies — have some great climactic moment, cry out loud, yell at the sky about how unfair it all was. Why Niles? He never did anything to anyone. He was the kindest, quietest, most invisible soul Eli had ever known, and someone had shot him in a library because — because what? Because he was there? Because he was studying? Because the world had decided that this particular Thursday afternoon, Niles Ashworth's life would end?

But the tears wouldn't come. They'd come later, or they wouldn't, and he had no control over which.

He rolled back on the sofa and stared at the ceiling — a crack he'd never noticed ran from the light fixture to the corner, a faint line in the plaster that looked like it had been there for years — before picking up his phone and hitting reply.

There's nothing you could say that you haven't already no matter how old you are Levi

love you too.

He hit send and put the phone down and took a breath. It was the first message he'd responded to since Graham brought him home Thursday. He thought about texting Donna, then decided against it. What could he offer her? He couldn't imagine what she and Brett were going through — then he called bullshit on himself. Of course he could. He was going through it too. The difference was that Donna's grief had a name. Mother. Everyone understood that. Everyone knew what to say to a mother. Nobody knew what to say to the boyfriend who wasn't a husband, who wasn't a fiancé, who wasn't anything the world had a word for.

His stomach growled, which made him feel like a traitor. He was alive. He needed to eat. Unlike Niles. It was Saturday evening. He had been planning to take Niles out tonight — somewhere quiet, away from the pressure of finals, where they could sit across from each other and Niles could order the same thing he always ordered and Eli could pretend to study the menu even though he always got the same thing too, and they'd eat and not talk very much and that would be enough. Just the two of them.

Now it was just him.

He finally got up and walked into the bathroom. God, he looked like shit. He stared at himself in the mirror — the dark hollows under his eyes, the stubble he hadn't dealt with, the general appearance of a man who had been lying on a sofa for two days and looked exactly like it. Niles would be annoyed with him, all mopey like this. Niles, who had spent his entire life quietly enduring things that would have broken most people and never once asked for sympathy. Was that what Eli wanted? Pity? No. He just wanted — he didn't know. For it to go away. To not have to deal with it or accept it or understand it or whatever came next.

He reached over and turned on the shower, but caught sight of Niles's toothbrush propped in the glass by the sink. Niles had never laid it down like a normal person — always stood it upright in the glass, like a soldier at attention. Eli had made fun of it once. *Why not just lay it on the side like mine?*

"Nope. It's statistically better to allow airflow and prevent bacterial growth among the bristles this way," Niles had said. Completely serious. As if toothbrush orientation were a matter of scientific rigor, which, for Niles, it was.

Eli remembered standing in this exact spot, so taken with the logic and the gravity with which Niles delivered it that he'd leaned over and kissed him right then and there. Which made Niles go red immediately — the way he always did, the flush climbing from his collar to his ears in a slow wave that Eli had come to love more than he'd ever told him. Then Eli had started working at Niles's buttons, which only made it worse, and pulled him into the shower until Niles stopped being flustered and started being something else entirely. That had been the first time.

He forced his attention from the toothbrush and stepped into the shower.

This time, *without Niles.*

Eli sat at his desk on the second floor, overlooking the parking lot at his office, staring at his car. Simon's car, technically — the car Graham had given him, the car that had belonged to a man who died on a plane and whose husband couldn't bear to look at it sitting in the driveway. Now it was Eli's. A gift from grief, sitting in a parking lot, waiting to carry him through more.

He wasn't sure why he'd come in today. Force of habit, maybe. Or maybe because he was tired of lying on the sofa staring at the ceiling and its crack and the robot in the corner and the toothbrush he still hadn't moved. This wasn't like him. Nothing was like him anymore. Nothing was like it was.

Before.

He'd already burned through a couple of vacation days, and he had enough banked to take more. But what was the point? So he could spend more hours doing what? Missing Niles. No — that wasn't the right word for it. He'd been thinking about that for days now. What had he and Niles been, exactly? They weren't married. That had still been somewhere far off in the distance, barely a thought. They were still new at this quiet little game of house they'd been playing.

Had they been playing? Or was it more?

He wanted to think so, even if they were still just learning what it meant to share a bathroom and negotiate whose turn it was to buy milk and deal with the specific challenge of living with a person whose emotional vocabulary consisted of approximately seven words, all of them deployed with surgical precision. Niles would have panicked at even a hint of something as permanent as marriage, Eli kept reminding himself. Would have needed months of preparation — spreadsheets, probably, with pros and cons columns and statistical analyses of successful partnerships. But now that he was gone, it was all Eli could think about. What if. Why not. Should he have.

The questions didn't have answers. That was the worst part. Not the grief itself, but the cruelty of being left with a conversation that could never be finished.

So after finally texting Graham back — *I'm here. Sort of.* — he'd driven out to Graham's house for dinner. He'd sat across from him at the dining room table, the one in the kitchen with the window overlooking the woods, pushing food around his plate for the better part of an hour. No appetite for any of it. The chicken could have been cardboard. The salad might as well have been paper. But Graham hadn't pushed him to eat. Hadn't pushed him to talk. Just sat there with him, and somewhere in that quiet, Eli had arrived at two things.

Life was moving with or without him. Try to appreciate what that does to you.

And don't pretend you'll get over it.

Graham knew. Graham had lived inside this exact silence for months before Eli ever met him — before the Whole Foods line where they first met, before the drive in the snow, before any of it. Eli hadn't really understood what Graham had gone through when Simon died. He'd met

Graham months after, when the worst of it had hardened, he supposed. But now he felt like he finally understood something about the shape of it. About Simon.

That he was never coming back. That the missing didn't end. That you just got better at walking with it, the way you got better at walking with a stone in your shoe — not because the stone got smaller, but because your foot changed shape around it.

Graham hadn't said any of that. He hadn't needed to. He'd just sat there, and Eli had understood.

Eli's phone buzzed in his pocket. He stared at his desk and debated whether to look. That was another thing he'd come to appreciate about grief — the sudden influx of people wanting to check in, to see how you were doing, to make sure you knew they were thinking of you. He knew they meant well. He'd probably do the same if it were someone else. But didn't they get it? How was he doing? Not very well, thanks. Should he say that? Probably not. They didn't deserve his anger, and he knew it. He knew a lot of things now, whether he wanted to or not. It was like Niles was finally getting him to learn something — kicking and screaming, the way Eli approached most forms of personal growth.

He still hadn't cried. The funeral wasn't until next Monday. Maybe then.

He looked at his phone.

MOM

> Hi Honey. Been a while. How have you been? Can you believe this weather? Your father and I are still debating driving down to the city, but worried about getting caught in a storm, so we might wait.

His mother. Terry Pelletier and her usual everything-at-once text — the kind she sent every week or two, paragraphs that wandered from weather to family gossip to unsolicited life advice without pausing for breath or punctuation. He sometimes longed for the days before texting, then remembered they had been worse. Growing up, she'd barely learned any sign — a few basics, enough to say *dinner* and *stop that* and *I love you,* though the last one always looked slightly wrong the way she did it. He could hear some of what she said, but often he'd let her talk and pretend to follow, nodding along, reading her face for cues. Except when she asked a question — then he'd have to work backward through whatever she'd been saying and reconstruct the conversation he hadn't actually heard. At least with text, he could scan for anything important.

> Did you see the news about that horrible event down at that library? Tragic. Of course, I'm sure everyone will try and twist it around like they always do. Why can't people realize what they really need is to help those poor people who do these kinds of things, not just come after the rights of good people who just happen to—

Eli stopped reading.

His mother was talking about Niles and didn't know it. Talking about the shooting as if it were a political debate, a cable news segment, something to have opinions about over dinner. She didn't know that the student who died was the person her son had been sleeping beside for months. She didn't know because Eli had never told her. Hadn't wanted to deal with what would follow — the silence, the careful change of subject, the weeks of pretending he'd never said anything.

He'd tried once, back in college. Introduced them to a guy he'd been seeing — a sweet kid who was even picking up a little ASL, who'd practiced fingerspelling Eli's parents' names in the car on the drive up. They'd been polite enough. Asked about his classes, where he was from, the usual. But the dinner felt off — something in the air, some frequency only Eli could detect — and afterward the guy told Eli he felt like they hated him. Eli had tried to reassure him. He knew better. His parents never mentioned the guy again. Never asked about him. Never said his name. And Eli, who had spent his whole life reading the things people chose not to say, understood perfectly what their silence meant.

> Anyway, when you come home next, I promised I'd take you down to the center I volunteer at to meet one of the new staff. She's so lovely and I think she even has a brother who has trouble with his ears like you.

Eli set the phone down.

In the space of a few sentences, his mother had moved from discussing the event in which her son's boyfriend had been killed to setting him up with a woman whose brother was hard of hearing. As if those two things occupied the same universe. As if his life were a series of problems she could solve with introductions and positive thinking and the assumption that what he really needed was a nice girl.

He stopped himself. Pressed it back. Not here. Not at work, where everyone thought he'd been out sick for a few days. Where he'd told people he was getting over something — a cold, maybe, a bug — like he'd taken an antibiotic and was nearly well. No bereavement leave. No explanation. No language for any of it, because the language didn't exist for what he'd lost. There was no word for it. *Boyfriend* was too small. *Partner* was too clinical. *The person I was building a life with who was shot in a library and died before I could say goodbye* didn't fit on a form.

He picked up the phone and read her messages again, for reasons he couldn't entirely explain. Maybe to convince himself he'd misread them. That something in there might have been — he didn't know. Helpful.

No.

Really busy. Little under the weather. I'll be fine.

He hit send and put the phone face down on his desk and looked back out the window at his car. At Simon's car.

Maybe he'd get in it and just drive somewhere. North. Anywhere. Up I-95, past Brunswick, past Bath, keep going. He just wanted to go.

The funeral was still six days away.

Five o'clock came and Eli was in no hurry to move. The parking lot below was emptying out — coats and bags, people heading somewhere. He watched them go and recognized that he hadn't a clue where most of them were headed. They were work friends. They didn't know him, not really. Didn't know about Niles. Didn't know that when they left to return home to their families — to the parent-teacher conference, the school play, the soccer practice — he was returning to an apartment where a toothbrush still stood upright in a glass and a half-finished robot sat in the corner with one hand reaching.

He couldn't. Not yet. Niles wasn't even in the ground yet. And that was what hurt the most — not the absence, exactly, but the limbo. Somewhere in Portland, in some facility he hadn't been told the name of, Niles lay in whatever state the dead are kept before the living decide what to do with them. Not beside Eli in their bed. Not anywhere Eli could reach. He hadn't been able to tell him how much he meant to him. How hard this was. How incredibly unfair it all was. And not a single person around him — not his colleagues packing up their bags, not his boss wishing him well, not his mother texting about the weather — knew.

"Stop. Just stop," Eli told himself. *"This will get you nowhere."* He packed up and left.

He stopped at Whole Foods on the way home — the one near Graham's, the same store where Graham had first offered him a ride in the snow the previous winter. Graham was just down the street. He could turn left, pull into the driveway, sit in that kitchen with the big windows and the woods out back and not say anything and Graham wouldn't need him to. But he couldn't make himself turn. He drove straight on to the apartment instead. He bought food because he knew he needed to eat. That was all it was. Survival, not living. There was a difference, and Niles

— who had spent his life cataloging differences — would have appreciated the distinction.

He caught himself in the rearview mirror at a red light and shook his head. "Do you hear yourself?" Then stopped. *Hear myself.* He looked away. Niles wouldn't have gotten that joke. Neither did Eli. Not anymore.

Inside, he dropped his bag by the door. The robot sat in the corner where he'd left it. He pulled the meatloaf out of the takeout container from the grocery and ate it standing at the kitchen counter. It was food. Nothing else.

Wednesday was the same. Maybe he'd stop by Graham's tomorrow. Maybe not.

Friday was worse. He had the whole weekend ahead of him — two days of nothing, of the apartment and the sofa and the toothbrush and the robot. He'd told his boss that a distant relative had passed and he'd need Monday for the funeral. A vacation day, since he wasn't immediate family. His boss said he was sorry, but at least it wasn't someone close.

"Yeah," was all Eli said.

The robot was still there when he got home that night. He still didn't go to Graham's. He didn't want to sit there looking pitiful. But he didn't want to talk either.

He thought about texting Donna again — he'd tried once and Brett had replied.

DONNA

She's not up for it yet. I'll let her know you reached out.

That had been all. Nothing about the funeral. No mention of what they needed. Not even a sign-off. Eli had understood. He hadn't written back. He wasn't even sure what he was supposed to do at the funeral — only that it was at the Cathedral of the Immaculate Conception, a name he'd had to look up twice because it wouldn't stay in his head.

Brett had texted him a few days ago with the details.

BRETT

Monday, ten o'clock.

Eli had replied saying he'd be there in whatever way they needed. Brett said he appreciated it. Donna wasn't doing well.

He knew the feeling.

Jesus, did he know the feeling.

Chapter Three

MAUREEN CALLAHAN LOOKED up as her son Kieran walked into the kitchen, which today — like most days — was scattered with bits of clothing in various stages of repair. A pair of men's trousers hung over the back of a chair, one leg pinned and waiting. A stack of dress shirts sat folded beside the sewing machine, each with a yellow sticky note marking the alteration: *shorten sleeves, take in sides, replace buttons (use the brass ones).* The kitchen table, which in theory was for eating, hadn't seen a proper meal since sometime around Easter.

Ever since Kieran could remember, she'd been a seamstress — first out of the back room of Petersen's dry cleaners down the street, where the old man let her set up her Singer in exchange for handling his overflow, and then, when Petersen closed during the pandemic, out of the kitchen. She'd carried the Singer home, set it up on the table, and informed the family that meals would now be served around the sewing machine or not at all. Made a few bucks shortening dress lengths, patching old blue jeans, or — especially lately — letting out the waist of men's trousers. Something about the men in Portland getting wider while the women stayed the same, she'd observed more than once. Kieran had learned not to comment on that.

"I can come back, ma," Kieran said upon seeing the state of the table. He worked tomorrow, so this was a once-a-month Friday off and he planned on getting his hair cut. It probably didn't need it, but he liked it short. Always had. Short hair meant less to deal with, less of himself in the mirror that he had to reckon with.

She'd been cutting his hair at this very table since he was able to walk, probably before — sitting in a highchair, he guessed, squirming while she tried to hold his head still. She did okay. Only took a few minutes. Used her good scissors, the ones she didn't let anyone else touch — not the barber's electric clippers, which he'd tried exactly once, at a place on Congress Street that smelled like burnt coffee, where the clippers pulled at his hair and the barber talked the entire time about the Red Sox. Kieran had walked out looking like he'd been in a fight with a lawn mower. His ma hadn't said a word. Just sat him down at the kitchen table the next morning and fixed it.

"No, sit down, I'll clear things." She stood and pushed the sewing machine to one end of the table, gathering the two pairs of jeans she'd been working on and draping them over the back of a chair. These weren't rich people dropping off dry cleaning. These were neighbors who couldn't afford new pants when the old ones got too tight.

The old AM radio she liked to keep on — a beige Panasonic that had been on that shelf since before Kieran could remember, its antenna held at the correct angle by a twist of electrical tape — was spouting out waves of commercials. She reached over and turned it down slightly, though "down" for Maureen still meant clearly audible from every room in the house. Kieran had never figured out whether she actually listened or if the radio was just her way of filling the silence when nobody else was home. Maybe both. His ma had always been more comfortable with noise than quiet.

Kieran took off his shirt and sat in the same kitchen chair his mother had just been using, feeling the warmth still in the seat. The kitchen smelled like the iron she'd been using earlier and, underneath that, something baking — bread, maybe, or one of her soda bread loaves that she made without a recipe and never the same way twice. He wanted to move out, find a place on his own, but there were some things he knew he'd miss. This being one.

Maureen draped a towel around his shoulders and began to run a comb through his hair, her fingers working through a knot at the crown with practiced patience.

"Newsradio 560 WGAN, eleven o'clock. The top story — USM has released the name of the student killed in last week's shooting at the Glickman Library. Twenty-one-year-old Niles Ashworth, a senior electrical engineering student, has been credited with intervening during the incident, an action campus police say likely prevented additional casualties. The suspect remains in custody at Cumberland County Jail. A funeral Mass for Ashworth is scheduled for Monday at the Cathedral of the Immaculate Conception on Cumberland Avenue. Services begin at ten a.m. USM has announced counseling services will be available through the remainder of the semester. In other news—"

"That's such a shame," she said, working the scissors along the back of his neck in small, careful strokes. "This world — I just don't know what's gotten into people."

Kieran didn't say a word. Just looked across the room at the stove — the old gas range that had a burner nobody used because Sean had once left a pot of water boiling until it went dry and scorched the enamel. Their mother had been furious.

They lived in an older house, the only one Kieran had ever known. A two-story on a street of two-stories, with a front porch that sagged slightly on the left side and a chain-link fence around a yard that was more dirt than grass. There wasn't much money — hadn't been since his dad's job went bust before Kieran was born, some construction thing that disappeared with the economy and never came back. Patrick had stopped coming home not long after — gone for good somewhere, the boys never asked where, Maureen never said. It was another reason Kieran hadn't pushed to move out. The mortgage was Maureen's to carry, and she carried it the way she carried everything — without complaint, without asking for help.

His older brother Sean had been seeing his girl since high school, and everyone was just waiting for when they finally got married. Sean had the room at the end of the hall, the biggest one, and his girlfriend stayed over often enough that her shampoo had permanent residency in the bathroom. His younger brother Danny had just turned seventeen and shared the wall with Kieran's room — the one through which Kieran could hear Danny's music, his phone calls, and the silence that meant Danny was awake but not sleeping.

Danny was the primary reason Kieran hadn't moved. Not just the company — though he liked having his brother next door — but the practical matter of Danny's future. Kieran was helping pay for Danny's college fund. Sean had been working as a lineman for CMP since he was nineteen, climbing poles and running cable in weather that would make most people stay home, and working his way up. Kieran had gone the paramedic route. So it was up to Danny to be the first Callahan to go to school. Kieran had made sure of that without ever saying it out loud, the same way he did most things — without expecting anyone to notice.

"Did you know anything about that poor boy?"

Kieran came back from his thoughts. "What boy, ma?"

"The one on the radio. I can't imagine his poor mother, what she must be going through."

Kieran hadn't been paying much attention — or rather, he'd been paying attention to everything except the radio. "Did they say who it was?"

"Honest to Pete, boy. Weren't you paying attention?"

His freckled face went red, which it did at the slightest provocation. He'd always been fair — the kind of Irish complexion that burned in June, peeled in July, and burned again in August, a cycle he'd long since stopped fighting. He used to joke in school that he was the happy leprechaun and had the Irish in him to prove it. The other kids laughed. He'd learned early that if you made the joke first, nobody else needed to.

"Uh — Niles — now, what was it they said?" She stopped, holding her scissors at the angle of a woman trying to remember something she'd only half heard. "Ashland — no — Ash — Ashworthy! That's it."

Niles Ashworthy? His phone said *Eli* when he was leaving the hospital. The screen lighting up, the name appearing, the small bright rectangle in the officer's hands. He wondered if maybe Eli was Niles's brother. Or a friend. Or something.

"Poor kid. At least Monsignor Flaherty will send him into the Good Lord's arms, rest his soul." She crossed herself — forehead, chest, left, right — a motion so practiced it was almost invisible.

Kieran nodded, which was a mistake because his mother was holding scissors.

"You want me to nick you, Kieran Patrick Callahan? Hold still."

"Sorry, ma."

She resumed cutting, and the radio switched to another commercial — something about a mattress sale that promised to change your life, which Kieran doubted — and he sat there in the kitchen chair replaying the events of that Thursday over a week ago. It had bothered him. Couldn't quite shake it off. He'd had a few of those in his years on the job — calls that stayed, that followed him home and sat in the corner of his room like uninvited guests. Usually kids were the hardest to let go of. The little ones who looked up at you with that absolute trust, as if you could fix anything, and sometimes you couldn't.

But this one was different. This one was a year younger than him. Holding his hand, Kieran couldn't help but feel like he was looking at some version of himself — another young guy with his whole life ahead of him who'd gone to a library on a Thursday afternoon and never walked out. Kieran had watched his face in the ambulance, trying to keep him focused, trying to keep him here. The man had tried to speak — his lips moving, forming words that never quite arrived — but Kieran needed him to breathe, not talk.

In the end, he knew it was coming. He could see it in the man's eyes. That look he'd been trained to recognize but had never gotten used to — the slow withdrawal, the tide going out.

Those eyes were what stuck with him. That, and the hand grasping at his like the man was going to be pulled up and away and Kieran was the only anchor he had left. Niles, huh? He wondered where he was from.

What he was studying. Whether anyone was waiting for him to come home that night.

"Where is that mind of yours now? You haven't heard a word I've been saying!" his mother chastised him from somewhere above his right ear.

"Sorry, ma," he said again. "What were you talking about?"

"I was saying that Patty Sullivan's daughter Katie is home from college this weekend. Perhaps you can walk down there and ask her out to dinner?"

His ma did this often — had been doing it since he was in ninth grade, cycling through every eligible girl within a six-block radius. At least Sean kept her occupied with his girlfriend and out of Kieran's hair — well, unless she was cutting it.

"What's so funny, Mr. Callahan? Katie is a lovely girl."

"Not her, ma — it's — never mind."

"Don't you never-mind me, Kieran. You're getting older and need someone to settle down with. Unlike that poor boy who lost his life. Just remember, you never know when the Good Lord is ready for you."

He hated arguing with her. Couldn't do it — couldn't stand up for himself, not with his ma, not about this. She'd look at him with that particular combination of love and disappointment that only Irish Catholic mothers had truly mastered, and whatever argument he'd prepared would dissolve. He knew she meant well. He knew she wanted him happy. But thinking about Niles — she had no idea that was his patient. He never spoke about them to her. Never brought work home in words, even when it came home in everything else. And she never asked. That was their arrangement, unspoken and carefully maintained.

But this time he wanted to. Didn't. But he wanted to. If nothing else, to say, "It was me, ma. I held his hand."

But he couldn't say any of that. Not to her. Not to anyone.

"I have to work tomorrow, ma. I can't go see Katie."

"Well, I'm sure we'll see her at church Sunday, then. Shame. She'd be perfect for you and —"

"Sorry, ma, I gotta run some errands." He shifted in his chair. She was finished clipping his hair — he could tell from the way she'd stepped back to assess, tilting her head the way she did when examining a hemline — and had now moved into things he'd rather not explain.

"Lands sakes, boy." She took the towel from him as he brushed out the stray hairs and pulled on his T-shirt.

"I gotta run, ma." He kissed her cheek and headed out the door.

He didn't know where he was going. But he knew it wasn't down the street to see Katie Sullivan.

Didn't matter. He just needed to move.

He enjoyed being on his bike — a Honda CB300R, used, paid for in cash. Nothing the guys at the station rode. Nothing he had to keep up. It was his own little zone — the engine vibrating through his hands, the road opening up, the world reduced to what was directly ahead. No radio. No dispatch. No one asking him where he was going or why. He loved that bike. His ma worried something fierce about it, naturally — worried about the roads, the cold, the ice, the other drivers, the entire state of Maine and its various threats to her son's survival. But she'd quit saying so after he'd finally mentioned he'd found a good offer on an apartment closer to work. She'd gone quiet for exactly one day before deciding, without discussion, that a motorcycle was a small price to pay for keeping her son under her roof. Kieran had figured as much. That was the trade, and they both knew it.

He rode south on Cottage Road, the houses thinning as the road curved toward the water. Shore Road wound along the edge of Cape Elizabeth, narrow and humped, the ocean appearing and disappearing through breaks in the trees. Mid-fifties. The kind of day that felt fine in a car and borderline hostile on a motorcycle.

He pulled into the lot at Fort Williams Park near Portland Head Light. The lighthouse sat out on its point the way it had for two hundred years, white and patient. Someone had to climb those stairs every day to keep the light going. Kieran liked that thought. Doing the job nobody noticed until you stopped.

He found a spot on the sea wall that wasn't too damp and sat. The ocean was gray-green, restless, the swells coming in at an angle that meant the wind was shifting. But his mind was elsewhere. On that guy. Niles.

He had all sorts of questions — the kind that came at him sideways, usually at night, usually when he was trying to sleep. Did Niles have a girlfriend who was somewhere right now, falling apart? Or maybe a boyfriend? He pushed that thought aside almost as quickly as it arrived. He hated that — the reflex to map his own life onto strangers, to see himself in every young man close to his age, to wonder. Kieran had read somewhere that only a small percentage of people were gay, and from his own experience, he had to agree. Aside from the few he'd met online — careful conversations on apps he kept hidden in a folder on his phone, ones that never went anywhere because he couldn't bring himself to follow through — he didn't know anyone like himself. Not in any real way. Portland was supposed to be progressive, the kind of city where it didn't matter. But it mattered to Maureen Callahan. And what mattered to his ma mattered to him, whether he liked it or not.

Maybe Niles was just a loner student. Maybe his family was hurting, but nobody else. Kieran didn't wish that kind of pain on anyone — didn't wish anyone the specific agony of getting that phone call, of hearing those words — but part of him hoped that Niles had been alone in the way that made this simpler. No girlfriend. No boyfriend. No one sitting on a sofa somewhere staring at a wall. Just his parents, the people whose grief the world already knew how to handle.

After all, Kieran didn't have anyone in his life other than his family. If it had been him on that library floor, the only phone that would light up would be his ma's.

God, he couldn't imagine what it would do to her.

He wondered if Niles felt pain. He hoped not. He'd spent the past week going over every step — the chest seal, the gauze packing, the IV, the hand. Trying to reassure himself he'd done everything right. Trying to let go. Pat had told him long ago that you couldn't relive someone's death — the job was to show up, do the work, and leave it at the door. She'd meant it.

And here he was, sitting on a sea wall in Cape Elizabeth, doing it again.

The next morning, he woke to rain coming down at a fair clip. "Jesus," he muttered, standing at his bedroom window in his boxers, staring out at the street below. The gutter was already running, carrying leaves and trash toward the drain at the corner that had been half-clogged since October. He had to meet Pat in half an hour, and the idea of riding the Honda in this was enough to make him consider calling in — which he would never do, but the thought had a nice shape to it.

"Want me to drop you off?"

Kieran turned to see Danny standing in the doorway in his boxers, holding his teddy bear like he was still six. The bear was missing an eye and had been re-stitched at the neck by their mother at least twice. Danny was seventeen and six feet tall and he still slept with it, a fact that Kieran knew and Sean did not, because some things between brothers were sacred.

"What are you doing up? It's Saturday."

"Couldn't sleep. Heard you getting dressed." Danny rubbed his eyes and yawned — a full-body yawn, the kind that made him look younger than he was — before shuffling in and sitting down on the edge of Kieran's twin bed. The bed creaked. Everything in this house creaked.

"Go back to sleep. It's not even —" He looked over at the clock radio on his nightstand, the same clock radio that had been there since Sean's room, before Sean moved down the hall and Kieran inherited it along with the bed and the dresser and the water stain on the ceiling that looked like Abraham Lincoln if you squinted. "Seven."

"I can drop you off if you want."

"You're not dressed."

Danny disappeared into his room next door — Kieran heard the thump of the dresser drawer, the rustle of clothes, a brief silence that probably meant Danny was checking his phone — and reappeared in last night's jeans and a hoodie that was too big for him in a way that made him look even younger. Kieran's hoodie, actually. He didn't mention it.

They both gave their ma a quick kiss on the cheek as they passed through the kitchen — she was already up, already at the sewing machine, the radio on and the coffee made — and avoided the questions that her raised eyebrow was clearly preparing. Why was Danny awake? Where were they going? Why couldn't her sons sit still for five minutes? They were out the door before she could get to any of it.

Danny had been driving the better part of a year — his learner's permit first, then his license, which Kieran had helped him practice for on Sunday mornings in the parking lot of the church after Mass let out. Sean was always too busy, and their dad — well, he wasn't around to teach anyone anything. Driving was one of many things Kieran had taught Danny without being asked, the same way he'd taught him to tie a tie and throw a punch and change a tire, filling in the gaps their father had left without ever calling them gaps.

This, however, was the first time Danny had volunteered to drive him. Especially at this hour. Especially on a Saturday. Kieran glanced over at his brother, hands on the wheel, squinting through the rain, and wondered if something was up.

"You hear about that guy over at —"

"Yeah." Kieran cut him off. He knew what Danny was thinking about. Or whom.

"Like, what the fuck?" Danny asked, squinting harder as if that would help him see through the rain. The wipers were losing their battle with the windshield — the passenger side blade had a streak in it that Kieran kept meaning to replace and kept forgetting, and the rain was coming down harder than the blades could handle.

Kieran listened. He and Danny could say things to each other they'd never in a million years say in front of their ma. That was the other side of the thin wall between their rooms — the side where you could be honest, where you didn't have to perform the version of yourself that your mother needed you to be.

"I mean, Jesus. Everyone at school is going all batshit crazy. I mean — I don't understand why the fuck that guy —"

"I took him in." Kieran said it quietly, still looking ahead through the rain-soaked windshield.

"What?" Danny looked over quickly — too quickly — then snapped his eyes back to the road.

"Pat and I. We got the call. Took him into Medical."

"Jesus, Kieran. You did?"

"Yeah." He turned to look out the passenger window, at the rain streaming down the glass, at the blurred shapes of houses and parked cars sliding past. "Held his hand as he —"

"Oh fuck, man. That — I can't —"

Kieran hadn't told anyone. Not until now. Not Sean, who wouldn't have known what to do with it. Not Danny, who he told everything else to. Not his ma, who would have cried and prayed and made it about the Good Lord's plan, which was the last thing Kieran needed to hear. It had been sitting in him all week — not growing, exactly, but not shrinking either. Just present. Like a stone he'd swallowed that wouldn't pass. It was work. Work that kept creeping inside, past the door Pat said you were supposed to leave it at.

"I'm so sorry, Kieran. That — that fucking sucks, man. Was he — like — bad?" Danny kept sneaking glances at his big brother while trying to stay on the road, the rain hammering the roof.

Kieran thought about the question. Was he bad? Of course he was. He died, didn't he? But that's not what Danny meant, and Kieran knew it. It was a natural question — the kind people asked because they needed to know if it was quick, if it was painful — and Kieran didn't want to answer it because the answer was yes. Yes, it was bad. Yes, the grip got weaker. Yes, the eyes dimmed. Yes, he was there for all of it.

He didn't respond.

"Are *you* okay, Kierp?"

Kierp. It knocked Kieran out of his head for a moment, the way a hand on your shoulder can pull you back from an edge you didn't realize you were standing on.

When Danny was little — two, maybe three — he couldn't say Kieran's name. The *an* at the end defeated him every time, and what came out instead was *Kierp,* which made no linguistic sense but had its own strange logic, the way children's mispronunciations always do. Nobody knew where the P came from. Danny himself had no memory of it. He'd figured the name out before kindergarten, and *Kierp* had disappeared into the archive of childhood things that fade without ceremony.

Except it hadn't. Not entirely. Every now and then — rarely, and only when it was just the two of them, and only when something was wrong — it would surface. When Danny broke his ankle in eighth grade and Kieran drove him to the ER, Danny white-faced and gripping the door handle, he'd said it: *It really hurts, Kierp.* When Kieran had his appendix out and Danny came to visit him in the hospital, standing in the doorway looking terrified at the IV and the monitors, he'd said it then too: *You okay, Kierp?*

Now he was saying it again. Not asking about Niles — not Niles the man who'd made the news, not Niles the engineering student turned hero, not Niles the man with gunshot wounds who died holding Kieran's hand, staring into his eyes. Danny was asking about his brother. Kierp.

"I will be." It was all he could say. Because it was true. He wasn't. But he'd get there. Like he always did.

"If — uh — you know — need anything, Kierp — I mean — I can —"

"It's okay, DanDan."

Danny turned to look at his brother — a quick look, startled, his eyes wider than they'd been all morning — with a hint of a smile that he couldn't quite suppress, before turning back to the rainy windshield.

Kieran hadn't called him that since Danny was probably three. Four, maybe. It just came out, the way *Kierp* had come out of Danny — unprompted, unplanned, pulled from some deep well of brotherhood that didn't operate on the level of conscious thought. Maybe because Danny had called him Kierp. Maybe because of something else.

They drove just a moment more — past the gas station on the corner, past the church where Maureen would be on Sunday morning, past the pharmacy where Kieran picked up his ma's prescriptions — before Danny pulled up to the station.

"Take it slow, Danny. Okay?" His brother nodded, uncertain, his hands still tight on the wheel.

Kieran opened the door to the rain, which had thankfully slowed to a gentle shower — the kind that hung in the air more than it fell, misting everything without the commitment of an actual downpour.

"Kieran?"

"Yeah?"

"I, uh — well — I hope you don't —"

"I'll be fine, Danny. Now, go home. It's early still." Kieran gave his brother a look and shut the door.

He didn't bother hurrying to the station door. Walked right past the rig — Medic 4, parked in the bay, washed and restocked and waiting for whatever the day would bring — and paused. The rain fell softly on his jacket. He could smell diesel and wet pavement and coffee from somewhere inside. He couldn't get Niles out of his head.

"Mornin'," Pat grumbled as he came through the door and shook the rain off his jacket. She was leaning against the counter in the break room, already in uniform, a box of doughnuts open beside her — the good kind, from Tony's, not the gas station ones.

"Ready?" She held one out to him.

Kieran took it and mumbled as he chewed on the chocolate glazed. His favorite. But he barely tasted it. He thought about Danny earlier — *Kierp* — and his ma in the kitchen with the radio on and the scissors in her hand. That radio report. The name. The funeral on Monday. He'd need to take some hours off to go, he told himself. He'd mention it to Pat later. She'd give him shit about getting too close to his work — *not healthy, Callahan, we've talked about this* — but she'd let him go. She always did. She understood more than she said, which was the thing about Pat that most people never figured out. Underneath all the gruffness was a woman who'd kept a box of his favorite doughnuts in the break room on a rainy Saturday morning without being asked.

He just mumbled thanks for the doughnut and kept his mouth shut. He'd tell her. He'd need to.

He was off on Sundays.

Chapter Four

ELI SAT in Anthony's Buick — a 2014 LaCrosse, dark charcoal, with leather seats that had softened over the years. Anthony had insisted on driving him to the cathedral. Had told Graham, in the quiet way Anthony told people things that were not up for discussion, that this was his role today. Taking care of Eli. Graham could come along, but Anthony was driving and there would be no debate. Graham, who knew Anthony well enough to recognize a closed door when he saw one, had simply nodded and climbed into the back seat.

Eli had never been in Anthony's car before. He'd seen it — you couldn't miss it, parked in the driveway of a man whose entire aesthetic suggested an earlier, more civilized era. Quintessential old man. Eli had always found it a little funny seeing Anthony behind the wheel, driving along at twenty miles an hour down the street like he had nowhere to be and all day to not get there. Like watching Santa coming back from the grocery store in a Buick. The image had made him smile the first time he'd thought of it, and he'd almost told Niles about it once, and Niles would have said something precise and unexpected about Buick's resale value or the engineering of the LaCrosse transmission, and Eli would have laughed, and that would have been a Tuesday.

But he obeyed. Didn't bother to resist. Didn't have the energy or the desire. He felt relieved, in some ways, that someone had decided things for him — that he didn't have to drive, didn't have to navigate, didn't have to figure out where to park or which door to use or what he was supposed to do when he got there. Anthony had decided. And Anthony, Eli was beginning to understand, had been deciding things for people during the worst moments of their lives for a very long time.

He'd been nothing but kind to Eli ever since that first night when Graham introduced him at the HanukkahChristmaKwanzika party — standing there in his Santa suspenders, white beard perfectly trimmed, pressing a glass of something into Eli's hand and telling him that Graham needed more friends who could keep up with him. That was the night Niles had shown Eli the miniature village he'd built for Sonya and Angie — getting down on his hands and knees to point out the individual windows he'd wired with LEDs, explaining the circuitry with the kind of enthusiasm he reserved for things that didn't require him to make eye contact. Eli had gotten down on the floor with him. Anthony had watched from across the room with a look Eli hadn't understood at the time. He understood it now.

Eli watched houses slide past the window as they made their way to the cathedral. The morning was overcast, the kind of flat gray sky that made everything in Portland look like a photograph someone had forgotten to develop. Graham sat in the back. Nobody spoke. The radio was off. The only sound was the engine and the soft hiss of the tires on pavement still damp from last night's rain.

He'd made it through the wake. Barely. The funeral home had been on Congress Street — one of those places that managed to look dignified and industrial at the same time, all dark carpet and brass fixtures and the particular hush of a building designed to contain grief without letting it spill. Seeing Niles laid out in the casket had been — he didn't have a word for it. They'd dressed him in a suit Eli had never seen before, probably something Donna had chosen, and they'd done something to his face that was supposed to make him look peaceful but instead made him look like a department store mannequin. Like someone had studied Niles from a photograph and recreated him from memory, getting all the details right except the one that mattered. He looked nothing like Niles. Niles never looked that still. Even in sleep, even in his quietest moments, there had been something alive in his face — some low-frequency hum of thought, of the mind behind the eyes working through whatever problem had captured it.

Donna had been seated off to one side of the viewing room, crying the way she did everything — openly, without apology. Brett stood beside her with a handkerchief in his hand. Eli wasn't sure if it was for Donna or himself. Neither looked like they'd slept. Neither looked like people who would sleep well again for a long time. Eli had kissed her on the cheek and shook Brett's hand, but knew this wasn't the place to do anything more. Others were behind him in the line — colleagues, neighbors, people from the university — and the machinery of the thing kept everyone moving forward, past the casket, past the family, past the flowers, out the other side. An assembly line of sympathy. Eli had never been to a funeral before. His grandparents were already gone by the time he was born, and death had simply never been part of his experience. He'd had no framework for this. No script. He hadn't known what else to do.

That was when Anthony had appeared at his shoulder and handed him a slip of paper. Something written in careful block letters, the handwriting of a man who wanted to be understood.

I'll drive tomorrow. 9 o'clock. No questions.

Eli had looked at it, wondering why Anthony had written it down instead of speaking. Then he'd looked up and seen Anthony's eyes — those old, steady eyes that held more than they showed — and glanced over at Graham, who stood a few feet away talking to someone Eli didn't recognize. He'd looked around the room. The crowd was larger than he'd expected — some seated in the white folding chairs arranged in rows before the casket, others standing in a line that wound back through the lobby, still others gathered in clusters near the doors, conversations happening that Eli couldn't pick up. In all of it, Anthony had chosen to write.

Eli had looked back down at the note, then back up at Anthony's face, and nodded. He'd handed the paper back. Anthony had folded it and put it in his pocket without a word.

Now they were driving along in a suit that Eli hadn't worn in two years and Anthony's old Buick, and Eli couldn't have wished for a worse Monday.

After they parked — Anthony taking two careful attempts to center the Buick between the lines, the way he did everything, with precision and no hurry — they walked up the stone steps of the Cathedral of the Immaculate Conception. Eli had looked it up twice over the past week and it still wouldn't stick in his head, which seemed appropriate. Nothing was sticking.

The cathedral was enormous. He hadn't expected that. Three steeples rose above the roofline, the tallest one piercing the overcast sky like a needle, and the Gothic arched entrance looked like something from a European city, not a street in Portland. A news truck was parked out front, its satellite dish raised, a reporter adjusting her hair near the steps. A fairly large crowd was gathered by the doors — more people than Eli could have imagined Niles knowing.

Did they all know him? He couldn't picture it. He and Niles were homebodies. Their social world consisted of Graham's circle, their apartment, the occasional dinner with Donna. Niles didn't have college friends, not really — acquaintances, lab partners, people who borrowed his notes and returned them without conversation. He wasn't the kind of person who drew crowds.

Must be Donna, he thought. She must know everyone in Cumberland County.

Once inside, he realized most of them were strangers. Here to see the hero — that was what the news had made of Niles, a word that would have mortified him. Here to report the story. Here to look, in the way people looked at tragedies they had no part in, drawn by the same impulse that slowed traffic past an accident.

The interior of the cathedral opened up above him and he stopped. He hadn't meant to — his feet simply quit moving on the third step inside. The nave stretched ahead, flanked by massive stone pillars that rose into a vaulted ceiling seventy feet overhead. Stained glass windows lined the walls — rich, saturated panels depicting scenes he didn't recognize, the light coming through them muted by the overcast sky outside but still casting faint washes of color across the stone floor. The space was built to make you feel small. It succeeded.

He felt a hand on his back — gentle, not pushing, just present — and Graham was on his right side, helping him forward. Anthony flanked his left. Neither spoke. Neither was approached by anyone, because nobody in this building knew who they were. They were invisible — three men walking into a cathedral full of nine hundred people, none of whom knew that the person who'd lost the most was the one in the middle.

It felt strange, Eli thought. Being invisible. He was used to it in certain ways — used to being overlooked in meetings when his voice drew stares, used to being left out of conversations that moved too fast for his ears. But this was different. This was the specific invisibility of grief that had no official standing. He wasn't family. He wasn't a fiancé or a spouse. He was — what? The boyfriend. The roommate. The young man who'd been sharing a bed and a bathroom and a half-finished robot with the person in the casket, and none of that had a name the world recognized.

They dipped their hands in the font of holy water near the entrance — Graham and Anthony automatically, Eli imitating a half-second behind — and moved toward the pews.

Graham saw them first. Eli saw them next. Brett walking in through the main entrance with Donna, a television camera following close enough that its operator nearly tripped on the threshold. Brett steered Donna past it with the practiced deflection of a man who'd been shielding his wife from things all week. They stepped into the vestibule and Donna's eyes found Eli immediately.

She came to him and pulled him into a hug. Not carefully, not politely — the way she hugged at parties, with her whole body, both arms around him, her face pressed against his shoulder. Except this wasn't a party. And the sound she made against his jacket wasn't laughter.

It was the first proper moment they'd had. Just the two of them. Brett stood a few feet behind, giving them the space. Graham and Anthony had moved off to the side, instinctively, the way people who understood grief knew to create room for the moments that mattered. Eli pulled his arms up around Donna and held her, and it struck him — suddenly, physically, like a change in air pressure — that this was real. This was permanent. Niles was in that casket and they were standing in this cathedral and nothing about this day would be undone. His eyes began to water. He hated this for her. Wanted to take her out to lunch instead — their bistro near the waterfront, their usual table, where she'd order wine and talk for two hours and he'd laugh until his face hurt. Go have a few drinks and laugh and go back to how they normally were.

But they would never be how they normally were. Not again.

Brett reached over and touched his wife's shoulder, gently moving her along. She looked up at Eli and nodded — the worst he'd ever seen her, her mascara ruined, her face swollen in a way that suggested she hadn't stopped crying long enough for the swelling to go down. Eli grimaced and forced himself to hold together.

Brett leaned in to speak to him, but Eli was having difficulty hearing anything. The cathedral's acoustics were a nightmare — every voice bounced off the stone and arrived at his ears from three directions at once, layered over the murmur of the crowd and the distant sound of the organ warming up. His eyes were so misty he'd begun wiping them, which made focusing on Brett's lips impossible. He caught fragments — *sorry* and *haven't called* and what he thought was *meant to reach out* — and assembled something close to an apology.

"It's okay," Eli managed. The first words he'd spoken all day. His voice — the voice he spent his whole life managing, modulating, trying to keep at a volume and tone that didn't draw attention — came out louder than he intended. A few people nearby looked over. The way people always looked. The quick glance, the slight widening of the eyes, the rapid recalibration. He knew that look. Had known it his entire life. But today, in this place, it landed differently.

Then arms surrounded his torso from the side — unexpected, firm, without preamble — and he looked over and saw Levi.

He'd come with Sonya and Angie — Eli could see them a few steps back, Sonya in a dark dress she looked uncomfortable in, Angie with her hand on Sonya's arm. But Levi hadn't waited. Hadn't said hello, hadn't offered condolences, hadn't done any of the things that adults did in these situations because Levi wasn't an adult and didn't have any interest in pretending. He'd just walked up and put his arms around Eli's charcoal suit jacket and held on.

Eli put his arm up and around Levi's shoulders in an unbalanced hug — the kid was taller than he'd remembered, nearly to his chin now — and looked over at Sonya and Angie. Sonya said something, but the cathedral swallowed it before it reached Eli's ears. He just looked back at Levi, who still held on. No words. No tears. Just holding. The way Levi had hugged him that first time, outside the apartment building in the snow, when Graham had driven them home from the shelter — that same rigid-then-surrender, the posture of a kid who'd been holding himself together so long he'd forgotten how to accept being held.

Eli felt him breathing.

Levi pulled back slightly and said something — Eli thought it was about sitting together — and then turned toward Anthony, speaking to him with the quiet confidence of someone negotiating a seat assignment on an airplane. Angie appeared to suggest that Levi could sit with them, give Eli some space. But Levi shook his head. He was sitting next to Eli. That was decided.

It was during this exchange — Levi's back to him, Anthony nodding, Sonya reaching out to touch Eli's arm — that Eli saw the paramedic.

A young man in uniform, standing a few feet away near the vestibule wall, watching. Eli's first thought was that something had happened. Why was a paramedic here? Did someone faint, or have a panic attack, or —

Then the man stepped forward.

"Hello," he signed. Deliberately, the way someone signs when they've learned the motions but haven't yet learned the rhythm. "My name is K-I-E-R-A-N." He finger-spelled it slowly, watching his own fingers.

Eli was taken aback. The man was — maybe his age. Maybe younger. He couldn't tell. Shorter than Eli, and given that Eli was barely five-nine, the man looked almost like a kid. Slim, red-headed, short hair that someone had recently cut with care. Slightly built, the way certain people are built — not fragile, just compact. He was wearing his paramedic uniform — navy pants, the patch on his sleeve, the radio clipped to his shoulder — and he looked nervous. Almost apologetic. Like he wasn't sure he had the right to be standing here, doing this.

But he signed. He'd seen Eli's hearing aids and he'd signed.

How did he know about my ears? Eli thought, and instinctively reached for his hearing aids, fiddling with the volume dial the way he always did when someone surprised him — a nervous habit, buying himself a half-second to adjust.

"Sorry," the man signed again and looked down at his shoes, as if the floor might offer him better language than his hands could.

Eli lifted his own hands and signed back. "I'm E-L-I."

Kieran shook his head — a small, quick shake that said *I know* — before lifting his hands to reply. He paused. His fingers hovered in the air, uncertain. "Sorry. New. Hard. Sign."

"Go slow," Eli said, speaking in his voice. Kieran seemed to breathe — his shoulders dropping a fraction, the way people's did when they realized Eli could speak, that this wouldn't have to happen entirely in a language the paramedic clearly hadn't mastered.

"I heard them call you Eli." Kieran nodded toward Levi, Sonya, and Angie. Eli followed his gaze and met the three of them looking back at Kieran with expressions ranging from curiosity to suspicion — Sonya's, naturally, being the most suspicious.

"I — tried to help Niles." Kieran spoke slowly, deliberately, his lips moving with the exaggerated care of someone who understood that his mouth was being read.

He forced himself to focus on Kieran's face — his lips, the shape of the words, the slight movement of his jaw — trying to will his ears, what little hearing he had in this echoing stone cavern, to really listen.

"Help." Kieran signed the word — one of the few he seemed confident in — and pointed at Niles's name printed in the funeral Mass program he held in his hand.

Eli looked down at the program, at the name in black ink — *Niles Ashworth* — and back up at Kieran. Confused.

Kieran realized he wasn't being clear. He pointed to the paramedic patch on his sleeve — the star of life, the word *PARAMEDIC* stitched beneath it — and then back at the program. At Niles's name.

"He — your name — phone." Kieran spoke slowly, pointing to Eli and then to his own iPhone to demonstrate, but Eli was only getting fragments. The organ had started playing — a low, resonant chord that filled the cathedral's stone interior and made Eli's hearing aids buzz with distortion. Everything was breaking apart.

"Sorry," Kieran signed one more time and looked down, the way he had each time — as though each failed attempt at communication was a personal failure, as though he'd come here with one thing to say and the building itself was conspiring against him.

The priest walked in through the main doors, vestments flowing, the funeral home staff behind him. The casket was being carried up the stone steps and into the nave. Six pallbearers — young men Eli didn't recognize, probably from the university — carrying Niles in a polished wooden box. Graham reached over and pulled gently on Eli's elbow, turning him toward the aisle, saying something to the paramedic that Eli couldn't hear. Everything was moving now. The organ swelled. People shifted in their pews. Levi had his hand again, pulling him forward.

Eli looked back at Kieran one last time. The paramedic stood where they'd left him, near the vestibule wall, looking sad in a way that seemed to have nothing to do with the ceremony and everything to do with what he'd failed to say. Their eyes locked for a moment — half a second, maybe less — before Graham and Levi turned him and he walked away.

• • •

Eli watched as Donna and Brett took their places in the front pew. He started walking toward them — toward the front, where he should be, where the people who loved Niles most were sitting — but Levi's hand pulled slightly and he looked over. Graham was guiding them into a pew halfway back. Anthony was already there, standing aside to let them in. Halfway back. In the middle of the cathedral.

Eli caught Graham's eyes, which seemed apologetic. As if to say: *I know. But this is where we are.* This was their spot. Not the front, where the family sat. Not the back, where the curious sat. The middle. The place reserved for people whose grief was real but whose claim was unofficial.

He looked around as others found their seats. The cathedral was full — nine hundred seats, and it seemed like all of them were taken. A sea of faces he didn't recognize, all turned forward, all waiting. A couple seated beside Donna that Eli assumed were extended family — he'd never met them, but they had Brett's jaw. A section on the opposite side sat empty, reserved for pallbearers who were now processing up the aisle. A choir assembled on the right, their robes a deep burgundy against the stone. The stained glass windows rose above everything, depicting scenes of faith and suffering that Eli couldn't name and didn't need to — the images communicated their meaning without language, which was something Eli understood better than most.

Levi took his left hand and pulled him gently back into the pew. Eli had assumed he'd do something today. Pallbearer, maybe. Or share some words — a story, a memory, something that would let the room know that Niles had been loved by someone beyond his parents — participate in some way that acknowledged what they had been to each other. But he stood in the middle of the pew, looking around at the hundreds of faces, and understood that this was as far as he was going. Nobody had asked him to speak. Nobody had asked him to carry the casket. Nobody had asked him anything at all.

He was a friend among friends. Invisible.

The crowd turned toward the back and Eli followed. He wasn't Catholic — wasn't anything, really. His family had probably been Catholic once, back in Quebec, generations ago, before the Pelletiers crossed the border and settled in Maine and stopped going to church and kept the last name and forgot the rest. He had no idea what he was supposed to do — when to stand, when to kneel, when to cross himself, any of it. He just followed along.

Levi seemed to sense the same problem and kept his hand firmly grasped on Eli's, as though he'd appointed himself a guide. Eli looked down at him — this kid who had shown up without being asked, who had refused to sit anywhere else, who was now holding his hand in a cathedral full of strangers as if it were the most natural thing in the world — and started to pull away, to let him know he'd be okay. But something in Levi's eyes stopped him. Something that said: *Don't. Not yet.* Eli squeezed his hand and turned toward the casket being wheeled forward.

Funny, he thought. This was so not Niles. The pageantry, the vestments, the incense, the organ, the hundreds of people watching. Niles could barely handle a dinner party with eight people. He'd have hated every second of this — the attention, the spectacle, the priest speaking about him in front of an audience he would never have chosen to face. Good thing he wasn't around to see it.

Eli paused at that thought. Turned it over. He didn't believe Niles was here — not in the way the priest would say, not in some better place or resting eternally or watching from above. Niles was a scientist. He believed in data and evidence and the observable universe. He would have said that consciousness was an emergent property of neural complexity, and when the neurons stopped firing, so did you. No heaven. No afterlife. No comfort. Just gone.

Eli missed him so much it took the air out of him.

He caught sight of the paramedic — Kieran — standing in the back of the cathedral, close to the vestibule wall, almost hidden behind the last pillar. The man was watching the casket being wheeled past, but Eli's focus had shifted entirely. Something was tugging at the back of his mind. Something about their conversation that he hadn't fully processed.

What was his name? He signed it. K-I-E-R-A-N. Kieran. The paramedic.

Eli shifted his gaze upward, toward the vaulted ceiling — the stone ribs arching overhead, the height of the space somehow both beautiful and oppressive — as if admiring the architecture. But he wasn't looking at the ceiling. He was looking inward, replaying.

Phone. Kieran had said something about a phone. Pointed to the program. To Niles's name. He'd signed *help* — that one was clear. And he'd pointed to his patch. Paramedic. He tried to help Niles.

But the other part. The fragments. *He – your name – phone.* Pointing to Eli, then to his iPhone. Something about Eli's name and a phone. Niles's phone?

Eli knew the sign for "sorry" — Kieran had said it three times. Four, maybe. Everyone seemed to say that. But underneath the apologies, underneath the fumbled signs and the nervous pauses, the man had been trying to tell Eli something specific. Something about how he knew Eli's name. How he'd known to approach him in this crowd of nine hundred people. How a paramedic in uniform had walked up to a stranger at a funeral and signed his name.

Eli looked back at Kieran, who was watching him. Not the casket, not the priest, not the ceremony. Watching Eli. Searching, like the paramedic was trying to understand whether Eli had heard him. Whether the message had landed.

His careful, uncertain fingers spelling it out. The letters coming back to Eli one at a time. Kieran.

Everyone else in the cathedral had turned to follow the casket to the front, past the marble steps up to the altar where Monsignor Flaherty waited in his vestments. But Eli kept his eyes on the back of the church. Levi tugged at his hand — gently, the way you'd steer someone who'd stopped in the middle of a sidewalk — but Eli looked a little longer. He thought he saw something in Kieran's eyes. Something that matched something in his own.

Eli turned forward. The priest was swinging the censer — a silver vessel trailing incense, the smoke climbing in thin white ribbons toward the ceiling, filling the nave with a smell that was sweet and ancient and had nothing to do with anything Eli believed. But he wasn't watching the ceremony. He was assembling.

Kieran. Phone. Eli. Niles. Paramedic.

And then it came — all at once, the way a word you've been trying to remember arrives not gradually but in a flood. Kieran was the paramedic. He was with Niles. He saw Eli's name on Niles's phone. He came to this funeral because he'd been there. He'd held Niles, or worked on him, or ridden in the ambulance with him. And the last thing he'd seen, before Niles slipped away or was taken into surgery or whatever had happened in those final minutes, was a phone screen lighting up with a name.

Eli's name.

Kieran was with Niles before he died.

Eli turned around fully in the pew, looking back toward the vestibule. Kieran was still there. Still watching. And now Eli was looking at him with new eyes — not confusion, not curiosity, but something raw and desperate and enormous. This man — this stranger in a paramedic uniform who'd tried to sign to him in a language he barely spoke — was the last person to hold Niles's hand.

The first thread. The first connection to the final moments of Niles's life. In eleven days, no one had been able to give Eli that. Not the hospital, not the police, not the news reports that called Niles a hero without ever mentioning who he'd left behind. And here was Kieran, standing in the back of a cathedral, looking like he wasn't sure he deserved to be here, having come because — why? Because a name on a phone screen had stayed with him.

Their eyes held for a moment. Then Levi pulled his hand, and Eli turned back to the altar, and the Mass continued around him like weather he couldn't feel.

• • •

Levi helped Eli know when to stand, to sit, to kneel — all those things the ceremony required, the choreography of Catholic mourning that meant nothing to Eli and everything to the people around him. He followed Levi's cues the way he followed most things in life — watching, imitating, half a beat behind. Stand. Sit. Kneel. He wasn't paying attention to any of it.

The priest spoke. Eli didn't try to follow. He watched the priest's mouth move, watched the congregation rise and sit when it was time, watched Donna lift a tissue to her face when something in the priest's words landed. He let the ritual happen around him.

Donna stood and walked to the lectern. Brett helped her forward. She gripped the edges of the wooden stand with both hands and opened her mouth and words came out. Eli watched her face. Watched it crumble. Watched Brett come forward and take her arm and guide her back to the pew, and watched Donna collapse into the space beside him, Brett's hand going immediately to her back.

Eli didn't bother walking up when everyone rose to receive communion — the wafer the priest was offering, the line of people shuffling forward in a procession that seemed to have its own gravity. He sat. Levi sat with him, their hands still linked on the pew between them.

Because he was watching Kieran.

Watched him join the line — walking past their pew, close enough that Eli could see the stitching on his sleeve, the radio on his shoulder, the tired lines around his eyes. Watched him receive the wafer from the priest with a small bow of his head. Watched him walk back along the side aisle and, as he passed, glance over. Their eyes met. Kieran nodded — a small nod, careful, the nod of someone saying *I'm still here.* Eli nodded back.

He wanted to get up and follow. Wanted to grab his arm and pull him into the vestibule and ask every question that had been building since the fragments assembled. Was Niles in pain? Did he say anything? Was he conscious? Was he afraid? Were you there at the end? Did he know what was happening to him? Did he ask for anyone? Did he ask for me?

But Kieran walked out of the cathedral before the priest was finished. Eli watched him go — watched him check his watch twice, the way someone does when they're running out of time they didn't have to begin with. He was in his uniform. Eli wondered if he'd come on his break. Or before a shift. Either way, he'd come.

Eli wanted to jump from the pew and follow him down the steps. Ask for a phone number, an address, anything. Could they talk later? Tomorrow? Next week? Whenever? He just needed — he needed to hear it from someone who was there. Someone who'd seen Niles in those last minutes. Someone who could tell him the one thing that nobody else in this building could tell him: what it was like at the end.

But Kieran was gone. Through the doors, down the steps, back to his rig. And Levi was pulling Eli to his feet for the final prayer or the final hymn or whatever came last. Eli didn't care about any of it. He stood because Levi stood. Bowed his head because everyone bowed their heads. But his mind was in the vestibule, following the paramedic out the door.

Kieran.

Anthony pulled the Buick into Graham's driveway. Graham got out first, walked ahead to unlock the door.

Eli had tried to ask where they were going when Anthony hadn't turned toward his apartment — had started to form the words, had even leaned forward from the back seat — but he didn't want to fight. Didn't have the fight in him. His heart was weak. His whole body was. He'd spent what little he had left at the cemetery.

They'd driven there from the cathedral in a procession — a line of cars with their headlights on, following the hearse through the streets of Portland like a slow parade for a city that had already moved on. At the cemetery, Eli had watched from the back of the small crowd as Monsignor Flaherty said the final prayers. Watched Graham step forward to say something to Donna — quiet, private, the kind of words that Graham knew how to say because he'd been on the other side of them. Watched Brett shake Graham's hand and hold it for a moment longer than a handshake required. Watched as Anthony and Levi began walking back toward the cars, Levi looking over his shoulder once at Eli with an expression that said *come on* and *take your time* simultaneously.

But Eli couldn't move. Everyone was leaving. The priest, the pallbearers, the mourners, the curious — all of them filtering away through the headstones toward their cars, their lives, their Monday afternoons. And Eli was standing at the edge of an open grave, finally alone with Niles. At least as close as he was going to get.

He walked forward. The casket sat on the lowering device, flowers strewn across the polished lid — white roses, lilies, something purple he couldn't name. He stared at it. At the wood. At the brass handles. At the small brass plate with Niles's name on it, which someone had engraved in a font that Niles would have had an opinion about.

He felt numb. Hollowed out. Like something essential had been scooped from his center and what remained was just the shell, still standing by force of habit. He reached into the inside pocket of his suit jacket — the jacket he hadn't worn in two years, the jacket that still had a movie ticket stub in the breast pocket from a date he'd forgotten about — and pulled out a small piece of metal and wire. A servo bracket, maybe. Or a joint connector. He wasn't an engineer. He didn't know what it was called. He only knew it was part of the robot Niles had been building — the humanoid project, the one with one completed hand and one still skeletal — and he'd grabbed it that morning while waiting for Anthony, standing in the apartment, staring at the unfinished machine in the corner, needing to bring something and not knowing what.

He placed it on top of a rose. A small piece of aluminum, barely an inch long, resting on a white petal. The grounds crew would throw it away when they came to fill the grave. But Eli didn't know what else to do. He'd never done this before. There was no protocol for leaving a piece of a robot on your boyfriend's casket. There was no protocol for any of this.

And now here it was. With Niles.

He felt someone take his hand — small fingers wrapping around his — and turned. Levi stood beside him, tears running down his face, looking up at Eli with an expression that was too old for his face and too young for the grief behind it. He wasn't making a sound. The tears just fell, the way rain fell — without effort, without decision, just gravity doing what it did.

Eli thought he should say something. Try to comfort him. Levi had known Niles — not well, but enough. They'd met at the New Year's party, the night Levi had taken Niles out to the patio when the room got to be too much for him. After that, dinners in Graham's kitchen where Niles would explain something about engineering and Levi would listen with the quiet intensity of a boy who understood what it meant to be underestimated. Niles had worried about Levi, Eli remembered. Had mentioned him, in that careful way Niles mentioned things that mattered — briefly, precisely. *I think he's going to be okay,* Niles had said. About Levi. As if he'd been running calculations in his head and the numbers had finally come out right.

Now Levi was standing at Niles's grave, crying without sound, holding Eli's hand. And Eli understood that the tears weren't only for Niles. They were for Eli, too. For what Eli had lost. For the particular cruelty of watching someone you loved stand alone at a grave while the rest of the world walked away.

Eli pulled him into a hug and looked out over the cemetery — the rows of headstones stretching across the green, the trees just beginning to leaf out in that tentative way Maine trees had in early May, the sky still gray above all of it.

Now at Graham's, pulling into the driveway, Eli hadn't realized how tired he'd been. He hadn't realized he'd been crying — silently, without the collapse he'd been expecting for days. The tears had just come, somewhere between the cemetery and here, along the quiet streets of Falmouth with Anthony driving and Graham in the back seat and nobody saying anything.

Chapter Five

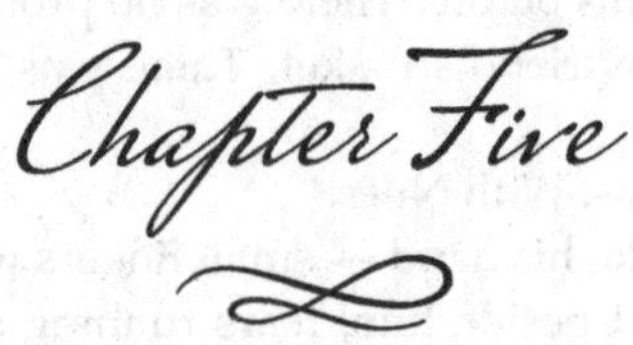

ELI WAS A SIDE SLEEPER. Always had been.

As a kid, he'd pull his teddy bear to his chest and turn on his side toward the window, gazing out at the night with the bear pressed against him like a shield. He didn't know what he was looking for out there — never had, even then. Just that the dark was easier to face with something to hold on to. When he moved out of his parents' house, the bear came with him, tucked into a duffel bag between his jeans and his hearing aid case, the last thing packed and the first thing unpacked. He'd clamp hold and roll to his side, same as always. Same window ritual, same need.

That was until Niles moved in. That first night they shared a bed, Eli had lain awake longer than he'd admit, worried about all the wrong things. Worried that Niles might not want to be touched — that the closeness Eli craved would feel like intrusion to a man who navigated the world with a carefully maintained perimeter of personal space. Worried that the sounds Eli made in his sleep — the heavy breathing, the occasional mumbled half-words that came from a man who couldn't hear himself dream — would keep Niles up. Worried, most of all, that he was too old to sleep with a stuffed toy animal and that Niles would see it and think less of him for it.

So the bear had been relegated to the chair in the bedroom corner — the one that accumulated the clothes Eli shed before crawling into bed. Jeans draped over the arm. Shirt tossed across the seat. The bear underneath it all, buried but present.

He'd gotten used to holding Niles instead. Not that Niles made it easy — he slept on his back, rigid as a plank, arms at his sides, in a posture that suggested he'd once read an article about optimal sleeping positions and was following it to the letter. But Eli would curl against him anyway, one arm across his chest, and eventually Niles would shift — not quite relaxing, more like accepting — and they'd find a configuration that worked. Not perfect. But theirs.

When everything fell apart almost two weeks ago, Eli had reached across the empty bed in the dark and found nothing. No warmth. No rigid back. No reluctant shift toward acceptance. Just sheets that still smelled like Niles's shampoo and a pillow that still held the shape of his head. Eli had lain there for perhaps thirty seconds before rolling over and reaching for the chair.

The bear resumed his usual post against Eli's chest. It wasn't the same — a stuffed animal was no Niles. But he wasn't the same as before Niles, either. Or Eli wasn't, anyway. That was probably closer to the truth, he thought, as he woke now in unfamiliar light, his hand searching for the bear that wasn't there.

He lay curled up in Graham's Eames lounger beside the fireplace — or as curled as a five-foot-nine man could manage in a chair designed more for contemplation than sleeping, his legs dangling off the ottoman at an angle that his lower back was already protesting. A wool blanket had been draped over him — Graham's doing, or Anthony's — and his shoes were gone. His hearing aids were gone. He lay there in his suit trousers and dress shirt, wrinkled and damp with the particular staleness of clothes that had been worn through the worst day of someone's life and then slept in. His jacket and tie were laid neatly over the arm of the sofa across the room, arranged with a care that suggested someone had removed them after he'd fallen asleep.

Sunlight was spilling into the window-lined hallway to his right — the hallway that led to Graham's office, the one with the floor-to-ceiling glass that turned the whole corridor into a greenhouse of morning light. But the house was still. No movement. No vibration through the floor that might tell him someone was walking. In the complete absence of his hearing aids, the world was as silent as it ever got for Eli, which was not truly silent — there was always the low hum, the blood-sound, the faint static of a nervous system processing nothing — but close enough.

He sat up. His back cracked. His mouth tasted of stale coffee. He needed to shower. Needed caffeine. Needed to wake up and make sense of why he was sitting in Graham Tierney's living room on a Tuesday morning in his ruined suit.

Standing, he turned and walked into the kitchen. He'd been to Graham's a hundred times — more, probably. He was practically more at home here than in his own apartment, which said something about the apartment and something else about Graham. The kitchen was the same as always: clean, organized, the counters bare except for the coffee maker and the wooden cutting board that Simon had made years ago — Graham had mentioned it once, casually, the way he mentioned Simon in everything, because Simon was in everything. The round table by the patio window where they'd sat last night still had a bowl on it. His soup, untouched. Someone had put plastic wrap over it.

No sign of Graham. He was a morning person — early bird, that was the expression. Gets the worm. Normally Graham would be up before the sun, either in his office or standing at this very counter with a cup of tea, looking out at the woods.

Eli stared through the patio window at the backyard — brown grass giving way to the tree line, the branches just beginning to carry the first haze of green that passed for spring in Maine. A pair of squirrels chased each other up the trunk of an oak near the bird feeder — the bird feeder Graham was perpetually at war with, the one the squirrels had conquered years ago and now occupied like they owned it. Eli smiled, wondering if Graham had waged this battle when Simon was alive, or if the squirrels had sensed the household's diminished defenses and moved in after.

Simon.

Eli had heard so much about him. Seen a couple of photos — the one on Graham's desk, the one in the hallway. He'd felt so sorry for Graham when he first told him, that night in the car driving home from Whole Foods, the word *husband* catching in Graham's throat. Eli couldn't have imagined losing someone like that — not then, not when his own life was still intact and the idea of that kind of loss was abstract, something that happened to other people, older people, people who'd had decades together and earned the right to grieve.

Now he could imagine it. Now he was living inside it. Sure, he and Niles hadn't been together that long — nowhere close to what Graham and Simon had built over thirty years. But the weight didn't scale with time. Grief didn't check your résumé before it moved in. It just arrived, and it was enormous, and it didn't care that you'd only been together for months instead of decades. Inside, it felt the same. At least, Eli thought it did. He'd never ask Graham to confirm.

He turned away from the window before the ghosts of Simon could keep pulling at him. He could feel them in this house. Not supernatural. Just the shape of two people that a home holds even when one is gone. Simon's cutting board. Simon's bird feeder. Simon's absence in every room.

Eli set down the coffee he'd poured — black, from a pot that must have been made earlier, which meant Graham had been up and had gone somewhere — and wandered back through the living room toward the office. Graham was probably in there. Working, maybe.

But when he stepped through the doorway, the office was empty. The same floor-to-ceiling windows showed the morning outside — the woods, the light filtering through new leaves, the amber quality that early sun took on in this room, warming the wood and the books and the papers on the desk. Graham's huge wooden desk sat in the center of it all — the mid-century Danish modern piece he and Simon had designed together, the one Simon said would give Graham great joy and help him write stories. It was covered in the organized chaos of a working writer: stacked pages, a cup of pens, reading glasses folded on top of a legal pad, and what Eli was certain was the manuscript of Graham's latest novel. The final Oltrarno.

He'd been secretive about it. Had deflected every question with the practiced ease of a man who'd spent decades protecting his work in progress from well-meaning curiosity. Eli hadn't pushed — partly out of respect, partly because he knew that pushing would only make Graham retreat further, and partly because he couldn't bear the thought of Graham clamming up about Marco and Alessandro entirely. Those characters — the two men whose story had unfolded across six novels, whose love had survived distance and politics and a world that would destroy them for it — were too important to Eli for him to risk losing access by being impatient.

He stood there in the empty office, coffee in hand, and remembered the first time he'd been in this room. Last year. Standing right here and seeing the Oltrarno novels on the shelf, not yet knowing that the man who'd driven him home from Whole Foods — the self-deprecating, impossibly kind man who'd offered him a ride in the snow — was Graham Tierney. The Graham Tierney. The author who had written Marco and Alessandro into existence and, in doing so, had given a lonely deaf kid from Maine the only two friends who'd ever truly understood him.

He still held that moment in his heart. The shock. The disbelief. Looking at the spines on the shelf and then looking at Graham, who stood there like it wasn't a big deal, like being the author of the books that had saved Eli's life was roughly as interesting as being the author of a grocery list. That was Graham. Incapable of seeing himself the way others saw him.

Eli instinctively reached up to adjust his hearing aid, only to realize again that he wasn't wearing them. He'd gotten so accustomed to the gesture — the small fidget, the recalibration — that his hand went to his ear even in silence. As if he somehow needed a soundtrack to the novels sitting right in front of him.

Where was Graham? Perhaps his bedroom? Eli had never gone further than the doorway — some boundaries he maintained without being asked, the way you maintained certain distances with people you respected. He looked down the hallway. Graham's door was open. The guest rooms were open, too. Was he the only one here?

He tried to reconstruct the night before. Anthony had brought him here instead of the apartment — he remembered that. The drive, mostly.

The trees along the road to Falmouth, black against a sky that was just beginning to darken. Graham had made soup. Bread, too — the dense, slightly lopsided kind Graham produced from a recipe he kept adjusting and never improving, though nobody had the heart to tell him. They'd sat at the round kitchen table by the patio window — Anthony on one side, Graham on the other, Eli in between. The two older men had spoken to each other across him, but Eli had been elsewhere. Lost. Not hearing, not reading lips, not participating. Just sitting in a kitchen that smelled like bread, wearing a suit he'd put on that morning to bury someone he loved, and feeling nothing.

His hearing aids. That was the other thing. They'd been terrible all day — buzzing in the cathedral, distorting at the cemetery, unable to handle the acoustics of grief-filled spaces designed for people with functioning ears. At some point during dinner, he'd gotten up from the table without a word, walked to the powder room off the front hall, taken the aids out, and set them on the folded hand towel beside the sink. Just set them down the way you'd set down a heavy bag. Done with them. Done with trying to hear a world that had nothing left to say to him.

He turned now and walked back to the powder room. There they were — right where he'd left them, two small devices sitting on a pale blue towel. He didn't put them in. Just noted where they were, the way you'd note an exit in a building you weren't ready to leave. Turning, he saw his shoes by the front door — kicked off, apparently, at some point he couldn't remember. Graham hadn't moved them. Hadn't tidied up after him. Had just let Eli's shoes sit where they'd landed.

He stood looking back at the living room. The fireplace. The Eames lounger. The blanket pooled on the ottoman where his legs had been.

That's right. He'd just wanted to sit down after dinner. Rest his eyes. His head had been pounding — the particular headache that came from crying without producing tears, the pressure building behind his sinuses with nowhere to go — and he'd just needed a few moments.

Obviously, those few moments had turned into all night. He was surprised he'd slept at all. He hadn't slept through a full night since — well. Since Niles. At the apartment, sleep came in fragments: an hour here, two hours there, then wide awake at three a.m. staring at the ceiling crack while the toothbrush stood vigil in the bathroom and the robot reached in the corner. But here, in Graham's chair, wrapped in someone's blanket, he'd slept until morning.

He didn't want to think about what that meant.

Niles.

Eli carried his coffee back into the office.

The morning light had shifted while he'd been wandering — moving from the early amber into something brighter, sharper, the sun clearing the tree line and flooding the room through those enormous windows. Everything looked warmer than it was. The desk. The shelves. The stack of manuscript pages he would not touch. The reading glasses Graham had probably been wearing last night while Eli stared at untouched soup.

He stood with his mug and remembered Levi in this room. Last year — the snowstorm, the night everyone had stayed over. Levi sitting in one of the leather chairs that flanked the bookshelves, legs tucked under him, reading the original Oltrarno manuscript with the intensity of a boy who'd found a door to a place he didn't want to leave. Graham had allowed Levi access to the handwritten pages — the early drafts, the crossed-out lines, the margin notes — and Eli had teased him about it. Playfully, the way he and Graham handled most things: *So Levi gets the behind-the-scenes tour and I don't even get a peek?* Graham had smiled and said something about earning it, and Eli had laughed, and that had been that.

But inside, there'd been a tinge of something he wasn't proud of. Not jealousy, exactly — or if it was, not the kind that wanted to take something from Levi. More like recognition. Eli had been Levi's age once. Had been lost in those same books, for many of the same reasons. Had sat in his own bedroom — not a car, not a shelter, he'd had a home and parents who fed him and a bed to sleep in, he knew his situation and Levi's weren't the same — but he'd been drowning in his own way. Lonely in the way that being different made you lonely. The only voices that reached him had been the ones in books.

Marco and Alessandro had been those voices. He'd found them when he was — what, fifteen? Sixteen? Around Levi's age. Found the first Oltrarno novel in the library, pulled it from the shelf for no reason. He'd read it in two days. Then read it again. Then went looking for the rest.

They'd been like brothers to him. That was the word he'd used at the time, though even then he'd known it wasn't quite right. Brothers didn't look at each other the way Marco looked at Alessandro. Brothers didn't write letters that did to you what those letters did, in ways you couldn't explain to your mother, your friends, your guidance counselor, or anyone else in your life who might have helped if you'd known how to ask. But *brothers* was the safe word. The word that let Eli love them without having to examine what that love meant about himself.

That came later. Slowly, and then all at once — the way understanding works when you've been circling something for years, afraid to look at it directly. He'd read the scene where Marco kisses Alessandro for the first time — really read it, not skimming, not looking away — and something had unlocked inside him with a click so quiet and so final that he'd sat in his bedroom holding the book and understood that he was not going to marry a girl. Was not going to bring home a nice woman for his parents to approve of. Was not going to be the son Terry Pelletier had been preparing for, with her volunteer center introductions and her casual mentions of daughters and nieces and the brother who had *trouble with his ears like you.*

He was Marco. He'd always been Marco. And the thing he felt when he read about Alessandro — that ache, that longing, that desperate hope that someone like that existed somewhere in the real world — was not admiration or friendship or the bond between brothers.

It was love. The wanting kind. The kind he'd eventually find with Niles, years later, in the most unlikely of packages — a quiet, rigid, beautiful boy who couldn't handle a grocery store but could build a robot from scratch and who blushed every single time Eli kissed him.

He hadn't told Levi any of that. Not the full story. He and Michael had been figuring themselves out last year — two boys navigating what they were to each other with the clumsy earnestness of people who don't yet have the vocabulary for what they're feeling — and they'd both looked up to Eli for guidance. Which was absurd. Eli, the wise elder. He barely had his own life together, and these two kids thought he was Graham — always knowing the right thing to say, always steady, always there. Graham had told him once that he didn't feel like he knew what he was doing either. Eli had been surprised by that. Graham of all people — the man who simply *looked* like a person you could go to, the person who would be there, who would know what to do. If Graham was faking it, then everyone was faking it.

But Eli had started taking the role more seriously after that. Levi and Michael needed someone, and he was going to be that someone, however imperfectly. They deserved that. He owed them that. He owed Niles that — Niles, who had worried about Levi, who had seen something in the boy that reminded him of himself.

The sun was climbing now, its light reaching the shelves where Graham kept his most treasured books. The Oltrarno novels sat in a row — six spines, each one a different color, each one a door Eli had walked through at a different point in his life.

He reached up instinctively to adjust a hearing aid that wasn't there. The habit again. The phantom reach.

His hand went to the shelf instead. His fingers found the spine of the first novel — the one he and Levi and Michael had talked about last year, the one Levi had read in this very chair, the one that had started everything. He almost pulled it out. Almost opened it to the first page, to Marco arriving in Florence with his drawings and his mother's tears, to the beginning of everything.

But something held his hand. Some pull — not a thought, exactly, more like a nudge from outside himself. His fingers slid to the right. Past the first novel. To the second.

The Novice's Chapel.

He pulled it from the shelf. The cover was simpler than he remembered — a muted painting of a church interior, candles burning low, shadows gathering in the nave. He opened to the frontispiece illustration: Marco standing at the edge of a chapel, the Vatican behind him, while Alessandro, dressed in traveling clothes, turned back from the road to look at him. Two figures caught in the moment between staying and leaving. Marco watching. Alessandro already going.

Eli had been devastated by this novel. Had hated it, initially — hated Graham for writing it, hated the story for going where it went, hated the feeling of being pulled along toward something he couldn't stop and didn't want to see. He'd wanted to write Graham a letter. *How dare you do this to them. How dare you take Alessandro away. You can't. You can't kill him.*

But Alessandro wasn't dead. The novel never said he was. It just — it *felt* that way. The silence. The absence. The letters that stopped coming. Marco alone in Rome, painting because painting was all he had, waiting for a word that didn't arrive. The novel had ended there — not with death, not with confirmation, not with anything so merciful as certainty. Just the not knowing. The worst of all possible states.

Eli remembered sitting in his bedroom at home — fifteen, maybe sixteen, the house quiet, his parents asleep — reading by the light of the lamp on his nightstand, unable to stop. Three nights straight he'd stayed up, unable to think about anything at school in between, unable to concentrate on anything but getting back to Marco. He'd lived inside that book the way you live inside a fever — completely, involuntarily, without the ability to step outside it and see it for what it was.

And when he'd finished — when the last page turned and there was nothing left and Alessandro was gone and Marco was standing in the chapel alone — Eli had cried. Not quietly. Not the dignified tears of someone processing literature. He'd cried the way children cry when something breaks that they don't know how to fix. Because it hurt. Because he'd been so used to seeing himself as Marco, walking beside him through every chapter, that Marco's loss felt like his own. He'd wanted to travel back in time and find Marco and tell him it would be okay. They'd go looking for Alessandro together. He *couldn't* be dead.

It had been past three in the morning. He was wiping his eyes, furious, ready to compose a letter to Graham Tierney telling him exactly what he could do with his novel. But then he'd remembered: there were more books. The series continued. Alessandro couldn't be dead — not really, not permanently — because Graham had more story to tell. He must have some plan for them. He must.

Eli had fallen asleep that night holding the bear, turned on his side toward the window, thinking about Marco alone in a chapel in Rome. And the next morning, before school, before breakfast, before anything, he'd checked the library's catalog to see if the third novel was available.

It was important. More important than school, more important than breakfast, more important than anything in his small, quiet, lonely life. Because if Alessandro was alive, then hope was alive. And if hope was alive, then maybe — just maybe — the world had room in it for people like Marco. And people like Eli.

He smiled now, standing in Graham's office, holding the book. Smiled at his own expense, at the boy he'd been — so earnest, so desperate, so certain that fictional characters could save him. So silly, he supposed. So young.

But he'd been right, hadn't he?

He took the book and sat down in the leather chair beside the shelves — the same chair Levi had curled up in last year, reading the first novel with that expression of ravenous need that Eli recognized because he'd worn it himself. He set his coffee mug on the side table, opened the book to the first page, and began to read.

He remembered this. Remembered the night in his bedroom when these same words had pulled him in and held him under. But he was different now. He was twenty-four, and the man he loved was dead, and the author of this book was somewhere in this house, and the chair he was sitting in still held the warmth of a boy who'd needed these words as badly as Eli had once needed them.

He turned the page.

Weather in Venice

THE COMMISSION WAS GOING WELL, which was the problem.

Marco stood on the scaffolding twelve feet above the chapel floor, his brush loaded with a mixture of terre verte and lead white he'd spent the better part of an hour grinding to the exact consistency he needed — thin enough to flow, thick enough to hold the line. The underpainting for the eastern lunette was nearly complete: a scene of the Annunciation, the angel arriving, the Virgin turning from her reading with an expression Marco was still fighting to get right. Surprise, yes. But not shock. Something closer to recognition — as if she'd been expecting the news without knowing she'd been expecting it.

He'd been painting for three months now. Every morning he climbed the scaffolding at first light, when the chapel was empty and the only sound was the scrape of his own breathing and the distant bells of the city marking the hours. By midmorning, the other artists arrived — two Romans who kept to themselves and a Venetian named Girolamo who talked incessantly about the superiority of Venetian color and whose own work, Marco privately observed, did not support the argument. A team of plasterers rotated in and out, preparing the surfaces Marco would paint next. Occasionally a priest would pass through, inspect the progress, murmur something noncommittal, and leave.

It was good work. The chapel was small but beautifully proportioned, the kind of space where light behaved with intention — entering through the high eastern window in the morning, tracking across the walls as the hours passed, arriving at the western lunette precisely at vespers, as if the architect had conspired with God to make the building tell time. Marco loved painting in it. Loved the quiet of the early hours, the way the plaster received his pigments, the slow emergence of figures from the wall as if they'd been waiting inside the stone for someone to find them.

He should have been happy.

In many ways, he was. The work was the finest he'd ever done — better than the altarpiece in Florence, better than the small commissions he'd taken after the Academy closed. Something about Rome had sharpened him. The light, maybe. Or the competition — knowing that Perugino was painting three streets away, that the ghost of Giotto haunted every church in the city, that the standard here was not competence but transcendence. Whatever it was, Marco was painting beyond himself, and he knew it, and on the days when the work went well, he climbed down from the scaffolding in the late afternoon feeling something close to whole.

And then he would return to his room. And the room would be empty. And the feeling would end.

Alessandro had been gone for six weeks.

The first weeks in Rome — the weeks before — had been something Marco hadn't known was possible. Not happiness, exactly. He didn't trust that word. It was too large, too certain, too easily taken away. What he'd felt was closer to steadiness. A settling. As though some essential tremor he'd carried since boyhood — a vibration of fear, of displacement, of never quite belonging — had finally gone still.

They were careful. Of course they were. In public, Alessandro was who he had always been — the Rinaldi heir, polished, composed, his bearing calibrated to the precise degree of warmth that his station required and no more. He spoke to Marco the way he spoke to the other artists: with courtesy, with a professional interest in the work, with the polite distance of a man whose family had funded the commission and who therefore had opinions about its progress. He addressed him as *Maestro di Benedetto,* which Marco found both absurd and slightly thrilling, coming from a mouth that had whispered entirely different things the night before.

In private, the distance vanished like a candle blown out. Alessandro would arrive at Marco's room after the household had settled — late, always late, when the corridors were empty and the guards were drowsy — and the door would close and he would become someone else entirely. Not a different person. Just the rest of the one he was. The version of himself he could only be in a locked room with the curtains drawn, where the Rinaldi name and the Vatican politics and the constant, exhausting performance of being the man the world expected him to be could be set aside like a coat hung on a hook.

He'd told Marco once, early on, lying in the narrow bed with the moonlight laid across the floor in pale bars: "You must never take to heart what I say to you out there. I hate it. I hate the way I sound when I speak to you as though you're beneath me. You are not beneath me. You are not beneath anyone."

Marco had nodded. He understood. He did. The rules of their world were not ambiguous — a Rinaldi son and a painter from Greve did not occupy the same tier of God's creation, regardless of what they did behind a locked door. Alessandro's public distance was not cruelty. It was survival.

But understanding it did not make it painless. Some mornings, crossing the courtyard to the chapel, Marco would pass Alessandro walking with his father, or with one of the cardinals, and Alessandro would glance at him — briefly, neutrally, with the same mild acknowledgment he gave the plasterers and the cleaning women — and something in Marco would clench. He knew the look was a performance. Knew that behind it, Alessandro was thinking of the night before, of Marco's hands, of words spoken in the dark. Knew all of it. And still the look landed like a stone.

He was admired for his talent. That much was clear. The cardinal overseeing the commission had praised the Annunciation sketch publicly, a compliment so rare from a man known for his silence that the other artists had stared. Visiting priests stopped to watch him work. A monsignor whose name Marco never learned had requested that he paint a small Madonna for his private quarters, which was both flattering and lucrative.

But admiration was not inclusion. He remained what he had always been — an outsider. Welcomed for his hands, tolerated for his origins, invisible in every other way. Some of the Vatican clergy were friendly enough. A novice monk assigned to the commission had taken to bringing Marco water during the long painting hours, sitting quietly on the floor below the scaffolding, watching the figures emerge from the plaster with an expression of such unguarded wonder that Marco sometimes forgot to be lonely.

Others barely registered his existence. He was the painter. The help. A pair of gifted hands attached to a person who didn't matter.

Alessandro was the one who mattered, in their eyes. And that was the distance Marco could never quite cross, no matter how many hours they spent tangled in his sheets.

The night before Alessandro left for Venice, Marco couldn't let go of him.

They lay in Marco's bed — the same narrow bed where everything had begun — and Marco held him with an urgency he couldn't explain and didn't try to. His hands moved across Alessandro's skin as if cataloging it, memorizing the geography of collarbone and ribcage and the hollow at the base of his throat where Marco liked to press his lips. He pulled him closer. Closer. As if proximity could prevent departure.

Alessandro was patient with it. He always was — patient in the particular way of a man who had learned to read another person's fear even when that person couldn't articulate it. He held Marco back, matched his intensity, gave him what he needed. But afterward, lying in the cooling dark, he propped himself on one elbow and looked down at

Marco with the expression he used when something needed to be addressed.

"What is this about?"

Marco shook his head. "Nothing."

"It's not nothing. You're holding me like I'm going to war. I'm going to Venice. My father has business with the Doge's court. Trade negotiations, banking arrangements — you know how these things work."

"I don't, actually."

Alessandro smiled. "That's because they're unspeakably dull. You'd last ten minutes before painting on someone's wall uninvited."

Marco didn't smile. Couldn't. Something was sitting low in him — a weight, a dread, a premonition he had no basis for and could not argue away.

"The last time you left —"

"Was different," Alessandro said, his voice gentle but firm. "My family was fleeing the collapse of the Medici. This is a business trip, Marco. A few weeks. A month at most."

"You said a few weeks or a month. That's already a range."

"Travel to Venice takes time. You know this."

"I know what it's like to wait for you." Marco's voice came out quieter than he'd intended. "I know what it's like to count the days and then stop counting because counting makes it worse."

Alessandro was silent for a moment. His hand found Marco's jaw and turned his face so their eyes met.

"I will write. We've arranged how. The phrases we agreed on — simple, ordinary. A letter about the weather means I'm well. A question about the commission means I miss you. You remember."

"I remember."

"Then trust me. This is not Florence again. No one is falling. No one is fleeing. I'm going to sit in a series of rooms with a series of men in expensive clothes who will argue about money, and I will think about you the entire time, and when it's done I will come home."

Home. The word hung in the air between them. Alessandro had never used it before — not for Rome, not for anywhere. Home had always been something in the past for both of them. Florence, before it fell apart. The Academy, before it scattered. Marco's village, before he'd left it. Home was a place you could no longer return to.

But Alessandro had said it now. *I will come home.*

"A few weeks," Marco repeated.

"A few weeks."

"And if the weather in your letters turns to storms?"

Alessandro leaned down and kissed him — slowly, deliberately, with the precision he brought to everything. "Then I'll write about sunshine until the storms pass."

They lay together for a while after that. Not speaking. The city was quiet outside the shuttered window — Rome at its gentlest, the small hours when even the eternal city allowed itself to rest. Marco listened to Alessandro's breathing slow toward sleep and tried to memorize the sound, the rhythm, the specific cadence of this particular night, as if storing it against whatever silence might follow.

He told himself he was being foolish. Alessandro was right. This was not Florence. No one was fleeing. It was a business trip. A few weeks. A month.

He told himself this, and fell asleep holding on.

Six weeks now. The letters had come — three of them, spaced at careful intervals. The weather in Venice was fine. The negotiations were proceeding. Alessandro asked after the commission — was the eastern lunette complete?

He was well. He missed Marco. He was thinking of him.

Marco wrote back. The commission was progressing. The weather in Rome was warm. He asked about the architecture of Venice.

But the letters had stopped. The last one had arrived three weeks ago. Twenty-one days. Marco had counted, despite having promised himself he wouldn't, because counting was something he did when the fear was winning and the rational mind had gone quiet.

Twenty-one days was not forever. He knew that. Letters were lost. Couriers were unreliable. Venice was far. There were a hundred ordinary reasons for a delay.

But Marco had spent his whole life reading the distance between what people said and what they meant, between the presence they performed and the absence underneath, and he knew — in the way you knew things without evidence, in the way your body knew a season was changing before the calendar confirmed it — that something was wrong.

He did not know what. He did not know how. He only knew that the silence had a different quality now — not the silence of two people who didn't need to speak, but the held-breath silence of a room in which something has fallen and not yet shattered.

He climbed the scaffolding each morning. He painted. The Annunciation was nearly finished — the angel's wings iridescent, the Virgin's face finally holding the expression he'd been chasing for weeks. Recognition. Not shock. The knowledge of something arriving that had always been coming.

He painted because it was the only thing he could do. Because the brush in his hand was steady even when the rest of him was not. Because the chapel didn't ask questions, didn't need him to perform composure, didn't require him to pretend he was fine when the room he returned to each night was empty and the letters had stopped and the man who had called Rome *home* had not come back to it.

The novice brought water at midmorning, as always. Sat below the scaffolding, as always. Looked up at the emerging figures on the wall with that expression of quiet astonishment that had become, without Marco's permission, one of the few things he looked forward to each day.

"It's beautiful," the novice said.

Marco didn't answer. He was painting the angel's hand — the one extended toward the Virgin, the gesture of announcement, of revelation. A hand reaching toward someone with news that would change everything.

He painted it carefully. Precisely. The way Alessandro would have done anything — with patience, with attention, with the faith that the work itself was enough to hold you when everything else was uncertain.

Then he climbed down, drank the water, and waited for a letter that did not come.

Chapter Six

GRAHAM TIERNEY WAS nothing if not a pragmatist.

Simon would call him on it constantly. Why use a paper cup when you could simply bring a coffee mug? Sounded reasonable, Simon would respond, but when an office has five hundred employees, where are you going to store all those mugs? And who is going to clean them? The employees themselves? Sure, perhaps a third would dutifully comply. Another third would barely rinse water over it and call it a day. But the rest? Come on, Graham. People are barely able to properly dress themselves, let alone tidy up after their morning caffeine ritual.

Life, Simon would remind him, was more nuanced than it appeared.

Graham had never fully accepted this. Nuance was for philosophers and politicians and people who had time to sit around considering the multiple angles of a situation before acting. Graham preferred to act. See the problem, solve the problem, move on. It was how he wrote — straightforward, no wasted words, every sentence earning its place. It was how he lived — or how he'd lived before Simon died, when the problems were simpler and the solutions presented themselves with reassuring clarity.

Now the problems were enormous and the solutions were nowhere, and Graham was learning, slowly and against his will, that Simon had been right about the nuance.

He stood in the hallway in the early dark, the sun not yet above the horizon but the sky already beginning to lighten in that gradual way Maine mornings had in May — the blue-black giving way to gray, the gray to something almost lavender at the edges. He'd been up since five. Hadn't slept well.

He'd walked to the kitchen first. Made a pot of coffee — not for himself, of course. Coffee was the devil's water, as far as Graham was concerned. He'd tried it exactly twice in his life, both times at Simon's insistence, both times to Simon's delight. But Eli would need it. He'd want it waiting when he woke up.

Now, on his way out, car keys in hand, Graham paused at the edge of the hallway and looked into the living room. Eli's sleeping frame was just visible in the growing light — curled in the Eames lounger, his legs hanging off the ottoman at an angle that made Graham's lower back ache just looking at it. The wool blanket they'd draped over him had slipped to one side. His suit trousers were wrinkled beyond recovery. His face, turned toward the window, looked younger in sleep than it did awake.

Graham had wanted to wake him last night. Put him to bed in one of the guest rooms. The lounger, while comfortable for reading, was not designed for a full night's sleep, and Eli was going to wake up with a back that felt like it had been folded in half. Straightforward. Easy enough. Move the young man to a proper bed. Problem, solution, done.

But Anthony had stopped him. "Let him rest. He needs it."

"He looks so uncomfortable," Graham had protested. "He'll be more comfortable in bed."

"That chair isn't where the pain is coming from, Graham. You know that."

Nuanced. Simon would have said exactly that.

So he'd left Eli where he was. He and Anthony had carefully removed the tie and draped it over the arm of the sofa with his suit jacket, noticing as they did that his hearing aids had already been removed. Graham had always noticed Eli's hearing aids. They were too large to ignore, even in today's world of miniaturized electronics — visible behind each ear, the small curved casings that Eli adjusted constantly, fiddling with the volume. Eli had always complained about them — too bulky, too obvious, too prone to buzzing in crowded rooms and screeching in wind. But he kept wearing them. Every day, first thing.

Sometimes Graham wondered why he didn't just take them out. Leave them off. Let the world be quiet. He'd never asked, exactly — but Eli had told him things, here and there. That the world through the aids was effortful. That it was sometimes exhausting. That hearing some sound was better than hearing none, even when the cost was high. Graham knew that much. The rest was Eli's, and Graham knew not to push.

He stood there in the morning light, watching Eli breathe, and then turned and left for his car.

Easier to run errands early, before the world woke up and filled the roads with people who drove as if they were the only ones on them. Eli had been to the house often enough that he no longer counted as a guest. He might as well have his mail delivered here — he had as much run of the place as Graham, if he wanted, and that meant he knew where the cereal was, the extra towels, the spare key to the back door that Graham kept in the drawer with the takeout menus Simon had never gotten around to throwing away.

Pulling out of the garage, he heard the squeak of the door closing behind him and worried for a moment that it would wake Eli. Then he remembered Eli couldn't hear it.

Graham knew that. He hadn't forgotten. He just — got so accustomed to having conversations with him, to treating him as someone who heard and responded and laughed at the right moments, that the hearing loss simply disappeared from Graham's awareness. Eli made it disappear. The jokes about his "deaf voice," the self-deprecating comments about misread lips, the way he positioned himself at dinner tables so he could see everyone's faces — all of it smoothed the edges so well that the edges seemed not to be there.

And it dawned on Graham, driving down the quiet morning roads toward the store, how much that took. How much energy Eli spent every day accommodating everyone else's way of communicating. He'd never once asked Graham to sign to him. Not once. Graham could sign a few words — Eli had taught him, with that patient amusement he brought to everything — but Eli never asked him to use them. Never made his hearing the other person's problem. He carried it the way he carried his grief — without asking anyone to meet him where he was.

Graham couldn't remember a single time Eli had asked the world to adjust for him. Instead, Eli adjusted for the world. Every single day.

Whole Foods was nearly empty at this hour — just a few early risers and the staff restocking shelves in that unhurried predawn rhythm that made the store feel like a different place entirely from the chaos of evening shopping. Graham wandered the aisles without a list, looking for something — anything — that might bring Eli a small moment of comfort. A token. A gesture. But nothing jumped off the shelves. What did you buy for someone whose boyfriend had been buried yesterday? There was no aisle for that. No endcap display reading *For the Grieving: 20% Off.*

He found himself in the coffee section and stopped. He remembered — months ago, maybe longer, back when the world was still intact — he and Eli wandering these same aisles around the holidays, Eli excited about a particular bag. *This one. Trust me. It's the only thing getting me through December.* Graham had made a face — his standard coffee face — and Eli had laughed.

He picked up a bag and put it in the cart. It wasn't enough. It wasn't anything, really. But it was what he had.

The drive home was quiet. The same streets he'd driven for years — past the turn for the gym, past the intersection where he'd first picked up Eli at the bus stop in the snow, past the neighborhood where nothing looked different. Nothing ever did.

His mind stayed on Eli. He'd asked Anthony about it last night — after they'd found Eli asleep in the lounger, after they'd removed his tie and draped the blanket and stood in the kitchen speaking in low voices over untouched cups of tea. "I feel like I should say something," Graham had said. "Especially since I went through this a year ago."

What he meant was: *I should know how to do this. I should be able to help. I survived Simon. I should be able to guide him.*

But Anthony had reminded him, in that gentle yet inflexible way of his — the voice that was warm but did not bend: "What you feel and what you do aren't always in agreement, Graham. I spent many a night feeling the same for you. Simon is still inside your heart like Theodore is in mine. And nothing I could say would ever make that emptiness go away. Just being there was much more important, don't you agree?"

Graham had looked at him — this man who had buried his own husband, who had sat in the ruins of his own life, who had come to Graham's house after Simon died and simply been there without explaining why or asking if it was wanted. Anthony didn't offer many opinions. But when he did, they arrived with weight.

"And now Niles has become that ghost for Eli. You know how that haunts."

Graham had bristled slightly at the word. Not *feels*. Not *hurts*. Haunts. And that was precisely the word. Not *pain*. Not *sadness*. Haunts. The continuous presence of an absence.

He just hated that life required that word. Hated that the world needed ghosts in order to weave one soul to the next.

Graham had been thinking too much — turning Anthony's words over, turning Simon's memory over, turning everything over and finding nothing new on the underside — and he parked and closed the garage door and slammed the mudroom door before realizing how much noise he'd made. The sound echoed through the house.

Graham carried the canvas grocery bag from the car — the one Simon had sewn on the old Singer years ago, telling him they needed to "reduce and reuse" while drinking a gin and tonic. The stitching was crooked. Graham could remember Simon cursing at the bobbin, declaring the whole project a monument to futility, and then presenting the finished bag with pride. The bag was ugly. Graham had used it every week since.

He walked down the hall toward the kitchen, and something caught the corner of his eye.

He stopped. Pivoted. Looked through the office doorway.

There, just around the corner, next to the bookshelves, sitting in the leather chair bathed in morning sun, still in his wrinkled suit sat Eli reading. Hadn't heard anything — not the garage door, not the mudroom slam, not Graham's boots on the hardwood. He was absorbed. Lost in whatever he was holding.

Graham instinctively backed away. Stepped quietly out of the doorway and continued to the kitchen, setting the grocery bag on the counter before glancing at the clock. Nearly nine. The world outside was going to work, to school, to whatever their days held. He had planned to spend the morning attempting another round of what had become his daily attempt at the Oltrarno.

How am I going to write this?

The final book. The last Marco and Alessandro novel. The one that was supposed to bring everything together — six novels' worth of story, of love, of separation and reunion and the slow, hard education of two men learning what it meant to belong to each other in a world that would never let them belong openly. It was supposed to have some grand ending, he kept telling himself, but couldn't find it.

It hadn't gone well from the start. He'd written fragments — a chapter here, a scene there, notes on scraps of paper that he filed in a folder and then forgot about. He thought he knew the shape of the story. Knew where Marco needed to go. Knew what Alessandro needed to become. But knowing the shape and writing it were different things.

Since Simon died — a year ago now, fourteen months if he was counting, and he was always counting — the writing had stopped. And now this. Niles. Eli in his living room. The world demonstrating once again that it had no interest in waiting for Graham to sort himself out before delivering the next catastrophe.

He knew those were excuses. He could have written before. He'd written through worse — the middle chapters where the story sagged and Simon kept him going. But Simon had always been the story. Graham had written Marco as Simon — not literally, not in the biographical sense, but in the way that mattered. Marco's steadiness was Simon's. Marco's quiet courage, his refusal to be diminished, his insistence on being present in a world that wanted him invisible — all of it came from watching Simon live. They'd never spoken of it directly. Not really. Graham suspected Simon knew, though.

Simon barely had any notes on Alessandro. A word here, a suggestion there, nothing that required more than a pencil mark in the margin. But Marco? Simon would flag the slightest phrase that smelled like surrender, the faintest hint of Marco pitying himself or giving in to despair. "Marco *has to be strong,* Graham," he'd say — not request, not suggest, but plead, with an urgency that went beyond editorial opinion. "There are too many people out there who *need* Marco to be strong for them."

Graham hadn't understood that fully at the time. Had taken it as Simon being Simon — exacting, demanding, pushing Graham to write better than he thought he could. But he understood it now. Standing in his kitchen, fourteen months after Simon's death, understanding arrived the way understanding always did — late, and all at once. Simon hadn't been editing a character. He'd been protecting the people who needed that character. The readers who would find Marco the way Eli had found him — alone, afraid, looking for proof that someone like them could survive.

Now Simon was gone. Had been for over a year. And while Graham had reached a place where he could say Simon's name without his throat closing, it still hurt. Time hadn't healed it. Anthony was right about that, as he was right about most things. It just got you accustomed to the haunting.

Except — while Simon was gone, Marco was not.

And Graham was not about to kill off his beloved Marco. He couldn't do that. Not to Alessandro. Not to the readers who needed them. Not to Simon, whose voice still lived inside Graham's head, still editing, still insisting: *Marco has to be strong, Graham.* Better. Braver. More.

He took off his coat, hung it on the hook in the mudroom, and walked back through the hall toward the office. The melancholy came with him just as he stopped at the doorway.

Eli was still in the chair. Still reading. Still so deeply inside the book that the world around him had ceased to exist. Graham had seen people read before — at book signings, at festivals, in the corners of cafés where strangers tucked into novels he'd written. But this was something else. Something he didn't have a word for yet.

Eli had a small tear rolling down his left cheek. He was rocking slightly — a gentle, almost imperceptible motion, forward and back, as if trying to comfort himself the way a child does when no one else is there to do it. He didn't know he was doing it. Graham was sure of that.

Graham took a step into the room, thinking Eli would notice, but Eli didn't look up. His hearing aids weren't in. Graham reminded himself that he knew that. Had known it since last night. Had known it ten minutes ago, when the slamming door hadn't registered. But somehow his brain still didn't default to Eli being deaf. He was just — Eli. The man who laughed too loud and made jokes at his own expense and could read Graham's face from across a room with an accuracy that bordered on clairvoyance. The hearing loss was always there, but it wasn't what Graham saw when he looked at him. It was the least interesting thing about him.

For a moment, he considered stepping back out. Letting Eli be. He didn't want to startle him — didn't want to be the thing that interrupted whatever was happening between Eli and the book, whatever private reckoning was taking place in that chair.

But Eli looked up.

Their eyes met, and Graham saw just how glassy Eli's were — red and swollen, the whites threaded with the particular pink that came from sustained crying. It went straight through him. He wanted to cross the room, pull Eli into his arms, hold him the way he'd held Simon's friends at the funeral.

But he held still. Anthony's voice was already in his head — Simon's, too — telling him not to move. He hated them for it. He wanted to *help*. But he knew. Eli didn't need fixing. Didn't need advice. He needed someone to stand in the doorway and not leave. That was all.

He gave Eli a small smile — trying to say, without words, that he didn't want to intrude, but also: *How are you, really?*

Eli laid the open book on his lap, and Graham saw the cover. *The Novice's Chapel.* His second novel. The Marco and Alessandro book about separation, about silence, about waiting for a letter that didn't come.

He winced. Internally, briefly, but he felt it. Of all the books on that shelf — six novels, any of which Eli could have reached for — he'd pulled that one. The one Graham had always considered his most difficult, the one that had nearly broken him to write.

He'd been riding the unexpected success of the first novel — the reviews, the readers, the letters from people he'd never met telling him that Marco and Alessandro had meant something to them. And then Simon had suggested that the second book needed to separate them. That Marco and Alessandro needed to learn what their connection meant by losing it.

Graham had spent weeks in quiet panic, convinced that Simon was speaking in code — that the suggestion to separate the characters was really a suggestion to separate themselves. That Simon was trying to tell him that *they* needed time apart. That *they* needed to know what their connection really meant. Graham couldn't say it. Couldn't bring himself to ask, because asking would make the fear real.

Simon had finally called him on it. Cornered him in the kitchen and asked why he'd been so cagey. Why he couldn't talk. Why he'd retreated into a silence that Simon could feel through the walls.

Graham couldn't answer. Stood there, unable to look at the man he loved because looking would mean admitting what he was afraid of, and admitting it might make it true.

Simon tugged at his hand the way he used to when they were students. He kissed him. Wiped his eyes with the pad of his thumb.

"If I didn't believe in you — in *us* — I would never have suggested that Marco and Alessandro learn how to love each other. Truly love."

Graham had looked at him. His precious Simon. Standing in that terrible kitchen with the overhead light buzzing, looking at Graham with the patience of a man who, as it turned out, didn't have all the time in the world.

"Graham. You can write this. You *need* to write this. Because those two boys need to learn how to make this work. The same way we learned."

Graham had stood there, flooded with relief but still afraid. How was he going to take readers who had come to love Marco, who had embraced

Alessandro as one of their own, and test them? How was he going to separate two characters that people had invested in without turning those people against the story — or worse, against hope? This was going to be a test of his readers as much as his characters. And Graham, who had spent his whole life being a pragmatist, knew that people sometimes failed exams.

He'd written it anyway. Because Simon told him to. And because Marco had to be strong.

"You okay?" Graham said.

As soon as the words left his mouth, he felt stupid. Simon had chastised him endlessly for using that word — *stupid.* "Only stupid people use it," he'd say, which was itself a kind of Simon joke, delivered with a straight face and a raised eyebrow.

But Graham felt it now. Not because the question was wrong, but because Eli couldn't hear him. Wouldn't have caught the words, wouldn't have been able to read his lips from that angle, with Graham mumbling the question into the doorframe. He wanted to step out of the room and come back in again, pretending the last few seconds hadn't happened. A do-over. A rewrite.

Eli set the book on the end table and stood, holding up one finger — *wait* — before walking past Graham and out of the office. Graham stepped aside, watching him disappear down the hall toward the powder room. He was gone for a few moments. Then he returned, fussing with the hearing aids — pressing them in, adjusting the volume. Then he spoke, and Graham heard his voice — the one with its particular cadence and slightly uncertain volume, the voice Graham realized he had missed hearing.

"I hated you, you know."

Graham's heart dropped — a physical sensation, the floor giving way beneath him.

"When I was fifteen and read this book —" Eli turned to look at the novel lying on the table, wiping at his eyes with the heel of his hand, "— and you took Alessandro away from me."

He couldn't finish the sentence. His voice caught — not a gentle faltering but a hard stop, the words breaking apart. He forced himself to breathe, visibly working at it.

"I sat down and started to write you a letter back then."

"You did?"

Eli nodded, still wiping at his eyes. His hand was shaking. "I finally had someone who understood me. I would lie in bed and pretend I was Marco — nobody able to understand me, nobody wanting me." His voice broke again. He paused. Breathed. Tried again. "And then you —"

Graham wanted desperately to walk over. Surround him in his arms. Rub his back. Let him cry against his chest. Tell him it would be okay. All his problems and worries would disappear, and the world would right itself, and everything would be fine.

But Anthony's voice whispered in one ear. Simon's in the other. *Just be.*

Goddammit, he hated them for this. He didn't want *just be.* He wanted *to help.* Wanted to do the thing his body was built to do — protect, comfort, solve. Every instinct in him was screaming to move, to close the distance, to hold this man.

"When Alessandro left for Venice — and he didn't come back —" Eli was crying now, openly, his voice raw and uncontrolled. "I cried. I kept waiting for him to return. Or a letter. *Something.* But you — you killed him. YOU KILLED HIM!"

The words tore out of him and filled the room. Eli fell back into the chair, his head in his hands, his shoulders shaking.

Graham's eyes watered. His vision blurred. But his feet were planted on the hardwood floor of his own office, and he could not move them. Could not have moved them if someone had offered to carry him. He stood there and watched.

A twenty-four-year-old man grieving a fifteen-year-old's heartbreak. The fifteen-year-old's heartbreak was really the twenty-four-year-old's. The fictional character's loss was really the loss of a person named Niles Ashworth, who had been buried yesterday in a cemetery in Portland while a piece of his unfinished robot sat on top of a rose.

"And —" Eli looked up, trying to speak, his face wrecked, and Graham was having difficulty understanding him. The words were waterlogged, coming out in fragments. "I wrote a letter to you — why did you kill Alessandro? Marco didn't deserve that. He never asked for much. Just wanted someone to love him. And you took him away —" He wiped his eyes, trying to see. "It was in my book bag. To mail from school. But I didn't."

Eli turned to look out through the office windows. The sun was rising higher now, casting long shadows across the room, the light moving the way it did every morning — tracking across the walls, finding the shelves, illuminating the spines of the books that held his life's work. He sat in that light, looking out at the woods, and Graham watched him and said nothing.

"Why didn't you?"

Eli didn't turn. Didn't respond. Graham wondered if he hadn't heard, but Eli replied.

"I realized that night, lying in bed —" His voice was quieter now. "— there were other books. Alessandro can't be dead. He *just can't.* You wouldn't kill him." He paused. "He'd come back somehow, right? Marco wasn't going to be alone forever, right?"

Eli looked at him. His red face. Swollen eyes. Hair plastered to his forehead from where his hands had been pressing against his skull. He looked like a boy.

All Graham could do was shake his head. He knew these worries. He'd had them himself, writing *The Novice's Chapel* — the fear that he'd gone too far, that the separation was too painful, that readers would abandon Marco the way Marco feared Alessandro had abandoned him. But Simon had assured him. Had told him to keep going, keep writing. Marco isn't done yet. Neither is Alessandro. But the work must be honest. There is no rescue. There is only survival.

And when Graham had finished the last chapter — the chapter that ended not with reunion, not with death, not with any answer at all, but with Marco painting an angel's hand in an empty chapel, waiting for a letter that didn't come — he'd felt sad. Depleted. There was no happy ending. Just a hint. A suggestion that the story continued beyond the page, that Marco's hope was still breathing even if the novel had stopped.

"Just like life," Simon had said when he read it. He'd set the manuscript down on the kitchen table and looked at Graham with an expression that held the simple conviction of a man who had read something true. He'd called it the most powerful work Graham had ever written. And he'd maintained that position until — until he died. Simon had always said that Book Two was Graham's best. His masterpiece.

Graham hadn't agreed. It didn't feel like a masterpiece. It felt like a wound. Too much of Marco in his head. Too much worry in his heart. The book hadn't given him pleasure the way the first one had.

"You can't get your characters out of a mess simply by having them say the right things," Simon had told him, years ago, sitting across from him with a red pen and a glass of wine. "They have to *feel* it, Graham. They're feeling. *Feeling*. That's what makes it real. That's how they survive."

Survive.

It hit Graham now, standing in his office doorway, watching Eli cry over a book he'd written decades ago. Simon had been teaching him how to survive. Not Marco — *Graham.* The novels weren't just stories. They were instructions. A manual for endurance, written in the language of Renaissance Italy, disguised as fiction, delivered by a man who must have known, on some level Graham couldn't fathom — that Graham would need them one day. That Marco's strength would become Graham's strength. That the lessons written on the page would eventually have to be lived off it.

Now Eli was learning the same lesson. Graham's story was no longer his own. Hadn't been for some time, though he was only now understanding that. Eli had taken it. Levi had taken it. Readers he would never meet, in rooms he would never enter, at three in the morning in bedrooms he would never see — they had taken it too. Graham had written Marco for Simon. But Marco didn't belong to Simon anymore. He didn't belong to Graham.

Stories don't belong to the people who write them. They belong to the people who need them.

Graham was not the author. He was the channel. The voice of Simon.

Eli stood abruptly and pressed at his hair. Rubbed his eyes with both palms. Straightened his wrinkled shirt and then left the office without a word. Graham heard — felt, more accurately, through the floorboards — his footsteps heading down the hall. The bathroom door closing. Water running.

He turned and looked at his desk. The pile of papers he'd been trying to mold into a book. The folder of notes. The legal pad with its lists and arrows and crossed-out ideas. A sample chapter he'd written last month that didn't sound like Marco.

"I killed him," Graham whispered to himself. He looked at his hands — the hands that had typed those chapters, that had written Alessandro's departure, that had ended a novel with silence instead of reunion. He took a deep breath and sat down. Put on his glasses. Pulled the stack of manuscript pages toward him and began to sort through them before stopping and looking out the windows. The woods. The bird feeder. The squirrels conducting their daily siege.

This wasn't his book anymore. None of them were, probably, though he hadn't truly understood that until now. He'd always thought that readers enjoyed a quick read — a good story, something to pass the time on a plane or a beach. Nothing more. He could never quite believe the people at book signings who told him how important the novels were. The woman in Chicago who'd cried and held his hand — that one had stayed with him. He'd told himself she was overcome. Caught up in the emotion of meeting an author, the way people sometimes were.

But the college kid in Boston. *Marco was the reason he hadn't killed himself.*

That one Graham hadn't known what to do with. Hadn't known what to say in the moment beyond *thank you for telling me*. Hadn't been able to look at the kid's face for too long, because if he looked too long he'd have had to ask the question that would not have been right to ask — *what was happening in your life that a book about a Renaissance painter became the thing that kept you here?* So he'd thanked the kid. And signed the book. And the kid had moved on, and Graham had gone back to his hotel room, called Simon and told him that surely the kid had meant *Marco* in some looser sense, some figurative sense, that the books had been one of many small things and not the thing.

Simon had listened. Then said, in the quiet way he said things that were not negotiable: "He meant it, Graham. They all do."

Graham had argued. Of course he had. They'd gone back and forth on the hotel phone for a long time, Simon patient, Graham insistent — that Simon was being kind, that the books were just books, that no one's actual life turned on whether a fictional Renaissance painter survived a fictional plague. Simon had eventually said *I love you* and *get some sleep* and hung up, and Graham had lain awake in that hotel bed and decided, in the way he decided most uncomfortable things, that Simon was wrong this once. That Simon's belief in the books was the loyalty of a husband, not a verdict on the work.

He had told himself that for two years. Because anything else was too much weight to carry. Silly little books, he'd thought. Stories about an Italian painter and the man he loved. They couldn't possibly mean what the kid had said they meant.

But Eli — just now — standing in this room, shaking, telling Graham about a letter he'd written at fifteen because a fictional character's loss had felt like his own. Crying now because —

Graham couldn't finish the thought. Didn't dare presume to know what level of hell Eli was navigating. He knew it was hell — he'd been on his own journey since Simon died — but he also knew there was no one-size-fits-all. Grief was custom-tailored. It fit no one else.

He turned and looked back at the leather chair where Eli had been sitting. The book lay on the end table where he'd left it — *The Novice's Chapel,* open, facedown, the spine gently cracked. He remembered Levi sitting in that same chair last year, reading the first manuscript, getting so lost in Marco's story that Graham had to touch his shoulder to bring him back for dinner. It had been different for Levi. But perhaps not so different. Levi had told him once that the book was his lifeline — that when they were living in the car, when Susan was looking for work and Lucy was too young to understand and Levi didn't know what lay ahead, Marco was the one who kept him company. Who made him feel less alone.

Graham had been moved by that. But he'd also, in some quiet corner of himself, not quite believed it. Levi was being nice. Being generous. The same way those people at the book signings were generous.

He thought about that night at the library last winter — the snowstorm, Eli texting him about Levi and Lucy, Graham driving through the worst weather of the year to find Susan and her children in a building that was about to close. How he'd summoned Simon's courage — Simon, who had always known how to talk to people, how to find the words that didn't condescend or diminish — and found a way to offer Susan help without undermining her pride. Levi had said it was the book that saved him. The Oltrarno. Graham had smiled.

But Levi had meant it.

And Eli meant it.

And the people at the signings — the woman in Chicago, the college kid in Boston — they had meant it too.

Graham looked at the manuscript pages and understood that the story he'd been trying to finish — the final Marco and Alessandro novel — wasn't stuck because he didn't know the plot. It was stuck because the ending required something he hadn't yet arrived at. He knew something he hadn't known an hour ago: the book's purpose was larger than his grief. Larger than Simon. Larger than Marco or Alessandro or any single reader in any single chair. The story would end the way it needed to end — not because Graham decided, but because the people who carried it forward would show him how.

He looked at the chair. At the book. At the window.

At his hands.

Alessandro's Last Letter

THE LETTER ARRIVED ON A TUESDAY, carried by a courier Marco had never seen before — a boy, perhaps fourteen, dust-covered and breathless, who handed it over without a word and disappeared back into the Via dei Coronari before Marco could ask who had sent him.

It was not in the usual hand.

The three previous letters had arrived through the cloth merchant in Prato — the circuitous route they'd established, the careful chain of hands that kept any single link from knowing the full path. Those letters had been written on Alessandro's good paper, the heavy cream stock his family used for correspondence, folded precisely into thirds and sealed with plain wax — no crest, no insignia, nothing that could identify the sender if the letter were opened by the wrong person. The handwriting on the outside had been the merchant's. The handwriting inside had been Alessandro's, but measured — controlled, written in the coded language they'd agreed upon, every sentence performing its innocence.

This letter was different.

The paper was thin — not Alessandro's stock but something cheaper, rougher, the kind you bought in a market stall when you needed to write something quickly and didn't have your own supplies. It was folded unevenly, one corner bent where it had been creased in haste. There was no seal. The handwriting on the outside — Marco's name, the chapel address — was Alessandro's own. Not the merchant's. Alessandro's. Unmediated. As if he'd written the address and handed it directly to the boy without thinking about what that meant, or thinking about it and not caring.

Marco stood in the courtyard outside the chapel, holding the letter. The midmorning light was hard and flat — the Roman sun at its least forgiving, the kind that erased shadows and made everything look exposed. The novice was somewhere inside, sweeping. The other artists hadn't arrived yet. Marco was alone, which was fortunate, because his hands were shaking.

Marco –

I have perhaps ten minutes before this letter must leave my hand, so I will not waste them on weather.

Something has changed here. I cannot say what, not in writing, not even in this letter which I am sending outside our arrangement because the arrangement may no longer be safe. I don't know that. I suspect it. The suspicion is enough.

The negotiations are not what my father described. I knew that within the first week, though I couldn't say how – something in the way the Doge's men spoke to us, the rooms we were given, the particular quality of courtesy that is really surveillance. My father sees it too. He has not said so. We do not discuss it. We discuss the terms, the trade routes, the banking arrangements. We discuss the weather.

The weather in Venice is not fine.

I have been trying to write this letter for six days. Every version I started sounded like a coded message, and I am tired of codes. I am tired of ordinary language carrying extraordinary weight. I am tired of asking about the commission when what I mean is: are you still mine? I am tired of writing about weather when what I mean is: I am afraid.

So I will say it without code, without metaphor, without the careful architecture of language that has kept us hidden for years. If someone intercepts this letter, then what follows will condemn us both, and I have decided that the risk of silence is greater than the risk of truth.

I think of you constantly. Not in the way that phrase is usually meant – not as sentiment, not as longing prettified for the page. I mean that my mind returns to you the way a compass returns to north. Involuntarily. Mechanically. As though the instrument of my thought has been calibrated to your coordinates and cannot be reset.

I think of you in the mornings. I have told you this. But I did not tell you that I think of you in the negotiations, too – sitting across from men who are deciding the fate of my family's influence, and thinking instead about the way your hand moves when you are painting. The sureness of it. How your whole body changes when you are working – how the uncertainty that lives in you every other hour of the day disappears entirely when there is a brush in your hand. I have watched you paint more than you know. I have stood in doorways you didn't know I was standing in. I have memorized you the way you memorize pigments – by studying what happens when the light changes.

Do you remember the evening by the Arno?

I know you do. You will say: which evening? We had many. But you know the one I mean. The evening before my family left Florence. The evening you came to the riverbank and we sat on the wall and watched the water and said nothing for a very long time. The light was doing that thing it does in Florence in autumn – turning everything the color of old gold, making the buildings across the river look like they were painted rather than built. You said the Arno was the only honest thing in the city. I asked what you meant. You said: it doesn't pretend to be anything other than what it is. It just moves. It just carries things from one place to the next.

I have thought about that every day since. The river as a carrier. As a passage between one bank and the other. And I have come to understand what you meant, though I don't think you knew you meant it yet – that love is not a destination. It is not the far bank, the place you arrive at and stay. Love is the crossing. The movement. The willingness to step into the current not knowing what waits on the other side.

That evening is my vanishing point.

You will understand the term. You taught it to me – the point in a painting where all parallel lines converge, where the eye is drawn, where the entire composition resolves into a single, distant truth. Every painting has one. Every life, perhaps, has one too. Mine is that evening. The wall. The water. Your voice saying something true without knowing it was true.

Everything I have done since – every letter, every arrangement, every careful manipulation of my family's influence to bring you to Rome, to keep you painting, to build a life around you without anyone seeing the architecture of it – all of it converges on that point. That evening. That wall. You.

I do not know what is happening here. I do not know why the negotiations have shifted, or what the Doge's men want from my father, or whether the courtesy that surrounds us is hospitality or captivity. I know only that I cannot write again for some time. Perhaps a long time.

And I needed you to have this letter – not a coded one, not a careful one, but this one – before the silence returns.

Remain hopeful. Not blindly – deliberately. Hope as an act of will, the way you paint as an act of will – not because the world has given you reason to, but because the alternative is to stop, and stopping is not something you know how to do.

Permission to remain hopeful. I grant it to you.

I grant it to myself.

– A.

Marco read the letter three times standing in the courtyard. Then he sat on the low stone wall beside the chapel entrance and read it twice more. The novice appeared in the doorway with a broom and saw him there and turned around without speaking, which was the novice's particular gift — the ability to recognize a moment that did not require his presence and to remove himself from it with a grace that most monks spent decades trying to achieve.

The sun moved. The shadows shortened. The bells of a nearby church marked the quarter hour, then the half, then the hour. Marco did not hear them. He was reading the letter again — the sixth time, the seventh — his eyes returning to the same passages, wearing grooves in the sentences the way water wore grooves in stone.

I have memorized you the way you memorize pigments – by studying what happens when the light changes.

He pressed the paper flat against his thigh and looked up at the sky. The blue was deep and absolute — the particular blue of Roman midday that admitted no clouds, no ambiguity, no softness. Everything was sharp. Everything was clear. Except the one thing that mattered, which was obscured behind a wall of words that said everything and explained nothing.

The weather in Venice is not fine.

What did that mean? The code they'd agreed upon — weather meant wellbeing. Fine meant safe. If the weather wasn't fine, then Alessandro wasn't safe. But the letter contradicted itself — he said he suspected, not that he knew. He said the courtesy might be surveillance. He said he couldn't write again for some time. He said *perhaps a long time.*

Perhaps. The most dangerous word in any language. A door left open just wide enough to let hope through, and fear with it.

Marco folded the letter. Not into thirds, the way Alessandro's letters usually arrived, but into a small, tight square — the smallest he could make it without creasing through the words. He placed it inside his shirt, against his chest, where it sat like a second heartbeat. Then he stood and walked back into the chapel and climbed the scaffolding and picked up his brush.

He painted for six hours without stopping. The angel's face. The Virgin's hands. The lilies in the foreground that symbolized purity but that Marco had always privately thought looked like they were reaching for something just out of frame. He painted with a precision that bordered on violence — every stroke deliberate, every line controlled, the brush moving across the plaster with the intensity of a man who understood that if he stopped moving, the stillness would consume him.

The novice brought water at the usual time. Set it on the floor below the scaffolding. Sat and watched.

"You seem different today," the novice said. He was a young man, with the angular face and serious eyes of someone who paid closer attention than his quiet demeanor implied. He rarely spoke, but when he did, his observations landed with an accuracy that suggested he had been listening for some time.

Marco didn't answer immediately. He was working on the angel's hand — the same hand he'd been painting for days, the one extended toward the Virgin. But today the hand looked different. Today it looked like it was reaching not to announce but to hold on.

"I received a letter," Marco said. He didn't know why he said it. He'd told no one about the letters — not the other artists, not the priests, certainly not the cardinal who oversaw the commission. The letters were the most dangerous thing Marco possessed, more dangerous than the memories they referenced, because memories could be denied but ink on paper could not.

The novice nodded. "Good news?"

Marco considered the question. The letter was pressed against his chest. He could feel it there — the thin paper, the hasty fold, the words he'd already memorized.

"I don't know yet," he said. And it was the truest thing he'd said in weeks.

He climbed down at vespers, when the light through the western window turned the chapel wall to gold. He ate alone in his room. He took the letter out and unfolded it and read it again — the eighth time, the ninth, the edges already softening from the handling, the ink already beginning to blur where his thumb had pressed against the words he kept returning to.

That evening is my vanishing point.

Marco lay on the narrow bed and held the letter against his chest and stared at the ceiling. The plaster was plain and white, unmarked — the same ceiling he'd stared at on his first night in Rome, when Alessandro had appeared in the doorway and said *Hello, Marco* and changed everything.

He thought about vanishing points. The painter's trick — the illusion of depth on a flat surface, the convergence of lines toward a single point that existed only in the mathematics of perspective. Every composition needed one. A fixed point that organized everything around it, that gave the eye a place to rest, that made the flat world appear to have dimension.

Alessandro was his. Had always been. The fixed point toward which every line of Marco's life converged. Without him, the composition fell apart. The parallel lines ran wild. The painting lost its depth and became what it had always been underneath — a flat surface, pigment on plaster, the illusion of meaning on a wall that was just a wall.

Remain hopeful. Not blindly – deliberately.

Marco folded the letter and placed it with the others — the small stack inside the oilcloth, the archive of love written in a hand that had grown steadier with the years. Three coded letters and this. Four pieces of paper. Everything he had.

He pressed his hand against the oilcloth and closed his eyes.

Outside, Rome settled into its evening. The bells marked compline. Somewhere in the building, the novice was praying. Somewhere far to the north, beyond the mountains and the plains and the lagoon, Alessandro was — Marco did not finish the thought. Could not. Would not.

He would remain hopeful. Deliberately. As an act of will.

He would paint the angel's hand tomorrow. And the day after. And the day after that.

And he would wait.

"WHAT'S THIS?"

Eli looked up from the paper Claire had handed him. He'd been sitting on the sofa when she and Derek walked into the living room together — a configuration that was unusual enough to make him close the book he'd been reading, set it on the end table, and turn to face them. Claire had the posture of someone delivering news. Derek had the posture of someone who'd been dragged along.

"It's — I thought it would be easier if I wrote it down, so —" She stumbled over the words. Eli noticed she was having a hard time looking at him, which didn't make it easier at all. Eye contact with Claire had always been one of the reassurances of this apartment — she was the roommate who looked at him when she talked, who turned her face toward his when she spoke so he could read her lips, who had learned these things without being asked. Claire not looking at him was its own kind of warning.

He looked back at the paper. A series of bullet points, really. Typed. Printed from whatever laptop she kept in her bedroom. The font was something sensible — Arial, probably — and the formatting suggested she'd agonized over it. Claire was a nurse. She wrote patient notes for a living. She knew how to structure information. What he was holding was not a casual memo. It was a carefully prepared document, and the care itself told him how serious this was.

Both Claire and Derek were moving out at the end of the lease.

Eli looked up and over toward the calendar hanging on the kitchen wall above the thrift-store table they'd all chipped in to buy two years ago — the round oak one with the scratch across the top from when Derek had dropped a cast-iron skillet, the one they'd bought at Goodwill for forty-five dollars and split three ways and now nobody would be taking because nobody could agree whose it was. The end of the lease was nearly six weeks away. The end of July. Somehow that date, which had always been abstract, suddenly had weight.

Eli looked at Derek. Derek was looking out the window. That was a Derek move — he'd always been good at being physically present without being available. Claire had clearly pulled him along to make this a joint meeting rather than two separate blows, and Derek had agreed to come, but that was as far as his participation was going to extend.

Eli had driven home maybe fifteen minutes earlier. Pulled into the lot, climbed the stairs, shed his work clothes, thrown on sweatpants and an old t-shirt, and come out to the living room with the intention of picking up Graham's book and reading another chapter of *The Novice's Chapel*. He'd already known what was coming next — he'd read the novel when he was fifteen, after all, remembered the broad shape of it. But he'd found that a chapter here or there was all he could take these past several weeks. Like a very expensive bottle of something he knew to pace himself with, a single pour at a time. Besides, he was finally starting to feel a little more himself. Not fully there. But he'd straightened his bedroom back toward something resembling civility. He'd even finally boxed up Niles's things — the engineering textbooks, the neatly folded shirts, the charger cords, the books on machine learning he'd been working through — and pushed the box to the back of his closet. He'd thought about taking it over to Donna and Brett's, but he didn't think they were ready yet. Donna hadn't reached out in a couple of weeks. Brett, neither.

Honestly, he admitted to himself, neither was he.

But at least he was on the right path this week. One more day of work, then the weekend. Work hadn't been particularly difficult — his coworkers had been nice, even though most of them still had no idea what had happened. He'd told a few people that someone close to him had passed, vaguely. He hadn't named Niles. Hadn't named their relationship. That felt like a conversation he'd have when he had the energy for it, which had not yet arrived. His spreadsheet work had been, unexpectedly, a form of comfort. The cells balanced. The formulas resolved. The routine didn't require him to feel anything. Still not quite the same as before. But he was getting there.

He looked back at the other bullet points on the paper.

Each was giving him $250 toward the security deposit, for cleaning or whatever.

He could keep the furniture if he wanted. Or sell it. They weren't taking it.

Claire had handwritten the last bit, probably just after she printed the rest. Eli wasn't sure if she'd forgotten to include it when she typed or if she'd wanted to make it more personal. Knowing Claire, it was the second.

I'm finally moving in with Justin. We're getting married at the end of the year.

He looked up, temporarily forgetting everything. "Awww, Claire! Congratulations!" He stood — really stood, pushed off the sofa entirely — and pulled her into a hug. "I'm so happy for you."

She was finally able to look at him once he stepped back, the worry in her face seemingly forgotten. The relief of being met where she'd been bracing herself to be rejected. "I'm sorry, Eli. I know there was never a good time, and — "

He waved his hand, only catching part of what she was saying. But he knew. "You go be a princess, girl!"

He was genuinely happy for her. Claire had told him, when she first moved in almost three years ago, that she was done with men. *There are no good ones left, Eli. Just – none. I'm going to adopt a cat and call it a life.* And then she'd met Justin at a coffee shop four months later — the nurse and the graphic designer, she'd summarized it, with an almost aggrieved precision, as if she resented being the protagonist of such a predictable story. Eli had laughed until his sides hurt. He was surprised, honestly, that it had taken them this long to get to the next step.

He looked over at Derek. Derek was watching now — with his usual subtle distance, the way he watched everything. Claire had known Derek before Eli; she'd been the one who recommended him as the third roommate back when they'd needed someone to fill the empty bedroom. Derek was quiet. Clean. Paid his rent on time. Kept his dishes washed and his portion of the fridge organized and his social commentary to himself. Otherwise, Eli didn't see much of him. They'd lived in the same apartment for two and a half years and Eli could not, if pressed, name a single one of Derek's friends.

Claire said something and Eli turned back to look at her, this time angling his face so he could catch her lips.

"Derek is moving to Chicago."

Eli looked over at him, surprised.

Derek shrugged, like it wasn't noteworthy.

"He's been offered a job at —" Eli turned to hear Claire — "— and the timing just worked out." He returned his attention to Derek's face. Moving across the country. Eli hadn't even known Derek was looking. Then again, there were plenty of things Eli didn't know about Derek.

"Congrats on your new gig, Derek."

He noticed Derek's slight wince — the small, almost invisible contraction at the corners of his mouth. Derek always did that when Eli spoke to him, as if Eli's deaf voice were a problem Derek was politely enduring. Eli had asked Claire about it once, years ago. *It's just Derek,* she'd said. *He's like that with everyone. Don't take it personally.* Eli hadn't bothered worrying about it after that — life was too short to make a project out of a roommate's unexplained micro-expressions — but he had never stopped feeling self-conscious when he spoke to Derek. Some things you couldn't un-notice.

Eli heard Claire's voice again, turning in time to catch her saying, "—sorry it's short notice."

"No, it's okay."

"I wanted to — "

"It's okay, Claire. I'm excited for your wedding."

She smiled. "Really? You sure?"

"Of course. I'll be okay."

Claire gave him another hug and began speaking again — something about invitations, something about the venue in Camden, something else he caught fragments of. He understood what she was getting at. He was tired of trying to keep up with every little word. Derek had already walked out of the living room by the time they both looked over — not a word of goodbye, not a handshake, not even a nod. Just gone. Back to his bedroom. Back to wherever Derek went when he wanted to not be here.

Claire gave a *sorry* shrug. Eli rolled his eyes and smiled. "That's Derek for you," he said, tilting his head — and Claire, to her credit, gave a little embarrassed smile in return, the acknowledgment of a shared joke that had been running for two and a half years and was now, apparently, ending.

She squeezed his arm and headed back to her room. Eli returned to the sofa. He set the paper on the coffee table beside Graham's book — the paper and the book side by side, Claire's bullet points and Marco's silence.

Everyone was leaving.

Eli's phone buzzed in his pocket, pulling him out of his head.

He'd practically gotten used to ignoring it since —

He needed to come up with a better phrase. *Since Niles.* The words only ever brought back everything at once, a wave that had no bottom. And something about the phrase itself felt disrespectful, like Niles was being relegated to a category, a chronological marker. *Before Niles. Since Niles.* As if Niles were an event in a timeline rather than a person who had sat at this very kitchen table eating cereal and explaining the specific pleasures of the Dewey Decimal System.

He shook his head — the small, physical gesture he sometimes used to move his brain along, like a stuck record getting a gentle nudge back onto the groove. Silly, probably. But it worked.

He pulled out the phone and found a message from Levi.

Another one.

Levi had been texting him every day since —

He scolded himself. *Goddammit.* There was that phrase again.

Since Niles. Since Niles died. Since his boyfriend had been shot through the chest in a library on a Thursday afternoon while reading a book. That was the phrase. Those were the words. He might as well start using them. They weren't going to get smaller by being avoided.

He swiped up to read today's edition.

LEVI

Can you help me with driver's ed?

Eli perked up. It wasn't what he was expecting.

Levi had been texting him to check in, to tell him he loved him, to send a meme or a photo of something Lucy had done. Small, regular, without demand. The kind of texts you could respond to with a single emoji without feeling like you'd failed. Eli had been doing exactly that for weeks — responding, when he responded, in the smallest possible ways, the minimum viable acknowledgments. He hadn't felt like he had anything to say. And if he did respond, it was usually something small. He didn't want to hurt Levi's feelings. He knew what Levi was trying to do. And — well — Eli still felt a need to keep an eye on him. Levi might have a home now and be going to school, but it hadn't been that long ago that he and Susan and Lucy had been sleeping in a Honda Civic in the parking lot of a grocery store. Levi carried that with him, whether he knew it or not. Eli recognized it because he'd grown up watching his own version of survival — different, less severe, but similar enough in shape that he understood the posture.

He also knew Levi and Michael were still… something. Levi hadn't volunteered much. Eli hadn't pushed.

But driver's ed? He hadn't even thought about Levi driving. Levi had never seemed particularly interested. Of course, to be fair, Eli hadn't spent all that much time with Levi since the holidays. He'd been so focused on Niles that —

Niles.

He shook his head again. *Nope. Not going there. This is about Levi.*

Hey. Isn't school over?

He texted — more to redirect his own brain than because he actually needed the answer.

Last week.

Oh. He hadn't realized. Of course, he hadn't realized a lot of things lately.

But taking summer school. Want to get my license.

Eli remembered learning to drive. He'd been late to it — used to say so to his friends, who had all been driving since sophomore year. It had taken him until nearly the end of his senior year to finally get that shiny plastic ID with his face on it. He remembered getting his hair trimmed specifically for the photo and taking his hearing aids out before the picture. His hearing aids back then had been enormous — this was seven years ago, the technology hadn't been as miniaturized as it was now — and Eli had painted them bright green with nail polish his sophomore year, a decision that had mortified his mother and delighted him in roughly equal measure. He'd loved it when people saw them. Took the conversational pressure off — nobody had to pretend they hadn't noticed, and nobody had to make Eli explain himself. Just there they were, bright green behind each ear, saying everything before Eli had to open his mouth. For the license photo, though, he'd taken them out. He hadn't wanted to look different in it. He'd wanted the ID to show a boy who looked like every other boy.

He didn't give a damn about that anymore. Hadn't for years. Funny how the things that had felt so pressing at seventeen turned out to be the things you outgrew without noticing.

Uh… sure. What do you need me to do?

Mom needs her car to go to work so I was wondering if I could use your car to practice?

A second message chased the first before Eli could respond.

Only if you don't mind. I don't want to be a burden or anything.

Typical Levi. The apology preceding the request, the preemptive offer to absolve anyone of the obligation of saying yes. It popped into Eli's head without effort: *Levi will always apologize before he's finished asking for something.* Funny how certain things about people just crystallized into shorthand once you'd known them long enough. *Never trust the guy in the shitty old white van. All Instagram photos are fake. Levi will always apologize before he's finished asking for something.*

Stop. Of course I'll help. And yes you are a big ol' burden, but I GUESS.

He hit send and smiled to himself. It felt… normal. The first normal thing in weeks. The small muscle of banter flexing again, tentatively.

He watched Levi's typing dots flash, then stop. *Oh, shit,* he thought. *I hope he understood I was joking.* Maybe he was out of practice. Maybe the joke had landed wrong. He started typing something more serious — a clarification, a walk-back — when Levi's reply beat him to it.

Great. I live to be a pain in your ass.

Eli looked at it for a moment before the smile crept fully across his face. *You little shit,* he thought, laughing aloud at the empty living room. Okay. Fine. Two could play that game. He deleted his serious follow-up.

It's good to have goals. Why the license all the sudden? Hot date?

Oh yeah. I've got so many lined up!

Tell me about it! I keep fighting off all those hot mens, but you know how it is.

Eli felt a twinge of guilt for being cheeky. Maybe he needed to be more serious. Maybe it was too soon for this kind of talk. Maybe grief had rules he was supposed to be following. But then —

Oh, I do. Got all those hot boys lined up outside my door just waiting.

Slut.

Eli hit send before he could censor himself and then panicked. Had he gone too far? Levi's typing dots appeared immediately. *Oh shit.* He wished there was an unsend button. Levi had been messaging him for weeks, trying to be there for him, and here Eli was pushing too hard trying to be funny, like he was learning how to walk on old legs again. Rusty. Creaking.

I learned from you.

Eli laughed aloud. The apartment was empty — Derek behind his bedroom door, Claire probably on the phone with Justin — and Eli laughed into the silence of it. He pulled his legs up onto the sofa and leaned forward over his phone.

Maybe he was fine. Maybe he'd been overthinking himself. Levi wasn't a kid — well, he *was,* in some ways, he was seventeen — but he was more mature than most adults Eli knew. And he could obviously hold his own. Eli just hadn't given much thought to how Levi really was... inside. Not lately. Not since Niles. Not since —

Gurl — you got so much to learn. But Miss Eli is here to learn ya.

Levi responded with a laughing emoji before adding:

So, will you teach me to drive then? PUULLLEEEAASSEEE?

Eli smiled. A normal conversation. It felt — free. Like sliding a window open for the first time after a long winter, the air coming in cold and sharp and alive.

Fine. Fine. But don't crash Simon's car. His ghost will come out of the organically sourced cloth seats and mess up your hair.

Simon's ghost lives in your car?

Don't tell Graham. He'll want it back.

Levi sent a zipped-lips emoji.

When do you get your permit?

Saturday.

Fine. 1st lesson is Sunday then. I'll come get you.

REALLY?

Eli laughed. Levi seemed excited.

YES GURL. CALM DOWN.

Levi sent a rainbow flag and a car emoji, causing Eli to snicker to himself.

Are you trying to imply my car is gay?

Not implying.

I'm telling Simon's ghost on you

Eli replied, adding a ghost emoji.

I'll be a good boy. I'm scared of g-g-g-ghosts.

Eli laughed aloud just as another text came through — this one from Graham. Eli swiped up to read it.

GRAHAM

Nashville says they miss you. How you holding up?

Nashville?

I'm here, remember? For Michael's graduation.

???

Last week... Saturday. I messaged you. We talked about it when you were over.

Eli sort of remembered. Honestly, he hadn't been thinking much about anything for weeks — his short-term memory had been sitting this season out, coming in only when absolutely necessary.

Oh... yea...

You don't remember. Don't bullshit a professional bullshit artist.

I thought you were an author.

Same difference.

Eli laughed. Why was he laughing? Shouldn't he still be sad? Or at least solemn? There was a guilt that came with any moment of lightness, the small voice that asked if he was allowed yet. He wasn't sure. But the laughing had happened before the voice could stop it, and maybe that was the point.

I'm happy to read you're feeling a little better, Eli.

He didn't know what to say. How would Graham know how he was?

I didn't say I was.

You didn't have to.

That's the first joke you and I have shared in a long time.

Eli paused. Was it? Probably. Was it okay to joke yet? He admitted to himself that it felt like diving back into the pool after the spring thaw. Good. A little chilly yet.

His phone buzzed — Levi again.

LEVI

What time?

Eli switched threads.

2am. Might as well start learning how to drive home from the gay bars.

I'M ONLY 17!

Eli laughed.

Besides, aren't you NOT supposed to drive when drunk?

YOU'RE not drinking. I meant driving ME home from the bars. Get it straight!

But I'm gay!

WHAT? YOU ARE? LORDY LORD!

Eli was smiling without knowing it. Everyone knew that Levi and Michael were *a thing*. But Levi hadn't had the movie moment — the formal coming out, the announcement, the sit-down with Susan. It had just been assumed. Even Levi treated it like everyone already knew — which, in fairness, everyone did. But Levi had not yet claimed the word — *gay* — at least not that Eli knew of.

Shut up!

Never! So... tell me about this gay thing... I want to know all...

Another text from Graham arrived as he hit send.

GRAHAM

Are you able to pick me up Sunday?

What time? Where? Deets?

LEVI

I CAN'T BELIEVE YOU

Levi had texted, prompting Eli to switch back.

Oh, you can believe in me. I'm better than Santa

Eli typed out with his thumbs, which were finally coming back to life after weeks of stiffness.

GRAHAM

Southwest, 4:18pm

Anthony dropped me off, but I thought I'd ask you first.

Eli had an idea. An excellent, terrible, perfect idea.

We'll be there

We'll? Are you bringing Anthony?

You'll see.

He switched back to Levi.

I'll be at your place at 2. And we're going to pick up Graham at the airport at 4. M'kay?

LEVI

We're picking up Graham?

YOU'RE picking up Graham. I'm just going to be in the passenger seat.

I don't think I can drive to the airport yet. It's like my first time.

And I'm the BEST at taking virginity! I'll be gentle!

ELI!!!

Eli could picture Levi — sitting on his bed, embarrassed, face going red, Susan probably calling from the kitchen to ask what was so funny.

Graham's coming back from Nashville. Which, btw, why didn't you go?

He watched Levi's typing dots come and go before another message from Graham covered the screen.

GRAHAM

Ok. Just text me if there is a problem.

Eli sent a thumbs-up and followed it with:

How was it?

Typical. Too hot. Too long. Boring speeches. But Michael was... excited.

Eli's eyebrow rose involuntarily.

Excited?

Before he could follow up, Levi's response finally came.

LEVI

I had school until Tuesday and mom said I couldn't go.

Cost too much anyway.

Eli read it twice. The simple facts. Susan's budget. The cost of a flight to Nashville. The fact that Levi's mother could not afford to send him to his boyfriend's graduation, and Levi was writing it the way he wrote most things — plainly, without self-pity, as if the facts spoke for themselves and needed no editorial. Eli had read texts like this from Levi before. He knew the tone. A kid who had learned early not to get upset about money.

You and Michael doing okay?

He hit send before thinking it through. His focus was still coming back online. This was the most he had spoken — texted, whatever — with anyone in... well. In a while. He'd skip past that thought.

I dunno.

Eli's eyebrow did another involuntary curl.

We can talk about it if you want.

Maybe Sunday. Text is hard.

He stopped himself from typing a risqué joke. Not because Levi was seventeen — that wasn't the issue, they'd been joking freely for twenty minutes. It was that this felt like something more important. He wasn't sure what, exactly. But he felt it. Levi had just said *I dunno,* and *I dunno* was not a Levi word. Levi said yes or no. Levi said *cost too much anyway.* Levi said *mom said I couldn't go. I dunno* meant something was too big and too tangled for text. Levi needed to say it with his face showing.

I'm here for you.

Thanks. Same for you.

Eli read the response and remembered all those texts Levi had sent over the past month — the check-ins, the memes, the *love you* at the end of nothing in particular. He'd read them. Replied to many. But now he was *feeling* them, the cumulative weight of them, the quiet persistence of a kid who had decided, without being asked, to be there. Eli wasn't that much older than Levi, technically — six, seven years — but he'd been through a thing or two. Especially now. And it sort of felt like he needed to be there for this kid. Levi was growing up — already had, in most of the ways that mattered — and maybe he just needed some help. It felt kind of good to be able to be that for him. Or, Eli hoped it did.

He had felt similar about Michael last winter, when Michael was coming out to him at the New Year's Eve party. But Michael had parents and an uncle who was one of the best role models around, even if Graham didn't think so himself. Michael had scaffolding. Levi had only his mother — Susan, who was doing her best and doing it alone — and a fragile, rebuilding life. Still learning to trust that things wouldn't always go to shit. Eli knew that feeling. Knew it quite well.

He sent a heart emoji, followed by:

See you Sunday at 2. I'll be the one in the fabulous car out front.

Gay car!

That's it! I'm pulling the Ouija board out and telling Simon on you!

Don't! I'm sca-sca-scared of g-g-ghosts!

Eli laughed.

Cya.

Bye.

Eli realized Graham had sent a couple of messages while he was finishing up with Levi. He scrolled up.

GRAHAM

Let's just say those closet doors have been taken off.

Burned down, more like it.

Becca has no idea what to think, although I think David is handling it just fine.

Eli read them and could only imagine Michael in short shorts and a skimpy tank with glitter makeup, strutting around David and Becca's living room like he was about to be interviewed on late-night TV.

We've created a monster!

WE? You!

I have no idea what you're implying. I am but a conservative professional who prides himself on being demure.

Demure, my ass! My nephew seems to have found a friend or two down here that... well... let's just say, have taught him how to fit in online.

WHAT?

Eli was genuinely surprised. He hadn't been on Instagram in forever — not since — but he swiped open the app and searched for Michael's account.

Again. The phrase. He needed a better one.

Michael's page came up and his profile picture had obviously been changed. It was still Michael, but a close-up of his upper body — shirtless — wearing what looked like a botanical bucket hat, green eyeshadow, rouge, painted lips, the whole arrangement framed like a magazine shoot. Eli stared at it for a second before scrolling down.

Several posts. Michael with other guys his age. Some at a garden somewhere — maybe Cheekwood, if Eli was remembering the Nashville landmarks right. One of Michael sitting in sunglasses in a convertible, his head tilted back and laughing. Another of a guy lifting Michael up from behind, Michael's legs dangling, both of them mid-laugh, Michael looking genuinely surprised. The guy was attractive — tall, dark hair, a little older-seeming, maybe a freshman in college rather than a high school senior. He appeared in more posts than the others. One with his arm around Michael at a restaurant. Another of them at what looked like a pool party, side by side, shoulders touching.

Is he okay?

Eli texted back to Graham.

I think so. I know he's been worried about you.

Eli paused. It wasn't a surprise — Graham had mentioned it before, and Michael had sent texts Eli hadn't answered. But reading it now, in plain words from Graham, it landed differently. *Michael was worried about me.* Eli was still getting used to the idea that people were worried about him, loved him, in ways that weren't performative. That had been Niles's gift — being so quietly and specifically loved had taught Eli that it was possible. Now the world was demonstrating it had been possible all along.

Tell him I'll text him soon. And I'm sorry for not before.

I'll pass it along, but I'm sure he understands. We talked a little already.

Eli was tempted to ask what they'd talked about. But he knew. Inside, he knew. Or thought he did. Graham and Michael had spoken as uncle and nephew, which meant they'd spoken as a man who had lost his husband and a kid who had watched it happen from the outside. Eli was not going to push into that. It was not his to know.

Gotta run. Dinner soon. Taking everyone out tonight.

Eli checked the time — 6:47 in Portland, which made it 5:47 in Nashville, dinnertime in the South. He remembered being in Nashville with Niles. The restaurant Graham's sister had insisted on, the hot chicken that had ruined both of their mouths for twenty-four hours, the way Niles had been charming and polite and had said almost nothing the entire meal while still somehow making Becca fall in love with him.

He paused. The thought of Niles had come through — but it didn't sting the way it had a week ago, a month ago. It was still present. Still hurt. But it had — softened. Become less of a wound and more of a presence. He hadn't flinched.

Have fun. Love to Becca and David.

Graham sent a thumbs-up.

See you Sunday.

Cya.

He set the phone down on the coffee table. Sat there for a minute.

Then he got up and walked to the bedroom.

The box was where he'd left it — at the back of the closet, under the spare comforter, the way he'd shoved it the day he'd packed it. He didn't think about it. He pulled the comforter off, picked the box up, carried it down the stairs and out to the car, and put it in the back. Closed the door. Walked back upstairs.

That was all he could do.

Barely an hour later, Eli's phone buzzed again. He pulled it up while standing in front of the microwave, waiting for his leftovers to finish reheating — chili from last weekend, the second-to-last serving from the big pot he'd made on Sunday because cooking for one still hadn't become routine.

Michael.

But Michael had obviously been sailing the HMS I'm Gay! while Eli had been —

Fine, he thought. *Hurting.* There. He'd said it. Well — thought it. He'd resisted the urge to admit this for six weeks. The whole damn thing had been horrible. Just awful. Catastrophic in the particular way that losing the one person who made your life make sense was catastrophic. He'd needed to be tough. To be strong. For — he didn't actually know who. Maybe for himself. Maybe for Donna and Brett, who were the parents, while he was just the boyfriend. Maybe for Graham, who had already lived through this and didn't deserve to watch someone he cared about repeat the performance.

But now, with the microwave humming and the evening light slanting through the kitchen window, he could step back and admit the whole thing just —

"Fucking sucks," he said aloud to the empty kitchen.

The microwave beeped, as if to punctuate it.

He set the phone on the counter and pulled out the bowl — too hot, of course, he'd set it for too long — and grabbed a spoon and a paper towel. Sat at the thrift-store table. Balanced the bowl on the paper towel like an amateur. Read Michael's text.

Well — looked.

It was a picture. A family selfie at some chain restaurant, obviously. Eli snickered before he'd fully processed it — Graham seated at the end of the booth looking perfectly miserable, his usual face in those situations. Graham hated chain restaurants on principle. Graham hated photographs of himself on a related principle. The combination of the two produced, reliably, an expression of patient suffering that Eli could have identified from across a football field.

Eli zoomed in to see everyone.

David was seated between Maddie and Jack. Maddie was fifteen, looking at the camera with the specific aggressive disinterest of a teenager who had been instructed to smile and had decided to comply only technically. Jack, ten, had stuck two straws up his nose for the picture, which was exactly the move you'd expect from a ten-year-old whose older brother had put him up to it. Becca sat on the other side next to Graham — her big brother, Eli always had to remind himself — leaning in and holding onto his arm. Eli smiled at that.

Sometimes — very rarely, but sometimes — Eli wondered what it would have been like to have a sibling.

Then there was Michael, up front, holding the camera for the family selfie.

Eli set the spoon down so he could pinch the screen and bring Michael into the full frame. He was wearing a tight navy t-shirt with big bold white letters across the chest: *G-A-Y.* And — Eli zoomed in closer — was that an earring? A small silver hoop in his left ear. Tasteful. But definitely new.

Wow, Eli thought. He set the phone down and took a bite of his dinner. Michael was really going all-in.

He snickered at himself. He couldn't have imagined doing anything like that when he was Michael's age. He stopped and reminded himself — he was only six years older. It wasn't *that* long ago. He'd been a painfully cautious college freshman, the kid who volunteered at the hearing loss resource center and studied accounting because it was practical. He hadn't worn a shirt that said *GAY* in his life. Hadn't worn an earring. Had not, as far as he could recall, ever painted his nails. The closest he'd gotten to any of this was a trip to Boston with friends when he was nineteen.

He picked up the phone, saved the photo, and replied.

Miss you all. Wish I were there.

It was the first real text he'd sent Michael since —

Since Niles died.

He paused. Let himself think it. *Niles died.* He said it, aloud, to the empty kitchen. Like it was finally time.

Life fucking sucked, he reminded himself. Again.

The phone buzzed.

MICHAEL

YOU'RE ALIVE.

Eli winced. He knew what Michael meant. Just — bad timing. Bad metaphor. In fairness to Michael, though, he hadn't had much practice choosing his metaphors around grief.

The follow-up came quickly.

Sorry.. I mean.. Thank you for texting back.

The sting went away. He needed to start returning Michael's attention. Niles would want him to.

He paused. Repeated the thought. *Niles would want him to.*

He was already at that stage, was he? Saying things that people said when someone important was gone forever. *They'd want that. He used to love this.* The grammar of loss. The language of bereavement as a set of stock phrases that came pre-formed, like laminated cards. Eli had always hated them in the mouths of other people. And here he was, using one in his own head without flinching.

He abandoned the chili and sat back in the kitchen chair.

I'm sorry I haven't been a good friend.

He felt it as he sent it. He hadn't been. Niles would have yelled at him for not keeping up with Michael, especially with what Michael was going through. Well — Niles never yelled. But Niles would have known. Would have said something small and specific and unavoidable, like: *Michael is seventeen. He has been alone in Tennessee for seven months. He is also going through something. You are not the only one going through something.* Niles had been like that. Precise. Quiet. Impossible to argue with.

The more Eli thought these things — the *Niles would* and the *Niles wouldn't have* — the more he felt like Niles was sitting there with him. Not across the table, exactly. More like beside him. Unable to look him in the eyes, but present. Looking toward him so Eli could read him. Understand him.

Eli unconsciously reached up and pulled out his hearing aids. He'd been doing that lately when he was at home. He didn't need them here. Not anymore. Niles had been the only person he'd ever lived with who'd let him not wear them — who'd learned to turn toward Eli when speaking, without being asked. Derek and Claire never quite had. But they were leaving, and Niles was gone, and the apartment was becoming a place where Eli could simply be deaf.

The way he'd wanted to be as a kid.

He set the aids on the table next to the chili bowl.

It's okay.

You should've seen Uncle Graham's face when we got him on the Mystery Mine in Dollywood last week.

Mystery Mine?

Coaster at Dollywood. Uncle Graham took us.

Pics?

Eli watched as his phone lit up with photos — the family decked out for a day at the amusement park. The first was them in front of the big Dollywood sign, everyone in shorts and loose clothes except for Graham, who was in his usual khakis and polo but had added a sun hat, which made him look less like a man at a theme park and more like a man about to embark on a short expedition to photograph birds. Other photos: Jack and Becca on a merry-go-round, Becca holding the pole like she was the one who might fall off. Graham and Maddie eating ice cream together at a picnic table, Maddie looking uncharacteristically relaxed, Graham looking uncharacteristically pleased with himself. Maddie had clearly warmed to her uncle over the week.

Then one of Graham flanked by Michael and Jack, the three of them just stepping off a roller coaster. Graham's face was — Eli actually laughed aloud. Graham looked like he had literally seen a ghost. His eyes were wide. His mouth was slightly open. His hair looked like the wind had won. Michael and Jack were both laughing — Michael openly, Jack to the point of doubling over. The photo was clearly taken about four seconds after they'd disembarked, and Graham had not yet recovered. Maddie had probably ambushed him with her phone. Graham had not yet been able to form the word *no*.

Eli saved all the photos and replied.

I wanna go! I love coasters.

OMG YOU SHOULD COME DOWN!

Eli smiled. Maybe he should. Get away. A real change of scenery. But he had shit to figure out first — especially now that his roommates were leaving.

Maybe after I get some shit done up here.

Michael's status showed he was typing.

I tried to come up.

Had he? Eli didn't remember. He felt a flash of guilt that he'd probably left a message from Michael unread. He hadn't read most of what Michael had sent. Hadn't read most of what anyone had sent, honestly.

I'm sorry. I know.

Can I ask a question?

Sure.

Well.. I guess it's not a question. Just.. I can't imagine like losing someone...

Eli read it. Read it again. Michael wasn't giving him the usual *how are you* that required a sanitized reply. Michael was saying the thing everyone else had been quietly refusing to say — that what had happened was unimaginable.

I couldn't either not until

He paused again before he sent it. Then added:

Niles died.

He hit send and waited. Staring at the phone. He'd finally written it.

He texted me the day before.

Eli looked at the words.

He did?

Said he was almost finished with his robot.
Wanted to show me when I was back.

He gulped.

I told him I couldn't wait to see it.

The picture surfaced before he could stop it: Niles at this table during breakfast, knocking out texts the way he always did. Check his emails. Send texts. Eat. Go to class. The order was the stabilizer. He would have been here — maybe Wednesday morning — texting Michael in Nashville about a robot he wouldn't live to finish. Eli would have been across from him, probably, or still in bed, or in the bathroom getting ready. The last morning.

I still have it

He texted, thinking about the robot pieces and the other small artifacts of Niles he'd put in the box at the back of his closet. He hadn't thrown any of it away. Couldn't.

I can imagine him yelling at you for stuffing it in a box.

Eli sniffed and half-smiled, mostly grimaced. That was exactly Niles. Not yelled, exactly. But he would have looked at him with that particular expression — the *are you sure this is optimal* expression — and Eli would have laughed and kissed him and moved the box anyway.

He probably would have.

Niles was always nice to me.

Eli paused.

He wasn't upset. Just — remembering. Everyone had been so focused on how he, Eli, was doing since Niles died, and almost no one had simply stated a fact about Niles himself. The small true things. The way he was in rooms. Michael had noticed. Michael had filed it away. And now Michael was offering it back, a simple observation without agenda, the way you'd tell someone about a color their friend had worn that suited them.

Niles *was* always nice to Michael. Worried about Levi. Thought deeply about Graham and Donna and Brett and this little gang of people Eli had pulled him into. At night, in bed, Niles wouldn't say much. But he would always — *always* — hold Eli's hand and ask him how he was doing.

Not a performance. Not a box to check. Just: *How are you? What happened today? Is there anything you need?*

That was what Eli missed most. The unsung question. The quiet hand in the dark. And he choked back tears — happy to remember those moments and equally devastated because they were no longer there. Never would be. Not like that. Not from Niles.

Yes.. He was.

Was.

As if Michael understood what was happening on the other end of the phone, he texted a little heart emoji. Eli stared at it. Looked through it.

Gurl, we need to get you outta that house! Getting too damn real up in here!

Eli did a double take. Michael's message was followed by a disco dancer emoji with rainbow spotlights behind it. A complete 180 from the previous beat. Eli laughed — couldn't help it. He remembered a line from a movie — *Steel Magnolias,* maybe — about how laughter through tears was one of the better emotions. How right that was.

Okay. Michael wanted to play that game. Eli leaned forward, scrolling through his photo app, searching for the specific picture he was looking for. It had been buried in there for years. He hadn't sent it to anyone. Hadn't had the balls. But Michael was the right audience. Michael had earned it.

He found it. Attached it. Hit send.

A moment later:

OMG GURL!

Followed by:

YAAASS QUEEN!

And a cascade of rainbow flag emojis that filled the entire screen.

Eli laughed aloud. He'd known it would work.

The photo was a rare shot of him at nineteen, in Boston, at the clubs during a long weekend with two college friends. A skintight crop top in hot pink with *TWINK* emblazoned across the front in rhinestones. His naturally dark, almost-curly hair cut short for the occasion, gelled into something approximating intentional. Skinny shorts that left essentially nothing to the imagination. A forearm-full of colored bracelets. Eyeliner. Highlighter on his cheekbones. He was posing on the dance floor with a vodka cranberry in his hand — courtesy of someone's older brother's ID — sunglasses covering his eyes in a dark club because that was the look. The one weekend of his life in which he had ever been, objectively, a twink.

He looked back at the photo and laughed at himself. His gay phase, he'd always called it. He'd told Graham about it once over dinner but hadn't had the courage to share the picture.

Michael was seeing it first.

Then it struck him.

Michael — in that selfie, tonight, with the GAY t-shirt and the earring — looked a lot like that nineteen-year-old Eli in Boston. Same energy. Same shimmer. Same willingness to take up space.

Maybe Michael was starting his gay moment. Whatever it was, Eli had been there. And there was comfort in that.

Seriously, you should come down here.

My friend and I can take you out. We can get in this club that's 18+.

Eli raised an eyebrow. Graham had mentioned Michael's changes. The Instagram posts had shown some guys Eli didn't recognize. One in particular — the tall dark-haired one — appeared in more photos than the others.

Friend? Anyone I know?

He pushed, gently.

Michael's response took longer.

He's cool. Met at school after we got back from Christmas break. He's gay too.

Nice.

It was all Eli could think to say. He wanted to ask about Levi. About whether Michael was still — whatever they were. But he remembered Levi's *I dunno* and decided not to push. Not in text. Not tonight. He preferred Michael open to Michael closed off. The friend from school wasn't his to name. Michael would, when he was ready. Or Eli would hear it from Levi on Sunday.

I was really pissed off for you, btw.

Another 180. What now?

Why? For what?

Levi told me about the funeral. You having to sit in the middle.

Fucking bullshit! Niles was your boyfriend!

Eli hadn't even been that upset. In the moment, he'd been too out of it to register anything beyond the stone floor and Levi's hand and that guy… uh… Kieran? Him signing in the vestibule. The seating had only registered later, and even then felt like a fact, not an injury. *This is how the Catholic Church works. I am not family. I am not a spouse. There is no line on the form for what I was to him.*

But Michael had been pissed off. On his behalf. Weeks ago. Still.

I was too out of it to notice, honestly

Just because you're gay doesn't mean you shouldn't be up there with everyone.

I'm tired of straights oppressing us!

Eli paused. Read the sentence again.

He had never been much of an activist. He'd signed a petition once in college for a change in bookstore fees and felt like a rebel, and that was approximately the extent of his political engagement. Michael seemed to have turned into what Eli had, in college, called a *political gay* — showing up at every Pride meeting, using words like *oppression* in text messages, having very specific opinions about rainbow capitalism. Eli was noticing a more out-and-proud Michael than he'd seen even six months ago.

I'm fine.

Really.

He wasn't going to stoke the fire. Niles and he had been opposite in many ways, but they'd shared one thing absolutely — neither of them had wanted to be in the spotlight. Not like that. Not as a political example. Not as a cause. The funeral had been what it had been. Eli had walked out with Levi's hand in his and a small piece of unfinished robot in his pocket. That had been enough. That was still enough.

Well, I just hate it for you.

Thank you, Michael. I will be okay. So, have you decided what you're doing for college now?

A subject change. Not subtle. But Michael would take it.

The last time they'd talked about college — really talked — had been before Niles died. Michael had gotten into a couple of schools. He'd been leaning toward Portland University, with the stated reason being that he wanted to live with Graham, wanted a change of scenery, wanted some independence from his parents. The unstated reason had been Levi.

Everyone had known it. Even Becca had known it.

Still debating. I got a couple of scholarships.

Congrats.

Thx.

Well, if you need help deciding, I'm here for you.

I have to decide soon coz the dorm paperwork is due.

Oh. I thought you were talking about staying at Graham's.

We talked. Still thinking.

Eli imagined a family meeting in Nashville. Graham, David, Becca, Michael. Eli could picture it. If Michael was *still thinking*, that sounded a lot like Michael was no longer as certain about Portland as he had been. Which meant he was no longer as certain about Levi.

Eli looked over at the chili bowl on the table — crusted around the sides, the spoon stuck to the paper towel he'd used as a napkin. The sun was already below the horizon outside the window, the sky going that particular late-evening blue that meant the day was officially over. He hadn't realized how long they'd been talking. He leaned forward and stretched, his spine cracking in three places. Today was different. Like the batteries had finally started charging again. He was still mostly drained. But underneath, something close to happy. Closer than he'd been in weeks.

Well, congrats on graduating, Michael.

Thx Eli. I wanna come see you regardless of school, mkay?

Eli smiled.

mkay, Gurl.

He added a winking emoji.

Michael replied with a snapping-fingers emoji. Then a kiss emoji.

Had he created a little gay monster?

Possibly. Probably. He couldn't stop smiling. Almost certainly.

And the little gay monster had just asked about his apartment, his friends, his grief, his boyfriend's final morning, and had sent him a disco dancer picture when the moment got too heavy, which was exactly the intervention Eli needed, and the intervention no one else had been able to deliver.

Niles would have approved.

Eli picked up the phone one more time. Looked at the photo Michael had sent. Then the photo he'd sent Michael in return.

He favorited both before turning off the kitchen light and going to bed.

Chapter Eight

SIMON'S VOLVO took the onramp to 295 South just a little after eleven on a Friday morning. Eli had decided to take the day off, figuring he had the vacation time and could use a three-day weekend. Besides, he needed to get ready for Claire and Derek's move-out, run errands — the usual excuses he knew he was making to keep himself busy. At least the weather had turned in his favor.

Late June in Portland was his second-favorite season, mid-October reigning supreme. He loved the change of the seasons, the anticipation of the holidays just ahead. That was something he'd looked forward to as a kid and still perked him up annually. But late June was the moment he stopped worrying about the weather — when summer was truly here. School out. Pool open. Bikes on the road. Things just felt brighter, and that, too, had stayed with him as he got older.

He slowed with traffic as he made his way down to the little place he and Donna would usually have lunch at before —

Before Niles died.

Eli felt himself scrunch his shoulders like he was holding something inside every time he mentally said those words. It had been devastating. Purely surreal, he thought, those first few days after Graham told him. Then he'd felt like nothing mattered anymore. Because, at least at the time, nothing did.

And just like Graham had shared way back when they were first getting to know each other, people were trying to cheer him up, or be overly nice to him — bringing him food, texting, Graham himself dropping off groceries one Friday after the funeral. Back then, when Graham had explained how, after Simon died, he'd both appreciated and tried to avoid people coming around to be 'nice,' Eli had nodded along. He hadn't really gotten it. He really got it now.

The guy in front slammed on his brakes, forcing Eli to pay attention. *Niles is dead. You're alive. Stay alert.* He'd lain awake last night thinking about all of it. How somebody recently had tried to comfort him and really pissed him off. He'd chosen not to push back, but something inside him had been bugging the shit out of him ever since. Eli was pretty sure they'd been trying to suggest that since he and Niles hadn't known each other but six months, it might get easier as time went on. *It's not like you were married for 30 years,* they'd said. Eli had smiled and agreed and watched them feel better for thinking they'd helped. They had suggested something he hadn't even known was sitting there. Inside, he hadn't wanted to fight with them.

Instead, his brain had started fighting with him last night. Lying there, he'd kept turning it over. *It's not like you were married for 30 years. Fuck you.* He'd sat up, teeth clenched. *What the fuck does that matter?* He stared at the dark window, but all he saw was the made-up version of the conversation, the one he wished he'd had.

Just because we only knew each other since last Christmas doesn't make it easier, you dumb bitch! It's actually fucking harder! he imagined saying. *We were just figuring out how to live together and then he's fucking gone! Like, Bam! Gone!* He slapped his hands together in this conversation he wished he could've thought of then.

That same *wished he would've thought of it* conversation played out as he exited the highway and drove into the parking garage. He wondered if Graham ever had pretend conversations with himself after Simon died. He'd never wanted to push and ask about things like that before — it had seemed like something you just didn't do. But now he wanted to. He at least knew now what it was like. He couldn't picture Graham yelling at anyone, so maybe Graham hadn't been as angry as Eli felt the past day or so. But everything was really starting to wear him down.

The booth was theirs, which is to say Eli didn't bother checking in with the host stand and walked straight to where he knew Donna would be. She was always the first there — telling him 11:45 but arriving at 11:30. He'd always found it odd that she was the opposite of fashionably late, but after months around her son, he wondered if maybe Niles hadn't been the only one in that family who needed things in life *just so.*

"Eli..." Donna stood and reached for him the way she always did, like she always had before. She looked thinner, tired around the eyes. Eli picked up on it all because he saw it in himself, too. A simple air kiss and he claimed his usual space in the booth. A waiter immediately appeared with a cocktail menu, but he raised his hand, signaling now wasn't the time.

Donna looked at him, but Eli turned to take in the restaurant — people gathering for business luncheons, men in suits and professional attire, the corporate monkey-suit he sometimes described to Graham and Anthony when Donna's lunches came up. Eli fiddled with his hearing aid, then noticed he was doing it and pulled his hand down, reaching for the linen napkin and draping it across his lap. Leaning back into the dark leather, he looked over at her. She was staring. This was the first time they'd been together since the funeral.

"You look tired, sweetheart."

Eli tilted his head slightly. On the best of days it was a struggle to hear in this restaurant. But he caught most of it.

"I am tired."

Donna looked at him as if regrouping. He figured she'd expected him to pass as himself — *I'll be fine* or *Long week.* The usual bullshit that meant nothing but was easy to say. Instead he felt like being completely honest. His *I'm in public* censor hadn't come along for lunch.

She nodded, dismissing what she didn't want to look at, and reached for her wine. She took a sip and surveyed him over the rim, the way she'd always surveyed him, with the look that said *I have already decided what we are doing today and you are going to enjoy it.*

"Brett and I are going to Maine Maritime in August. The benefit. He's been doing committee work for them and they've roped him into emceeing, which is hilarious, you know how Brett is at a microphone. I told him I'd come and run interference. So that's August. Then I'm going to make him take me to that little inn in Rockport in September because if I don't get out of the city for a long weekend I am going to *commit something.*"

Eli nodded.

A basket of bread appeared on their table. Eli watched Donna cast her eyes down to it before gesturing he should begin, while taking another sip of wine.

Donna had suggested they meet. More like commanded. He'd *finally* heard back from her yesterday, after weeks since they'd really talked. He'd reached out, heard back from Brett, knew things were difficult. Hadn't wanted to push. Told himself he couldn't imagine what she was going through.

He'd sent another check-in earlier this week, not expecting a reply, and didn't get one. But added onto it yesterday, deciding he was taking Friday off. Her reply was simple, classic Donna, really.

It's been too long. Our usual. 11:45.

He'd replied with an *ok* and tossed the phone. It was what really got his brain fighting with him last night, thinking about what she must have been going through, as Niles's mother. And his brain came back around saying *so. You're going through some heavy shit, too. It's not a competition, Eli.*

That voice kept interrupting him as they sat there and chit-chatted about being busy, telling him to get to it. *She's not well. You're not well.*

"What are we doing?" Eli raised his voice, unable to control it, unwilling to care. Donna paused and looked at him over her wine glass.

Eli shook his head and stared through her.

"I don't —"

"Donna. Niles is dead."

Eli watched her wince, the glass nearly clinking her nose as she regained herself and set it down without bothering to look him in the eye.

"He's dead, Donna," he continued. "And I don't know about you, but I'm just fucking awful." Eli gritted his teeth, squeezing his nose and eyes, trying to force himself to remain in control.

He saw her look at him — a definite *Don't you do this to me, Eli. Not here* — but he countered: he was going to do this. Here. Now.

"You know, I at least expected to be there with you."

"Eli…" She reached for her glass, but he reached over and moved it away. She sat stunned. Eli saw a waiter coming over and raised his palm. The man stopped in his tracks.

"I never got to tell anyone how much Niles meant to me. Nobody came and even asked if I would help out at the funeral. They didn't ask me to speak. They didn't ask me *anything*. And the fucking strange thing is, Donna, I didn't even realize I was upset. I was too fucking stunned at that awful —" Eli shook his head, forcing something out. "— just fucking horrible funeral, knowing Niles was lying up there instead of in bed next to me."

He saw Donna begin to break, her watering eyes staring a hole into him, but she stayed silent.

"I know —"

She lifted her hand, gesturing he was being too loud, but he stared even harder and continued.

"Eli, nobody would understand —"

"I know you're his mom, Donna. And I *only* was his boyfriend. And it was church, and what would people say, and you were hurting *too*. Blah blah blah." He waved his hand dismissively. "But just because we only lived together a couple of months doesn't mean I didn't *love him*." Eli gulped back his breath and counted to three in his mind, pushing back down everything that was trying to escape.

"You and Brett *have* to be going through so much right now. I get that." He nodded like he wanted her to as well. *"But so am I, Donna…"* The tears finally came trailing down his cheeks. *"So am I."*

"Eli —"

"Hold on. Hold on. I need to say this once because I haven't said it once and I'm tired of carrying it."

She was very still.

"Six months with Niles doesn't make it anything less. Everyone's been assuming that because I didn't have him long, I shouldn't be — what, this devastated. That a few months of dating isn't the same as —" Eli waved his hand her way. "And I have been waiting, this whole time, for somebody to say it out loud so I could fight them. But nobody will. Everyone is so fucking quiet, or *supportive.*" He used air quotes. "So I've been having the fight by myself, in my head, ever since —" Eli paused and gulped. "— Niles died."

Eli broke down. He didn't give a damn who saw, how uncomfortable it made anyone around them. He needed to.

A few moments later, he felt Donna's hand on his. Looking up, he saw her ruined mascara, her watering swollen eyes, the confidence she always had gone.

"I love you, Donna. That's why this hurts to say. I would not bother to say it to somebody I didn't love."

Eli watched her look away. "It's not gonna be the same, Donna. It's not." He pulled his hand back to grab the linen napkin and clear his eyes.

"Everyone means well, but I'm tired of pretending. I *know* it'll get better." He raised his voice again, and she looked over.

"But I don't *want it to.*" He closed his eyes and counted down again to try and calm himself. "Not yet." He stopped and looked right at her.

"The only one who gets it is you, Donna. Graham lost Simon, and Anthony his husband before. I never knew them. Maybe you did. But I didn't. So I can only imagine how they figured out how to move on." He leaned forward, realizing he was grabbing her hand again, thinking it looked like he was almost pleading. He didn't care.

"But you, Donna. You *know* what it's like. You knew Niles." He stopped. Then looked down and felt angry before turning back to her. "*Knew* Niles."

Eli felt Donna pull her hand away, watching her reach for something in her purse. Dabbing a tissue to her eyes, she just watched him.

"You know, you haven't said his name since I got here."

He saw Donna look puzzled.

"You haven't."

"Eli, I don't —"

"I bet you haven't been able to say it aloud, have you?"

"Eli, what in the world are you —"

"Say it, Donna." Eli felt himself sit straighter, focused on her.

"Eli —"

"Donna… you need to —"

"You're upset, Eli, and —"

"Donna."

Eli watched her face begin to collapse again, tears starting to roll over the ones she'd just wiped away. Eli kept his focus.

"Eli —"

He didn't move.

"Niles. *Niles. Niles!*" she spat at him before breaking down into her palms. Eli reached over and touched her arm.

"Niles is —" he began.

"Dead. My son is dead."

Eli slid over and let her fall into his shoulder, feeling her shaking. He watched as people in other booths cast their gaze before abruptly looking away when they saw him watching back. *Let 'em look,* he thought. *This fucking hurts.*

And the only person who understands that is in my arms right now.

Chapter Nine

KIERAN SAT on his bike across the street from Blackstones holding his helmet against his chest and asking himself, under his breath, why he had even agreed to this.

The bar sat low on the corner of Pine Street where it always did, the small front window glowing dim and yellow, a rainbow flag in the upper left corner of the glass that was older than Kieran was. He had been here once before, years ago, in the back of a friend's car who had been giving someone else a ride and had pulled over to let them run inside for a thing — Kieran had stayed in the car, not wanting to seem too curious, his eyes on the door for the whole eight minutes. He had been nineteen then and not ready to know what was inside. He was twenty-two now and he was apparently still not ready, because he had been sitting on his Honda for a full minute and twenty seconds and had not yet swung his leg off the bike to walk in.

He'd been lonely. That was always how it started. Typical Saturday night, everyone else either at work or asleep or doing whatever twenty-two-year-olds with friends did. Kieran had pulled out the phone he kept the app on and had scrolled with the same reluctant thumb he scrolled with every time, telling himself for the umpteenth Saturday in as many years that he wasn't going to find anyone there, that the app was a black hole, that everyone on it was either a creep or a tourist. Three guys had pinged him within the first ten minutes. None had a profile picture of a face. All abs and torsos and one disembodied chest that Kieran had to admit, looking at it, was interested in but also somehow wasn't, which was the contradiction he'd been trying to resolve for years and hadn't yet.

The first guy came right out of the gate with what he wanted Kieran to do to him. No hello. No how are you. Just an instruction, in three words, written in lowercase, with no punctuation. Kieran had blocked him without typing back.

The second seemed more polite at first.

How are you this fine evening?

Kieran had read it twice to make sure it wasn't sarcastic, then replied.

Hello. Doing okay. You?

Horny.

Block.

The third guy was different. Kieran had read the opening message four times because it actually sounded like it had been typed by someone with thoughts.

Hi. I haven't done this much. Sorry if I'm awkward.
Trying to figure things out.

College sophomore. Nineteen. Closeted. Said there were creeps everywhere on the app but he didn't know where else to meet people, and he'd seen Kieran's face in his profile picture and decided to take a chance.

Kieran had related to every word. Had felt seen, in a small and embarrassing way. Had typed back. They'd chatted for fifteen minutes — quick back-and-forth, the kid asking what Kieran did for work, Kieran saying paramedic, the kid replying with a

Whoa, that's cool, I was thinking about pre-med.

The kid had suggested they meet. Just for a drink. No expectations. Kieran had hesitated, then suggested Blackstones — somewhere two guys could have a beer and leave and that was that. The kid had said yes immediately. They'd agreed on ten-thirty.

The kid had asked Kieran to send a picture. Kieran had sent one — not the gym selfie everyone sent, just his face, a normal photo from Pat's birthday party last year. The kid had sent back a row of green check marks.

Can't wait.

He hadn't sent a picture of himself. Told him he'd be in a green shirt and jeans, blond hair. That his phone was acting weird and he couldn't get the camera to upload. He'd see Kieran at the bar.

Kieran knew, sitting on the bike now, that the picture-not-uploading had been the first red flag and that he had let himself ignore it because the rest of the conversation had been so good.

He swung off the bike, locked the helmet to the seat, and crossed Pine Street.

Blackstones was small and dim inside, smaller than Kieran remembered from the eight minutes he had spent looking at its door from a car. A wooden bar ran the length of the right wall, lit underneath in a way that made the bottles glow. A pool table sat in the back. Maybe fifteen people in the place, mostly older men in pairs or threes, a few in leather vests, one in what Kieran would later swear was a cowboy hat. The jukebox was playing something seventies. Nobody looked up when he walked in. Which was its own kind of welcome.

He scanned for a green shirt and blond hair.

He didn't find it. Not in any of the booths along the left wall, not at the bar, not at the pool table. A few of the men were blond or had been blond once, but they were all in their fifties and sixties — regulars, probably, here every Saturday because it was their Saturday. There was no nineteen-year-old in a green shirt anywhere in this room.

Kieran stood near the door for a moment, the disappointment beginning to land. He had been stood up. The kid hadn't —

He felt a hand on his shoulder.

He turned, and the man behind him was wearing a green t-shirt.

Green t-shirt and skinny jeans that were fifteen years too young for the body inside them. Blond hair shot through with grey, the kind of blond that had been fading for two decades. Late fifties at the most generous estimate. The face wore the long fine wrinkles of a habitual smoker, and the hands — Kieran's eyes always went to hands first, professional habit — the hands looked like they had spent thirty years working machinery. Calluses on the fingertips, scars along the backs of the knuckles, a tattoo on one forearm that had blurred into a soft blue cloud Kieran couldn't read.

The man smiled and threw his hands up like he'd just finished a dance number.

"Surprise!"

Kieran felt his heart sink so fast it was almost audible. He understood the entire situation in the time it took him to take a breath. The man had not been the nineteen-year-old who couldn't get his camera to upload. There was no nineteen-year-old. There had probably never been one. The man had probably been doing this for years — running a profile of a kid Kieran's age or younger, charming guys into agreeing to meet, then showing up himself and watching their faces. Kieran wondered, briefly, what came next in the script. Did the man pretend it had been a misunderstanding? Did he offer to buy Kieran a drink anyway? Did he get angry when Kieran turned to leave?

Kieran would not be staying long enough to find out.

He turned without a word and walked out.

The man didn't follow. Didn't call after him. Didn't say *wait* or *stop* or *I can explain*. Which told Kieran everything he needed to know — that this was the man's regular Saturday night, that Kieran was the third or fourth or twentieth man to walk out on him this month, and that the man had built up the necessary calluses to receive that walk-out without flinching.

Kieran crossed Pine Street and got back on the bike. He sat with his gloves on and his helmet on his lap and gritted his teeth so hard he could feel the muscles in his jaw protest. He was not going to cry. He was too angry with himself to cry. He sat with the ache until it became manageable.

He had really thought, sitting on his bed in the lamplight typing back to that profile, that someone his age might also be looking. Someone who was figuring it out. Someone who could meet him halfway. He had let himself believe it for fifteen minutes. And then he had paid for those fifteen minutes by spending the next forty-five thinking he was going on a date.

Not tonight. Probably not ever. He slid the helmet on and fastened the strap and started the engine.

The ride home was ten minutes — back across the Casco Bay Bridge, the lights of Portland behind him, the lights of South Portland ahead, the harbor dark on either side. Ten minutes was not enough time. He spent the whole ride taking inventory of all the reasons it would never work — his mother, who would die first, his ma who had told him at fifteen that the priesthood was a beautiful calling and he should pray about it, his ma who still cut his hair at the kitchen table and would not be cutting it the same way if she knew. He spent the ride enumerating the men on the app he had blocked over the years and the men he hadn't blocked but should have. He spent the ride thinking about Pat, who he'd never once asked about a husband or a boyfriend or a life outside the rig, because asking would have meant being asked back.

He killed the engine half a block before the house, the way he always did, and coasted the last hundred feet so the neighbors wouldn't have to listen to him at midnight. He parked the bike in its usual spot under the side awning and quietly let himself in through the kitchen door, expecting the house to be dark.

The Owl clock at the top of the stairs read 11:32. The stove lamp was on. Danny was sitting at the kitchen table eating ice cream out of the carton, scrolling through his phone in the dim light.

Kieran froze for a half second in the doorway.

"Out late?" Danny said without looking up.

Kieran wasn't sure what to say. He hadn't rehearsed an excuse. He was twenty-two and he was still, apparently, a kid who had to invent a story when his sixteen-year-old brother caught him sneaking in.

"Uh — Pat had a party, and —"

"Oh," Danny said, returning to his phone, the syllable carrying nothing in particular.

Kieran looked at him for a second longer than he should have. Danny didn't look up. Danny was either uninterested or pretending to be uninterested, and Kieran had been Danny's brother long enough to suspect it was the second. He let it pass and walked down the hall to his bedroom.

He flipped on the nightstand lamp and sat on the edge of the twin bed. Pulled off his riding boots — left first, then right, the way he always did, lining them up by the chair without thinking about it. Stood and shed the leather jacket and tossed it across the chair back where it landed in a black slump. He was about to start unbuttoning his shirt when Danny appeared in the doorway.

"You okay?"

Kieran looked up. He hadn't heard Danny coming down the hall.

"Yeah. Why?"

Danny shrugged. "Dunno. You just look angry."

Kieran hadn't realized he looked anything. He was angry, but he hadn't thought it was on his face. He filed that away — Danny reading him at midnight from a kitchen doorway, picking up what Kieran had thought he was successfully concealing.

"I'm okay."

Danny held the look for another beat — the *okay, suit yourself* beat — said *g'nite* and went next door to his own room. Kieran heard the door close, then the muted thump of Danny landing on his bed, then nothing. The thin wall between their rooms going about its business.

Kieran shut his own door, finished undressing down to his boxers, and didn't bother brushing his teeth. He didn't want to look himself in the eye in the bathroom mirror tonight. Not after that. He climbed onto the bed without pulling the covers back and lay on his stomach looking at his pillow.

The night replayed itself in fragments. The man's hand on his shoulder. *Surprise!* The hands like a mechanic's. The dance-number wave. The walk out. The ride home. Danny in the kitchen. The conversation at the door. None of it added up to anything except another Saturday spent in proof of what Kieran already knew.

He flipped onto his back and stared at the ceiling. He'd painted the ceiling himself when he was fourteen — his ma had let him pick the color and he had picked, with great thought, white, because he had wanted to be the kind of kid who didn't have a ceiling preference. He could still see the brushstrokes if the light hit it right.

His mind drifted toward work because work was always where his mind drifted when nothing else was working. Pat. Medic 4. The runs they'd been on this week. The old man in Westbrook who'd fallen off the porch. The kid with the asthma attack on Brackett Street who'd thrown up on Pat's boots. The lady whose dog wouldn't let them near her after she'd had the seizure. The rhythm of the days. The thing that anchored him.

And then, the way it always did when he wasn't being careful, his mind went back to the boy on the road.

The first call he'd ever taken with Pat. Years ago — almost three years now. A boy, ten or maybe twelve, hit by a car on a residential street in Westbrook. Riding his bicycle down a hill. Driver had been backing out of a driveway and hadn't checked. The boy had gone over the trunk and landed in the street twenty feet behind the car. By the time Kieran and Pat had arrived, the driver was on the curb crying with her phone in her hand and the boy was on his back in the road and his bicycle was lying ten feet away with the front wheel still spinning.

Kieran had done everything right. Everything he'd been trained to do. He had checked airway. He had checked breathing. He had started compressions when the boy went into arrest, and Pat had counted aloud beside him because Pat always counted aloud for the new ones, and Kieran had pressed two inches deep, the way he'd been taught — not the shallow TV bullshit, the real thing, the depth that cracked ribs but kept blood moving. He had counted with Pat. He had felt the boy's chest under his hands. He had not stopped when Pat said *Kieran, we need to load him.* He had kept going while they got the board under and lifted, and he had kept going in the rig with Pat driving fast and the siren on, and he had been doing compressions when they wheeled the boy into the trauma bay at Maine Med.

The trauma team had taken over. Kieran had stepped back, his arms shaking. The doctors had worked for another four minutes. Then the senior physician had called it.

Kieran still dreamed about the boy. Not often. Not every week. But often enough that the dream had a shape. He was always doing compressions and the boy was always slipping further away no matter how hard Kieran pressed. He had never told Pat about the dream. He was afraid Pat would say he wasn't strong enough for the job. Which Pat probably wouldn't say, because Pat was Pat, but Kieran couldn't risk it. He needed the job. He needed the direction the job gave him. He knew he could do it. So he kept the dream to himself.

For some reason, lying on the bed at almost midnight on the worst Saturday in a string of bad Saturdays, the boy's eyes came back to him. The dark brown of them. The way they had looked up at the sky and not at Kieran's face. As if to remind him: your shitty date was a shitty date, Kieran, but at least you came home.

He felt grateful and he felt alone and the two feelings did not cancel each other out. They sat side by side, the way they always did.

He looked down at his hands and realized he had been wringing them, and he suddenly remembered Niles. He had held Niles's hand in the rig the way he held all of them, ever since the boy on the road. He didn't want them feeling alone or scared. The boy on the road had taught him that. Every patient since had inherited the lesson.

Niles hadn't seemed scared, exactly. More worried. He had kept trying to talk. Kieran hadn't been able to make out what he was saying — the sounds were wet and shapeless and Kieran had been focused on keeping him alive — but Niles had been trying. Kieran had thought, after the funeral, after meeting Eli in the vestibule, that maybe Niles had been trying to say *Eli*. Maybe Niles had been trying to say something to Eli through Kieran. Kieran couldn't know. But the possibility had been sitting in him for three months.

He closed his eyes and saw the whole scene in his mind again — the library doors, the sound of feet on concrete, Niles on the floor with his white shirt going dark — and felt the familiar weariness of having seen it too many times. He wasn't being haunted, exactly. He was being tired. He wondered if he should see someone. People said you could go talk to people about this. But it cost money he didn't have, and besides, he was just sad for what had happened to a stranger and the stranger's boyfriend. He couldn't imagine how Eli had been doing.

Kieran paused. *Eli was his boyfriend, right?* He thought so. He hadn't had any conversation that established it directly — the funeral program had not said the word — but the way Eli had stood in the vestibule, the way Eli's eyes had moved when Kieran said Niles's name, the way Eli had walked back from their brief exchange and taken a seat in the middle of the church rather than the front, had told Kieran what he needed to know. Eli was Niles's boyfriend. Or had been. Kieran didn't even know what the right word was now. *Boyfriend* didn't quite fit when one of them was gone. *Widower* was wrong because they hadn't been married. The English language did not have a clean noun for what Eli was, which was typical. The English language did not have clean nouns for most things that mattered.

He had meant to try and catch up with Eli sometime after the funeral. He had thought about it on the ride home that day in his uniform, the wind in his sleeves. But he had a shift the next morning and the funeral had been a funeral, and besides — what was he going to say? What did he even want to say? He didn't know the man's last name.

Kieran rolled onto his side and reached for his phone where it was charging on the nightstand. He'd been thinking about this on and off for three months and had done absolutely nothing about it, which was approximately the speed at which Kieran did everything that involved courage. It was already August. School would be starting up again at USM in a few weeks. Niles's friends would be moving on. And Kieran would still be lying in this bed having done nothing.

But where to start. He knew Eli's first name. He knew Eli was deaf, or hearing-impaired, or whatever the right word was. He knew Eli had been Niles's boyfriend. He knew Eli had been seated in the middle of the church next to a tall thin older man who was probably a friend.

That was approximately everything he knew.

He was pretty sure Eli wasn't a member of the Cathedral parish. Not that there was much to arrange — a Catholic funeral Mass was a Catholic funeral Mass, the readings and prayers and order of things all prescribed — but the homily had given it away. The monsignor had leaned on scripture and general language about grief and the communion of saints. He hadn't said much about Niles himself. A priest who had actually known Niles would have had specifics. This one had not.

The Catholic Church was not a place where Niles and Eli would have been received together as a couple, and it definitely wasn't a place where the priest was going to invite them up to receive Communion side by side. Kieran had his own quiet feelings about all of that.

He went to Holy Cross every Sunday because his ma expected him to, and because Holy Cross was Holy Cross — he had been baptized there, made his first Communion there, been confirmed there, served Mass there as an altar boy in the year his father was the most absent. Holy Cross was woven into him.

But the Catholic Church as an institution was something he and the institution were not on the same page about, and he had not figured out yet what to do with that disagreement except to keep showing up anyway because it would crush his mother if he didn't.

He pulled open the desk drawer and rooted around in the back amongst old papers — receipts, two birthday cards from his mother that he'd never thrown away, a folded program from his grandfather's funeral five years ago — until he found Niles's program. He had kept it. He hadn't been sure why at the time. It was a glossy folded card with Niles's photo on the front, a photo Kieran could now barely look at, and the words *In Loving Memory* in a curlicue script that someone at the funeral home had probably chosen from a menu.

Niles Christopher Ashworth.

Kieran lay back on the bed with the program and his phone and started typing the name into Google.

The results came up the way he'd expected — the news articles about the shooting, the local coverage, the syndicated AP version that had run in newspapers across the country, a USM press release about counseling services, two short pieces on the funeral. Kieran scrolled through them. He didn't see Eli's name in any of them. Of course he didn't. Eli was the boyfriend, and the boyfriend wasn't in the news coverage because the news coverage took its information from the funeral home and the family, and the family had not wanted a boyfriend in the obituary he figured. That was how it worked. Kieran knew it was how it worked. He had read enough obituaries in his life to know that the survived by section listed wives and husbands and children but rarely listed boyfriends and almost never listed boyfriends of dead twenty-one-year-olds. It was unspoken. It was the standard erasure. It was bullshit.

He went back to Google and tried a different search. *Niles Ashworth boyfriend Portland.* Nothing. *Niles Ashworth Eli.* Nothing. *Eli Niles Portland Maine.* Nothing.

He paused. If Niles had been on social media at all, he might have a tagged photo somewhere. But Niles probably hadn't been — Kieran had built a profile of him in his head over three months and had decided Niles was probably a careful, bookish, quiet kid who put his actual life on the actual real-world side of the screen. Kieran searched for Niles on Instagram. Nothing came up. On Facebook. Nothing under that name. Niles had been off the grid. Which figured.

Kieran stared at the ceiling. *Eli Portland ME.*

He typed it into Google with very low expectations.

The results: a real estate agent in Falmouth named Eli something. A musician named Eli who played acoustic guitar at Bull Feeney's. The Executive Leadership Institute. A few LinkedIn profiles for men named Eli who worked in finance or insurance. Kieran scrolled.

And then, near the bottom of the second page of results, an Instagram link. *Eli Pelletier. @elip.*

Pelletier. Kieran said it under his breath, the way he'd been taught to say French words from a year of high school French he'd mostly slept through. *Pell-eh-tee-yay.* Or maybe *Pell-eh-tier* — he wasn't sure how Eli pronounced it. He'd find out.

He clicked the link.

He had to log into his own Instagram, which took a minute because he couldn't remember the password. He used Instagram approximately twice a year — to post a picture of the bike along the coast, or a deer he'd come across on a run in Riverside Park that had stared at him long enough for him to get the phone out. Otherwise the app sat on his phone gathering digital dust.

The login finally went through, and there was Eli's profile.

Kieran sat up in bed.

The profile picture was a candid shot of a young man laughing — head tilted slightly back, dark wavy hair falling across his forehead and partly obscuring one eye, a wide unrehearsed smile. Whoever had taken the picture had caught Eli mid-laugh. It looked like he didn't know the camera was there. There was something about his face that made Kieran want to know what the joke had been.

Kieran almost blushed at his own reaction. He scrolled.

Eli didn't have many posts. A picture of the ocean. A picture of a piano keyboard with hands on it. A picture of a snowy walk in what Kieran thought might be Falmouth. A picture of Eli with what looked like a small dog, maybe a friend's. And then, several months back, a picture of Eli with another young man, both of them sitting on a couch, the other man slightly turned toward Eli, their shoulders touching, both of them smiling. Eli was leaning his head against the other man's shoulder.

The other man was Niles.

Kieran studied the photo. It was Niles, definitely. The face he'd seen for forty minutes in the worst forty minutes of his summer. Niles looked younger here, healthier, present in a way Kieran would never get to see him in person. Eli was leaning into him. They were in love. The picture made it obvious without needing to announce it.

Kieran felt the guilt arrive on schedule. He had been admiring Eli's profile picture and now he was looking at a picture of Eli with the man Kieran had failed to save. He needed to be respectful. He needed to remember why he was here. Eli was a man who had lost his boyfriend three months ago, and Kieran was a stranger with a useful piece of information and that was the entire shape of this exchange.

But another part of Kieran was not having it. Another part was saying: I was the last person Niles ever saw. I'm the one whose hand he held. If Eli wants to know what that was like, I'm the only one who can tell him. And if I don't reach out, Eli will spend the rest of his life wondering, and I'll spend the rest of my life knowing I had something to give and didn't.

Kieran clicked Follow.

He set the phone on his bare chest, the cold glass tingling against his skin, and stared at the ceiling for another minute. The ceiling fan was off. The room smelled faintly like leather from the jacket on the chair. Outside his window, the streetlight at the corner of the block was buzzing in its usual broken way.

He picked up the phone again and opened a direct message to Eli.

He typed:

> Hi Eli. This is Kieran Callahan. We met quickly at the Cathedral for

He paused. *For the funeral* sounded too blunt. *For Niles* sounded presumptuous. He wrote *the funeral* and kept going.

> the funeral. I was the paramedic. I'm sorry if I am interrupting you, but I found your profile and wanted to reach out. I don't know if you would want to, but I was with Niles that day and wanted to offer to share if that would help at all. I don't want to cause any pain, so if it's too much, please don't feel you need to respond. I hope you are doing as well as you can. I hope I am not troubling you. Thank you. Kieran.

He hit send before he could read it again, because he knew if he read it he would not send it.

Then he read it. He felt like a complete idiot. *Thank you?* Why had he written *thank you?* Thank Eli for what? For existing? For being someone he had a message to send to? And how many times was he going to apologize? Three? Four? He counted. Four. He had apologized four times in one paragraph.

He plugged the phone in, turned off the lamp, and rolled over to face the window. The streetlight was still buzzing. It was nearly midnight. His ma would wake him for Mass at 8:00.

Like always.

He was starting to drift off when he could've sworn he heard a buzzing. Then it buzzed again. Looking up, he saw the dim glow of blue light reflecting off the curtains flanking his window, turning them from gray-blue to pale white for a moment before going away.

His phone.

Kieran turned and unplugged it, swiping up. A notification from Instagram. It was Eli.

He hadn't been asleep that long, he thought. Still drifting. But the clock on the phone read 11:58 — almost midnight. He opened the message.

His first thought was that he hoped he hadn't woken Eli. He pictured Eli's phone going off, the buzz against a nightstand, the disturbance — and then he reminded himself, with a small internal nudge, that Eli was deaf. He wouldn't have heard the buzz. He might have seen the screen light up. But it wasn't the same. Kieran had to remember everyone wasn't like himself. He had always been that way. When his best friend in second grade had come back from getting his cast off after breaking his leg, Kieran had spent the walk to school that morning physically reminding himself: *Paul can't run as fast as we used to. Not yet. His leg is still healing.* Kieran had said it under his breath the whole way, like a small prayer. He still did versions of that, three decades on. Adjusting his expectations of other people quietly, internally, in advance, so that nobody would have to ask him to.

He read the message.

> Hi Kieran! Thank you for writing me. I had wondered if I would ever hear from you. I'm sorry we couldn't talk after the funeral.

Kieran paused. It had been three months since Niles died. Eli had said *the funeral* without it seeming to be a big deal. Maybe that was a sign that Eli was past the worst of it. Or maybe it was just words on a screen and Kieran couldn't read what was behind them. He chastised himself for trying to. Words on a screen were hard to figure out. He should know that.

The message continued.

> I didn't know how to contact you. But thank you for being so kind to me that day. I never got to say that. I know it's late and you've probably gone to bed already, but if you want, maybe you can write me back sometime. I'd like to know a few things about your time with Niles, if you don't mind. I think I'm ready. Good night.

Kieran read it twice. *I think I'm ready.* Ready for what, exactly? To hear how Niles died? Eli already knew that part. To hear how it had happened? To hear what Niles had been like in those forty minutes? Kieran wasn't sure. He felt suddenly unprepared, trying to catalog what he could even tell Eli, what Eli might want, what Kieran could responsibly offer. Maybe Eli just wanted to talk. Maybe something totally different.

He hit reply and typed quickly, before he could overthink it.

> Hi Eli! Thanks for writing me back. Sorry if I woke you. I hadn't realized how late it was before I sent you the message. If I did, I'm sorry. Yes, I'd like to chat. Just let me know whenever. I'm pretty boring, so not a lot going on other than work. Take care.

He hit send and immediately regretted every sentence. Why had he apologized again? Twice, this time. *Sorry if I woke you. If I did, I'm sorry.* Why had he said *take care,* like a man closing out a Hallmark card? Why had he called himself boring? *He replied to you,* Kieran's brain nagged. *He could've waited. If he had been annoyed, he probably would've told you to fuck off. Or just not responded. Stop apologizing.*

The phone lit up again.

> You up?

Eli.

Kieran exhaled and typed.

Yeah. Hi.

Smooth, Kieran, he thought, rolling his eyes in the dark. His face was illuminated by the phone screen and probably a delicate shade of dim-room red.

Night owl?

I'm in bed, but it's okay.

Oh, we can chat tomorrow. Go back to sleep.

No, I wasn't asleep. I want to chat.

He hit send and immediately worried he sounded pushy. He had wanted to communicate availability and instead had communicated need. There was probably a class somewhere on how to text without sounding like a hostage situation, and he had not taken it.

Okay. I'm usually awake late, which sucks because I have to be at work by 8.

What do you do?

Accountant. Boring.

I'm the boring one ;)

I think I have you beat. You get to save lives. I get to save margins on a spreadsheet.

Kieran read it. Eli had followed it with a laughing emoji. Eli clearly hadn't connected the dots Kieran had connected, which was that Kieran hadn't been able to save Niles's life and was now chatting friendly with the man Niles had loved. Eli was treating this like a normal conversation. Kieran had to learn to do the same. He couldn't carry both grief and guilt into every line.

Most of the time we're just helping people who have fallen or that sort of thing. Usually we're just driving, or eating.

Eating? If I remember correctly, you looked skinny.

A pause.

I mean that in a good way.

Kieran smirked at his pillow. He was skinny. He knew he was skinny. Short and skinny and looked maybe eighteen on a good day and fourteen if the light was wrong. Most patients looked at him like he was on a bring-your-kid-to-work program, or like he was a child genius who'd finished college early and was now driving around in an ambulance because there was nothing left to learn. Kieran imagined that — being a child genius. He laughed quietly. He didn't think he'd be an EMT if he'd gone that route. Probably some kind of surgeon. Or a guy who shorted stocks. Some terrible career he'd hate.

I have a high metabolism. I'm trying to break 125, but all those doughnuts just seem to go right through me.

If I even look at a doughnut I gain 2 pounds.

That's not true. You look great!

Kieran read his own reply and immediately second-guessed it. *Look great?* Was there a right way to say that to a man you'd met once at a funeral and were now texting at midnight? Probably not. He waited.

A blushing emoji from Eli, then:

Thank you. Flattery will get you everywhere.

Kieran's eyes popped open. He sat up and kicked the covers off and stared at the screen.

Did Eli just — ?

It was a line. A classic line. From an old movie. Eli was joking. He was joking. Right? Kieran wasn't sure. He waited for the next message.

You're funny.

He typed it back, trying to keep things on solid ground.

Looking?

Kieran froze.

Looking was a Grindr word. *Looking?* meant *are you looking right now, are you available, are you down to meet up*. He had seen *looking?* dozens of times in his app inbox. He had typed it himself once, a year and a half ago, to a guy whose profile he'd been staring at for six weeks before he worked up the nerve. The guy had responded not tonight and Kieran had not used the word again.

But Eli wasn't on Grindr. Eli was sending him an Instagram DM. Eli wouldn't—

What?

He typed it carefully. He had to know what Eli meant.

Funny looking? Get it? Guess I'm still not back to my usual self if I have to explain my jokes. lol

Kieran exhaled into his pillow, the relief sudden and embarrassing. Of course. *Funny looking.* It was a joke. Eli had set up the line and Kieran had read it as something else entirely because his brain was apparently still in Pine Street parking-lot mode.

You are funny. But you look good.

He hit send and immediately panicked. He was flirting. He hadn't meant to flirt. Or maybe he had meant to flirt and was now panicking about having succeeded. Either way, his stomach was doing a thing.

Can I ask you a question?

Sure.

You were with Niles that day, right? You found him?

Kieran shifted onto his side.

Yeah.

Are you okay to talk about it?

Kieran was puzzled. Shouldn't he be the one asking Eli that question?

Sure.

Was he in pain?

There it was. The question Kieran had known was coming since he'd hit send to his original message. Everyone wanted to know. Everyone always wanted to know. And Kieran had thought about this exact question many times over three years of doing the job, because he had been in the position before — not often, but often enough — of being the last person to be physically with someone who didn't make it.

Most cases ended okay. The patient was discharged, the patient went home, the patient sent a Christmas card sometimes. But sometimes they didn't. And Kieran had decided early in his career that when they didn't, he owed it to whoever loved them to remember as much as he could. Most families never knew Kieran existed. Most never asked. But occasionally one did, and Kieran wanted to be ready, because the truth was the only thing he could give them. He thought of himself, in those moments, as an unofficial proxy — the person who had been there in place of the one who couldn't be.

I tried to make him as comfortable as I could.

It was true. He had no way to know exactly how much pain Niles had been in. They had needed Niles awake, and pain was sometimes the price of awake. But he had tried.

I held his hand along the way. He kept trying to talk.

He hit send and waited. The dots appeared, then disappeared. Then appeared again.

Did he die with you?

A well of something rushed up into Kieran's eyes. He didn't know Niles. He didn't know Eli. He had pieced together a few things over the months but he had not really known any of them. And yet — sitting in the dark of his bedroom at almost twelve-thirty in the morning, reading those five words on a screen — Kieran felt something open in him that he had not known was closed.

He was drifting off when we arrived at trauma unit.

He'd wanted to write something gentler. Something that would let Eli have the answer he needed without it costing him anything. But Eli had asked. And Eli deserved the truth.

So, he did?

I think so.

Think?

Kieran knew Eli wanted clarity. Wanted clear responses. Wanted to know what the last moments of his boyfriend's life had been. And Kieran was the only person who could give that to him. Anyone else would have soft-pedaled. Kieran had decided, three months ago, sitting on his bike at the cathedral with his uniform on, that if he ever talked to Eli he would not soft-pedal.

His heart stopped just as we arrived. Yes.

He set the phone on his lap and felt the tears come down without warning. Just a quiet drip of them, sliding down his cheeks. He wiped them with the back of his hand and felt the cold trail they left. He had been carrying a man he had not known for three months. The man had had a name and a boyfriend and a college and a mother, and Kieran had carried him all summer because he had not had anyone to give him to.

The phone buzzed against his bare leg.

You held his hand?

Yes. Kept talking to him. I'm sorry.

What did he say?

Kieran remembered Niles trying to say something. He hadn't been able to make it out. The words had been wet and shapeless and the rig had been loud and Kieran had been focused on chest rise and pulse and pressure. But Niles had been trying. And Kieran had thought, at the time and since, that Niles had been trying to say something specific. Maybe a name. Maybe the name Kieran would later attach to the man in the vestibule. Maybe Kieran was projecting.

He tried to speak, but he couldn't.

He hit send. Then added:

I like to think it was about you. But that's just my gut.

The phone went silent. Kieran watched the dots come and go and come and go.

Thank you.

Thank me? For what? For not having been able to give Eli what he was looking for? He hadn't been able to give him *He said he loved you* or *Tell Eli*

I'll always be with him. None of that. Just: he held his hand. He thinks Niles was trying to say something.

I wish I could've done more. I'm sorry.

He wiped another tear away.

You held his hand. That's the most important. At least he had you to be with him. I can't imagine if he were alone.

Kieran had no idea how Eli was holding up on the other end. Was Eli crying? Just thoughtful? Somewhere in between? Kieran reread the message. *That's the most important.*

I wish I could've done more

He repeated himself. He felt it. Had for months. Something about Niles and Eli and the small life he had glimpsed in the back of an ambulance had stuck in him in a way he couldn't articulate.

Me, too. But you did the most important thing. He was not alone.

Kieran put the phone down on the bed and brought his hands to his eyes and cried again.

Eli had reached through the screen, somehow, and told him it was okay to let Niles go. Kieran hadn't realized how much of that day was still with him. He had never met Niles. Had never spoken to him in any way Niles could understand. And yet had been carrying him. For weeks. For months.

He felt the phone buzz against his thigh where it had fallen a second time. Then it buzzed again. Then a third time.

He picked it up and wiped his eyes.

I don't know how you do it. I would be a mess everyday doing what you do.

You there?

Kieran? I'm worried.

He hadn't realized — the clock said it had been almost five minutes since he'd dropped the phone. He typed quickly.

Sorry. I'm here. I didn't know how emotional I was.

A hug emoji from Eli.

🤗

Did you know him?

No. I'm a complete stranger.

Well, that was Niles. So.. I've introduced you. Now you're not a stranger.

Kieran gave a half-laugh, half-sniff, trying to pull himself together.

Thank you. Nice to meet you, Niles, wherever you are.

I'm sure he would think we're being silly. He was very scientific and not emotional.

Kieran smiled into the dark. The first smile of the night.

Then nice to meet you Eli. Better?

Nice to meet you too Kieran. Yes. Niles would approve.

Kieran's smile deepened. The second smile of the night. He typed without thinking.

Can I ask you a question?

Sure.

Does it hurt? I mean sorry, I know that's stupid I mean How are you able to talk about it like this? If my boyfriend died I don't know if I could go on.

He hit send before he could correct himself. The grammar was awful. He didn't care. He needed to know.

It's taken me a while. Like a really fucking long time... but I'm getting better. Not great. But better.

Kieran nodded at the screen as if Eli could see him. Then a follow-up arrived.

How does your boyfriend deal with you having that job? He must really find it tough with all that you go through.

Kieran reread his last few messages. *If my boyfriend died.* He saw, suddenly, how Eli had read that — as a hypothetical referring to a boyfriend who existed.

He could leave it. He could clarify later. He could let Eli think there was a boyfriend and not bother correcting it.

He typed.

I don't have a boyfriend. I only meant if I did.

He stared at the screen.

He had just come out to Eli.

Not to a stranger on an app. Not to a man in a parking lot whose face he would never see again. To Eli — who was a stranger, technically, but who somehow already wasn't. Kieran had typed I don't have a boyfriend in a way that took for granted he would, eventually, possibly, want one. Which was a thing he had never said out loud to anyone in his life. Including, until just now, himself.

He kept typing, before the moment could acquire weight.

I imagine it'd be tough if you did. At least in my job, the worst that I normally deal with is tracking down missing invoices.

I think if I had a boyfriend, I'd want to tell him about my day, but I'd be worried to share too much, you know?

He realized, even as he hit send, that they had come full circle — back to the joke about whose job was worse. He smiled.

I'd listen. I'd rather know and help, even if it was simply being there, you know?

Kieran imagined it. Coming home from a particularly bad shift to a person who would listen. He hadn't realized, until reading those words, that he didn't have that. Didn't have anyone he could talk to that way. His ma would have been horrified by the details. Sean wouldn't have been interested. Danny was seventeen and shouldn't have to be anyone's emotional dumping ground while he was trying to finish high school. Pat was the closest thing Kieran had, but Pat already lived with the same job and didn't need to bring it home twice.

I sometimes wish I had one.

Why don't you? You're good looking and seem stable.

Kieran's face heated. He wasn't used to being called good-looking. By anyone.

I'm not all that. Besides, it's a little hard still living at home.

You're not out to your parents?

It'd kill ma. She's way catholic and I can't just —

My parents too

You're not out? Did they know about Niles?

I'm out. Have been since high school. But they don't talk about it. No, they didn't know about Niles.

Kieran sat with that. Eli had been carrying this whole grief without his parents even knowing the boyfriend had existed. Kieran imagined his own mother in that scenario. Imagined her at a funeral for someone she didn't know was someone, sitting next to Kieran in a black dress with no idea why he was crying. The image was unbearable.

OMG. Sorry. Do you live with them still? I can't imagine going through this with them not knowing.

No, I moved out long time ago. I had roommates, but they left last month.

Sorry.

It's okay.

You gonna get more?

Don't know. I had been saving for a house, but at least I have some $ to tie myself over. What about you?

I want to have my own place, but trying to help my brother with college. He'll be the first to go.

He's not in school yet?

In high school. Saving money to help him.

You're a good brother.

Kieran read the line and felt something small lift in him. Nobody had ever said that to him before. His ma probably thought it but wouldn't have said it. Sean wouldn't have said it because saying it would have implicated Sean in not being one. Danny was Danny and didn't say things like that because Danny had not yet learned how to. Eli, who was a stranger he had been speaking to for forty minutes, had said it.

You have any brothers or sisters?

No. Sometimes I wish I did, but I'm okay. How many you have?

I have an older brother, but he's getting married soon and moving out. Then there's me and Danny. That's it.

Irish, right? You sure you're a catholic family? lol.

Kieran laughed quietly into his pillow.

How'd you know?

You already told me your mom is catholic.

I meant, irish. But, I guess my joke wasn't good either.

Oh! Duh! Redhead and freckles, party of one!

Kieran snickered aloud. He heard a small thump on the other side of the wall — Danny shifting, maybe. He reminded himself to keep it down. Danny was sleeping. Or possibly listening. Or possibly both.

I'm like a leprechaun. Only, I can't stand corned beef and cabbage!

You're funny.

I try.

Kieran, would you like to meet up? Just to talk? Like, for real? I... my friends are great, but everyone is still worried about me and it'd be nice to have a friend who is just there, you know?

Kieran read it twice.

Sure, if you want. I don't want to intrude or anything.

You're too polite, Irish boy.

At least you didn't call me a mick!

I'm French canadian or some shit. My great whoevers were. So I'm sure you can call me something too. Kids probably did when I was in school.

Beat them up?

No, I never heard them. Advantage of being deaf.

Kieran paused. He'd been wondering. He typed carefully.

Do you call it deaf or hearing impaired or what? I never know and want to be polite.

Deaf. But I have a little hearing. Can't really hear without my aids, but I hate them tbh.

I can imagine.

Betcha can't. Not being mean, but it's hard for people who are hearing to know.

Sorry. I didn't mean to hurt.

You didn't. AND stop apologizing. It's sweet, but snap outta it. Don't make me get out of bed and drive over there!

A car emoji and a running emoji, in that order.

Hey! I run!

Run?

Yeah.. I don't own a car so I bike. And I run sometimes.

You run to like the grocery store?

Kieran laughed, then caught himself and pressed his mouth into the pillow to muffle it.

No. Just for fun.

Oh god. Those words don't go together. I only run when being chased.

Kieran laughed again, this time a little louder than he intended. Something brushed against the wall on Danny's side. Kieran went still for a second, then lay back down on his pillow and held the phone up.

I always have. Maybe you and I can meet out at my favorite park. There's places we could eat around there if you want.

I am not going to go run with you. I wouldn't make two minutes.

Oh? Sorry.. I didn't mean to push.

But I will go walk with you.

Kieran exhaled. He had thought, for a half-second, that he had pushed too hard. The relief he felt at but I will go walk with you was disproportionate to the stakes.

Deal. No running required.

Where at?

You know South Portland?

I live up in North Falmouth area.

That's like 25 minutes, if you're okay coming down this way. Or I can ride up somewhere closer.

Your bike? That's like a long way to bicycle.

No, motorcycle. Honda. It's not much, but paid for.

Oooohhh! A biker! Hawt!

Kieran blushed at his phone.

I'm nothing.

How tall are you?

What?

He typed it before he understood.

How tall? I'm 5'9 and always thought short guys did it better ;p

His face heated all the way down to his neck.

I'm 5'6. 5'7 if I am wearing my boots.

Black leather jacket?

Yeah.

Hawt!

Stop it. I'm not.

Nope. And I'm just calling it.

Kieran did not know what to say. He was, again, technically being flirted with. He wasn't sure if Eli was being serious or being silly. He suspected — and the suspicion came with another wave of heat — that it was both at once.

So, I'll meet you. Where are we going?

He sent the address — Bug Light Park, on Madison Street.

There's a place that goes out into the bay where you can see downtown. It's nice.

So I don't need to be worried that you'll take me out to the woods and have your way.

Kieran's eyes bulged. He typed quickly.

Uh, no. I'm a gentleman. Besides, there's lots of people walking and biking etc.

Pity.

He coughed into his pillow. He had not been prepared to read that.

You're something, you know that?

100% Eli.

Kieran smiled at the dark.

Well, 100% Eli, Meet tomorrow?

Sure. You have church with mommy?

yeah.. Ma will wake me at 8.

Good catholic boy.

I try. Nothing to confess, tho. Like I said. I'm boring.

Those are the ones to worry about.

I promise to keep my hands to myself.

We'll see.

Kieran wondered if Eli was being for real. He wasn't sure.

Thanks for reaching out. Here's my phone so we don't have to use insta.

Eli sent his phone number. Kieran saved it and texted him back from his actual phone:

ELI PELLETIER

Who dis?

Kieran almost wrote *it's me, Kieran* before he caught the joke.

Your grindr date.

He didn't know why he said it. It had just come out. Maybe because he had been thinking about the disaster all night and saying it as a joke to Eli was the first form it had taken that didn't sting.

Which one?

Kieran laughed, then clamped his hand over his own mouth to keep Danny from hearing through the wall. Eli had snapped back without pause. Eli was a person who could make the worst night of Kieran's recent year into a punchline that Kieran himself could laugh at.

You are too much.

I'm just the right amount.

A pause.

Go to sleep. Church in the morning. Pray hard. On your knees!

Kieran's grin came easily.

I will. Still practicing.

I'll be the judge of that. Good night, Kieran.

Kieran's mouth hung open.

Did he just — ?

He stared at the screen. The blue bubble stared back. The streetlight outside continued its broken buzz. The wall between his room and Danny's sat between them like it always did. The clock said 1:14.

He typed.

Goodnight, Eli.

He plugged the phone back in, set it on the nightstand, and lay on his back looking at the ceiling. He could feel his heart beating in his throat. He had not flirted with anyone in his life — not really, not in person, not in a way that had been received and returned. He had been flirted with tonight. He had flirted back. He had cried twice. He had come out, in casual passing, to a man he had met once at a funeral. He had agreed to meet that man tomorrow at a park.

He was meeting Eli tomorrow.

He was meeting Eli.

He pulled the covers up over his bare chest because the room had gone cold somehow, and he turned on his side facing the wall, and he closed his eyes, and he was still smiling when he fell asleep.

The Bug Light, as the Portland Breakwater Light had been called for as long as anyone could remember, had been built in 1875. Kieran had read that on the brass plaque near the base when he had first started coming out here to run, back in high school. He didn't come down this way often anymore — the park was a fifteen-minute drive from home and his usual run was Mill Creek, easier, out and back. But on the Sundays when he wanted a longer route or a view of the water that pushed him, he came here.

He pulled into the park's small paved lot at 3:45, fifteen minutes early.

They had agreed to meet at four. Late enough to give Kieran time to be a good boy and go to Mass and do all the Sunday dinner things. Early enough that the sun would still be up — assuming it didn't rain, which it had not — and that the park would have other people in it. Kieran had insisted on the timing in his morning text. He had wanted Eli to feel safe.

> I want to make sure it's a public time of day. Just so you're comfortable.

Eli had texted back:

> Kieran, I've been driving since I was 17. I'll be fine. But thank you.

Kieran parked the Honda at the end of the first row, closest to the paved walkway that led out toward the lighthouse. He pulled off his helmet but didn't get off the bike. He set the helmet on his thigh and watched the entrance to the lot.

He had read once that the Bug Light had gotten its name because it was the runt of all the proper Maine lighthouses — only twenty-six feet tall, which made it one of the smallest working lighthouses in the country. Most lighthouses were giants — eighty feet, ninety feet, the Portland Head Light pushing a hundred and a half. The Bug Light was just a little white thing perched at the end of a short stone breakwater, designed in the style of an ancient Greek monument, with six fluted columns ringing a small central tower painted white. It looked, Kieran had always thought, like a lighthouse trying to make up for its size by being more elegant than the bigger ones. Whoever had designed it in 1875 had decided that if it was going to be small, it was going to be beautiful. And it was.

Kieran would run by it on his loop and think to himself that he knew the feeling. The little thing trying to shine. He had wondered, sometimes, if that song was about this lighthouse. It probably wasn't. But he had liked thinking it might be.

He was wearing his leather jacket, which he always wore on the bike even in summer. He had seen too many guys come into the ER with road rash that went down to bone because they hadn't bothered to put on long sleeves for a quick ride. The jacket was his armor. It also, he had to admit, made him look a little older. A little more like he was supposed to be on the bike. A little like that George Michael video he had watched too many times when he was sixteen and not yet ready to know why he was watching it. The jacket gave him a man he liked better than his actual self.

A few minutes before four, a white Volvo pulled in off Madison Street.

Kieran spotted Eli's hair first — dark and curly and longer than it had been in May, almost to his shoulders, falling across his eyes as he leaned forward to peer through the windshield. Eli was pushing the hair out of his face with one hand while he steered into a spot two rows over and three cars down. He hadn't seen Kieran yet.

Kieran sat on the bike with his sunglasses still on, holding the helmet, and watched.

Eli put the car in park. Looked at his phone. Lifted his hands, typed in something — Kieran couldn't tell what — and then opened the door, stepped out, locked the car with the key fob, and looked up at the lot.

His eyes landed on Kieran and slid past him for a half-second before snapping back. The double-take. Eli's eyebrows lifted and his face opened into a smile that grew the longer it was on. He started walking toward the bike.

Kieran felt the phone buzz in his pocket — Eli sending the I'm here text he hadn't needed to send. He didn't pull the phone out. He brushed his short hair back with one hand — without realizing he was doing it — and pulled off his sunglasses and tucked them into the collar of his t-shirt under the jacket. Then he held up one finger to Eli — *one second* — and pulled off his gloves.

Eli stopped a few feet from the bike and waited. His eyes traveled the length of the Honda, then back up to Kieran. The smile had not gone anywhere.

Kieran lifted his hands.

Hello E-L-I.

He had practiced it twice in his bathroom mirror that morning before church. He had spelled the name slowly and deliberately, each letter formed with care, the way he would have written a thank-you note to someone who had given him something.

Eli's smile shifted into something that wasn't quite the same. Softer. Not surprised exactly, but moved. It hadn't mattered if his signing was perfect. It had mattered that he had done it.

Eli signed back.

Hello K-I-E-R-A-N.

He paused, then signed something faster — Kieran caught only fragments. Something about *signing* and *nobody* and *for me*. Kieran had picked up enough ASL on the job over the years to handle a basic medical assessment — *are you hurt, where, can you breathe, do you take medications* — but Eli was speaking the actual language and Kieran was a novice.

Eli giggled at Kieran's frozen face. "I said nobody had ever signed like that for me," he said in his distinctive voice — the voice that carried the texture of partial hearing, the words shaped slightly differently than they would be from a hearing speaker, the consonants softer in some places and harder in others.

Kieran watched him part his hair over one ear and fidget for a moment with what he assumed was a hearing aid.

"I want to learn more," Kieran said, slowly and clearly.

"You don't have to speak that slow. I understand. Just let me see your lips."

"You like my lips?"

It came out before Kieran could stop it.

Eli's head lifted slightly, his eyes lifted with it, and the smile took on a new dimension. "Depends on how today goes."

Kieran's body went into immediate-shutdown mode. His face flushed. His hands found something to do with the sunglasses in his collar. He was twenty-two years old and he had just flirted with a man in a parking lot in the middle of the afternoon and the man had flirted back, and Kieran had no manual for what to do next.

"I love a man who blushes!" Eli said, with delight.

Kieran stole a glance. Eli was smiling right at him — not at the bike, not at the air, at him. Kieran ducked his eyes back to the gloves.

"You really look like a badass biker," Eli said. He stepped closer and reached out and touched the leather sleeve of Kieran's jacket, fingers brushing the worn edge of the cuff like he was confirming the leather was real. Kieran felt the touch through the leather — couldn't have actually felt anything, the leather was thick — but felt it anyway. Felt his own arm under the jacket. Felt his own skin under the sleeve of his t-shirt under the jacket. Felt every layer between him and Eli's hand.

He swung his leg off the bike, locked the helmet to the seat, and stood. He was aware, suddenly, of how short he was — Eli had three inches on him, maybe more in those sneakers Eli was wearing. He tilted his face up slightly so Eli could see his lips and tried to figure out the right volume to speak at. Not loud. Not slow. Just normal. Easier said than done.

"Relax," Eli said, reading his face. "I'll tell you if I can't understand."

"Okay." Kieran nodded and shrugged out of the jacket.

"Wow. You're really built. You work out?" Eli reached out and squeezed lightly on Kieran's bicep, then let his hand rest for a moment on Kieran's shoulder, testing the firmness through the t-shirt.

Kieran lost the ability to speak for a second. He had been touched on the arm by other people — Pat slapped his shoulder all the time, Maureen had pressed his bicep just last week and tutted that he was too thin — but the touches had not gone through him the way this one was going through him.

"No," he managed. "Just — work, I guess. Dunno."

"You're really a cute guy, you know?"

Eli was being obvious now. Kieran felt the heat climb his neck again and worked very hard not to look at Eli's face. He failed. Eli was looking right at him and laughing, a small private laugh like he knew what he was doing.

Kieran suspected Eli always knew exactly what he was doing.

He motioned vaguely toward the path. They began walking, going in no particular direction, Kieran pointing toward the lighthouse at the end of the breakwater because it was the obvious destination. The afternoon light was soft and slanted. The harbor was busy with small boats. A kite was flying somewhere off to the right, just visible above the trees, and a woman with a stroller passed them going the other way and gave Kieran a polite nod that he returned without thinking about it.

They reached one of the benches that lined the seawall — wooden, a little weathered, facing across the harbor toward Portland's downtown skyline. Eli sat down and stretched his legs out in front of him.

"I cannot believe you run for fun around this place. I'm already tired."

Kieran laughed and tried to sign back. He got as far as *I run* and stopped. He had no idea how to sign *for fun*.

Eli held his hands up and showed him. Two signs. Eli demonstrated each one, then nodded for Kieran to repeat.

Kieran tried. Eli reached over and gently took Kieran's hand and adjusted the position of his fingers, slightly. Kieran felt the gentleness of it. Eli's fingers were warm.

"Try the whole sentence."

Kieran did. Eli laughed midway through and nodded.

"Perfect."

Then Eli signed something else that Kieran didn't catch, and Eli laughed again. "I knew you wouldn't get it."

"What?" Kieran signed, hoping he had got the question right.

Evidently he had, because Eli signed something back. Kieran tried to follow. Eli giggled before saying aloud: "I'll teach you if you want."

"Yes," Kieran signed. Enthusiastically. He knew that one.

Eli signed something Kieran was unfamiliar with and then taught him how to do it — correcting the position of Kieran's fingers twice before Kieran got it right.

"What's it mean?" Kieran finally asked aloud. He had not yet learned how to sign *what does that mean* and he suspected it might be a while before he did.

Eli laughed. "Dinner."

"Dinner?" Kieran asked, signing it again. Eli reached over and adjusted Kieran's hand slightly, and Kieran was suddenly, acutely aware of the contact. Eli wasn't scolding. Eli was teaching. There was a difference, and the difference was making Kieran's wrist warm.

Eli signed yes and then another sign Kieran didn't recognize.

"What's that?" Kieran asked.

"Where?"

"The sign," Kieran said, pointing to Eli's fingers. Eli smiled.

"No. It's how to ask where you want to go for dinner."

Kieran felt slightly dumb and looked at his own hands, which were still in the wrong position from his last attempt. He noticed Eli's hands move into his peripheral vision and looked over. Eli had turned on the bench to face him fully. This time Eli signed as he spoke aloud: "You will learn. It's sweet you are trying for me."

Kieran looked down again. He had not been trying for Eli — he had been trying because Eli was teaching him and he wanted to learn — but having Eli describe it as a thing Kieran was doing for him made Kieran's chest do something he wasn't ready for. Eli was the one being sweet, not him.

"I want to," he said. Then he remembered he had been looking down and repeated himself with his face up. He thought he was learning the rhythm of it. Not too loud. Not too soft. Not too fast or slow. He laughed inwardly. Eli was Goldilocks and he was the three bears, all of them at once.

"What's funny?" Eli signed as he spoke.

Kieran explained. Eli wiggled his eyebrows.

"That bitch isn't as fabulous as me."

Kieran laughed and leaned forward and slapped Eli's knee. It was a friendly, instinctive slap — the kind of slap you gave a friend who had just made a good joke. He had done it before he thought about it.

Eli looked down at Kieran's hand on his knee. Then up to Kieran's eyes. Then smiled — broadly.

"Can't keep your hands off me, huh?"

Kieran pulled his hand back as if it had been spring-loaded and felt his face go from pink to scarlet to a color that probably required a name from a paint chip catalogue. Eli laughed aloud at him — a laugh that was, Kieran was beginning to understand, an Eli kind of laugh. Not controlled. Not pretty in any conventional sense. Different from a hearing person's laugh, the way Eli's voice was different. But so unmistakably Eli that Kieran could not imagine anyone else laughing it. It was infectious. He started laughing too.

Eli returned the slap on Kieran's knee — payback — and asked again about dinner. Kieran fought off the heat in his face and tried to think.

"Pizza?"

Eli nodded, then signed something. Kieran watched and guessed it was that's good or something close.

"*Yes,*" Eli signed, this time without voice.

Kieran laughed. "*Yes,*" he repeated aloud and signed it back. He was learning.

They got up from the bench and started toward the parking lot, then through it toward Madison Street. Kieran suggested Foulmouthed

Brewing in Knightville — about a ten-minute walk straight up Madison — and Eli agreed immediately, saying he hadn't been there but had heard about it. They walked side by side along the shoulder of Madison, the houses thickening as they moved away from the park and into the residential streets of Knightville. Eli walked fast for someone who had announced himself an hour earlier as a non-runner. Kieran had to lengthen his stride to keep up, which he found himself doing without complaint.

Foulmouthed sat on Ocean Street in Knightville's small commercial cluster — a low brick building with the brewery's logo painted on the front window, the door propped open in the late-afternoon warmth. Inside, the bar ran along the right wall. The room was scattered with mismatched tables and chairs that looked like they had been collected over years from estate sales. The blue-checkered tablecloths had been wiped down so many times the pattern had faded in the middle of each one. Several beer signs hung on the walls — some current, some from breweries that had closed years ago. A place where two guys eating pizza and drinking cider would be the least interesting thing in the room.

They found a four-top near the back and sat across from each other. A waitress in her thirties came over with menus and a tired-but-real smile. Kieran ordered the standard Portland-style — thin crust, completely different from New York (folded — no thank you) or Chicago (which wasn't pizza, it was a cheese-and-sauce cake). Eli added an order of fries.

"Fries with pizza?" Kieran asked.

"Sue me," Eli shot back. He gave Kieran a ten dollar smile.

Kieran held the smile for a moment longer than he should have.

The waitress asked about drinks. Kieran ordered a beer — a session IPA Foulmouthed was running. Eli asked for a hard cider. Kieran had never had cider before. He'd had beer, he'd had whiskey at his uncle Frank's wake, he'd had his ma's Christmas wine that came out of a box. Cider was new. He changed his order.

The waitress brought two pint glasses of cider — pale gold, slightly cloudy — and disappeared.

They clinked.

Kieran took a sip and was surprised. It tasted like a spicy apple juice, which he supposed was what it was, but the alcohol was hidden — the kind that caught up with you when you stood. He didn't feel anything yet. He wasn't planning to ride the bike home anytime soon, so he figured he had time.

While they waited for the food, they picked up the signing lesson where they had left off. The brewery was loud — a mix of conversation, the clink of glasses, music playing softly from a speaker behind the bar — and Kieran could see Eli straining slightly. Kieran tried to lean in closer, to position himself so Eli could see his lips clearly, to keep his words slow without overdoing it. Eli was patient with him.

When Kieran stood to go to the bathroom, he was suddenly aware that the bottom of his glass was much closer than he remembered. Half-empty. He swayed slightly as he stood. Eli laughed and reached out to steady him with a hand on his arm.

"Can't take you anywhere."

Kieran heard it — or read it, or some combination — and saw the joy on Eli's face that he hadn't expected to see. Not pity. Not concern. Joy.

He made it to the bathroom, peed, and washed his hands. Kieran stood looking at himself in the mirror. His face was flushed. His eyes looked too bright. He had been having fun. He had been having so much fun he had almost forgotten the night before — the parking lot, the man's hand on his shoulder, the ride home in the dark. He had been laughing. He had been flirting. He had been — there was no other word — happy.

Then Niles came flooding into his head as if he had been staring back from the other side of the mirror.

Kieran scolded himself.

He had forgotten Niles. For a moment, in the middle of the cider and the fries-not-yet-arrived and Eli's hand on his arm, he had forgotten that Niles had ever existed. And the forgetting felt like a betrayal. Of a man Kieran had not known and the man across the table who had loved him.

He splashed water on his face. Took a paper towel. Dried off. Looked at his reflection — flushed, alcohol contributing — and said quietly, to the version of himself in the mirror: *Just be a friend. You can't do more.*

It wasn't his place. Eli was three months out from losing the love of his life. Kieran was a paramedic who had held that man's hand in an ambulance. The line was clear. Friend. That was the line. That was the entire line.

He nodded at himself and walked back out.

The pizza had arrived — a thin-crust round of everything a carnivore could ask for, sausage and pepperoni and bacon and onion in a careful geometry across the cheese — and Eli already had his hand in the basket of fries.

"Better?" Eli asked, holding three fries aimed at his mouth.

Kieran nodded and reached for one. Eli, for reasons that defied protocol, shoved one into Kieran's mouth instead. Kieran almost choked. Recovered. Chewed.

"Good, huh?" Eli slapped him on the back, then stopped — looked at his own greasy fingers — gave Kieran an apologetic face — grabbed a wad of napkins — and proceeded to dab at the small French fry fingerprints of grease on Kieran's shirt with the focused care of a mother.

Kieran waved him off, still chewing. The fries were genuinely good.

He took the opportunity Eli's distraction provided and reached into the basket for more.

"Hey! My fries!" Eli mock-protested.

"Says who?" Kieran shot back, pushing another into his mouth, feeling — for reasons he didn't try to identify — bold.

Eli reached over and pulled the half-fry still in Kieran's fingers and popped it into his own mouth. Kieran laughed, which made Eli laugh, and they sat there laughing at each other across a basket of fries like two people who had known each other longer than four hours.

This was wonderful.

He froze for a half-second. *Friend,* he reminded himself. *Just a friend.*

He had never had a date like this. He had to keep stopping himself from thinking the word — date — because it wasn't a date and Eli had specifically said it wasn't a date and Kieran had specifically agreed. But it had the texture of a date. They were just clicking. He was getting Eli's jokes. Eli was understanding him. They weren't talking about *I'm so sorry for your loss* or *did you come out in high school* or *was it hard for you growing up.* They were eating fries and stealing each other's food and laughing at jokes. It was — and he refused to call it a date— fun.

Eli held up his cider glass — half full — and proposed a toast.

Kieran missed some of it. The brewery had gotten louder. He thought he caught the words. Something like:

"To my first real dinner out with a new good friend."

Kieran clinked. Took a long sip. The cider was, he was willing to admit, delicious. It was also deceptive. He could feel himself growing warmer than before, looser. The pizza was tasting better with each bite. The fries were better too, even fries he had to steal from Eli to get. But it was the company — Eli being Eli, whatever that was — that was making him sit back in his chair and smile.

Eli signed something. Kieran wasn't ready for it. He sat up and gave Eli his best *do that again, please* face.

Eli set his glass down — almost empty now — and lifted his hands. He signed slower this time, and spoke aloud, the way they had been doing all afternoon.

"You look drunk."

Kieran giggled. He probably was. He rarely got this way. When he had too much, he didn't get loud — he got quiet, and everything got funny. Like now. He giggled again and that made Eli giggle, and the two of them sat there giggling at a four-top with a half-eaten pizza between them.

Kieran tried to mimic the sign. Eli shook his head and reached over and gently took both of Kieran's hands in his own.

"Let me show you."

Eli walked him through the signs slowly, his hands wrapped around Kieran's, positioning the fingers, guiding the wrists. Kieran leaned in to watch. He was concentrating on his fingers and not concentrating on anything else.

Then he looked up, by accident, and caught Eli's eyes.

Eli was looking right at him. Not at his lips. Not at his fingers. At his eyes.

Kieran said nothing. Eli said nothing. The brewery kept being loud around them. Then Eli looked down — at the fingers, at the table, at something — and Kieran could've sworn he saw Eli blush.

Or maybe it was the cider. Probably it was the cider.

Eli let go of Kieran's hands.

"Okay. Try now."

Kieran made it through the signs. Not perfectly. Probably he was slurring. He giggled again at his own joke — *was this how deaf people signed when they were drunk, slurring their fingers?* — and immediately worried he was being insensitive and stopped.

"What?"

Kieran told him.

Eli started laughing. "Good one." He reached over and squeezed Kieran's shoulder lightly.

They both knew they needed to slow down and eat. They picked at the pizza. Drank water. Let the cider work its way back through their systems. The conversation drifted, naturally, toward Eli's hearing.

He told Kieran about always being this way. That he could hear some things — that it wasn't an all-or-nothing situation, the way most hearing people assumed. That sometimes it was just easier to sign and be done with it. That he had stopped wearing his hearing aids at home over the past couple of months and had found it surprisingly freeing — to not be performing hearing for anyone, to let the world be the volume it actually was for him. Kieran listened carefully. He thought about whether he had an equivalent, a thing he had been performing his whole life that he could imagine setting down. He couldn't think of one immediately. But he understood what Eli meant.

"Can I ask how you knew?" Kieran said.

"Knew what?"

"About liking guys."

Eli leaned back and grinned, his half-eaten slice abandoned on the paper plate.

"Sorry if I'm being too forward," Kieran added.

"No. I just hadn't really thought about it in a long time."

He told Kieran a story. Sixth grade. His father, with the best of intentions, had signed him up for elementary school basketball tryouts. Eli hadn't wanted to go. He suspected his dad thought it would help him fit in — that being on a team would normalize him in some way, would make him one of the boys, would maybe even improve his hearing situation by giving him peers. Eli wasn't athletic at all, and he couldn't hear the coach yelling instructions over the squeaking sneakers and shouting boys, and everyone was moving so fast around him that he was constantly half a beat behind everyone else. He had been horrible. He had wanted to quit immediately.

"Oh my god, that sucks."

"It did. But Dad let me quit, finally."

"He did?"

Eli's eyes beamed. He gave Kieran a sly grin.

"What did you do?" Kieran asked, watching Eli build to the punchline.

"Let's just say the coach called and suggested to Dad that I might not be right for basketball."

Kieran shrugged. *Obviously.* He shook his head — was he missing something?

"Because I was watching the other boys changing too much in the locker room."

Eli laughed at the look on Kieran's face.

Kieran's eyes went wide. *"No."*

Eli laughed harder and picked his pizza back up and took a bite, nodding.

"You were in *sixth grade?"*

Eli nodded with his mouth full.

"Damn."

Eli giggled. "Always been fabulous, baby!" He snapped his fingers in a small dramatic flourish.

Kieran nearly fell off his chair. He had not been prepared. The snap was so unexpected, so casually theatrical, so completely Eli — and Eli had performed it at full volume in the middle of a busy brewery on a Sunday evening. Someone at a nearby table looked over. Eli didn't notice or didn't care. Kieran, on Eli's behalf, blushed for him.

"You're cute when you're embarrassed," Eli remarked, finishing his slice.

Kieran dropped his eyes to the table and added another layer of red to his face. Eli was, at some level, just having a good time at Kieran's expense — but the having-a-good-time was so warm, so without malice, that Kieran couldn't be upset. He was being teased the way Pat teased him, except this wasn't friendship — or wasn't only friendship. He didn't know what it was exactly, but it wasn't unkind. It wasn't anything close to unkind.

"Feeling better?" Eli stretched and looked at his watch.

Kieran checked his own. It was nearly 8:00. They had been sitting there for hours. Kieran could not remember the last time he had been out this late on a Sunday night with anyone — with anyone at all, let alone with someone he had only met once before. Pat sometimes made him stay for an extra cup of coffee at the station, but that was different. That was work. This was —

This wasn't a date. He reminded himself.

"Wanna walk back?" Eli asked, glancing toward the windows. The sky outside had gone dark blue. The streetlights along Ocean Street were on.

The cider had mostly worn off by the time they got outside. The August air was cooler now, the evening dropping toward night, and Kieran felt his face start to come down from the flush. They started back toward Madison and the park. Eli kept talking — about his younger days after the basketball *incident*, as he called it. About how he had spent his early teens sneaking onto websites his parents didn't know how to monitor, looking up pictures of guys without anyone noticing. His parents had not understood the internet yet. Eli had used that to his advantage.

Kieran laughed. He had done his own version of the same — except his version had been complicated by Sean, who had shared the family computer and had a habit of looking through the browser history. Kieran had become an expert at clearing it.

The walk got quieter as they approached the park. Madison Street was quiet on a Sunday night, the houses dark or dimly lit through curtains. The sidewalk was uneven in places — old concrete, frost-heaved — and they had to step carefully. The streetlights were spaced far enough apart that they walked through alternating pools of light and dark.

Kieran realized, as the dark stretched longer, that he wasn't sure how Eli would understand him in the dark. Eli needed Kieran's lips. Kieran's lips were difficult to see in the spaces between streetlights.

They reached a crosswalk. The light was about to change.

Kieran reached over and gently took Eli's elbow, giving him a small tug to the right — a *come this way* signal — so they could cross safely.

Eli looked over. The streetlight caught Kieran's face for a second.

Then Eli reached down and took Kieran's hand.

Kieran felt the warmth of it again before he understood. Eli's hand was slightly larger than his and held on with a confidence Kieran had not expected. Kieran held on back as they crossed the street together.

When they got to the other side, Kieran started to let go.

Eli reached over and took his hand again.

He didn't say anything. Just took it. Then kept walking. Kept talking, his voice picking up where it had paused before the crosswalk — about growing up in Lewiston, about coming out to his parents at sixteen, about his mother's polite silence and his father's three-word we love you that had been the entirety of the family's response to it. Kieran was making mental notes of questions he wanted to ask — when they had a moment with proper space — but he wasn't holding most of the words. He was holding the hand. Eli's warm hand in the dark on a Knightville sidewalk. Kieran's first.

He had never done this before. Held a guy's hand. Ever. Not in passing. Not as a joke. Not at all.

Especially not while walking back to a parking lot on a Sunday night after dinner with a man who had just told Kieran the story of finding out he was gay in a sixth-grade locker room. Which Kieran had also never done.

Kieran looked down at their hands and back up at the sidewalk in front of them. The Bug Light Park entrance was three blocks ahead. Eli's car was in the lot. So was Kieran's bike. They had thirty more minutes, give or take, before they had to part. Kieran could already feel himself trying to make those minutes last longer than they would.

This wasn't a date, right?

Permission

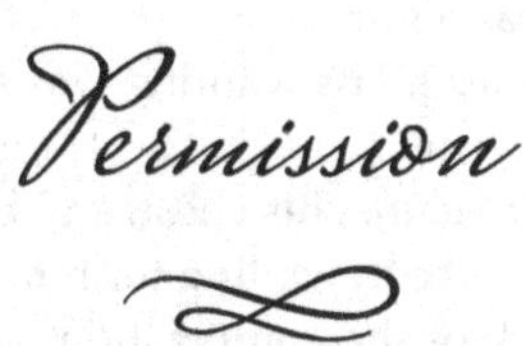

THREE WEEKS PASSED. Then four. Then the days stopped announcing themselves and became simply days, which was its own kind of mercy.

Marco had developed a rhythm that kept him upright. The bells of Sant'Agostino at prime — he rose. He dressed in the same plain shirt, the same linen breeches, the same leather apron stained with a decade of pigment. He ate what the kitchen provided — bread, cheese, sometimes a piece of fruit — standing at the small window of his cell with his back to the bed, because sitting to eat was what one did in company, and Marco was no longer in company.

By terce he was on the scaffolding. By sext he had finished the day's giornata — the patch of fresh plaster that had to be painted before it dried. By vespers he climbed down. By compline he was in his room with the door closed, the oil lamp lit, the letter against his chest where it had lived for weeks now, folded into a small square that had gone soft at the edges from his own reading.

Four letters, in total. Three in the cabinet. One on his person. The one on his person was the uncoded one. The one where Alessandro had said everything and nothing.

Permission to remain hopeful. I grant it to you. I grant it to myself.

Marco had been conducting an argument with those two sentences for six weeks. He could not make them hold still.

Some evenings he read them and they meant *wait for me.* Some evenings they meant *live without me.* The language was the same either way. The grammar did not disclose itself. A man granting permission could be granting permission to hope for return, or granting permission to release the demand of return and love anyway. Those were different permissions. They pointed in opposite directions.

Marco had always trusted his ear for text — he had learned to read late, from the priest who taught him Latin grace before teaching him how to mix gesso, and he had come to language the way a man comes to a new country: late enough to be grateful for its particulars. But he could not read this. The sentence was a mirror.

He wanted it to mean *wait.* His wanting was so loud he could not trust his own reading.

So he carried the letter against his chest, and he painted.

The Virgin's mantle had been waiting for him for a week.

It was the sacred work of the composition — ultramarine, lapis lazuli ground to powder, the single most expensive substance in any chapel the cardinal was funding. Marco had measured out the stone himself on the first morning of the commission, his hands careful the way they had been careful when he first held a brush he had been told cost more than a man's annual wage. The lapis had traveled from Afghanistan. It had crossed more land and sea than Marco would ever see.

You did not waste ultramarine. You did not mix too much and let it dry. You did not mix too little and find yourself, mid-giornata, with the plaster setting and the brush going dry in your hand.

Marco had mixed too little.

He noticed it first as a lightness at the tip of the brush. Then as a thinness in the blue itself — the stroke not depositing what it should. Then as the absolute refusal of the bristles to carry any pigment at all. He looked at the shallow dish on his scaffolding shelf. Empty. The rim smeared with what had been and was not.

He looked at his hands. They were blue to the second knuckle. Below, the section of the Virgin's mantle he had been working on — the inner fold, where the garment gathered at her wrist — was half-done. The plaster was drying. He had perhaps an hour before it set. Possibly less.

Marco's chest went cold. He did not move. He stood on the scaffolding with the empty brush in his hand and tried to recall when he had last crushed stone, and realized he could not remember. Not this week. Not last. He did not know when he had last ground lapis. Which meant he had been painting out of a preparation he had made at some prior time and had not replenished, because his mind had been elsewhere, and he had not noticed.

Forgetful. The word arrived in him with its own weight. He had been forgetful. He had been forgetful for weeks. The forgetfulness had been crawling in around the edges of his days — the brush left unwashed overnight, the shirt put on inside out and not corrected until midday, the Thursday he had lost entirely and never found. He had been telling himself, when he noticed at all, that he was merely tired.

He had not been tired. He had been grieving. Grief had been coming out of him sideways because he had refused to let it out the front door.

And now it was going to cost him the Virgin's mantle. Which would mean chipping out a half-finished giornata, explaining the loss, absorbing the cardinal's displeasure, absorbing the cost of lapis used and wasted — a sum Marco could not repay in a year of commissions.

He heard a footfall below.

Tommaso.

The novice was standing at the foot of the scaffolding with a broom in one hand and a dustpan in the other, looking up. He had been sweeping the apse, the way he swept the apse every afternoon. Marco had grown so accustomed to his quiet presence that he no longer registered the novice's movements — Tommaso had become a piece of the chapel itself, the way the drafts and the bells and the particular slant of the afternoon light were pieces.

Now he was looking up at Marco, and there was no surprise in his face.

"You have run out," Tommaso said. It was not a question.

Marco stared down at him. He had not told Tommaso he was running out. He had not told anyone anything in weeks. He had barely spoken, except to the priests who stopped in to check on the progress, and then only the minimum.

"Yes," Marco said.

"I can grind for you."

It landed on Marco as something he did not at first understand. Then, when he did understand, he understood too many things at once. That Tommaso had been watching him work. That Tommaso had watched him long enough to know how Marco mixed his pigments. That Tommaso had apparently been prepared to offer this for some time, and had been waiting for an opening — possibly this one, possibly any of a half-dozen others Marco had missed — and had finally seen his chance.

"It is lapis," Marco said. He meant: *it is not ordinary pigment. You cannot grind it as you would grind earth. It will be ruined if you are imprecise.* He said none of that. He said *it is lapis,* and Tommaso understood.

"I have been watching," Tommaso said. "I can do it."

Marco looked at the plaster drying under his brush. He looked at the novice standing below. The novice was calm. He was not offering from vanity. He was offering because he had decided, at some earlier point, that if the moment came he would be ready for it.

"Come up," Marco said. "I will show you where the stone is."

Marco climbed down. Tommaso climbed up partway, took the small linen-wrapped bundle Marco handed him, and climbed down again with it. He carried it to the low wooden table at the edge of the chapel where Marco kept his mortar and his muller and his slab of porphyry. He set the bundle down and unwrapped it — the stone inside a clear deep blue, veined with the small white threads that told you it was good lapis, the kind the Afghan traders did not always part with.

Tommaso looked at the stone. Looked at the mortar. Looked at Marco.

"You crush first to the size of a grain of rice," Marco said. "Then finer. Then you move it to the slab and work it with the muller, with water, in small quantities. You do not hurry. If you hurry, the grain is not even, and the blue will be dull. The darker you grind it, the more the color opens. Do you understand?"

"Yes."

"If you ruin it I cannot replace it."

"I will not ruin it."

Marco returned to the scaffolding. He began working the section he already had paint for — the outer fold of the mantle, where the blue was less critical, where the plaster was still wet enough to receive. He worked quickly and with focus. He did not look down. He trusted Tommaso not to look up, not to feel watched, not to have his hands unsteadied by Marco's attention.

He could hear the small sounds of the work. The dry crunch of the first crush. The patient scrape of stone on stone. The silence as Tommaso moved the ground pigment from the mortar to the slab. The slow, unhurried grinding on the porphyry — the sound a man makes who is paying the material the respect it requires.

Twenty minutes passed. Thirty.

"Maestro."

Marco looked down. Tommaso was holding up the shallow dish. Inside it, a small mound of paint the color of a clear evening sky just before it went indigo — the deep, saturated blue of lapis properly ground, properly bound, properly ready.

Marco climbed down to look at it. He took the dish and tilted it under the window light. The pigment caught the light the way only good ultramarine caught it — not reflecting, exactly, but absorbing and returning something richer than it had received.

He looked at Tommaso.

"Who taught you to grind?"

"No one. I watched you."

"For how long?"

Tommaso considered. "Since the second week."

Marco said nothing. The second week had been in April. It was now the last week of August. Tommaso had been watching him mix pigments for more than four months, silently, from whatever corner of the chapel he happened to be sweeping, and had taught himself the craft by observation alone.

Marco took the dish up the scaffolding. The plaster had nearly set at the edges but the center was still receptive. He finished the inner fold of the Virgin's mantle. The blue was true. The giornata held.

When he climbed down it was nearly vespers, and Tommaso was cleaning the mortar and the muller the way Marco would have cleaned them himself.

"Come to my room tonight," Marco said. "After the last bell. I have bread. I have a little wine."

He said it without having decided to say it. The words arrived in his mouth and then in the air between them, and only after they were spoken did Marco understand that he had made an invitation he had not made to anyone since Alessandro had left.

Tommaso looked up from the mortar. He was perhaps Marco's age — Marco had never actually looked closely enough to decide. Now, looking, he saw a young man, with a long thin face and dark eyes that were held steady by whatever interior discipline had taught him not to volunteer more than was asked.

"Yes, Maestro."

"Not Maestro. Here. Tonight. Not Maestro."

Tommaso almost smiled. It was the smallest adjustment of the corners of his mouth.

"Marco," he said, testing it.

"Yes."

He came when the last bell had finished ringing. He had washed his hands and his face. He had changed from the plain gray of his working habit into the plain gray of his evening habit, which was the same cloth but cleaner. He carried nothing. He stood in the doorway of Marco's room and looked in at it with a careful, unintrusive attention — the way a man looks at a painting he has not seen before and wants to understand before commenting.

"Sit," Marco said.

He had set out bread on the small table. A round of hard cheese. A clay jug of the thin red wine the kitchen gave the artists. Two cups. He had taken the sketches off the walls — not all of them, but the ones of Alessandro, the ones Marco had pinned up in the first weeks of the commission and had kept there because removing them had felt worse than leaving them. Tonight he had removed them. He did not want Tommaso to ask. He did not want to explain. He did not yet know what he was doing, only that he was doing it with some intention he had not yet named for himself.

Tommaso sat.

They ate. Marco poured the wine. They talked, at first, about the chapel — the progress, the sections remaining, the cardinal's visits and what each one signaled. Tommaso spoke about the priests in a voice that was careful but not reverent. He had opinions. He did not share all of them.

Marco asked where he was from.

A village north of Arezzo, Tommaso said. Small. The kind that did not appear on any map a Roman would own. His father kept sheep. His older brother would inherit the flock. Tommaso had been placed in the order at twelve — not because anyone had sensed a vocation in him, but because there had been no bread for a second son, and the priest who rode through their region twice a year had mentioned that the scriptorium at Arezzo needed boys with careful hands. Tommaso had careful hands. He had gone.

He had copied manuscripts for three years. He had not disliked it. He had not loved it. He had developed a steady way of sitting and a steady way of breathing, and the prior had noted this, and when the chapel project required additional novices of a quiet disposition, Tommaso had been sent.

"And your vows?" Marco asked.

Tommaso looked at his cup.

"I have not taken the final ones."

"When will you?"

"I do not know."

Marco did not press. He understood, by the careful way Tommaso set down his cup, that this was a question Tommaso had not yet been able to answer even to himself, and that asking him to answer it in a borrowed room on a warm August night over a jug of thin wine was beyond what any friendship could fairly ask.

He changed the subject.

He told Tommaso about Florence. About walking into the city as a boy with his drawings rolled under his arm and his shoes worn through. About the Academy, where he had been allowed to sweep in exchange for instruction, and where he had learned to grind pigments and prepare panels and to look at light the way a painter learned to look at light — slowly, and again, and again. About the old painter who had kept him on after the Academy dissolved with the Medici, who had taught him what the Academy had not, and who had died in February and left him his brushes. He did not mention Alessandro. Tommaso did not ask. They talked instead about the way light behaved in Florence and the way it behaved in Rome, and how Florentine light was a gentle collaborator and Roman light was a demanding patron, and how a painter spent his first year in a new city learning how to negotiate with its weather.

The bells marked the hour. Then the half. Then, eventually, the hour after that.

Tommaso stood.

"I should return."

"Yes."

"Thank you for the bread."

"Come again."

Tommaso paused in the doorway. "When?"

Marco considered. He did not know what he was agreeing to, or promising, or beginning. He knew only that he did not want to close the door on it tonight.

"When you would like to," he said.

Tommaso nodded, and went.

Marco sat on the edge of the bed.

The room was quiet in the way rooms are quiet after guests. The two cups stood on the table, one emptied, one half-full. The bread was broken. The wine had softened him in ways he had not expected. He felt warmth across the breadth of his chest, and in the muscles of his face, and in a place low in his belly that he could not locate more precisely than to say it was where loneliness had been living, and was no longer, or was less.

He had been warm for three hours, and had not known, while it was happening, that he was warm.

He sat with that.

He thought of Alessandro. He thought of the letter against his chest. He thought of the ten minutes in a Venetian room during which Alessandro had written *permission to remain hopeful* and had not explained what he was granting permission for.

Is this permitted, Marco asked, silently, of the shape of Alessandro he carried in his head. *A friend. A man my age who has been watching me. An hour of bread at a table I had not set for anyone since you. Is this permitted, or is it betrayal dressed as kindness?*

The shape of Alessandro did not answer. Marco had not expected it to. The dead answered; the absent did not. Alessandro was absent, and the silence of his absence was the exact silence Marco had been listening to for weeks, and no amount of listening would turn it into a voice.

He decided, sitting on the edge of the bed with his hands in his lap, that if Alessandro had meant *live,* then tonight had been permitted. If Alessandro had meant *wait,* then tonight had been a betrayal. He could not know which was meant. Therefore he would find out by continuing. Permission, if he had it, would be granted by the living of it. Love, if it had survived, would survive this too. If it had not survived — if Alessandro had meant *release me* — then Marco would discover that by the slow failure of his heart to hold two things at once, and he would accept that failure when it came.

He had done something tonight that he had not done before. He would do it again, carefully, and see.

He stood.

He wanted to read a letter before he slept. Not the one on his chest —

he had been living inside that one for weeks. The first one from Venice. The earliest. The letter where Alessandro had still been writing about weather and had still meant weather. Marco wanted to hear that voice again, the voice before the shift, to see if he could locate the moment when the shift had begun, the moment when *the weather in Venice* had started to become *the weather in Venice is not fine.*

He went to the cabinet.

The cabinet was a narrow wooden cupboard set into the wall beside the bed, with a small iron lock and a key Marco kept on a leather cord at his waist. He had not opened it in weeks. There was no need. The letter he read was the letter on his chest.

He unlocked the cabinet.

The letters lay inside, wrapped in the oilcloth, at the back of the cubby beneath the small wooden cross he had carved at twelve and had carried from city to city. He unwrapped the oilcloth. Three letters. Folded alike, in thirds, the way Alessandro had folded all the Prato letters — the careful sameness that kept any one of them from seeming more important than another.

Marco reached for the top letter. He expected the third — the most recent of the Prato letters, the last one before the uncoded one, the one he kept on top because it was most recent. Most recent on top. Foreground. Composition.

The letter in his hand was not the third.

It was the first. The earliest. The one he had just been about to reach for — but expecting to find at the bottom, not the top.

Marco stood still.

He set the first letter down on the bed. Picked up the next. It was the third. Picked up the one beneath. It was the second.

First. Third. Second.

Not his order. Not the order he had left them in. Not the order he would ever have left them in, because Marco kept the recent on top and the oldest at the bottom. This was the order a man imposed on a stack when he had removed the letters to look at and had replaced them without knowing the system.

Marco sat down on the bed.

He tried, for perhaps thirty seconds, to tell himself that he had been forgetful. That he had opened the cabinet at some point in the past month and rearranged them without remembering. That the same forgetfulness that had cost him the lapis had cost him this.

The argument collapsed before he finished making it. The forgetfulness had been for tasks in motion — paint not replenished, shirts not corrected, a Thursday that dissolved into a Friday. He had not opened this cabinet. He would have remembered opening it. You did not forget opening a locked box whose key lived on your own belt.

Someone had.

His hand went to his chest.

He did not decide to move it. It moved. It rested against the shirt over the small square of paper that had lived there for six weeks, and his palm pressed there, and he understood — not yet fully, but at the edge of fully — that something had been searched for in this room, and had not been found, because the thing someone wanted was not in the cabinet.

He counted the letters again. Three. Nothing gone. Nothing taken. Only read, and returned, and misordered.

He restacked them. Third on top. Second in the middle. First at the bottom. The order he had left them in. He rewrapped the oilcloth. He closed the cabinet. He locked it. He put the key back on his belt.

He sat on the edge of the bed for a long time.

Outside, Rome settled into its evening. Somewhere, bells marked an hour he did not count. Somewhere far to the north, beyond the mountains and the lagoon, Alessandro was — Marco did not finish the thought. He had stopped finishing that thought six weeks ago.

He lay down on the bed without undressing. His hand remained on his chest, over the letter, where it had gone on its own.

He did not sleep.

Chapter Ten

ELI PULLED up to Graham's in a good mood.

It was Labor Day weekend, which meant he had Monday off. No plans to speak of — Kieran was working tonight and had church tomorrow, the usual — but he figured they'd get up to something Monday. If nothing else, maybe Kieran could come over tomorrow for dinner and a movie.

The Volvo practically parked itself, as if it knew where home was. Eli stepped out and noticed Graham's hydrangeas — flanking the front of the house, ringing the trees out front. They were just about tipping into pinks and blues like they always did. Tipping into Eli's favorite season.

He didn't know why, but he looked forward to the cooler days, maybe a flurry or two before winter. That'd be another month or so, but it helped his already good mood.

Graham opened the door and looked over at his car — well, Simon's old car. Eli had always felt like it would still be Simon's and he was simply taking care of it. The lightkeeper, so to speak. Which was why he had popped it through the car wash on the way over. Nice and sparkly. Just like he imagined Simon to be.

"You didn't have to bring anything," Graham said.

Eli looked confused. "I didn't."

"Yes — I know." Graham gave him *a look* and smiled.

"Bitch," Eli muttered, following Graham through the door. Graham turned.

"What did you say?"

"I said you're a bitch."

Graham gave him the most Eli of grins back.

"And don't you forget it," he teased.

Eli followed him into the kitchen, where nothing had been set up. Graham had insisted he come over when he texted yesterday. Steaks he'd bought for a cookout hadn't gotten used, and he needed Eli's stomach to save the day. He hated to throw away perfectly good protein.

"I'm all about the protein!" Eli had teased, knowing Graham would be rolling his eyes. He loved double entendres, especially around Graham. Used them just to get a reaction. And it was always predictable. Rolled eyes followed by a change of subject.

Eli had agreed, of course. Kieran had the noon-to-midnight one Saturday a month, and this was his night. Besides, Eli hadn't done any sort of socializing in forever. Well, except for the few times he and Kieran got together for dinner.

"Where's the food?" Eli asked, looking at bare countertops. Graham hadn't even put out plates or seasoning. It was like he'd forgotten he'd invited Eli over for a small cookout. Or a *save Graham's steak* event.

"Anthony's coming," Graham replied. "Thought we'd wait."

Eli started to pull up a chair at the kitchen table, but Graham walked by and tapped him on the shoulder to get his attention.

"Help me get the grill ready."

"By what? Turning the dial?" Eli asked, raising his brows — proud of that one.

Graham didn't reply. Opened the screen door to the patio and reached down to grab a heavy bag of charcoal, which he dumped into Eli's hands.

"You're welcome," Graham said, walking over to the edge of the stone patio to open up a black metal grill that looked like it hadn't been cleaned since the last cookout.

Eli followed, holding the bag of Kingsford and wondering what the hell to do with it. He'd never started a grill before. Other than the aforementioned dial turn and pressing the ignite button.

Graham began cleaning the stainless grill bars with a wire brush that materialized from somewhere while Eli stood holding the bag, watching. And watching. And watching some more.

"Anytime you're ready," Eli announced. Graham ignored him.

Graham finally looked up. "Cleanliness is next to Godliness."

"Judging by the state you left that grill, you must've had a vacation home in hell."

"Who's the bitch now?" Graham retorted.

"Me!" Eli smiled.

Graham shook his head and took the bag of briquettes out of Eli's hand, freeing him to wander.

Eli had been here before. Many times. But he didn't remember grilling outside. He looked out at the patio and the back yard that merged into the woods. Remembered Graham telling the story of Anthony as Santa Claus out in the snow with Levi and Lucy that first morning they'd brought them in off the streets. He smiled imagining Anthony being chased by Lucy.

Eli took a seat in one of the cushioned wrought-iron rockers arranged around a matching wrought-iron table with a blue-and-white striped umbrella mounted in the center. He didn't remember Graham hiring a gardener, but the flower pots were still blooming and the yard was mowed. He had never even thought to ask if Graham did it himself. He'd always thought perhaps Simon had been the one with the green thumb. Didn't know why. Just felt that way.

He looked over at Graham, who had somehow gotten a fire started in the grill, and realized there were plenty of things he didn't know about him — or had even thought to ask.

Graham wiped his hands on a rag and came over, settling into the rocker next to Eli's. The fire popped behind them.

"So. Kieran couldn't make it, huh?"

Eli looked over. Graham's tone was easy enough, but the name landed with a little weight. Like he'd been holding onto it for a few days.

"His weekend to work."

"Ah." Graham nodded, looking out toward the trees. "He seemed like a nice fellow."

Eli opened his mouth to answer — but the sliding screen door rolled open behind them.

"Tell 'em yourself," Graham said, his face turning toward the door.

"Hello, Eli." Anthony came over and leaned down so Eli could see his face. "I asked Graham to let you know I was here so as not to surprise you, but even though he may be a scholar, he is definitely not a proper gentleman." Anthony turned and shot a mock glare at Graham, who simply shrugged.

Eli laughed. He loved watching these two mess with each other.

Anthony set down a bottle of something red, along with a box of crackers and a hunk of cheese encased in something red to match the bottle, before leaning in and giving Eli a short hug.

Unlike Graham, Anthony seemed to be a hugger. Graham would hug, but Eli had to be the initiator. Anthony, on the other hand, lived up to his Santa Claus persona. Eli always felt like Anthony was his grandpa. He thought Anthony enjoyed the role, too.

"So, Graham, what was your nephew's decision?" Anthony asked as he made himself comfortable in the chair next to Eli.

"Dorms," Graham said, grabbing the bottle and walking off toward the kitchen, presumably to uncork it.

"Probably for the best." Anthony looked over at Eli and read his face. "Didn't Graham tell you? Our little Michael was debating whether to stay here with his uncle or move into the dorms. I gather the decision was made."

"I knew he said he was coming to college here. Kind of surprised," Eli said. He and Michael had texted a bit off and on since that night a month or two ago, but he hadn't really been up on all the details.

Anthony nodded as Graham returned with a couple of wine glasses and the bottle balanced in his hands. Anthony stood to help, but Eli beat him to it, handing Anthony a glass and setting one at Graham's spot directly across. Graham poured into Anthony's glass and set the bottle down in front of Eli.

"What about me?" Eli looked up at him as he sat.

"What? You have hands." Graham shrugged again.

Eli took the bottle and began filling his glass, turning to Anthony. "See what I have to put up with?"

"You? I've had to put up with — this —" Anthony waved his hand in Graham's direction while holding his wine glass in the other, "— for much longer than you."

Eli tipped his glass to Anthony to clink.

"Hey now. Two against one isn't fair," Graham protested, reaching for the bottle.

"I don't know, Graham. I'm rather enjoying the conversation," Anthony said.

Eli laughed. He loved being around these two. Especially when he got to see Graham — the quiet, intellectual sage — reduced to another one of the guys.

Anthony tipped his head back and worked at his wine. "So. Our little Michael." He set the glass down on the wrought-iron table.

"What about him?"

"You been keeping in touch with him, Eli?"

"Texts. Off and on."

"Texts." Anthony arched a brow. "Yes. That is a polite way of putting it."

Graham stood and walked over to the grill, picking up the long fork from where he'd set it on the table. He worked the coals with it, settling them down.

Eli laughed. Anthony's gossip-face had arrived — the pretending-not-to-gossip face he wore when he was about to.

"Have you seen the Instagram?" Anthony asked.

"I've seen *the Instagram,*" Eli teased.

"And the —" Anthony tugged at his own earlobe.

"The earring. Yeah."

"Tasteful little hoop. I'll grant it. But our boy is making — choices."

"Anthony." Graham didn't turn around. "He's eighteen. He's allowed."

"I'm not opposed to the choices, Graham. I'm simply observing that there is a — volume."

Eli took a sip. "There is… *a volume*." He smiled at Anthony.

"There is."

"I'm going to go see him." Eli set his glass down. "Some weekend soon. He's been asking. And — yeah, I want to. Haven't really seen him since spring."

Graham glanced back from the grill. "Good."

"Even if all I do is take him to lunch and let him show me the Instagram in person, that's something."

Anthony nodded. "He asks about you. Constantly. Graham, when's the last time he called and didn't ask after Eli?"

"He doesn't."

"He doesn't. Every call."

"I'm getting better about texting back."

"He understands."

Anthony lifted his glass again. "And how is our Levi?"

"Practicing." Eli said it without thinking, then realized neither of them knew.

Graham turned from the grill. "Practicing what?"

"Driving."

"Driving?"

"Yeah. He got his permit in June. We've been — you know. Parking lots first. Now back roads."

Graham looked at Eli, then over at the Volvo where it sat under the trees, then back. Didn't say anything for a moment.

"In Simon's car."

"In Simon's car."

Graham nodded once. He turned back to the grill.

"I taught a kid to drive once," Anthony offered. "It was a disaster. He's fine. I am not. Levi is in better hands than mine. Mine were not steady."

Eli grinned. "He's nervous. But he listens."

"He always listens." Graham's voice from the grill. Quiet.

Graham worked the coals a moment longer. Then, half-turned: "I heard from Donna this week."

Eli looked up.

"Been a while," Graham said.

"She okay?"

"She wants to have lunch. Next week. She asked me." Graham came back to his rocker, picked up his glass, took a sip. "Which is — well. New."

Eli nodded.

"You're welcome to come, by the way." Graham gave him a half-shrug. "That way you two can gang up on me like the old days."

"I don't think so." Eli paused. "I think you and her need it to be just the two of you."

Graham held the look. Didn't push. But Graham's eyes told you everything he wasn't saying. Eli had learned how to read them. *When did you and Donna talk?* and *How was it?* and *Why didn't you say?* — and a few others Eli couldn't name. None of them came out. Graham just nodded once and turned back to the grill.

"We had lunch," Eli offered. "A month or so ago. It was — overdue."

Graham nodded again. "I'm glad."

Anthony, who had given them the space, leaned forward. "She's been through a lot. Like our young man here." He reached over and patted Eli's hand. Twice. Warm.

Eli let his hand stay where it was.

"Graham's perfect for her right now," Anthony continued. "Just the two of them. None of us hovering."

"Agreed." Eli looked over at Graham, who was tending the grill and pretending he wasn't listening. "I was over at their house last week, actually."

Graham did look up at that. "Really?"

"Yeah. They're doing — better than I might have expected. Slowly. But getting there." Eli took a sip. "Brett's painting the living room."

Anthony blinked. "Brett."

"Yeah."

"Brett. Is painting. Their living room."

"Apparently." Eli was grinning. "With a roller. Drop cloths everywhere. Had paint on his ear."

"Brett." Anthony set his glass down. "I have known the man for eight years and would not have guessed handyman."

"Neither would I." Eli laughed. "Donna's making the room over. He had no choice."

"Of course he didn't." Graham was smiling.

"Sage walls. White trim." Eli took another sip. "She said the place needed something — clean and new."

Eli laughed and looked at his glass. "I dropped off some of Niles's things while I was over there."

Anthony's glass paused on its way to his mouth. Graham turned from the grill.

Eli kept his eyes on his wine. "Just figured they should have it." Then he looked up. "Been hauling the box around in the back of the car all summer. Just kept meaning to."

Anthony and Graham looked at each other.

Anthony picked up his glass.

"Sage," he said.

"Sage."

"Brett. With a roller. Painting their living room sage."

"Sage."

"I think it's going to look very nice. I think Brett is going to look very confused."

Graham laughed — a small short laugh that caught.

"Donna picked it," Eli added.

"Naturally."

"So, Graham tells me you're reading some of his old works." Anthony changed the subject, took a sip and leaned in.

Eli looked over at Graham.

"It came up." Graham shrugged again like it was out of his control. Eli gave him an *I'll talk to you later* look, which prompted Graham to go grab the steaks from the fridge.

Returning to Anthony, Eli answered. "Just *The Novice's Chapel*. Saw it a few months ago and hadn't read it in years, so..." He let his words fade, not knowing how to proceed.

Anthony nodded in agreement. "I remember that book. Simon and I used to talk about that monk."

"What?" Graham asked as he walked past to place the steaks on the grill.

"Simon. He and I spoke about that monk of yours." Anthony turned and raised his voice toward Graham, as if he couldn't hear. Eli's hearing aids spiked briefly and he instinctively reached up to adjust them.

"What about?" Graham asked as he sat, the steaks doing their job on the grill now.

"Speaking of — why did you make it so Marco had to be alone for so long?" Eli interrupted, then turned back to Anthony to apologize. Anthony waved him off. They were just chatting.

"What do you mean?" Graham turned to Eli.

"This book is the hardest. I remember back when I first read it and being so..."

"I know — you told me."

Eli instinctively looked at Anthony, who was watching intently.

"I still find it so hard to read, especially when you don't even know what happened to Alessandro. Not really. And Marco — it's almost cruel what you put him through."

Eli looked over again at Anthony and back to Graham, realizing he was becoming agitated. He took a breath to calm himself and apologized again, this time to the table.

"That was all Simon," Graham said, tapping Eli's hand lightly to get his attention. "Simon said Marco had to face losing Alessandro completely in order to know what he had."

Eli noticed Anthony nodding.

"Simon had a stick up his butt about that. Said it tested Marco's ability to remain hopeful. Because, without hope, what do we have?"

"You sure picked a hell of a way to test him." Eli folded his arms and then released them, realizing he looked like a toddler in a tantrum.

"That monk of yours —" Anthony began, as Eli pulled his chair out to see them both more easily.

"Novice."

"Same thing." Anthony waved him off and took a drink. "I remember asking Simon once about why he was there. Did you make him up for a reason, or was he supposed to fall in love with Marco?"

Eli thought the same thing. He wasn't through re-reading the book, but he knew exactly what Anthony was getting at.

Graham stood to check on the steaks. "Hang on."

Eli looked at Anthony, who simply raised his glass slightly as if starting a toast he didn't finish, then took another drink. Eli took the opportunity to move into Graham's spot, directly across. That way, he figured, he could watch them both without moving his head like he was following a tennis match.

Graham returned from turning the steaks and looked at Eli, who simply slid Graham's wine glass over to his former seat and shrugged. Graham kept his eyes on Eli as he walked around and sat next to Anthony.

"Anyway…" Graham extended the word, keeping his eyes on Eli, who simply took a drink and looked over the rim of his glass like he owned the table.

"Simon and I nearly had a conniption about the novice," Graham said.

"Really? Simon made it sound like it was always in the works," Anthony said gently, then took the last swig of his wine and set the glass down. Eli reached over and filled it again.

"I remember sitting out on this very patio with him one night. I don't remember where you were at, Graham, but it was just us two old farts and we got to talking about your books."

Graham leaned over. "Really?" Eli noticed he looked like this was news to him.

"And I have always been intrigued with that monk of yours."

"Novice," Graham corrected, but Anthony either hadn't heard or didn't care. Eli figured the latter as he took another drink and leaned back into the cushions, absorbing their words.

"Anyway, I asked that husband of yours — 'But why didn't Marco fall in love with him? They were practically made for each other!'" Anthony paused, Eli guessed, for dramatic effect. "And you know what he said?"

Graham shook his head. Clearly, he hadn't heard this story. Eli could tell because Graham looked younger, engaged, eager, like he was in school. Not the tired and worn eyes of a wise man who'd heard it all.

"Simon said — and I'll always remember this — he'd been on your case forever about writing a character who was just a friend. Said the novice was the first one he felt you got right. That you'd been trying to show friendship between men that wasn't brotherhood and wasn't romance. 'Just love,' he said."

The very story he was reading all over again seemed to take on a slightly different tone. Marco was lonely. Hurt. Unsure what to do with his life since Alessandro was gone. And confused. Was he allowed to meet other people? Or not? Was he destined to go through the rest of his life alone? Or would Alessandro want him to have a companion along the way? Marco didn't know.

Neither did Eli.

Graham reached over and touched Anthony's arm. "I never heard that story."

Eli noticed something in Graham settle into a slight melancholy. The way he had looked when they first met. Even if it had been a year and a half ago, Graham still melted at Simon's memory. He supposed he would be the same with Niles. Even if theirs hadn't been the same history.

"I need to pee." Eli stood to head back inside.

"Grab the tongs when you come back," Graham said, before turning back to Anthony as if preparing further questions.

Eli walked inside and turned to head to the powder room. After finishing up, he stepped out into the living room and pulled his phone out.

Kieran had texted.

KIERAN

Miss me? 😜

with a silly face emoji, which made him smile. Kieran was sweet, in a way that meant he was discovering things Eli had taken for granted — or had jaded him over the past few years. Even months.

Of course. Graham's cooking steak and Anthony is telling stories.

he replied — although he wasn't sure he'd ever formally introduced who Graham and Anthony were, exactly.

Steak. Yum!

Eli laughed. The wine had taken the shine off and made him a little more carefree. Or relaxed. Or both.

Graham's cooking, so I dunno

I'm gonna tell on you!

Don't you have a cape to wear? People to save?

Gave up the cape along with wearing my underwear on the outside.

Eli laughed.

Prolly good. People would freak.

Gotta boogie. Pat is giving me the look. We stopped for coffee.

I'll text when I get home ltr

Eli saw a thumbs-up emoji and almost put his phone back in his pocket, but quickly added:

Stop by after you get off if you want. I'll be awake.

It'll be after midnight.

So? You gonna turn into a pumpkin?

Kieran sent a laughing emoji.

Oh, you have church in the morning like a good boy.

Yep.

Do you have to go?

Eli pushed a little, and he knew it. Didn't care.

I'll stop by.

Good boy. Go save the world.

Kieran sent a hug emoji.

Eli pocketed his phone and almost walked back out onto the patio when he remembered the tongs. Circling back to pull them out of a kitchen drawer by the stove, he walked back to find Graham talking animatedly with Anthony over something.

"Eli, be a dear and pull off the steaks — if they haven't burnt already, please." Graham looked up mid-sentence before returning to his debate or inquisition or whatever it was those two were discussing.

Eli did as asked and set the plate of three steaks in the center of the table before returning to his chair.

"We can finish what Simon did or didn't say later. But let's eat, Graham. I'm starving." Anthony turned to look over at Eli.

"Where's the food?"

"What?" Eli responded. "The steaks are right there."

"No." Anthony turned toward Graham, who seemed to still be deep in thought. "Graham, didn't you make anything to go with the steak?"

"Huh?" He seemed to snap out of his thoughts and looked at the table where the single plate of meat sat, then up at Eli.

"Oh," he said. Then something crossed his mind. "Oh shit. I forgot the potatoes."

Graham jumped up and ran into the kitchen, both Eli and Anthony tracking his movements.

"So. Graham tells me you've been seeing this Kieran fella."

Eli coughed. Some of the wine had started going down the wrong pipe.

Graham returned with another plate holding three slightly overdone baked potatoes Eli presumed he pulled from the oven in the nick of time.

"You okay, Eli?" Graham walked over and patted his back.

"I was just asking about Kieran," Anthony said, his eyes focused on one of the steaming potatoes as he reached over to put one on his plate.

"Anthony!" Graham scolded him.

"What?"

"Ixnay on the Ierankay!"

Eli looked up at Graham, who was hovering by him, and then to Anthony, who set his butter knife down from its attack on the potato. "What in the hell are you saying, old man?"

Eli couldn't help but laugh. He looked over at Graham, who returned to his seat and went quiet, his eyes turning into a school principal's.

Graham made an obvious head nod toward Eli, but Anthony rolled his eyes.

"Oh, get over it, Graham. I'm happy for Eli. He deserves to have someone back in his life. He's too young to go around hanging out with us old folks all the time."

"I'll have you know I'm only fifty-three, thank you very much."

"Well, good for you," Anthony said, spreading butter liberally on his potato. "Eli, be a dear and top up Santa here, would you?"

Eli relaxed, even giggled as he poured more wine in Anthony's glass before returning to his own.

"So. How is Kieran? I only remember seeing him that one time."

Eli knew what he was referring to. Niles's funeral. But he was okay saying it now. Or acknowledging.

"He's well. At work."

"Ah. Well, invite him over next time," Anthony replied as he took a bite.

"Shouldn't I be the one with the invitations?" Graham asked Anthony.

"You're too worried about Eli to say it."

Eli's eyes widened, wondering how Graham was going to take that.

"'Sides. I know when it's time to push a little. Theodore taught me that when he died…" Anthony chewed and took a sip of wine. "…along with a few other things," he added softly, but Eli could read him. Graham's brows furrowed slightly, like they did when he was curious or confused but too polite to inquire.

"So. Are you two in love?" Anthony asked, taking another bite of steak.

Graham coughed, his turn for something to go down the wrong pipe. Eli reached over and returned the patting-back favor, using the distraction to not answer.

"Anthony. It's only been —" Graham finally exclaimed after coming up for air.

"Four months. Yes, I know. But I stand by my question."

Graham and Anthony looked over at Eli, who sat there staring.

"Niles —" he started.

He stopped. Looked down at his glass. Tried again.

"I don't know."

He hadn't considered it. Well, that wasn't true. He'd been brushing around the edges of it. Kieran had been so funny and sweet and… he was definitely not Niles, that was for sure. But he hadn't even thought to compare him. He wasn't looking for anything from him.

But, still. He remembered holding his hand walking back that first night they met. He felt Kieran pull away after they crossed the street, but he wanted it back. So he claimed it as his own. And Kieran didn't protest.

Since, it'd been sort of the same way. Eli hadn't planned to do anything. But when they'd meet up for dinner or go for a walk, something simple would happen — Kieran had dropped his fork at dinner two weeks back and teasingly grabbed Eli's to replace it, and they'd ended up sharing the one fork for the rest of the meal. Silly. But sweet.

Or just last Tuesday, Eli had invited him over. He could do that now, since he didn't have roommates anymore. They'd sat on the sofa and watched Netflix together. Kieran was sweet, ensuring the captions were on. Eli had microwaved some popcorn and plopped down, accidentally sitting right next to him, probably a little too close. Kieran had moved to give him space, but Eli scooted right back over and sat there, shoulders and legs practically glued together. By the end of the show, Eli's legs were draped over Kieran's lap, and Kieran was absently rubbing his feet.

"Lay off, Anthony. We don't need to pressure Eli this soon," Graham said, bringing Eli back to the conversation — which was apparently about him, but not with him.

"Graham, it's not being disrespectful to Niles for Eli to find joy," Anthony said calmly, with the authority of an older man who knew. "Would you want Niles to always feel chained to grief if it were the other way around, Eli?"

Before Eli could respond, Anthony turned to Graham.

"Would Simon?"

Eli saw Graham's face wrinkle slightly, his upper lip twitching almost imperceptibly. But Eli caught it. Thought Anthony did, too.

"Listen, Graham. I know how difficult it is to reconcile wanting to remember your lover when they're gone while hating the pain of living it alone. Lord knows I spent many nights feeling so lonely after Theodore died, but too goddamned afraid to even walk down here and bullshit with you and Simon because I was worried it was 'too soon.'" Anthony used little air quotes with his fingers.

Eli seemed to pick up features of Anthony he hadn't noticed before. Even in the September twilight on the patio, he could see the young man Anthony had been showing through.

"But Theodore wasn't a saint. I learned a lot about that after he died. And neither was Simon. Nor Niles. None of us are."

Eli noticed Graham leaning forward, listening. More like reliving it.

"I wasn't paying tribute to Theodore by being miserable. Neither are you, Graham. Simon would be yipping at you now, telling you to laugh, tell a funny story, tease. Spread some joy."

Eli noticed Graham wince a little when Anthony mentioned Simon's name. He knew now how it felt. At least he knew what the experience of trying to let go meant. Or — transform. Maybe that was a better word.

"And you, Eli. If Kieran treats you well, if you are finding joy in discovering each other — I say do it. You're too young not to."

Eli locked eyes with Anthony and held the beat.

"The past is not less true because we keep living. We carry it with us. But *we carry it.* It does not carry us."

Eli looked down at his steak, not really seeing it. He remembered Niles. He always remembered Niles. It surprised him how much he had. They hadn't been together years, like Anthony and Theodore, or even Graham and Simon. But they'd loved each other. Said it. And Eli felt it.

But he was starting to realize that he still wanted to love. Needed it. And who knew if Kieran was the man destined for this next round of life. But it felt reassuring to hear Anthony say it. Not that he needed permission. But it felt like he didn't have to hide.

Primarily from himself.

"These steaks are wonderful, Graham. Even if you aren't a cook." Anthony clearly knew when to change the subject, because Eli saw Graham do a double-take and then switch back into his sarcastic self — at least when it came to Anthony.

"I'll have you know I can boil water."

Eli smiled. Anthony rolled his eyes.

"Oh. Hang on." Anthony set his fork down, excited to share something.

"I hope there's enough light out here. You may need to turn on the porch lamp, Graham."

Eli wondered what Anthony was up to. Was he going to show a card trick or something?

Anthony held both his arms up as if preparing for surgery, then slowly moved his hands into position and began signing. *Hello. My name is A-N-T-H—* He paused. "Aw, shit. I can't remember the next one."

Eli's eyes lit up just about as fast as the smile spread across his face. He glanced at Graham, who seemed to be doing the same.

Eli raised his hands and finished it for him — *O-N-Y* — before saying *Anthony* aloud for his benefit.

"That's right." Anthony signed it again, this time the whole name.

"How did you know how to do that?" Eli asked, signing it as well. He hadn't realized his hands had gone into ASL mode.

"Not so fast, buster. I'm still learning." Anthony smiled before adding, "And I know this one, too." *How are you?* he signed. It was clumsy, but he seemed happy with himself.

I am happy, Eli signed, although he was sure Anthony hadn't understood, assuming he'd said *fine* or *good*.

"How in the hell —" Graham began, but Anthony cut him off.

"Been learning on YouTube. You should try it, Graham. Poor Eli here has to put up with our shit. I thought we needed to try and at least meet him halfway."

Eli had never heard Anthony say anything like that. Not even Graham. He never asked or expected it, but to have Anthony think of him like this — Eli fought off a tear, blaming it on a gnat or something as he rubbed his eye.

But Anthony gave him a wink and smiled. "I got lots more to learn. You and me should practice, Graham."

Eli looked over at Graham, who was smiling, as if he finally agreed with Anthony on something and was close to admitting it.

"Fine. But I don't want you teaching me something only to discover I'm signing dirty words and don't even know it."

"Aww, you're no fun," Anthony shot back, and gave another grin to Eli.

All he could do was laugh. He picked up his fork and continued with his dinner, listening to Graham and Anthony banter some more while they finished the steaks. Eli emptied the bottle, topping up their glasses, and looked out at the night sky. The sun had dipped below the horizon and the two old men across from him were badgering each other.

But he was thinking of what Anthony had said earlier.

Was he in love?

They sat for a while, Anthony and Graham trading barbs, telling stories, asking Eli questions. Nothing terribly important, but that felt right. It was as if he'd been inducted into the widowers club, and he snickered to himself. It was funny in his mind, not sad. Especially given his age.

"Care to share?" Graham asked.

They had all pulled their chairs out, watching the night sky together. Graham had turned on the porch light, which helped Eli see their faces, but they'd settled into the kind of quiet that comes at the end of a long evening.

Eli nodded. He hadn't fully heard Graham, but he guessed what he said. Didn't matter. Silly joke anyway.

"Well, this old man is getting tired." Anthony yawned and stood. Eli hadn't quite caught Anthony's words either. He loved the dark sky and the stars, but they were shit for reading faces.

They all chipped in to clear the table and made their way to the front door.

"You tell Kieran to come see us, okay?" Anthony gave Eli a strong hug, making sure Eli could see his face.

Graham reached over and gave a Graham hug — which Eli had come to know. And appreciate.

Goodbye, Anthony signed — imperfect, but Eli understood, signing it back properly, giving Anthony something to practice.

Eli walked out and got into Simon's car. Started it up and pulled out, the lights briefly illuminating Anthony and Graham standing on the porch waving. He loved those two old men, even if he didn't say it. Perhaps he'd teach them to sign that next.

Driving home, he let his brain go on autopilot. It was still several hours before Kieran got off his shift. He looked forward to seeing him. Didn't feel guilty for coaxing him to come over. He could be sleepy at St. Whatshisface parish in the morning for all he cared.

Kieran did bring him joy. Eli remembered what Anthony had been saying. And he felt that Niles would've liked Kieran, even if it took him a little while to warm up. And Kieran would've been fascinated by Niles's robots and tinkering and all that geeky stuff Eli had no interest in but loved anyway because he loved Niles.

Loved Niles.

That didn't feel like past tense anymore. Niles wasn't here. But he still loved him. It felt good to know that.

But did he love Kieran? He felt like he was old enough now to not deny his feelings, but wasn't sure yet if he was ready to acknowledge them either. That didn't need to be decided tonight, he thought, and put it aside.

Back home, he let himself into the apartment and turned on the end-table lamp next to the sofa. Keys and wallet into the candy dish his grandmother had once owned — the one he'd taken when he moved out of his parents' place. It was the only thing he took, aside from his clothes and some silly high school yearbooks he never looked at.

Taking his jacket off, he texted Kieran.

I'm home.

Good deal. Slow night here. Don't want to jinx it.
See you soon.

Eli read the message alongside another hug emoji. Wondered when a heart emoji might make its way onto the screen.

Smiling at himself, he caught the novel lying where he'd left it on the sofa, open face-down to keep his page. Since he was on his own, he could do that now. Leave his stuff wherever he pleased.

He plopped down and picked up *The Novice's Chapel,* flipping back a page or two to remind himself where he'd left off.

Marco had invited the novice to his room for bread and wine.

Eli grinned, remembering the wine at Graham's earlier. And Anthony telling them Simon's story about the novice. Hearing how he came to be made something shift.

Eli could see the novice's face now.

A real and true friend.

For Marco.

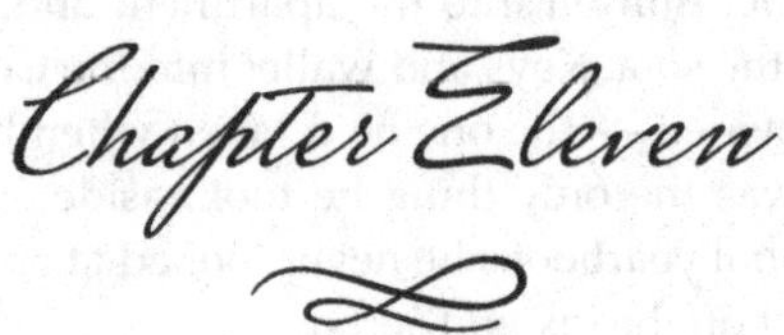

Chapter Eleven

LATE-MORNING SUN on a Saturday hit Eli's face as he stepped out of his apartment and looked at his car, dew burning off the windows. The defroster was probably in order — if nothing else, to help the sun along. It was nearing 10:30 and he needed to get a move on. He'd promised Michael he'd meet him around eleven, and according to Google Maps it was a good forty minutes to get there. He texted him before he put the car in Drive.

On my way.

Eli had never been uptight about punctuality, but today he wanted Michael to know he was coming. He hadn't seen Michael in person since the dorm move. They'd been texting back and forth all summer, with Michael finally confirming his plans to move to Portland after all. But they hadn't had a real conversation since the weekend he'd graduated high school.

It was nearly October now, and their schedules had only just lined up. Well, Michael's schedule, really. Eli had spent most of his free weekends with Kieran lately, but this Saturday Michael had finally landed clear of whatever orientation or student mixer or who-knew-what the school kept throwing at him.

Eli took the highway south past Portland, then west out toward Gorham. He'd never come out this way before. Kieran had suggested he give himself extra time to park, but Eli had found a visitor lot online last night that looked relatively close to Robie Hall, where Michael now lived.

Funny, he thought, turning right onto School Street. He'd read that Robie housed the Rainbow community, among others. Fitting.

Finding a spot, he pulled the Volvo in and stepped out. 11:12. Oh well.

Here

He texted Michael, and pulled up the map to see which direction to walk.

Heading up a path, he noticed a skinny kid practically skipping his way — hot pink Chuck Taylor high-tops, khaki shorts, a rainbow belt, and a white T-shirt with big bold black letters that said CHOOSE LIFE. Eli was pretty sure he'd seen that shirt in a Wham! video.

Eli stopped when he realized it was Michael heading his way. Wayfarers on. A shell necklace that looked a little tight around his neck. And — was his hair frosted?

Another guy was walking next to him — around the same height, skinny, his hair just a shade lighter than Michael's. Khaki shorts as well, but a plain T-shirt and white sneakers. Conservative, by comparison.

"Oh my Gawd, Gurl!" Michael opened his arms and ran into Eli's. "I haven't seen you in, like, forever!"

Eli heard that last part right in his ear, somewhat jumbled, his hearing aids whining as if Michael were screaming into a microphone.

He pulled back and gave him an obvious look up and down. Michael had changed since the last time. Going for it now, that was for damn sure.

Eli looked over at the other guy, who stood a step back and looked reluctant to butt into their reunion. Michael grabbed his hand and pulled him over, making him blush.

"This is Mike."

Eli smiled and shook his hand. "Nice to meet you." He could see Mike's eyes look into his momentarily before looking over at Michael.

"Eli's deaf, so make sure he can see your lips, okay?" Michael said, turning back to smile at Eli.

"I'm sorry," Mike said quickly. Eli patted his arm. "No need to be. Just talk like you would. I'll let you know if I can't follow." Mike gave a small nod.

Eli turned to Michael and took him in again. "I can't believe you're here."

"I know, right? It's so crazy! I almost didn't come, but I'm *so glad I did.*"

Michael looked at Mike, and Eli wondered if he had anything to do with that.

"So, did you know him before…" Eli began to ask Mike, but was interrupted.

"Oh my gawd, it was so funny! We met on the first day at orientation.

We were paired up accidentally because both our roommates didn't show and so they put us together and…"

Eli looked at Mike, who was watching Michael with a small smile. So they were roommates.

"So you both share your dorm?"

Mike nodded and looked around them like he had heard something, but Michael grabbed Eli's arm to pull him around and pointed up at a larger building in the distance. "That's home."

"Can I see?" Eli asked, but looked over at Mike, who nodded and led the way.

Michael kept his arm around Eli for a moment as they walked, pointing out something, but Eli was watching Mike walk ahead of them. Mike turned around occasionally, like he was checking they were keeping up.

Walking inside the building, Eli was brought back to his own dorm years ago. He'd been out of college for a couple of years already, but hadn't lived in a dorm since he was nineteen. The smell of it hit him. That and the furniture. He wondered if all college dorms bought their furnishing from the same place.

Eli watched as Mike took his key out to open their door while Michael pointed out the decorations.

Two nametags were taped to the door, both labeled "Michael," each with a small picture obviously taken at some orientation mixer. Someone had put a big & between them and pressed stickers all around — rainbows, smiley faces, hearts, and…

Eli leaned forward and squinted. Yep. Cartoon penises with happy faces, dancing.

Michael was laughing. "This was a joke!" He almost pleaded. "Guys down the hall and…"

Eli saw Mike shaking his head as he opened the door. Eli didn't say a word as he stepped into their room. It was a typical dorm, almost like the one he shared with his old roommate years ago. Industrial bunk bed slid against the corner, a window next, two desks and a small combination wardrobe and drawers with a mirror on the outside. A mini-fridge sat next to it with a microwave on top. A couple of hoodies and a jacket hung by the door along with a few posters along the walls.

"This is mine," Michael said, pointing to a black-and-white Calvin Klein ad — a dripping-wet guy staring off into nothing.

"Mine is less…" Mike made a point of looking right at Eli and pointing to a poster of the solar system.

"Gay, I know…" Michael explained for him.

Mike rolled his eyes — caught Eli looking, and turned away, slightly embarrassed.

"So, your name is Michael as well?" Eli asked Mike.

"Yeah.. I usually go by that, but.."

"But since I'm Michael, too, we did rock-paper-scissors to decide who changed." Michael finished it.

"And you got…" Eli looked at Mike.

"His paper covered my rock," he shrugged.

"I still call him Michael, tho," Mike added. Eli turned to look at his adopted nephew — that was how he'd started to think of him.

Turning around to take in the room, he noticed a few photos of Michael's family — and one of him and Niles when they'd visited. It caught him by surprise. It was sweet he had Niles there as well.

"I liked that photo. We had fun that day."

"Yeah," was all Eli could muster as he set the frame back down. He was fine. But he had his moments.

"Which one is yours?" Eli asked Mike about the bunk beds.

"I'm on top."

Eli looked up and saw a plain navy comforter with a pillow, the bed made up simply.

Below was another story. A pink-and-blue comforter with rainbows and butterflies, scrunched up to reveal sheets covered in cartoon animals. A furry body pillow. Too many stuffed animals to count.

"Yours, obviously," Eli turned to Michael, who beamed. "Did you do rock-paper-scissors for…" he pointed to the bunks, but Michael jumped onto his bed and enthusiastically declared he wanted the bottom bunk all along.

Eli turned to look at Mike, who shrugged again as if it hadn't mattered to him.

"I like your room," he said aloud as he turned to their desks, noticing a few photos taped on what obviously was Michael's whiteboard next to a stack of books.

Leaning down, they appeared to be more candids from that same day the pictures on their door were taken. One was Michael, Mike, and what looked like three or four others grouped together smiling, holding some sort of trophy.

"We won the tug-of-war during orientation," Michael said, coming over with pride. Eli looked at him before returning to the photos.

Another was of Michael running across a field. Someone must have been close by because he could see Michael's determination in his face.

"Mike took that. I was part of the relay. We had to —" Michael laughed. "— race across a field, up and back three times, holding a hot dog. Passing it like a baton! It was so gross, but so fun!"

Eli smiled and looked over at Mike, who was standing by his desk watching.

There were a few other photos, obviously from that orientation mixer. One caught Eli's eye: someone had taken a picture of Mike hugging

Michael from behind, his head resting on his shoulder as they both posed for the photo. It was cute. Sweet, actually.

Eli turned to Mike and looked at his desk, which was more ordered. He was starting to piece together their personalities.

"Is this your family?" he asked, looking at a small frame sitting just by the desk lamp.

"Yeah." Mike picked it up and pointed to each one. "That's my younger brother. My dad. My grandma."

His mother wasn't there. Eli didn't know him well enough to ask.

"So, lunch? My treat," Eli offered as Mike set the frame down.

"Sure! I'm starving anyway," Michael spoke up.

"I, uh.. I have a thing.. but.. you two go."

"What thing?" Michael asked, looking confused.

"I.. I'm supposed to be at my work study thing at 1 in the library and uh…"

"You sure, Mike?" Eli asked, but he caught a vibe that Mike was giving them an excuse to be alone.

"Yeah, maybe next time?" Mike looked right into his eyes and cocked his head a little.

Michael came around Eli and took Mike's hands. "You sure?"

Mike slowly pulled his hands away and nodded.

"It's okay, Mike." Eli stepped over and put a hand on Mike's shoulder with a small squeeze. "You and Michael can come visit sometime, and I'll treat you to dinner."

Mike gave him an appreciative look before Eli turned to Michael. "Where we headed?"

Michael continued to look at Mike, but Eli pushed him along.

"Well.. uh.. maybe we can walk down to… uh…"

"Miller's is pretty good," Mike jumped in. Both Eli and Michael looked over. "If you, uh, want sandwiches, maybe?" Eli noticed he sank into himself a little.

"That sounds good," Eli replied, watching Mike perk back.

"You buying?" Michael was quick to confirm.

"Me? I thought you were taking your favorite uncle out!" Eli teased.

"Graham's not here!" Michael gave it right back. Eli noticed Mike laugh. He was curious to know more about him, especially how the two of them got together.

Because it was obvious. He wasn't going to pry, but the look he gave to Michael said it all.

"Fine!" Eli clapped his hands. "Let's go. Lead the way."

Michael grabbed his wallet off his desk and turned to Mike but then stopped. Eli noticed and looked away, walking toward the door. He was pretty sure there was more to the goodbye than he was meant to see.

Before he made it to the hall, a tap on his arm. He turned. Mike was standing there.

"Thanks for coming, Eli."

It took him by surprise. "Of course. Happy to. And you come visit, too. You're always welcome." Eli reached over and gave him a hug.

Mike didn't hug like a first-time hugger. He settled into it like he knew how. *There's more to his story,* Eli thought. He let go and noticed Mike smiling, biting his lip.

"You sure you don't want to come?" Eli offered.

For a moment, it looked like he might, but Eli noticed him look at Michael and turn to shake his head. "I've got that thing..." he drifted.

Eli nodded. "Do we need to drive?" He turned to ask Michael, who was still looking at Mike.

"Uh.. oh, no. We can walk. It's not that far," he looked over at Eli and followed him out the door. Eli noticed him look back before closing it.

They walked until they reached a little deli and butcher shop nearby, with picnic tables out front along a railing.

"Michael!" The man behind the counter seemed to know his name. "Spicy Italian today? Or do you want a sandwich?" he joked.

Michael came alive at hearing his name like that. He'd only been a student here for — what, a month? — and he was already known.

"You should try the chicken Caesar wrap, Eli. It's a religious experience!"

Eli loved how Michael seemed to be over the top with everything. Nothing was good or fun or interesting. Instead it was The Most or Absolutely the best!

They ordered. Eli stepped in to pay. While their sandwiches were being made, he noticed how much older he felt. Not old, per se. Older. He was paying for Michael's lunch. He was quietly walking along as Michael pointed out his world. He was the passenger on this little adventure, not the driver. He felt like a dad.

To his super gay son.

"What's funny?" Michael took off his Wayfarers and looked him in the eye, a smile across his face like he wanted in on the punchline.

"I was thinking I feel like your gay dad."

Michael laughed.

"And I'm your super gay princess!" He did a little pirouette.

Eli pushed his shoulder. "Stop it or you'll get us kicked out."

"Nah, it's cool in here. You should've seen Mike last week. He was wearing these super cute but super short cutoffs and a tank top. OMG!" Michael laughed as he told it.

Eli pictured Mike exactly like that.

"Made me look butch!"

"Mike? *Your Mike*?"

Michael nodded while still laughing.

Eli shook his head. Michael had changed. Last winter he'd been a typical high school kid, afraid of even saying the word *gay* — and now he was practically a walking billboard.

They picked up their order and made their way outside to a picnic table.

"So, you seem to have fit in well," Eli mentioned before taking a bite.

Michael's mouth was full as he began nodding while reaching for napkins. "I'm really happy."

Eli noticed. He did seem happy.

"I almost didn't come, you know."

"Yeah, you mentioned it. Why?"

"Well.. it's a long story."

Eli gave him a look which said *go on*.

Michael set his sandwich down and looked up. He looked more like the Michael Eli remembered from last winter. None of the *super gay* elements. Just Michael, the way Eli felt he knew him.

"I was gonna, you know. Since like… spring break."

Eli nodded as he continued eating.

"Levi and I were…" Michael stopped as if thinking of his words.

"What?"

Michael looked down at his sandwich and mouthed something. Eli reached over and tapped his hand, making him look up. "I can't follow." Eli pointed to his own eyes. Michael nodded and began again.

"If I tell you something, will you swear not to tell anyone?"

Eli set his sandwich down.

"Okay," he said a little reluctantly. He hated hearing those words because they usually were followed by something that always should have been told to others.

"Levi was my first.. time." He looked up at Eli as if waiting for disappointment.

Eli sat looking at him. He wasn't surprised. Perhaps a little concerned, especially now that he'd seen Mike and knew there was more to the story. But he decided to remain quiet.

"But I got home after visiting, you know.. and.. well.. something happened."

Michael began fidgeting with his hands, unable to keep his eyes up. Eli waited, giving Michael room to talk. He had brought it up. Eli figured he'd let him take his time.

"I didn't mean to, but.. I got home and…"

Eli sat back.

"I met a guy."

There it is, Eli thought. The missing key. Eli raised his eyebrows. Michael noticed.

"It wasn't *like that*," Michael said quickly. But Eli kept his face straight. He'd reserve judgment.

"Well, I mean.. it sorta was I guess.. but.. " Michael looked down again before turning his face back to Eli. "I didn't mean it to, seriously."

Eli watched him look — like he was asking permission. Michael looked away, then back, and kept going.

"I went to this party. I didn't even know about it until like that day. And Stuart was there."

"Stuart?"

Michael nodded. "Mom didn't know about him, but dad did. I told him."

Eli remembered Graham texting from Nashville back in May — something about Michael's dad handling things better than Becca. Now it made sense.

"He was so nice. Was a freshman at Vanderbilt. You'd like him. I mean.. "

Michael looked away again, but Eli waited.

"I didn't mean to…" Michael repeated.

"What did you not mean to?" Eli finally asked. Michael couldn't look him in the eye. The table shook slightly. Eli looked down through the metal grating — Michael's leg was bouncing.

"We… we, uh.. "

"Slept together?" Eli asked blankly.

Michael's mouth pursed like he was holding back some emotions, but he nodded and looked down.

"So that's the reason for whatever is going on with you and Levi," Eli said aloud.

Michael looked off to his side, wiping his face slightly, unable to look at him directly.

"Michael," Eli reached over and touched him to gain his attention.

Michael turned. Eli could see he was struggling to keep his eyes on him — they kept darting away.

"Michael, I am not judging you."

Michael looked at him and paused.

"What happened to Stuart?"

Michael didn't say anything.

"I mean, you're here, not back in Nashville."

Michael looked down and back again.

"And it's obvious you and Mike are a thing."

Michael's eyes grew wider.

Eli leaned, stretching his back and shaking his head. "C'mon, Michael. I can see."

Michael's lips pursed again. This time he looked up, cocking his head and biting his lip.

Eli reached over and grabbed his hand and squeezed it gently before letting go.

"It's okay, Michael. You're young. I'm not judging. Really."

Michael looked back at him. Took a napkin and wiped at his eyes. What might have been makeup smudged off too.

Michael took a moment before he spoke.

"Stuart… I told him I was falling in love, and —" Michael started biting his lip again. He reached for Eli's hand and held on. It felt like he was clinging.

"He didn't love you?" Eli predicted.

Michael shook his head. He was holding himself together, Eli noticed, but wondered if he ever let himself out.

"I told him that night, after you and I texted. I was talking about going to Vanderbilt and he told me I should come here. 'Cause —" Michael choked and squeezed Eli's hand. "—'cause he liked me. But he had another guy he was dating, too. Said it was like —"

Michael turned again to look away, letting go of his hand and grabbing his chin, like the *Thinking Man,* only through tears.

Eli handed him a napkin and sat with the silence. Someone walked by on their way to the next table and Eli watched them look at Michael before moving on.

This seemed to explain a lot. Michael met Stuart. Had a good time. Stuart was *there,* not miles away like Levi. They had fun. Michael was finally having fun. Living. His dad knew.

But Levi didn't. Neither did Becca. Neither did he.

Eli imagined it. Michael falling in love — probably by the second date. Michael was the type to go from zero to love in six seconds. Stuart, a Vandy freshman, probably just enjoying him. Dating around. But then Michael named it. And Stuart redirected him to Portland.

Eli looked around at others eating, people pulling up to park out front. And Michael staring off into the distance.

"So you came to Portland."

Michael turned and set the balled-up napkin on the table.

"And you met Mike at Orientation."

Michael nodded.

"Have you talked to Levi?"

Michael's face turned away. He hated thinking it, but this was so predictable. Had he not been dealing with..

Eli took a breath.

Niles's death. He'd seen the pattern. Called it, probably. But it wasn't his to interfere with. Michael and Levi were young. Mike was too. Stuart probably. Eli was only twenty-four, but he'd spent several years learning what it was like to fall in love, to have sex for the first time, to want to be close to someone — and then meet someone else and feel torn. Kid stuff he was still learning himself. But with a head start on them.

"We text," was all Michael said, turning back to Eli.

"I think he knows," Eli said.

Michael looked scared.

"I don't mean specifics, but I think he knows, Michael."

He watched Michael close his eyes and look down, like he was ashamed. Eli supposed he might be.

"I think you owe it to him to say."

"I don't want to hurt him," he managed. Eli caught the gist; Michael was barely holding together.

Eli reached over and grabbed his hand again.

"Michael, I understand. I think you and Mike look really cute together."

Michael's eyes perked slightly.

"But I think Levi will be okay as long as you give him the chance to be."

Michael wrestled with that. Eli didn't push. He let go of his hand, packed up their wrappers, stood, and cleared the table.

"C'mon. Why don't you show me the campus?" Eli reached over and patted Michael's back, giving him a slight nudge up.

Michael wiped his eyes on the back of his arm as they walked across the street and back the way they came.

"So, tell me more about Mike. I want to know more about this boyfriend of yours."

"Eli…"

He stopped and turned directly to face Michael. "You are boyfriends, right?"

Michael nodded apologetically.

"Why are you so sad looking? Mike is cute. He seems really nice."

"He is, but.."

"But what, Michael?"

"I just.. Levi…"

"Yeah, Levi.. and you have some thinking to do about what you tell him, but that's not Mike's issue, right?"

Michael shook his head.

"So, don't take it out on him, okay?"

Michael look down, embarrassed.

"Besides, I know you."

"You *know me*?" Michael looked up.

Eli nodded. "Uh huh. And I know before too long you'll be head over heels in love with him." Eli smiled, watching Michael's own smile betray him.

"Eli!"

"It's true! You probably already are. Right?"

Michael's smile return brighter, but he didn't say anything.

"Thought so." Eli said, and continued walking, Michael catching up.

"Are you mad at me?" Michael tapped his arm and caught his attention.

"Why?"

Michael shrugged his shoulders. "Dunno.. I guess I just…"

"I'm not mad at you, Michael."

"Disappointed," he said and looked down, but Eli forced him to look back.

"Not disappointed either. I just want you to…" Eli thought for a second before continuing.

"I'm proud that you're learning to be open about being yourself. This whole — gay thing." Eli waved his hand at Michael's clothes and the persona. "But I think you might feel better if you were as comfortable being who you are on the inside."

Michael stared a hole in him, like he was trying to figure out something.

"Michael — it's super easy to fall in love. You've got that heart. That's a good thing. But you have to remember some people have a harder time trusting. And when you go silent on them, it just confirms what they're afraid of. Even when it's hard. They deserve the truth."

Michael stood listening as students walked past.

"You still love Levi?"

Michael nodded.

"Then he deserves your honesty."

"What if he hates me?"

Eli shrugged. "He might. But I don't think he will. He's just confused that you've gone quiet."

Michael looked away.

"Michael, just think about it this way: If you had moved here only to find he had fallen in love with someone else, but didn't tell you, didn't come see you.."

"I'd be devastated."

Eli pointed gently to his own heart. "Then put yourself in his shoes. Try walking in them next."

He watched Michael look down and then take a deep breath.

"C'mon. Show me where things are. I've never been here." Eli moved them along.

Chapter Twelve

SATURDAY. Eli took 295 south the way he used to — almost without thinking, the Volvo's lane changes mostly muscle memory, the early-October sun cutting across the dashboard and warming the back of his hand on the wheel. He hadn't been down to the waterfront since June. Their lunches had always been weekday lunches, Donna in her work-day uniform, the place full of men in suits. Saturday was new. He didn't know what to make of it yet. Maybe nothing.

He took the parking lot off Commercial and walked the two blocks, hands in his jacket pockets, watching the gulls work the trash by the curb. Bright day. Cold enough for the jacket. He could see his breath when he laughed at something a gull did with a paper cup.

The bistro looked the way it always did — dark wood, brass, the back wall of pressed tin Eli had once told Donna looked like a movie set for a wedding. Donna had told him that was exactly why she liked it. He pushed the door open and the host nodded at him before he could speak. He was a regular here in someone else's reservation. Always had been.

He didn't bother checking. He walked to the booth.

Donna was already there. Of course. Eleven thirty-eight, by his phone. She'd told him noon and he knew what that meant.

She looked up and her face did the thing it had always done when he walked in — that small lift, half a smile, the rest waiting until he was close enough to receive it properly. Less stage-managed than he remembered. Her hair was shorter. She was in an oatmeal sweater he'd never seen before, slouchy at the shoulder. No lipstick. He hadn't seen Donna without lipstick since the funeral, and even then she'd put it on between the wake and the burial. He didn't comment.

"Eli." She stood and reached for him. The air-kiss landed at his ear, not his cheek. She held him a half-second longer than the choreography asked for.

"Donna."

He slid into the booth. She slid back into hers.

"You look —" she started, and stopped, and tilted her head. "You look good."

"Don't sound so surprised."

"I'm not surprised. I'm pleased. There's a difference." She picked up her menu. "And do not let me order the bouillabaisse. Niles always made me get the bouillabaisse and then I'd be sorry for two days."

Eli laughed. "He did do that."

"He did. He was a tyrant about the bouillabaisse."

"He was a tyrant about a lot of things."

"He was." She set the menu down with the small precise motion that meant she had already decided what she wanted before he sat down. "Salad. I'm being good. Which is wretched. Brett has me being good."

"How's Brett?"

She gave him a look over her wine glass. The look said *don't get me started* and *thank you for asking* in equal measure.

"He's decided he likes the sage."

"No."

"Yes. He stood in the doorway last week and said it made the room *calmer*. That was the word. Calmer."

"Brett?"

"Brett." She took a sip. "I am not going to tell him I knew."

"You shouldn't."

"I won't."

The waiter came. Donna ordered the salad. Eli ordered the lobster roll because he could, and because Niles had loved the lobster roll here, and because saying it out loud to the waiter was — fine. It was fine. He could order a lobster roll at a restaurant in Portland.

When the waiter left, Donna folded her hands.

"So tell me things."

Eli scratched at the corner of the menu where it had started to come unglued. Thought about how to open it. There was no way to open it that wasn't going to sound like a confession, which was the part he didn't want it to sound like.

"I've been —" He paused. "I've been seeing someone."

He watched her face. It did not do any of the things he'd half-expected. No flinch. No closing. Just attention.

"Tell me."

"His name's Kieran. He's — Donna, I want you to know I didn't —"

"Eli." She put her hand flat on the table. Not on his hand. On the table, between them. "Don't do that."

"I —"

"Don't qualify it. Don't apologize for it. You are twenty-four years old. You are not asking me anything." She tipped her head. "I'm not the keeper of any of this. I won't be."

He let out a breath he hadn't realized he was holding.

"Okay."

"Okay. Now tell me."

So he did. He told her how they'd met — the paramedic at the wake, the same paramedic who'd come up to him at the cemetery, the messages later. He told her Kieran was twenty-two, a paramedic, lived with his mother and his brothers in South Portland. He told her about the popcorn night and the one fork at dinner. He told her about Kieran riding a motorcycle, which made her wince. About Kieran's church, which made her smile.

"A Catholic," she said.

"A Catholic."

"My mother would have approved."

"Mine doesn't know yet."

"Well." Donna picked up her wine again. "One thing at a time."

The food came. They ate. Eli realized, halfway through the lobster roll, that they had been talking for forty minutes without either of them pretending. Donna asked a follow-up about Kieran's mother that was sharper than he'd have expected, and he answered the way he used to answer her, before any of it.

"He sounds —" Donna paused. Looked for the word. "He sounds like someone who shows up."

"He does."

"Good." She set her fork down. "Bring him round. I want to meet him."

"Donna —"

"When you're ready. Not before. I'm not summoning. I'm asking."

He nodded.

She picked up the check before he'd noticed it had been put down.

"Donna."

"Don't."

"Donna —"

"Eli." She slid her card into the holder without looking. "I always pay. End of discussion."

He let her.

Out on the sidewalk, the wind off the harbor had picked up. Donna pulled her sweater closed at the neck and looked at him with the expression he remembered from a hundred lunches before this one — the *we'll do this again, and soon* expression. She didn't say it. She didn't have to.

She kissed his cheek. Proper this time.

"Saturday again sometime?" she said.

"Saturday again."

He watched her walk up Commercial toward where she'd parked. She didn't look back. She never did.

Eli's landlady was an elderly woman who lived in the top-floor apartment, down the hall from the others. He had no idea how old she was, but wondered, not for the first time, if she was going to make it up the steps — the building had no elevator. It was old enough that elevators hadn't yet been a thing, let alone ADA codes.

She was always nice to him. Never made a fuss. Always called her son to come over whenever something needed to be fixed. No questions. Sent along a handwritten note when, inevitably, rent needed to increase. Last year it had gone up twenty-five dollars a month and the note had read like an apology letter for hitting his dog with her car. Eli suspected she didn't need the money, but enjoyed being surrounded by her tenants, even if no one ever saw her.

Until today. He had arrived home after work, like always. Thursday the 15th. Two weekends until Sonya and Angie's Halloween party, and he still hadn't pulled together a costume. He was searching Amazon on his phone at the kitchen table when he noticed a light out in the living room turn on and then off. He almost missed it. Wondered what *that* was. And then it dawned on him.

Back when Claire lived here, she had found some doorbell contraption online — the kind that mounted outside with double-sided tape and had a wireless chime plugged into a box she had set on the TV stand. Looked like a beige nothing-or-other, but it had an LED light that flashed whenever someone rang. She had showed him, proud of herself for "installing it," meaning she pulled the tape off and stuck it to the doorframe, announcing that the light would flash to let him know when someone was at the door. Clever. But no one was ever at their door.

Apparently, someone was now.

Eli opened it and had to look down. His elderly landlady was standing patiently, holding a tin of what appeared to be cookies.

"Hello, E-L-I," she said, spacing out her letters, almost yelling. She knew about his deafness and tried, but overcompensated. In the few times he had spoken with her, it had always been the same. He didn't have the heart to correct her, so he tolerated it and smiled.

"Hi."

"I don't want to intrude, but I made you some cookies. Snickerdoodles. I hope you like them."

Eli took the tin, wondering why the gift. It wasn't Christmas yet, and she hadn't given him anything for the holidays before. Still, he thanked her, which made her smile. She stood in the doorway as if she was physically unable to walk inside.

"I know your roommates moved out and you're month-to-month, but I thought I'd ask if you plan on staying here yourself, or —" She stopped, as if this was a game show and Eli was supposed to complete the phrase for ten thousand dollars.

"Oh!" He finally spoke after waiting for her. "I — uh — I'd been saving for my own place, but —"

"Oh yes. That is a wonderful goal, dear. How far along are you?"

"Well — uh — the way prices are, not there yet," he offered, with the same forced laugh he used at work, as if he had told a joke.

She smiled. "Yes. It is expensive these days."

Eli nodded. "Is there a problem?"

"Oh no. No problem, dear. I just —"

Eli kept looking at her. She seemed so frail, yet obviously still had her wits.

"I was checking since you're month to month, and — well — my great niece and her fiancé are getting married soon. I was seeing if perhaps the timing would be right, was all."

Eli now understood.

"You were thinking of having them move in here?"

"Oh, I'd never put you in an awkward position, dear. You're such a good friend."

Eli didn't know they were that close, but she seemed legitimate.

"When do they need a place?"

"Oh, I'm not sure. I know it's going to be a Christmas wedding. I was thinking it'd be my little present for them, you know?"

"Ahh." He nodded, his mind now rolling.

"Well, there's a couple of others I'll check with. Don't you pay it any mind."

"No problem. I'll let you know if I win the lottery," Eli joked, and she smiled before turning to leave.

He closed the door and sat down on the sofa, thinking. He'd already been absorbing the rent that used to be split three ways. And going month-to-month added an extra hundred. At this rate, he was going backwards in his savings goal — and no sign of that winning lottery ticket, not that he played.

Graham had been on him about just moving in to his place. Had mentioned it months ago, before Niles had moved in. Said he had that big place, and without Simon there, it was too much room. Too quiet, he had said at the time, and Eli remembered making a joke about that. Something about his ears. He couldn't remember now.

But then Niles. And it looked like Michael was going to move in for the summer again. Go to school. Levi would be down all the time. Well, that was then.

Now it was still Graham and Simon's ghost. And Eli, here alone. He supposed with Niles's ghost, too.

He pulled out his phone and texted Graham.

Hey, old man

A moment later came his response:

GRAHAM

Yes, young man?

Eli smirked. He enjoyed coming up with ways to make Graham's feathers slightly ruffled.

Can I come over and talk... moving?

I don't know. Can you?

Be there in 15, bitch.

I'll hold my breath in anticipation.

Eli laughed. He grabbed his coat and keys out of his grandma's candy dish and headed down to his car.

"So — your landlady. The sweet and nice little old lady who literally bakes you cookies — told you to get the hell out?"

Eli laughed. "No! She didn't tell me to get the hell out, Graham. She said her great niece is getting married, and —"

"— and she needs the apartment." Graham said, finishing.

Eli nodded. "Something like that."

Graham sat at the kitchen table while Eli got up and grabbed himself something to drink from the fridge. Graham didn't even notice, still pondering.

"Well, then why don't you move in here? Take your old room."

Eli stopped at the chair, still standing, and looked down at him. "Old room? When did I ever have a room?"

"Well, you could sleep in the chair in the living room if you want, but I think your clothes would be better suited to the guest suite."

Eli remembered waking up in that chair. Beautiful to look at. Hard as nails on his back.

"Guest suite? You mean Michael's room?" Eli asked, taking his seat.

"He's over at school. So it's your room now."

"Michael didn't leave cooties or anything, did he?" Eli teased.

"I had it fumigated for cooties and icky stuff, too."

Eli smiled and set his glass down.

"How much?"

"I'm not a call boy," Graham replied, deadpan.

"No, you bitch." Eli pushed at his arm, making Graham smile. "How much for rent?"

"Well —" Graham leaned back in his chair and acted like he was calculating figures in mid-air, amusing Eli, who was watching him while taking another drink. "— how about an — oh — I dunno — three hundred a month?"

Eli nearly did a spit-take, set down the glass, and wiped his mouth with his sleeve. "Three hundred?"

"Too much?"

Eli's eyes bulged. "I pay twenty-five hundred now!"

"Oh." Graham pursed his lips as if seeing an opportunity. "Well, in that case —"

"Three hundred! Final answer. You already said." Eli teased.

"You have to help with grocery shopping. I'm getting tired of going there alone."

Eli perked up. "Oooh! Can we order a bunch of shit at Amazon and then stand in line again to return it?"

"Maybe I should rethink this," Graham teased back.

Eli stuck his tongue out.

"Flattered," Graham replied, before changing back to practical matters. "When do you want to move?"

"Oh — god —" Eli stretched in his chair. "I need to figure out what to do with the furniture. You've already got everything."

"Think your landlady's niece, or whoever she is, would want it? You could offer it up."

"Dunno. Maybe."

"Worth a shot. Besides, that'd leave you with just — what? Clothes? Whatever personal stuff."

"I don't have that much shit. Some boxes. Too many shoes."

Eli's mind started taking inventory. What to take. What to donate. The lighthouse photo. The little piece he'd kept from Niles's robot. Those came with him.

Keep or — Kieran signed, and stopped. He'd come over to help without being asked. Insisted when Eli mentioned moving.

Eli threw the collection of old *New Yorker* magazines from two years ago in the trash and taught him how to sign *donate* — a clawed finger in an arc. Kieran repeated it.

Eli looked at the denim jacket he had uncovered at the back of his closet. The one he'd had since high school and didn't want to give away. The same one he hadn't even worn because his chest and biceps had filled out since tenth grade, rendering it impossible to fit in.

Donate, he signed, and turned away.

He'd ridden up to Eli's place first thing that morning. Eli hadn't even had a chance to shower when he arrived. Graham and Anthony weren't far behind. They figured they could take the stuff Eli was keeping and deposit it in his new room at the house while Kieran helped Eli sort and pitch. Most of the stuff was staying.

Eli's landlady was delighted. Even showed up that morning with fresh cookies — Toll House, this time — and told him she'd give him the security deposit back in full, no matter. Insisted she pay him for the furniture and dishes. In the end, they agreed on fifteen hundred in total. Eli decided to keep the full deposit to himself. Claire wouldn't care, and Derek had already moved out of state.

Kieran reappeared from the bedroom with an actual clown outfit, complete with a set of extra-large red clown boots hanging around the hanger.

Donate, Eli signed immediately, before Kieran had the opportunity to ask. Kieran gave him a look that asked *what the hell is this,* but Eli just nodded. *Another day. Silly story,* he signed, hoping Kieran would understand. A remnant of a party from long ago for work. It was silly.

Eli felt a tap on his shoulder as he was finishing with the last of the items in the kitchen cupboards.

More? Anthony signed slowly to him — shaky hands, but Eli got the gist. He smiled and pointed toward the bedroom. Anthony nodded and walked that direction.

"How much more?" Graham spoke to Eli clearly.

"Not much. Just my backpack and luggage."

Graham nodded, but Eli stopped him before he walked off to find Anthony, handing him a set of keys. "You can put them in the car."

Graham looked down and paused for a moment. Simon's keys. Eli saw it. But Graham grabbed them and moved on. He supposed he would always be that way.

Twenty minutes later, everything had been packed, thrown out, or set aside in a couple of donation boxes the landlady had said she'd handle. Maybe some of the other tenants might like something. Eli didn't care. Have at it, as far as he was concerned. Especially the clown costume.

Anthony and Graham had taken off for the house, leaving Kieran standing with his jacket and helmet by his bike, waiting for Eli to hand over the keys to his landlady.

Cookies? he signed, as Eli emerged from the building with yet another tin. Eli had taught Kieran the word this morning, noticing the boy could eat all of them and lose a pound doing it. *All yours,* he signed, thrusting the tin into Kieran's hands with a smile. Kieran pointed toward the bike and wasn't sure how to reply in sign. Eli found it endearing that he'd been trying to sign everything since he came over, but he was still limited. Finally he broke out in speech. "How do you say — *I'm on my bike, you take them in the car?*" He looked serious, like a student.

Eli smiled.

"You just did," he laughed, grabbing the tin, throwing it into the front seat of the Volvo and closing the door.

Kieran gave him a look, but laughed.

"I'll follow."

Eli gave a thumbs up before getting in the car and taking off.

Along the way, Eli could see Kieran's motorcycle headlamp just behind. It felt like he was riding his own version of a lighthouse, letting him know he was there. It was reassuring, in a way. He paid careful attention to stop early at lights so Kieran wouldn't get caught and not know where to go.

Pulling into the driveway, the garage door was already open, Anthony and Graham both carrying in items. Kieran ran up, helmet still on, to grab Eli's luggage from Anthony. Eli smiled, noticing how gentle he was, taking the heavy bag from him before coming back out to take off his own gear.

You're sweet, he signed, but Kieran hadn't learned that yet. "Show you later," Eli said, and began unloading the last of his items from the car. Kieran smiled and reached in to grab a few bags, following him in.

They arrived at his room, just down the hall, as Graham was placing a box into the closet leading to the ensuite. Anthony stood at the end of the bed, watching — clearly finished with moving, but polite enough to watch.

Eli dumped the last of his things on the bed and sat down, patting the space next to him for Kieran.

Kieran looked at Anthony as if asking permission. Anthony simply smiled and extended his hand as if to say *go ahead.*

"Eli. I got a little something for your room," Graham came over and handed him a gift bag with tissue paper sticking out.

Eli looked puzzled. Kieran sat smiling, looking up at Graham, curious.

Reaching in, he felt a frame. Pulling it out, he turned it around to see what appeared to be an older photo of Graham and Simon. Back when they were both younger. Graham looked almost the same, his face perhaps a little less wrinkled, his hair more full. Or he had just needed a haircut. One of the two. But Simon — he looked radiant. That was the word for it.

Eli had only seen a couple of pictures of him before. Graham had a few around the house. But this was a candid.

Anthony stepped forward and leaned on Kieran's shoulder to have a look. Eli noticed Kieran looking up and saw Anthony's face practically between the two of them, analyzing the photo.

"I know that picture. I think I took it."

"Bingo." Graham smiled. "I thought Simon and I could spy on you in your room from time to time." He teased.

Anthony stepped back toward the door and paused, turning to Graham. "That was when you both first moved in. I remember that day like it was —"

"A long time ago?" Eli joked, getting both Graham and Anthony's attention.

"You know, Graham," Anthony said directly to his friend, "I think Eli is going to fit in nicely."

Kieran laughed, and laid his hand on Eli's knee, not moving it. Eli noticed it while he held the frame.

"Babe? Would you place this over on the desk for me, please?"

Kieran looked at him like he had proposed.

Eli looked up at Graham, then Anthony. Both their mouths slightly askew.

"What? Something wrong?" He asked the room, knowing exactly what.

Kieran's smile returned, along with the red in his cheeks indicating he was embarrassed. Or something more. Eli assumed the latter.

"No. No." Graham shook his head.

"Nothing." Anthony spoke over top, but gave Graham a look.

Eli knew what he was doing.

And it was time.

Kieran's phone buzzed just as they were finishing the pizza he had called in and paid for, pushing Graham's money away when he offered. He had to head home. His ma was asking about him. Anthony followed him out, said something to Graham about an early morning, kissed Eli on the cheek. The door closed behind them, and the house went quiet.

He went to his room — *his* room, that was going to take some getting used to — took his hearing aids out and put them in the charging case next to his bed and started unpacking the last of his bags. Sock drawer. Underwear. Hats he never wore, but wanted to keep. The framed photo of him and Niles at the lighthouse, which he placed on the dresser without thinking too hard about it. The picture Graham had given him went on the desk, where Graham had said it should go.

He didn't hear Graham come in. Didn't realize Graham was there until he turned around and he was standing in the doorway with two mugs of something, one held out toward him, his mouth moving.

Eli's brain ran the catch-up reflex it always ran when his aids were out — read the lips, fill in the blanks, guess the rest. But Graham wasn't quite facing him fully, and the hallway light behind him put his face in shadow, and Eli got nothing. A few words. *Tomorrow,* maybe. *Coffee.* The shapes of the sentence were there, but the meaning didn't land.

Graham noticed. He always noticed. He stepped further into the room, into the better light, and started again, slower.

Eli watched. Got most of it. Got *what time tomorrow* and *if you want.* Lost the rest.

He looked at Graham, standing in the doorway with the mugs and the patient face of a man waiting for him to ask for the sentence again.

Eli didn't ask.

Out in the world, he was the one who adjusted. Always. He read lips. He angled himself toward people. He made sure the lighting worked. He laughed off the times he missed a word and made jokes about his deaf voice and never, not once, asked anyone to slow down or repeat something or look at him while they spoke. That was the deal. That had always been the deal. The world ran on hearing, and Eli ran on whatever fraction of it he could catch, and he had spent his whole life making sure that no one around him ever felt the weight of it.

But this was his home now.

His room. His bed. His desk. His framed photo of him and Niles on the dresser. His clothes in the closet. His books on the shelf. His.

Out there, he would keep doing what he had always done. He'd keep meeting the world. Keep making it easy for everyone else.

But here, at night, tired, with Graham — he didn't have to. Not anymore.

Graham could learn to meet him.

Eli raised his hands.

Show me, he signed.

Graham watched the gesture. Set the mugs down on the dresser.

"I don't understand," he said aloud.

Eli went to the desk, where one of the boxes still hadn't been sorted, and dug out a notepad and a pen. He brought them back to the dresser and set the pad next to the mugs and wrote:

First lesson: what were you asking?

Graham raised an eyebrow. Looked at the notepad. Looked at Eli. Looked at the hearing aids on the nightstand. Then, slowly took the pen.

We can go to the store tomorrow if you need anything.

Eli read it. Nodded. And lifted his hands.

He signed *store* — both hands flat, palms down, tilting forward and back twice. Graham watched. Tried it. Got something close to *store* if *store* meant *waving at a wall.* Eli laughed. Couldn't help it. Pointed back at the notepad — *store* — and then signed it again, slower, exaggerating the wrist motion. Graham tried. Closer. Eli reached over and turned Graham's wrist so the angle was right.

Graham signed it again. Got it.

Good, Eli signed. Then thumbed up just to be sure Graham understood that one.

They moved through the sentence one piece at a time. *Tomorrow* — index finger sweeping forward from the chin. Graham got that one on the second try. *Need* — two hooked fingers tapping downward. That one took four tries. *Anything* — Eli had to write it on the pad and circle it before Graham believed him, because the sign looked too simple and Graham kept assuming he was being mocked.

By the time they had the whole sentence, Graham was sweating slightly. Eli could see it on his forehead. He laughed again — gentler this time — and signed: *Now both. Together.*

Graham stared at him.

Eli wrote on the pad: *Both. Together. The whole sentence.*

Graham sighed. Tried it. Got *we* and *go* and lost the rest. Eli walked him back through it. Pointed at the pad. Pointed at his hand. Repositioned a thumb. Graham tried again. Got most of it.

Again, Eli signed.

Graham did it again.

Again.

"You're enjoying this."

Again, Eli signed, smiling.

Graham did it again. This time the whole sentence held — clumsy, foreign, the shapes belonging to a language his hands had never spoken before — but it held.

Good, Eli signed.

He picked up the pen and wrote:

It's important to me.

Graham read it. Looked up. Looked at Eli for a moment longer than he might have. Then nodded — once, small.

He took the pen back, hesitated, then wrote:

How do you sign...?

Eli looked at it. Picked up the pen and wrote:

Sign what?

Graham shook his head. Took the pen again.

If I don't know how to sign something, how do I ask you how to?

Eli read it. Sat down on the edge of the bed. Thought for a moment.

Then he stood back up, pointed at himself — *I* — and then made the *don't know* sign, palm flicking out from the forehead, and then made a small *show me* gesture with both hands. *I don't know. Show me.*

Graham watched. Tried. The *don't know* came out as something halfway between *don't know* and *what*. Eli adjusted Graham's wrist again.

Graham tried again. Got it.

Good, Eli signed.

Then he wrote on the pad:

If you don't remember a sign, just point.
Or write it. I'll show you.
We figure it out.

Graham read that one twice. Eli put the pen down.

It had been — Eli wasn't sure how long. Forty minutes, maybe. An hour. The mugs on the dresser had gone cold. His hands were tired from the slow careful movements he'd been making. Graham looked tired in a different way.

Graham signed a close approximation of *How do you sign...?* He paused, picked up the pen and wrote on the pad:

I'm happy you're home.

Eli read it.

Held the pad for a moment longer than he needed to.

He set it down on the dresser. Lifted his hands. Started slowly.

Happy. Both hands brushing upward against the chest. *You.* Pointing at Graham. *Home.* Hand to mouth, then to cheek, like the place where you eat and sleep.

Graham watched. Tried.

His *happy* came out fine. His *you* was unmistakable. His *home* was wrong — the hand at the wrong height, the second touch missing.

Eli walked him through *home* again. Once. Twice.

Graham got it on the third try.

Then, hands moving carefully, he signed the whole thing. *Happy. You. Home.*

Eli watched him do it.

He didn't sign back right away. Instead he picked up the pen and wrote on the pad, in slightly larger letters than before:

Me too. Home.

Then he signed it.

The Trap Closes

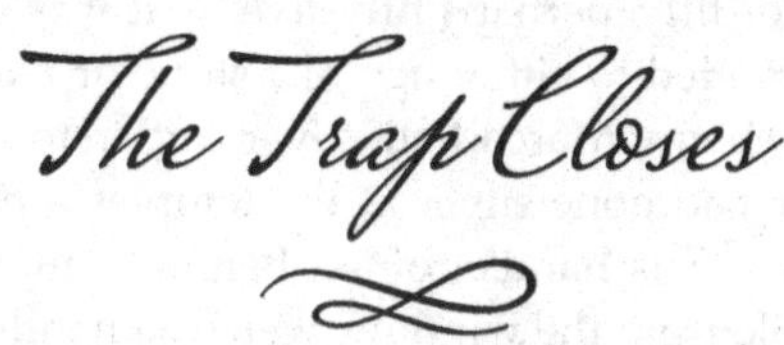

THE SUMMONS CAME ON A TUESDAY.

Marco received it the way a man in his position received anything from the cardinal's household — through a steward who arrived at the foot of the scaffolding, waited for Marco to notice him, and delivered the message in the formal phrasing the palazzo favored when it wished a thing to be unmistakable. *Sua Eminenza* would welcome the *maestro* in his private chamber at the hour of sext. It was not a request that permitted alternatives.

Marco thanked the steward. He kept his brush moving. He finished the section he had mixed paint for — one cannot waste lapis even for a cardinal, and the cardinal, of all men, would understand this — and climbed down when the plaster told him to and not a moment sooner. He washed his hands at the basin in the sacristy. He changed his shirt. He did not hurry.

Tommaso was in the apse, sweeping. He looked up as Marco passed.

"I am called to the cardinal," Marco said.

"Now?"

"Shortly."

Tommaso's expression did not change. He had the face of a man who had been raised in an institution that taught one not to ask questions in corridors. But his eyes held on Marco's for a beat longer than they usually did, and Marco understood the beat, and nodded, and kept walking.

The cardinal's private chamber sat on the piano nobile above the chapel, three doors down from the library, accessed by a corridor that Marco had walked perhaps twice before in all the months of the commission. The corridor was hung with tapestries Marco did not look at too closely. He had learned in his years among the wealthy that a man who admired the furnishings too openly was a man placing himself in a category the owner of the furnishings would then have to sort.

The door was open when he arrived. A secretary indicated the chamber with a small inclination of the head and withdrew.

Cardinal Rospigliosi was standing at the window.

He was a man of fifty, perhaps fifty-five — it was difficult to tell with ecclesiastics, who tended to either age like stone or like paper, depending on some private alchemy Marco had never understood. Rospigliosi aged like stone. His hair had gone silver at the temples a decade ago and had not progressed since. His hands, folded behind him now as he watched whatever was visible from the window, were the hands of a man who had not performed manual labor in forty years and still carried the strength of whatever labor had come before.

"Maestro di Benedetti," he said, without turning. "Come in."

Marco came in. He stopped at a respectful distance from the cardinal's desk. He did not know whether he was meant to sit. He waited.

Rospigliosi turned. His face was arranged into the expression it customarily wore in Marco's presence — warm, but not familiar. A patron's expression. A man pleased with what his money had bought him.

"Your work progresses beautifully."

"Your Eminence is kind."

"I am not kind. I am accurate." Rospigliosi crossed to his desk and gestured, finally, to the chair opposite. Marco sat. The cardinal did not sit. He remained standing, his hand resting on the back of his own chair, looking down at Marco with the slight elevation that the room's arrangement had always favored.

"The Virgin's mantle," Rospigliosi said. "The ultramarine. I stopped in yesterday when you were at your midday bread. I wished to see it in afternoon light."

"The afternoon light is best for lapis."

"So I am told. The color — " he paused, and his small smile arrived, " — the color is extraordinary. I have rarely seen ultramarine of this quality in any chapel I have funded. And I have funded seven."

"Your Eminence is generous."

"Your Eminence is observant. The two are not the same thing." He moved a small object on his desk — a bronze seal, which he touched and repositioned with the small motion of a man who enjoyed keeping his hands occupied. "I am told the novice has been grinding for you."

Marco performed the small adjustment a man performs when he realizes a conversation has just declared its direction.

"The novice has assisted with pigment preparation, yes."

"Tommaso."

"Yes."

"A competent boy. His prior was right to send him."

"He is careful with the stone."

"And you have grown fond of him."

Marco did not answer immediately. He was weighing the word *fond.* It was not an accusation. It was not even properly a question. It was a sentence laid on the table between them, and Rospigliosi was watching him to see what he did with it.

"The novice is a steady presence in the chapel," Marco said. "I have come to value his contributions."

"Of course." Rospigliosi's smile warmed by the smallest gradation. "One cannot complete work like this in isolation. The masters never did. The assistants are often what make the work possible. You and I both know this."

"Yes, Eminence."

Rospigliosi regarded him for a moment. Then he crossed the chamber — slowly, unhurriedly, the way a man walks when he has decided the conversation will proceed at his pace or not at all — and stopped at a small cabinet in the wall. He opened it. He removed something from inside. He returned to the desk holding a small object in his hand, which he did not yet show.

Marco had not moved.

"A man in my position," Rospigliosi said, "receives a great many letters. Some of them are addressed to me. Some of them are addressed to others who live within my palazzo. Some arrive through official channels, from priors and from bishops and from the households of families to whom I have obligations, and these I have read to me, or read myself, depending on the importance of the sender. Others arrive through less official channels. Merchants. Travelers. Friends of friends. These are of uncertain provenance and uncertain intent, and I have learned over the course of my life to treat them with the caution they invite."

He set the small object on the desk. It was a slip of folded paper. Marco could not see what was on it.

"Do you know, Maestro di Benedetti, how many letters have arrived at this palazzo addressed to you?"

Marco had not prepared for the question. He had thought he had prepared for every question. He had not thought the conversation would ask him to speak the number aloud.

"I have received letters from Venice," he said.

"From a particular correspondent."

"Yes."

"A correspondent with excellent handwriting. A trained hand. The hand of a man who was educated by tutors, not by parish priests — you can see it in the way he forms his uppercase *A.* There is a small confidence in the stem that is taught in certain academies and not in others."

Marco said nothing.

"Three letters arrived at the palazzo through the ordinary post." Rospigliosi rested his hand lightly on the slip of paper on the desk. "They were held in the gatekeeper's office until I was advised of them. As is the custom. I do not generally interest myself in the correspondence of my commissioned artists. But when the same hand arrives three times, over the course of several months, from a city in which that hand is presently a matter of some interest to persons I know — you understand, of course, that one cannot remain entirely uncurious."

Marco's hands had gone cold. He placed them on his knees beneath the desk, where the cardinal could not see them.

"The letters were delivered to you?"

"They were, Eminence. Each of them."

"And you preserved them."

"I did."

"In the cabinet in your room."

Marco did not answer. There was nothing to answer. The cardinal had already said it.

"A man," Rospigliosi continued, "keeps the letters he treasures. A man keeps the letters he cannot bear to discard. The impulse is human. I do not reproach you for it. I mention the cabinet only to establish that you and I share the same set of facts, which will make our conversation shorter."

The slip of paper was still beneath his hand. He had not yet lifted it. He did not lift it now. Marco understood that he was not going to lift it — that the paper's presence was all the cardinal needed, and that its content, whatever it was, would remain implicit. The cardinal was a man who did not need to produce evidence. He needed only to know that the evidence was within reach, and to let Marco know it also.

"The correspondent writes well," Rospigliosi said. "Of course he would. A man of his education. A certain cadence in the final letter — the one that came at the end of summer, I believe. He has a way with a sentence that carries its weight well."

Marco felt the muscles at the back of his neck go still.

Rospigliosi watched him.

"I will not ask you to confirm it," he said. "It does not matter whether you confirm it. What matters, Maestro di Benedetti, is that you understand I have not brought you here to diminish you. I admire your work. I have said so. The chapel will be the finest in Rome when it is complete. I wish for it to be complete on schedule. I wish for it to continue to receive the pigment, the plaster, the labor, the patronage it deserves. None of this need change. None of it need be disturbed."

He paused. Marco understood that the pause was a space the cardinal had left open for Marco to step into, and that the cardinal was watching to see whether Marco would.

Marco did not.

"You are a gifted painter," Rospigliosi continued, more gently. "You are also, I suspect, a man whose gifts do not sit easily with him. I have seen this before. Artists are often constituted in ways the world has made inconvenient. The church has long understood this about you. The church is not a tribunal in these matters. The church is a vessel. It carries what it carries."

He drew his hand back from the paper.

"There is, however, a matter of discretion. A household such as mine does not survive scrutiny. You understand. A painter in my employ does not wish to become — how shall I say it — a matter of interest to those who take interest. Neither do I. Neither, I would imagine, does your correspondent, who is in a city where he is at present not free to extend himself much further than his own four walls."

Marco's head lifted a fraction. Rospigliosi saw it.

"You are surprised that I know his circumstances."

"Yes, Eminence."

"I know many circumstances. A man in my position does. I know, for instance, that your correspondent has not written to you in some weeks. I know that this silence is a cause for you of considerable distress. I know that the distress has begun to affect your work — the forgetfulness of a month past, the unmixed pigment, the novice who intervened on a Friday afternoon to save a giornata you had nearly lost. I know these things because I know most things that occur in this palazzo. It is my house. I am responsible for it."

Marco sat with his hands on his knees. He did not move.

"I am telling you this, Maestro," Rospigliosi said, "because I wish you to understand that what you are doing in this chapel is precious to me. It is precious to me for its own sake. It is also precious to me as a demonstration. My colleagues in the Curia watch what I commission. They watch whom I commission. They watch how my commissions are completed. If the work falters — if the work becomes, through whatever cause, a matter of conversation — then I will no longer be able to shelter it. Or you. Or anyone who has assisted you. Do you understand me?"

"Yes, Eminence."

"Good." Rospigliosi moved his hand, finally, and the slip of paper on the desk went with it — back into the cabinet, into whatever drawer or compartment it had come from. The small click of the lock turning was the loudest sound in the room. "Then we have had our conversation. You will return to your work. I will return to mine. The chapel will be finished. The Virgin will wear her mantle. And the letters, if more arrive, will continue to be delivered to you. As will the post that passes through the ordinary channels of any house."

He let the last sentence hang.

Marco understood it. The letters would continue to be delivered. They had always been delivered. They had also, always, passed through the cardinal's hands first. What arrived in Marco's cabinet had already been read. What Marco kept against his chest in the folded square of paper the cardinal had not mentioned — the uncoded one — might or might not be known. The cardinal had not said. The cardinal did not say anything he did not have to.

"Maestro."

Marco rose. He bowed — the bow of a painter before his patron, practiced, formal, exact.

"Thank you, Eminence."

"Go with God."

Marco went.

The corridor was the same corridor. The tapestries were the same tapestries. Marco walked through them with the same composure with which he had walked in, because a man who let composure slip in the cardinal's corridors was a man who did not walk them for long.

He descended the stairs. He crossed the courtyard. He entered the chapel through the side door and passed into the nave as though returning from a midday errand.

Tommaso was at the low table. He was grinding lapis.

He looked up when Marco came in. He read Marco's face in one glance — as he read everything, with the quiet thoroughness of a boy who had learned to read faces before he learned to read Latin — and put down the muller.

Marco did not stop at the table. He crossed to the scaffolding. He began to climb.

"Maestro — "

"Keep grinding."

He climbed. He reached the platform. He took up the brush he had set down an hour earlier. The plaster was past working, of course. He had known it would be before he left. The giornata was lost — a thin patch of mantle he would have to chip out tomorrow and reprepare, one more day of schedule gone to something that was not painting.

He loaded the brush from the dish anyway. He moved it toward the wall. His hand shook. The brush touched the plaster and deposited nothing, because there was nothing there to deposit — the color had gone thin in the dish as the cardinal spoke, or Marco had not mixed enough, or his eyes could no longer see what was in front of him.

He loaded the brush again.

His hand shook more.

He had not cried in six weeks. He had kept himself upright through discipline and through the small architecture of Tommaso's presence and through the private, unreasoning hope that Alessandro was alive and writing and that the silence from Venice was the silence of a man temporarily prevented and not the silence of a man ended. He had held all of this in a balance as narrow as a single hair, and for six weeks the hair had held.

The cardinal had not broken the hair. The cardinal had simply shown Marco the hair. Had shown him that the hair had been threaded through a loom the cardinal held, and had always been, and that every private act of hope Marco had committed in his room with the letter against his chest had been committed within a house whose master had been counting his breaths.

The brush shook. Marco could not see the mantle. His eyes were wet. He was not sobbing — he had forgotten how to sob; it was an act that belonged to a Marco who had believed there were rooms in his life no one else could enter — but the tears had arrived anyway, from exhaustion or from rage or from the simple mechanical collapse of a man who had been held upright by a structure he now knew to be illusory.

He tried to load the brush once more. He could not see what he was doing. His hand would not steady.

He felt a weight.

The smallest weight at the end of his brush. A second hand, placed gently over his own.

Marco blinked. Tommaso was beside him. On the scaffolding. The novice had climbed up in silence, had settled himself on the narrow board beside Marco, and had placed his hand around Marco's hand where it held the brush — not taking the brush, not painting for him, only steadying him. Holding the brush steady so that the tremor in Marco's hand would not travel into the work.

Marco could not speak. He looked at the novice's hand on his own and could not speak.

"Take a breath," Tommaso said. "The plaster is dry. There is nothing to ruin now. Only breathe."

Marco breathed.

Tommaso kept his hand where it was.

Marco looked at him. He looked at the narrow, serious, unsurprised face of this boy who had climbed a scaffolding without being asked, who had watched Marco return from a corridor he had not walked before, and who had understood, somehow, at twenty years old with no correspondent in Venice and no letters folded against any chest, what Marco needed.

Marco had thought, walking back from the cardinal's chamber, that everything had been for nothing. Alessandro in Venice. The letters. The permission. The six weeks of holding himself upright. The chapel. The Virgin's mantle. The secret architecture of hope the cardinal had just shown him had never been secret at all.

He had thought all of it had been for nothing.

He looked at Tommaso's hand on his own.

Not nothing.

Not quite.

Below them, in the apse, the afternoon light moved across the stone the way it moved every day at this hour — indifferent to what had occurred in the chamber upstairs, indifferent to the cardinal and to the letters and to the slip of paper returned to the cabinet — and the two men on the scaffolding sat with their hands together on the brush, not painting, not speaking, only breathing.

The Virgin's face waited above them, unfinished.

Tomorrow there would be plaster to chip. Paint to mix. A giornata to reprepare. The work would continue. The cardinal would watch. The letters would arrive, if they arrived, already read. There would be no private room. There would not have been a private room for a long time.

But there would be this. A hand on a hand. A breath. A boy who climbed a scaffolding unbidden. An afternoon that passed as afternoons pass, carrying its small rebellions in the quiet places where patronage could not see.

Marco breathed.

Tommaso's hand steadied his own.

And, slowly, the trembling passed.

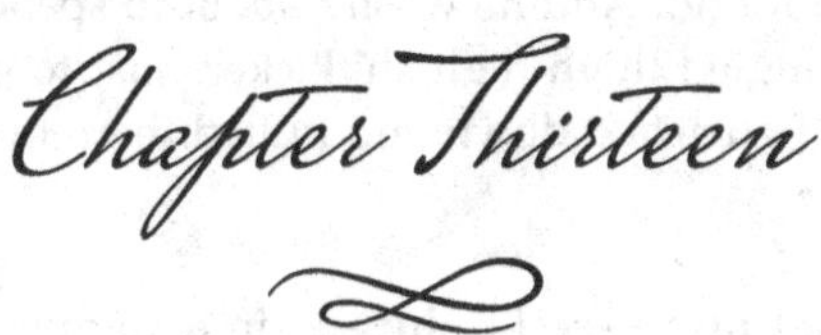

Chapter Thirteen

"I'M GETTING TOO old for this," Anthony mumbled to himself while trying to walk down the worn path to Graham's wearing a cape and boots. He hadn't put the eye mask on, instead holding it in his left hand while stopping periodically to fuss with the satin trousers Eli had forced him to wear.

They'd gone out costume shopping just the other night. Eli had driven, bringing along Kieran as his sidekick. Graham had reminded Anthony they were in this together. *You old fool* and *How I ever agreed to this* spilled from their mouths to each other, but Anthony saw how Kieran, especially, got a kick out of it. For Anthony, it was just how he and Graham worked together.

He had heard Kieran ask Eli something about how to sign *old married couple* when they were in the store, and stepped up to watch.

"Yes, Eli. I want to know as well."

Kieran looked embarrassed, but Eli smiled and demonstrated.

Anthony was the first to sign it back, however poorly, and then pointed to Kieran and himself. *Two can play at that game,* he signed, and rejoined Graham, who had been looking at *Sexy Kitten* costumes.

"What in the hell are you doing?"

He had to admonish Graham. He had no desire to even imagine Graham snug inside one of *those.* In the end, Graham was to be a mad scientist and Anthony was given the honorary role of *Captain Old Fart.* Fine. If that's what the group decided, then he was going to do his level best to live up to the part.

"And what are you two? Supertwink and Gayman?" he had shot back to Eli and Kieran, giving Graham a side-eye that clearly stated *us old gays can take care of our own.* Graham had to turn around to keep composure, but Anthony was sure he had scored more points with Eli than ever. He had no comeback. Rare, for a deaf man who just couldn't shut up. Anthony laughed at that one.

He wasn't laughing now, standing a few steps from Graham's front door, his goddamn boots slipping again. They were two sizes too big, but were what he had found. And he wasn't about to spend precious pension money on red spangled thigh-high shitkickers just to play dress-up for a couple of hours. He reached down and pulled them up for the tenth time since walking over.

"You're here!"

Anthony looked up to see Eli dressed in a vampire costume, painted face and all.

"And queer. Get used to it." Anthony retorted deadpan, and took his hand to walk up the step for fear those damn boots would fall off and then he'd break a hip. At his age, he figured, a hip gone was lights out for the rest of him.

"Yes, Shirley Temple." Eli spoke back in his voice that Anthony always found endearing, if a little muddled. He had asked him once if he took offense when Anthony asked him to repeat himself. His ears weren't what they used to be. *I always take offense from you,* Eli had replied. Anthony liked him even more.

"Ready, Captain whatever-the-hell-you-are?" Graham appeared in a white lab coat with thick-rimmed glasses.

"I thought you were supposed to be a mad scientist, not a nerd."

Anthony turned at the sound of Kieran's laughter.

"Now *he* appreciates my humor." Anthony smiled and made his way to Kieran for a hug. He wanted to make sure Kieran felt a part of their little group. He knew what it felt like, trying to come into your own with an established group of friends — well, family, more so.

"You told a joke?" Graham shot back. His usual.

Anthony loved the man like a kid brother. He was older than Graham, by a mile. But he felt like they had always known each other. He and Theodore had always had such good times with Graham and Simon. Of course, it was Simon who was the more outgoing of the two. Graham would somehow always navigate to Theodore with his quieter side, which seemed to parallel Theodore's. Anthony loved when he and Simon would gang up and tease their husbands. Even before it was legal, they had referred to each other as husbands.

Anthony took a beat, remembering them. He always allowed himself just a beat. Nothing more. Then it became nostalgic.

"Kieran, your costume looks —" Anthony gave him the once-over. "— missing."

Kieran laughed. "I'm gonna put it on when we get there. I can't ride in the car with it."

Anthony scrunched his face and looked at Eli, who gave a *you'll see* shrug.

"Let's get on with it." Graham clapped his hands. "Kieran, since you're not suffering in some silly costume, would you mind grabbing the party tray in the fridge, please?"

"You actually made something this time?" Anthony teased.

"*I did,*" Eli interjected. "Kieran and I last night."

Anthony raised his eyebrow.

"No. He did not stay over, old man. I'm a lady."

Anthony's grin came slow, but wide.

Graham shook his head. "They wouldn't let me get something at Whole Foods."

Anthony took Eli's hand and patted it. "You're a good man."

Then it came to him. "Oh, hold on." He stepped back from Eli. "I've been practicing."

Anthony extended his hands and slowly, in his shaky movements, signed *Nice to meet you.* Or, he hoped that's what he signed. It was the next thing he had worked on from a video series he'd been watching.

Eli grinned and signed it back, more precise and fluid, Anthony saw, but at least he had understood.

"Graham, when are you going to come over and learn with me?" Anthony turned to his best friend and partner in sarcasm.

"Is never good for you? I think I have that open on my calendar."

Eli laughed. He had caught it. Anthony thumbed back at Graham while speaking directly to Eli. "If I didn't love that old man, I'd kick his ass."

Eli's grin became a full laugh.

"C'mon, Captain Pain in the Ass. Let's go." Graham put his arm around Anthony's shoulders and escorted him to the car.

It was already dusk by the time they pulled up to Sonya and Angie's. Susan's car was parked to the side over by the house, along with perhaps a half-dozen others.

"Goddamn these boots," Anthony muttered as they slipped down again on the steps up. Eli grabbed his arm while Kieran reached down and pulled them up before Anthony knew what was happening.

"Wow, Graham. Your staff is really attentive," Anthony turned around to look at him. Kieran laughed, but Eli hadn't heard, Anthony guessed. He'd already rung the doorbell.

Before he knew what was happening, the door had flown open and what appeared to be a furry tiger — or perhaps a bear, or a large chipmunk, *something* — flew into Eli's arms for a hug.

"I saw you coming," Levi said, looking like a boy with a tiger face painted on.

"Levi, this is — Kieran." Eli pulled Kieran's arm to bring him closer for introductions.

Anthony noticed how he had paused for a moment when introducing him.

"Hi, Levi." Kieran smiled, still in his jeans and t-shirt and jacket.

Anthony couldn't tell who was taller. Kieran or Levi. But Levi came up and gave Kieran a hug, showing Anthony he seemed to have the edge.

"No costume?" Levi said.

"It's in the trunk."

"Ahem. Hello, Mr. Levi." Anthony cleared his throat, indicating he needed some attention too.

Levi turned and smiled. Anthony had always liked the boy. He reminded Anthony of himself at that age. "Hi, Santa."

Anthony beamed. But he noticed Kieran looked confused. He put his arm around Levi's shoulder and turned to explain, pointing to his white beard. "I'm living a double life." Levi giggled. Graham, he noticed, rolled his eyes. Like he always did.

Anthony turned back to Levi and stepped back to get a look at his costume. It was one of those pajama-looking things that he thought kids wore, like a onesie with a hood that looked like a tiger. Someone had painted his face to match.

"Lemme guess: kitty cat?" Anthony teased, but Levi grinned and gave a growl.

"Ooooh! Tiger!" Eli pulled Levi back over and into his side.

"Hello, Levi — I mean, Mr. Pussycat," Graham said finally.

"Did the party move out here?" Sonya belted out behind them at the doorway.

"Hello, old woman." Anthony turned and extended his hand, which she slapped away.

"I ain't no lady." She teased in her typical Sonya / Anthony banter.

"Not for you, woman. Me. I can't walk in these damn things." He looked down at his go-go boots, her eyes following. "I need help."

Sonya pulled him up the steps and into the house, where Angie waited, wearing her Mrs. Claus outfit.

"I thought we had to wait until Christmas for *that*," Anthony said. Not hello. Nor hi, Angie.

"What *are* you?" was her response, as if trying to figure out who put this ensemble together. Or why.

"He's the Old Curmudgeon," Graham appeared from behind him, resting his hands on Anthony's shoulders.

Sonya appeared next to them. "So you didn't dress up, then?"

"You look nice, Martha," Graham said to Angie.

"Martha?"

"Washington. President's wife, right?" Graham teased and walked toward the kitchen.

"Why on earth do we ever invite you two?" she said, more to Anthony, but looking at Sonya.

"You don't. We just arrive." He gave her a hug.

"Santa!" Lucy ran up and then stopped. "What happened to you?" She looked like Anthony had killed off the Jolly Old Elf and replaced him with a superhero wannabe.

"He's just playing along for Halloween, dear," Angie said, leaning down to comfort her. She nodded, but Anthony wasn't sure she bought it.

"Hey, Lucy Lou!" Eli stepped around Anthony and scooped her into his arms, much to her delight. And to Anthony's. She was distracted, so he could escape into the living room.

"Annnnthoonnnyyyy." Donna came over in her theatrical sway, leaning in for air kisses. "How arrreee you?" She was a perfect Morticia Addams.

"Apparently scaring children." He looked back at Eli, who seemed to be introducing Lucy to Kieran.

"At least you're doing that right." Donna deadpanned and handed him a glass.

Anthony never asked what anything she handed him was. Didn't need to. Not at his age.

"Brett." Anthony leaned over and shook his hand. He knew how to go into *straight guy* mode easily, having spent forty years in the insurance business.

"Hi, Anthony."

Anthony noticed Brett didn't seem fully himself. He understood.

"Well, I'll be." Anthony let it out as he turned toward the kitchen island separating the living room from where the real action was — and saw Susan. He hadn't seen her in months. God, probably since last New Year's, come to think of it. Had it already been ten months?

She was thinner. More joy-filled. Less riddled with — *something.* He knew the look, when the world's problems made their way into your skin, your eyes. But all that seemed erased. She looked like she was having fun. Good for her, he thought. Good for her.

"Oh, thank God. A Super Old Man come to save the day." She let out as he took a step toward her, prompting him to stop in his tracks.

Did she just chime in with a bout of sarcasm? Miss *scaredy cat* Susan? The one who last party looked like she wasn't sure she belonged? Now she was preparing some sort of dip and veggie combo while smacking Graham's hands as he stood next to her trying to steal pieces of celery and cream cheese. She certainly had come a long way.

"And what are you supposed to be, Susan? Short order cook?" He gave it back to her.

"I'm off the clock. Ask your boyfriend here if you want someone to make you a cheeseburger." She countered and let out a laugh.

Graham took a step back and gave her a *did you just say that* look.

Anthony's smile registered hard. She *was* fitting in nicely.

He took a seat in what he thought might be Sonya's recliner. There were two, both angled around an end table with a lamp, TV remote laying close. Didn't matter. He needed to get out of these damn boots.

"Coming through." Kieran announced as he made his way with the party tray apparently he and Eli had made the night before.

"What grocery did you all pick this one up at, Graham?" Sonya walked behind Kieran, inspecting.

"Not me. That was all them," Graham replied between bites of a celery stick, pointing it at Kieran and Eli, who was following along with Lucy and Levi in tow.

"Hey, Angie!" Sonya yelled out across the room. "Did you hear? We have a proper party tray this time. Graham didn't help, thank God."

The room laughed. Graham pretended like he hadn't heard and opened up the fridge to inspect for other items he could nibble on.

"Mommy! When are we gonna go trick-or-treating?"

Lucy had run over to Susan at the island, jumping up and down.

"Ask your brother. It's already getting dark."

Lucy ran past Anthony like it was a race and practically ran into Levi.

"I don't want to go, Lucy. Can't you just —"

"I'll go!" Kieran said, a little excited.

Lucy became quiet. She seemed to still be sizing him up.

"Lucy?" Anthony got her attention and she ran over to his chair.

"Kieran here is one of my personal elf friends. He has the best trick-or-treating skills of anyone I know."

Lucy's eyes lit up, turning to look at Kieran, who was standing next to her brother.

"Really?"

"Mmhmm. And if you don't tell your brother — as he might get jealous — I think he'll give you all his candy if you ask nicely."

Levi and Kieran both heard, but turned away as if whistling in some other direction when she looked over at them.

"You're not even dressed!" Lucy turned and pointed out to Kieran.

"Oh! You're right. Hang on. Let me go get my costume. It's still in the car." He pretended not to realize. "Can you help me, Levi?"

Levi looked over at him like a little brother. "Uh — sure."

"Lucy." Anthony commanded her attention again while Levi and Kieran left for the front door. "See your uncles Eli and Graham over there?" he whispered, pointing over to the two who were watching from the island.

She nodded.

"I'll give you a whole dollar if you go up and tell them that Uncle Anth — I mean, Santa's costume is the best of all."

Her eyes lit up.

"Don't you be getting her in trouble, Mr. Claus." Angie came over and scolded him with a smile.

Anthony turned and put his fingers to his lips. This was between him, Lucy, and the boys. Angie stood watching as Lucy walked over to Graham, who leaned down as she whispered something in his ear and pointed his way.

Graham gave a mischievous grin toward Anthony, who smiled innocently, before leaning back up and explaining to Eli what Lucy had said.

Eli turned and pointed to Anthony and signed something before laughing. Then he said something to Graham, who let out a laugh aloud before whispering something back to Lucy.

"Okay, what are they up to now?" Angie said while standing by Anthony's chair.

"Uncle Grammy and — uh — Uncle Eli — said —" She looked back for assurance at the two of them. Eli waved his hands like *go on.* Lucy turned back to Anthony.

"They uh said to uh — ask you — if —" She looked back at Eli, confused. He nodded encouragingly. "They asked if you wanted your pills and uh — jello cup now, or — after activity time?"

Angie stifled a laugh. Graham's grin sat on that smartass face of his. But Eli's took the cake. He yelled out for Lucy, who ran over to him and he made a show of handing her a five-dollar bill from his wallet.

"I think you've met your match — Santa." Angie snickered.

Suddenly the crowd erupted in laughter and delight, turning their attention to the front hall. Anthony saw Levi walking through with a great smile on his face, followed by —

He sat up in his chair to get a better look. Was that — Kieran?

Walking — well, waddling was the better word — behind Levi was a seven-foot inflatable walking dinosaur with Kieran's face somewhere behind the eyes.

"It's a dinosaur!" Lucy yelled, running over to see.

Eli seemed delighted himself. Graham looked as surprised as Anthony.

Kieran let out a growl from inside, which caused Lucy to jump back into her brother's arms. Levi seemed to be enjoying the moment, because his *do I have to* attitude earlier seemed to have vanished.

"Ready to go trick-or-treating, Lucy?" the dinosaur asked.

Lucy nodded and turned to Anthony, yelling out from across the room. "You were right, Santa! He is the best trick-or-treater!"

Anthony couldn't help but smile. He wondered, decades ago, if he might be a good father. He knew that would never happen, of course, but he loved seeing the joy of little kids. Their curiosity. Theodore had nieces and nephews who lived across the country, so they barely knew them. Anthony was a solo child, so no experience like that for him either. But when he got older and his hair turned white, the *Mr. Claus* thing happened over dinner with everyone one night, when someone commented how Angie and he were perfect together as the two. It sort of stuck. And the kids loved it. He loved being the kind old elf, even if he wouldn't admit to Graham that his heart was soft.

Susan had begun giving Lucy and Levi the ground rules — stick to the neighborhood. No going out onto the main street. Be back in thirty minutes. Usual worried-mom stuff. But Kieran — the dinosaur — assured her he would keep them safe. He was a paramedic.

"You are? Oh, that makes me feel so much better. I get worried about —"

"Kieran will take care of them, Susan." Eli had yelled out from his perch with Graham, nibbling on snacks.

Anthony noticed how, even behind the costume, Kieran was watching and protective of the kids.

Was Levi still a kid? he asked himself. Anthony remembered standing with Graham over by the fireplace last year, watching him and Michael together. Perhaps Levi wasn't a kid anymore. But then Anthony noticed Michael wasn't there either. Another observation. He'd ask Graham about that later.

"We're off! Back in a half hour," Kieran the dinosaur yelled out. "Levi, why don't you lead. I can't quite see well enough in this thing." He added it as they made their way up to the front door and left.

Anthony watched as Donna made her way over to the island, directly toward Eli. *He's a keeper*, he heard her say, but was distracted by Graham walking his way.

"Want anything?"

"New boots?"

Graham laughed. "I meant food."

"I'll get it. I may be old, but I need to keep active. Don't want to end up looking like you."

"Oh, you two!" Angie laughed and walked into the crowd.

No sooner had the trick-or-treaters left than Thomas and Jason arrived. Thomas was wearing a suit and holding a briefcase, while Jason had on a Fairy Godmother outfit complete with tiara and wand — which complemented his graying beard.

Thomas made a beeline for Eli. "How's my favorite accountant?"

Anthony wandered over to Jason and leaned in for a hug. "Pink's not your color, dear," he said, but Jason waved his wand.

"Be careful, or I'll turn you into a pumpkin."

Anthony pulled himself into one of the kitchen chairs with a small grunt and waved Jason into the one next to him. Jason settled in, tiara slightly askew, wand laid flat on the table between them.

"How long has it been?" Jason asked.

"Since I last sat? An hour."

"Since we last had a proper catch-up, you fool."

Anthony considered. "I'm afraid to count."

They had lunch, Jason told him, planned for the week after next — *if you'***re free, and don'***t pretend you have a calendar full of obligations.* Thomas had a thing in Boston that Saturday and Jason was bored already at the prospect of it. Anthony agreed to lunch with the dignity of a man who was, in fact, free every Saturday for the foreseeable future.

Across the room, Donna was telling Sonya something that involved a lot of hand-waving and a dramatic widening of eyes. Brett stood beside her looking, Anthony thought, like he was holding on. Susan and Angie had moved to the sink and were laughing about something neither of them seemed fully able to explain. Graham had reappeared at the snack table with a small plate, eating one cracker at a time as if doing penance for his earlier raids.

"It's nice," Jason said, watching the room. "All of them."

"It is."

"Even him?" Jason gestured with his chin toward Graham.

"Even him."

They sat. Anthony's drink found its bottom. Jason waved a hand at Thomas across the room and signaled for a refill, which Thomas pretended not to see. Behind them, the front door rattled and swung open.

Anthony turned.

In came Lucy, skipping, followed by Tony the Tiger — as Anthony decided he must be — and Dino bringing up the rear.

"What in gay hell?" Jason stood holding his tiara. Sonya laughed and slapped his back, causing him to stumble for a moment.

"That's Eli's boyfriend."

"Eli has a boyfriend? After —" Jason turned and whispered loud enough that Sonya picked it up. She looked interested in knowing as well. Anthony assumed everyone was, but they weren't going to pry. Not when both Eli *and* Donna were here.

"I don't know that they are, officially. But might as well be."

"Huh."

"I think it's good for Eli. Don't you?" Anthony turned to Jason, but addressed Sonya as well.

"Oh — yes. Of course. He's much too young to be —" Jason started to say.

"I like 'em!" Sonya finished.

"I thought you were repulsed by anyone with a penis," Jason narrowed his eyes and threw at Sonya.

"Oh, men are useful sometimes. Still trying to figure out what for, but I'll let you know," she quipped, wandering over to find Thomas.

"What does Angie see in her?" Jason stood next to Anthony as they watched her wander across the room.

Anthony shrugged.

"Levi, can you help me, please?"

Anthony and Jason turned to see Dino, trying to unzip himself. Levi ran over and did the honors as Lucy watched in amazement. Stepping out of the costume, Kieran fixed his hair, but Anthony laughed — his hair was so short, what was to fix?

"Levi seems to be taken with him," Jason spoke softly in Anthony's ear. Anthony looked over quizzically.

"Not *that* way, perverted old man. I meant, look how much he is —"

"What?"

"I dunno. It's like this Kieran fellow has become his new best friend. See it?"

Anthony turned as Jason pointed his wand their direction. Levi was smiling, eager to help Kieran fold up the costume, and even stepped up to fix something in his hair. Anthony nodded in agreement.

"Speaking of which, what's the scoop on Graham's nephew? Are he and Levi still an item?" Jason gossiped.

"Graham said it's complicated. I'm inclined to believe that anything before the age of fifty is complicated."

"Fifty?"

"Yes." Anthony turned to look Jason in the eye. "After that point, you've lived long enough to not give a shit about petty things."

He saw Jason shrug, his face following. "True."

"How are you and Thomas?"

"Oh, same. It's such a dull life. Paris last month was rainy, and Geneva will be cold in two weeks."

"Such a struggle," Anthony added, trying to emphasize the sarcasm, but Jason simply agreed.

Both watched as Eli walked over to Lucy and knelt down. "Thanks for bringing me candy!" he teased her.

She pulled her plastic jack-o-lantern away, giggling. "My candy, Uncle Eli."

"Should I give him mine?" Kieran knelt down and asked.

"No! It's *my* candy too!" She reached for his bag.

"Lucy. Be nice." Susan walked up, correcting her.

"Okay, Mommy." Anthony could see her look down like she'd been in trouble.

"It's okay, Lucy. You can have mine," Kieran handed her the bag, but Eli pulled out a Tootsie Roll Pop quickly.

"You can have that one, Uncle Eli."

"Thank you, Lucy."

"See, Mommy, I shared!" She turned to ensure Susan saw. Anthony giggled, watching the interaction.

Eli turned to Levi's bag and started to root around, but Levi pulled it to his chest. "'Scuse me?" He teased.

"Did you sneeze?" Eli countered and reached for it.

"I didn't see you out trick-or-treating with us," Levi protested, but he was smiling.

"Candy tax." Eli added it, but Levi turned toward Kieran as if asking for help.

"C'mon, Eli, before we get in trouble again." Kieran stood and grabbed Eli's arms to pull him away.

Levi giggled as Eli made a gesture that he was watching him — or his candy.

Kieran walked Eli out onto the deck. Anthony turned back to Lucy, who was standing proudly, sharing with anyone who would listen how she had gotten a one-dollar bill at one house, too.

"Some guy forgot it was trick-or-treat, so he handed us cash." Levi offered the explanation.

"Perhaps we should've gone with them," Jason said to Anthony and took another drink.

Anthony shrugged and walked over to the kitchen to find something to nibble on, saying hello to Thomas. Thomas had been busy hitting up Graham on when he was going to publish another book, but Graham looked like he would rather talk tax tables. Anthony decided he wasn't getting involved in *that* and turned to see Levi standing over by the back deck window, away from where the rest of the crowd was.

Walking over, Anthony saw a curious expression on his face.

"I thought you were taking inventory of your candy stash from —"

Anthony turned to follow his gaze out the window.

Off in the moonlight, at the end of Sonya and Angie's deck — the spot by the stairs that went down into the yard, away from the house, away from where everyone was gathered — Eli and Kieran were together.

In a kiss.

Anthony looked over at Levi, who was watching as if unaware of him standing there. Unaware of anything other than the private moment cast in moonlight outside through the window.

He reached over and gently squeezed Levi's shoulder, causing him to jump just slightly, looking up at him as if being caught. Anthony gave him a reassuring smile and looked back out as he saw the simple kiss Eli and Kieran were sharing.

It brought him back to when he had been nearly twenty, and the guy he'd been roommates with in college — the one who always spoke of his girlfriend back home, the one who got along so well with Anthony despite his lack of interest in football, *chicks,* cars, and whatever else his roommate went on about — got drunk with him one night in their room and ended up leaning in to kiss Anthony.

He was the one who initiated it. Anthony had been still too scared to even think of it. But it was late. And they were seated on the floor, his desk lamp the only light in the room. The radio had been on, he remembered, and they'd been laughing over something meaningless. And his roommate poked him, which caused Anthony to be tickled, laughing. That led to more horseplay, and before he knew it Anthony lay on the floor, pinned by his roommate.

There was no magical moment. No passionate kiss. It didn't last long. But his roommate leaned down and pressed his lips to Anthony's, which shocked him initially, followed by relaxing into it — smelling the alcohol, feeling the stubble on his chin, the heat on his body. Anthony had reached up and pulled him into it slightly before his roommate broke away and began laughing. *Got you,* he teased, and got up, playing like it was a continuation of their horseplay. Anthony had been confused, but played along, forcing a laugh and carrying on as well.

They never spoke of it and never drank together again.

But it had been his first kiss.

Looking back at the window, he saw how gentle Eli seemed to be, holding Kieran's face. How sweet it was. No passion and groping. It was as if Kieran was just as nervous. Yet both were finding each other. Slowly.

The doorbell chimed behind them and Anthony turned, catching Levi doing the same. Several folks had been milling up around the front hallway when the door opened, so he couldn't imagine who it'd be. He was pretty sure all of Sonya and Angie's friends were already here. But Levi took a step forward as if recognizing a friend of his, but then stopped.

"We're the Ambiguously Gay Duo!" Anthony heard one of the pair say as the group laughed. Two twinks, both about the same height, in skin-tight superhero costumes that left little to the imagination, in black eye masks, were standing there smiling. Frosted tips on their hair. One of them looked incredibly familiar to Anthony.

Levi had taken a step back and bumped into him. Anthony looked over.

Levi's eyes were on the figure in the doorway. He hadn't moved.

"Michael?"

Chapter Fourteen

LEVI LOCKED eyes with Michael from across the room. Even through the black eye mask, he could tell Michael was different.

He'd invited Michael to come up. DM'd him. Said he should bring friends. Anyone, really. He hadn't seen him, and everyone would be there. Michael had been reluctant for some reason. Kept asking if he was sure. But Levi said Eli was going to be there. And maybe Kieran. That seemed to be the clincher, which kinda made him feel a little down.

They had messaged off and on over the summer. And when Michael finally moved up to Portland, Levi had offered to come help him move into the dorms. But Michael said he had it covered. Didn't need much. Gonna be busy with orientation. Levi would probably be bored. He didn't say *no*, but he might as well have, Levi thought. It wasn't a surprise. He had known something was going on ever since Michael's spring break last year. He'd changed. Not drastically. But he really got into the whole *gay thing*, which was fine. But it wasn't Levi.

Then Niles.

When all that happened, Levi knew Michael wasn't happy that he couldn't come. But he had really gotten upset when Levi told him over the phone that night after the funeral about how Eli sat in the middle next to him and Anthony. Michael had yelled into the phone. Yelled. He could still hear him. Levi had been kinda scared for a moment, but Michael had apologized. He was upset, he said. Just because Eli was gay didn't mean he should be *shit on for loving a guy*. Levi just listened. Agreed, but it didn't matter now. Niles was buried, and Levi was more concerned about helping Eli not feel so hurt. He knew what feeling like you're all alone in the world was like. But he never said that. Not to Eli. It wasn't appropriate. But he didn't say it to Michael either. He was too upset on the phone.

Levi had actually been even more surprised that Michael came to Portland for college. He'd messaged earlier in the summer that he was still thinking about it. He'd actually gotten a scholarship to Vanderbilt, just down the way from where they lived in Nashville. Levi wasn't up on colleges, but he'd heard of that school before somewhere and knew it was quite an accomplishment for Michael. But he told him he had decided to move on up to Portland anyway. Loved his family and all, but wanted to move in with his Uncle Graham, like he had talked about last Christmas.

That had confused Levi, to be honest. Did that mean he still wanted to *be with him?* Or was he coming up just to get away from Nashville? Michael didn't say.

But now, looking into his eyes from across the living room, he saw everything he felt he needed to know.

Anthony put his hand on his shoulder, like he was trying to comfort him. But Levi didn't need comfort. He actually felt at ease. At least now he knew what he and Michael *were.*

Friends.

That was it.

He still loved him. He knew inside. But he also knew that wasn't the same feeling he had back last winter. Back when he thought they'd be together.

Whatever that had meant.

Levi nodded to Anthony slightly and walked over toward Michael.

"Hey."

Michael seemed quiet. Or embarrassed. Shy, maybe? He didn't know.

Levi saw his friend, the other half of the *Gay Duo* — or whatever Michael had said they were — standing around with the gang.

"Hey. I'm Levi." He extended his hand.

"Mike." He shook it. "I'm really Michael as well, but he got there first, so —" He thumbed to Michael standing next to him and smiled.

Levi noticed Michael's eyes dart between him and Mike, nervous.

Mike was cute. He could see that. He stood just slightly shorter than Michael, but about the same build. His hair was almost the same color as Michael's, and Levi turned and saw Michael's frosted, short-cut hair, gelled and stiff with something else. Was that *glitter?*

"Michael's told me so much about you." Mike continued.

Levi looked at him in that superhero body suit. The boy looked really good. Like, he must have worked out — but not buff, exactly. Toned. Tight. Levi blushed thinking about the rest as he glanced down his body. The suit wasn't really hiding much.

And it dawned on him. This was Michael's boyfriend.

Boyfriend.

"All lies," Levi teased and laughed. Mike followed suit, but Michael seemed worried.

"What's wrong?" Mike asked Michael.

Levi realized now why he was acting this way. He hadn't said anything about having a boyfriend. Levi had known Michael had met friends. Michael had said as much in messages they had traded. Levi had suspected he was meeting other guys, but hadn't really allowed himself to piece it all together.

"Nothing." Michael quickly replied and darted his eyes between Mike and Levi again.

Now Michael is freaking out, Levi thought. *Probably worried what I think.*

Part of him wanted to take Michael aside and yell at him. Tell him he could've at least let him know. Not string him along all these months. It was okay if he didn't want to be together. He'd already prepared himself for that a long time ago. Both a blessing and a curse — he remembered thinking back when he suspected they were drifting apart — was that he'd spent so much of his life preparing for the worst that when it did happen, at least it wasn't a surprise. It still hurt like hell, but he could start to prepare for the pain early. Make it easier to get over.

He was still waiting for something bad to happen to him, or his family, and they'd have to move back into his mom's car again. Eli had finally gotten him to admit that a couple of weeks ago when he helped him move into Graham's. Kieran had to go home, and Eli had given Levi a lift. Eli had asked about Michael. Levi talked, unsure if Eli had heard.

When he pulled up outside, Eli looked over at him and spoke slowly.

"People you love sometimes go away, Levi. And — and it hurts. Really hurts. But —"

Levi remembered Eli looking so — open. He didn't know the right word, but he wasn't the easy, cool, always-*on* Eli.

"But you can't live your life thinking something bad is just around the corner, Levi. Even if everything fucks up, I'm still here. Just like you've been there for me since Niles — since Niles died."

Levi hadn't worried about his own life when Niles died. He simply ceased to consider anything truly important. All he cared about now was Eli. Because Eli needed someone to carry his pain for a little while. And that was all Levi could think to do. Help carry him.

Now Eli was telling him he noticed. And it meant more than perhaps he realized.

And — Eli was there for him, too. Let up, a little. Try and see the joy in life, even through the pain.

Because, Eli had said, *Nothing else matters, really.*

"Michael's a great friend. I'm so happy you two are here," Levi said directly to Mike, who smiled.

"Want something to drink?" Levi turned toward the kitchen and began walking. Mike alongside, Michael behind them.

"I love your costumes, Mike."

"Michael's idea. They're kinda tight, and —" He leaned in and whispered as they were walking toward the kitchen island. "I feel like everyone can see my balls."

Levi laughed. "It's true!"

Mike laughed along, looking down at himself. Levi fought the urge to follow suit. He didn't need to see them.

"There's the super nephew." Graham walked up and placed his arm around Michael's shoulders. "I haven't seen you since —"

"I'm sorry. It's been busy and —"

"This is Mike. Michael's boyfriend." Levi introduced him.

Mike looked over at Michael, whose eyes bulged.

"Sorry. Are you not — uh —" Levi thought maybe he had mistaken them being together, by the look in Mike's eyes.

"Nice to meet you, Mike. Love the costumes." Graham deflected. "Can I get you something to drink?" He took Mike over toward the counter with bottles and cans, while Levi looked over at Michael, who was staring at him.

"I thought —" Levi began, but Michael looked down and spoke.

"I should've told you."

"So, he *is* your boyfriend?"

Michael nodded, as if ashamed.

"C'mere." Levi grabbed Michael's hand and pulled him out onto the deck, just outside the door. Michael seemed confused.

"Listen, Michael. I'm happy for you."

Michael looked at him like he had been prepared for a fight and then thrown off course by Levi's kindness.

"What? You are?"

"He's cute. How long have you officially been —"

"Levi, you don't have —"

"I'm serious, Michael. I really am."

"I'd be so mad if it were —"

"I'm not."

"I didn't want to come. At least — not with Mike."

"Why not?" Levi asked. But he knew the answer. Anyone would know the answer.

"'Cause you invited me. And — well — it's like *Hey, Levi! Meet my boyfriend. Oh, by the way, we*'re through."

Levi looked up at the moon and then back at Michael.

"Listen. I — I loved you. I — I thought I did — *still do.* But it's different. And — I don't know how to say it, Michael. But — ever since Niles — I just —"

Levi saw Michael's face change. He became more — the only word that came to mind was *shadowy*.

"Stop that."

"What?" Michael didn't look at him.

Levi reached over and took Michael's chin, turning his face to look at him. He had no idea where this side of him was coming from, but he felt this need to get Michael to snap out of it.

"I loved you, Michael. But I know shit changes. And I want to be friends. Need to be. Okay? Okay?"

Michael nodded slightly, looking like he was going to cry.

"And don't you start crying on me out here, 'cause I can't handle that right now. Okay?"

Michael bit his lip, fighting it back.

"Mike is really nice. And I can see you both together. So why are you afraid of me with him?"

"I'm not afraid."

"Bullshit."

"Bull true."

"Then admit you're boyfriends. What was *that* back in there when I told Graham he was your boyfriend?"

Michael started to look down again, shaking his head, embarrassed. Levi reached over and grabbed his chin again, forcing him to look in his eyes.

"Look at me, goddammit."

Michael began to cry.

"I'm sorry, Michael. I didn't mean —"

"I don't want to hurt you —" Michael let out. "I just don't know what to do."

Levi took a step and pulled Michael into his arms, pulling him close. Michael's body stiffened, but Levi didn't care. It'd been months — felt like years — that he'd been wanting to hold onto Michael. At least one more time. He could smell him. That unmistakable Michael scent. His shoulder that felt so warm to rest his head upon. But he wasn't here to relive love lost.

"Michael. I am truly happy for you. I really am. So please — be happy, too. And don't let Mike feel like he's second best."

Michael pulled back slightly, wiped his eyes with his costume sleeve, and nodded.

"Mike's been asking me if we're boyfriends, and I haven't been able to say it."

"Why?"

"Because — I —"

"There you both are. I got you a Coke, Michael. Hope that's —" Mike appeared by the door and stopped, noticing Michael's face, Levi standing next to him. "Sorry. I can go."

"No. We were just talking about you." Levi gestured for him to join.

Mike shut the door and walked a few steps out to meet them, a little curious.

"I've known Michael for — well — I know him, and I was just asking why the weirdness about the boyfriend thing," Levi said.

He noticed Mike look down, side-glancing at Michael, as if wondering whether he should be quiet.

"It's okay, Mike. I don't mean to get into your business. I'm just a friend, and —"

"Best friend." Michael spoke up.

"Huh?" Levi asked.

"You're my best friend. Don't sell yourself short." Michael's voice strengthened.

Levi raised his head, looking back at Michael to be sure what he'd heard matched what he saw.

"Best friend." He smiled. "I was just trying to make sure I got it right, was all."

Michael reached over and took Mike's hand. Levi watched as Mike seemed uncertain as to what was happening.

"Levi. Mike is my — my boyfriend."

Mike's eyes opened wide again. Levi could see them clearly in the moonlight, the windows illuminating their spot on the deck from the party inside.

"Sorry, Mike. I just didn't know how —"

"It's okay."

"Is it? You sure?"

"Yeah. Of course. It's a big step."

Michael looked like he wanted to cry again. Levi could see it. And he watched Mike forget he was there, watching, because he pulled Michael into his arms — not too differently from what Levi had done moments before — and held him tight. This time, Michael's arms came up around his, and he cried.

Levi debated saying anything — *I'll let you two be,* something like that. But he decided it was best to quietly walk back inside. As he began to open the door, he caught something in his peripheral vision. At the other end of the deck, back by the steps. He'd forgotten.

Kieran and Eli stood quietly, holding each other in the cold.

Watching.

Levi walked back into the party, his mom stopping him halfway through the living room.

"Honey, I'm walking home with your sister. It's past bedtime."

He nodded.

"Everything okay?" She stopped and fussed with his hair, like she always did whenever she was worried about him.

"I'll be okay."

She gave him a look before he pushed her along. "Don't worry. I'll probably head home once Eli and Kieran leave."

"Don't be too late. Tell them I said hello. I couldn't find them earlier."

"I will," he said, and closed the front door, watching her and Lucy leave before he felt a hand rest on his shoulder.

"Wanna join me?" Eli asked as Levi turned to look over.

Eli nodded toward the front door, which confused him a little. Did he mean he was leaving? Join him? Home?

Eli reached around him and opened the front door and stepped outside. Levi followed, shutting the door behind, and noticed Eli walking toward the other end of the porch — to the rockers angled in front of Sonya and Angie's picture window. Light from the formal living room spilled through, coating the porch with enough light to see easily, a warm yellow. The porch itself was flanked by tall shrubs that protected it from the yard and street ahead, offering some privacy, but allowing one to enjoy a nice Maine evening outside, rocking in silence.

Eli sat down on the far chair and looked at Levi, who took the other.

"We saw you outside earlier." He began.

Levi looked around. He loved Eli and wouldn't want to change anything about him, but he didn't have an ability to whisper or gauge the volume of his voice well, he guessed. But everyone was in the back of the house for the party. They were alone.

"I had forgotten you two were there. Sorry if I scared you," Levi said.

"You didn't. We didn't have enough time to leave when you and Michael came out."

"It's okay. I was just —"

"I know."

They rocked in silence, both looking off into the night sky. The cold air was already chilling Levi's skin without a jacket.

"You're a brave man, Levi."

"I'm just a boy still."

"I don't think so."

Levi blushed. He always felt weird accepting compliments.

"Letting go of Michael like that."

"I wasn't letting him go."

Eli looked at him, silently asking for more.

"I just remember what you told me coming home the other night."

Eli nodded, but remained silent.

Levi scrunched his face, like he felt tears coming and didn't want that. He was legitimately happy for Michael. And Mike. But —

"It still hurts, though."

Levi nodded, losing his fight with the tears. He wiped at his eyes, but fought to remain in control.

"You really helped Michael tonight. He'll always be a better man because of you."

Levi shook his head. He wouldn't go that far, he thought.

"It's true. Look at me, Levi."

He forced himself to look over at Eli, biting at his lip, trying to get his emotions to die down.

Eli leaned forward in his rocker and spoke slowly, in his own Eli way.

"You gave Michael a gift tonight. You helped him know he is loved. *And* — he knows he can and *should* give Mike all of himself. You not just telling him, but *showing* — that's rare, Levi. And special. Just like you."

Eli leaned over and patted his knee before leaning back into his chair, his eyes fixed on Levi's.

"I'm not anything special."

"You know that's not true," Eli said.

Levi had expected him to fight him on it. Or joke. Or do whatever Eli normally did to get him to laugh and accept it. But he didn't. He simply called him out on it. He knew it wasn't true. It just felt weird thinking it. Feeling it.

"Eli?"

He looked at him.

"Do you love Kieran?"

Levi really wanted to know. He needed to know. Not because he was curious. Or prying. Or comparing to Niles. It was hard to know why, but he felt he needed to.

"I'm on my way," Eli said. No banter. No deflection. No jokes.

Levi nodded, accepting.

"I like him. He's really nice."

"He is."

"And he was really kind to Lucy."

"He's a family man, that's for sure."

"You gonna adopt kids together?"

Levi knew that'd get him. And it did. Finally. Eli's eyes bulged and he stopped rocking.

"I'm just teasing. I like Kieran, though. For real."

Eli's mouth perked into a smile. "You're a little shit sometimes, you know?"

"Uh huh. I'm the best. I'm — *Special!*" He teased.

"*Your highness,*" Eli added, and they both laughed.

The front door opened, and Levi noticed Michael stepping outside as if looking for something.

"Oh. I was — sorry if I interrupted." He paused once he saw Eli and Levi sitting.

"No. We were just talking is all. It's cold anyway. My nips are getting hard," Levi joked as Eli stood and headed over toward Michael, pulling him into a hug.

"Oh my god. Look at your outfit," Eli said, stepping back and giving him the once-over, causing Michael to smile and Levi to laugh.

"You're such a queen!" Levi walked up and snarked.

Michael laughed loudly while Eli took a step back. "That's *Your highness*, mmmkay?"

"Where's that boyfriend of yours?" Eli turned to Michael, who looked at Levi for a moment and then seemed to relax.

"C'mon." Michael grabbed Eli's hand and pulled him inside. Levi followed.

"Hey, Mike," Michael called, and his near look-alike came practically skipping in from the living room. He saw Eli and grinned, walking straight into the hug Eli was already opening for him. Long, the way the family hugged. Levi caught Mike blushing as they stepped back from each other.

"Hey. Hands off! You already have a boyfriend."

Levi looked over Mike's shoulder. Kieran had come down the hall and stood next to Eli, pulling him close.

Michael turned in time with Mike to see him.

"I'm Kieran. And you must be Michael," he said to Mike.

"Well, yeah — but no."

Michael grinned, but Kieran looked confused.

"I'm Michael," Michael said, "and he's Michael, too." He pointed to Mike.

"But I'm Mike to make things easier."

Kieran nodded, but Levi wasn't sure he got all that. He wasn't even sure he understood himself. But it didn't matter.

Kieran stepped around them and came over to hold Eli's back, just like Michael had resumed doing with Mike. Levi watched as the two couples got to know each other briefly while he stood on the side. He felt a little pity for himself, if he was honest, but decided that didn't help, so he just listened to the conversation. He'd find someone later, maybe. Didn't matter. At least not yet.

"Did you dress up?" Mike asked Kieran.

"My dinosaur outfit is back in the car. Little hard seeing in that thing."

"And you're Count Dracula?" Mike turned to Eli.

"More like Count Chocula," Michael teased, and Eli gave him a look.

"Watch it. You know I can suck your blood."

"Bet that's not the only thing you can suck," Michael teased back. Levi burst out laughing alongside Mike. Kieran's face turned redder than his hair while Michael looked like he had won the competition, his smile saying it all.

Eli looked stunned before leaning in and hugging Michael. "You've been awarded ten points for that one." He waved his hand like it was a wand. Michael genuflected.

"We've got another party to get to," Michael finally said.

"Get out!" Eli pointed toward the door, but Michael laughed. Mike was grinning.

"I expect to see you both soon. And none of this *We're busy* shit," Eli proclaimed. "Kieran and I will take his ambulance up to your dorm with lights and sirens going if we have to."

"Oh my god, you're an ambulance guy?"

"Paramedic, but yeah."

"That's so cool," Mike said.

Eli was already hugging Michael goodbye before moving on to Mike, who seemed to appreciate the gesture, judging by his face. Kieran followed suit before Michael stepped over to Levi and pulled him close, this time wrapping his arms around him.

"Thank you, Levi. I love you."

"Love you, too. Bestie."

Michael stepped back smiling, with a little water in his eyes. "Bestie."

Mike stepped forward and pulled Levi into a hug as well, following everyone's lead. Levi was surprised at first, but then relaxed and hugged him back before letting go.

"I'm really glad you and Michael are together."

"Thanks for helping — uh — us."

"You'll be okay. Oh — DM me if you need anything, okay? I'm on Michael's friends list."

"Really?"

Levi nodded. Mike gave him another quick hug, and then they both left.

Levi watched from the front porch as they headed toward what he guessed was Mike's car.

He felt a hand on his shoulder, and then, a moment later, on the other. Looking up, both Eli and Kieran were quietly holding him as they watched Levi's best friend drive away.

Chapter Fifteen

MIKE WAS in his Corolla driving up to meet Levi. They'd agreed to meet at Cafe Luna on Route 1 — about a forty minute drive on 295. Levi had said it wasn't too far from his high school. He sometimes walked the mile up just to think.

Mike wondered about what.

It had been a couple of weeks since Halloween — that party Michael had dragged him to where they'd met. Mike still couldn't believe he'd been talked into that ridiculous getup. Gay superheroes or something. Michael had come up with it, said it was funny, showed him clips on YouTube. *Mike* had been self-conscious — the outfit showing off his junk — but Michael had insisted. That, and frosting his hair. He'd never done anything like that before.

He hadn't even known exactly where they were going. They'd been invited to a party some of the guys down the hall were going to, out at one of their older brothers' houses up north. Michael had said at the last minute they were going to stop by a Halloween party to meet his uncle. And Eli.

And Levi.

Mike knew Levi was Michael's friend who lived up here in Portland. Michael had told him they'd met last Thanksgiving but never got into details. *Mike* had wondered if something was up between them — but didn't want to push.

When they arrived, everyone was older and he felt out of place. Especially since he and Michael were obviously screaming gay while everyone else was in vampire or witch costumes, the usual. But Eli had hugged him just like when he'd come by the dorm — *of course you came, get in here* — and introduced him to his boyfriend, Kieran.

Mike smiled remembering it. He hadn't met many friends since moving from Atlanta — Michael, a few of the guys at the dorm. Eli was the first guy who wasn't *one of the bros.* Michael had said Eli had lost his boyfriend last spring. He wasn't sure what happened, but Eli had seemed okay when they met at the dorm. And now, seeing him with Kieran, Mike was glad. He liked the idea of Eli having someone who loved him.

Mike pulled the Corolla into an open spot on the street and locked the door. A 2012 Toyota with a hundred and twenty-some-thousand miles on it. His grandma had driven it easy until she gave it to him for his seventeenth birthday last year. It wasn't a Civic, but he didn't care. Cheap on gas. No dents. No rust.

Down the sidewalk a guy was waving. A few steps closer and Mike recognized Levi — out of the tiger paint he'd worn for his costume at the party. Mike walked up and hesitated, uncertain if he should hug him. Levi had been okay with it at the party. Mike had always liked hugs. Ever since he could remember, he'd hugged everyone. Never understood why people freaked out about it.

Levi made the decision for him with a quick hug. "I almost didn't recognize you," he said.

"I'm not in that awful costume!" Mike laughed.

"Well, it *did show everything,*" Levi teased.

Mike turned red. "God, I was gonna kill Michael when he made me put it on."

Levi smiled and turned toward the cafe.

Inside, they ordered drinks and split a brownie, taking a small table near the window.

"Michael didn't want to come?" Levi asked, cutting off a corner for himself.

"He doesn't know I'm here."

Levi looked up.

"I didn't want him to think I was snooping on him."

"Snooping?"

Mike shrugged and took a bite of brownie. Chewed. Wiped his lips with a napkin.

"I wanted to ask something and I knew if I told him I was coming to see you, he'd freak."

"About?"

Mike wasn't sure if he was referring to his question or the idea of Michael freaking.

"Listen, I — uh. Well. Thanks for replying to my DM first. I wasn't sure you'd know it was me."

"I already looked you up."

"You did?"

Levi nodded. "Stalked Michael's Insta after you all left. Found you." He looked a little proud.

Mike smiled and reached for his drink. He supposed he'd do the same thing.

"Your account is so different from Michael's."

Mike grinned. The guys on the dorm floor had said the same, calling Michael's Insta the *gayest page ever*. Michael had taken it as a badge of honor. By comparison, Mike's was just a couple of pictures of the sunset over on campus, a few older ones of his dog back home, a picture of his car when he first got it, and a recent one of him and Michael standing outside somewhere. Levi had liked that one.

"He's — more out than I am."

"Me too."

Mike noticed Levi glance out the window before taking a drink and looking over at him.

"Are you out at school?" Mike asked.

"Yeah, but I don't really talk much. I don't have many school friends."

Mike nodded. "I didn't either."

"Really?"

"Used to. But —"

"What happened?"

Mike looked out the window toward where Levi had just glanced.

"Sorry, I'm being nosy."

"No — it's okay. I — it's boring."

"That's okay."

Mike half-grinned and set his cup down.

"Just — well." He shrugged. "My old boyfriend."

"Oh? What happened?" Levi asked. Then quickly: "If you don't mind saying."

Mike shrugged again. "I don't mind. It's just —" He reached for his cup and took another drink. "I haven't really talked about it since."

"Doesn't Michael know?"

Mike shook his head. "Not really. He just knows the general thing."

"Oh."

"It's stupid."

Mike looked over at Levi who sat there looking at him.

"Brandon and I were really — well —"

"Love?"

"What?"

"In love?"

Mike felt his face flush. It'd been almost a year now and he still felt that way when thinking of him.

"I take that as a yes," Levi said. Mike didn't deny it. "So, what happened?"

Mike thought about it and spoke, but looked off at the napkin dispenser rather than Levi.

"He was on varsity basketball, so we had to keep it quiet. He wasn't out."

He glanced over at Levi, who was taking another drink but had his eyes locked on him.

"Anyway, someone caught us together at a party —" Mike stopped, remembering that night.

"Doing it?"

"What?" Mike sat up, surprised and a little embarrassed. "No. God no. I've never —" He shut his mouth, realizing he'd said too much. Levi looked embarrassed, like he knew he'd overstepped.

"We were just making out, is all," Mike said. Levi nodded, mouthed *sorry*, and sat back.

"It's okay," Mike said. "The thing was, I didn't care if anyone saw us. Brandon did."

"Lost his shit?"

Mike looked at Levi who was setting his empty cup down before looking over at him.

"Yeah."

"Sorry," Levi added again, but Mike shook his head slightly. "It's okay."

"So. You and your boyfriend were caught kissing and you didn't care but Brandon did."

Mike nodded.

"So what happened? He get upset?"

"He told everyone I forced myself on him. That he wasn't gay. Made it seem like I was — some rapist or something." Mike belted it out, still angry. Levi's eyes widened. Leaned into the table.

"No way. That asshole."

Mike nodded.

"Oh my god. What did everyone do?"

Mike looked down, remembering that next week.

"Dad got called to school. Principal said Brandon's folks weren't going to press charges — as long as I was out of his classes. No games. No lunch period. Nothing near him."

"Oh my god, Mike. I'm so sorry. I can't —"

Mike shook his head. "It was the last week before Christmas break. Everyone at school thought I was a stalker. I was so glad when we got out for Christmas break. At least I wouldn't have to be there again until January."

"Damn. That — that makes me angry."

"It's okay, Levi. I'm — over it."

"I wouldn't be. I mean —"

"I don't know why I told you that."

"What did you tell Michael?"

"He knows that something happened last semester and I couldn't wait to graduate. We were talking about being out at school."

Mike watched Levi look out the window again. "So you had to go back last January to everyone thinking you were some perv or something while your boyfriend —"

"Ex."

"Ex-boyfriend was all high and mighty? That fucking sucks."

Mike closed his eyes for a second. He'd heard words like that for years. Everyone at school said cuss words. He tried not to, even when he was angry. No religious thing — his own dad cussed plenty. He just liked saying exactly what he meant. Not hiding behind some nonsense word for shock. He'd been trying lately not to judge people who did.

Levi must have understood somehow. He said *sorry* again and looked away.

"It's okay." Mike finished the last of his drink and set the cup down, trying to remember what they'd been talking about before he went down memory lane.

"You wanna walk? I sometimes do around the track down at school."

"Uh, sure. Is it far?"

"About a mile. It's easy to get to."

"Why don't I drive? I can drop you off after." Mike offered before quickly adding, "If you want."

"You don't have to."

"I don't mind. Besides, you agreed to come meet me."

Mike helped Levi bus their table before walking outside and down to the car.

"Must be nice to have your own car," Levi said. Teasing, Mike could tell.

"My grandma's first. She gave it to me last year after I got my license."

"Eli's been helping me get my hours in. I should be able to take the test next month."

"If you need my car, I can —"

"Thanks. But I think it helps Eli as much as me."

Mike tilted his head a little. He wasn't sure what Levi meant. He didn't know Levi well enough to ask. He got in and closed the door, looking over at Levi who did the same.

"Michael told you about him, right?"

"You mean Kieran? I met him, remember? At the party."

"No. About Niles."

"He mentioned someone from before. Didn't say his name. Said he'd lost him."

"He died."

Mike's hands stopped on the key in the ignition.

"Died?"

"Yeah. Michael didn't tell you?"

"No. I had no idea. I thought he meant they broke up or — something."

"No, it was horrible. Some guy tried to shoot up the library and —"

"*That* was Eli's boyfriend? I saw the news back home about some guy —"

"Yeah." Levi nodded, looking right at him.

"Jesus."

"Yeah."

"I — I didn't — Eli. He and Kieran looked so —"

"Kieran was the paramedic who found Niles."

"No way." Mike sat back into the seat.

"Yeah. Last person who saw him. That's how they met."

"I — I can't —"

"Michael was calling me freaked out. His folks wouldn't let him come up for the funeral, which pissed him off. It was a whole thing."

Mike's head started cataloging Michael's stories from around that time. They'd talked a lot about their past — but not in much detail. Not this stuff.

"I thought you knew. I'm surprised Michael didn't tell you." Levi looked like maybe he should have stopped talking.

"No. I — Eli hugged me when I met him."

"Yeah, he's a hugger. I used to hate it, but —"

"You did?" Mike turned to look at him.

"Well — I wasn't — not — used to being touched. You know. Like that."

"Oh God, I love hugs. Ever since my mom —"

Mike stopped. This was getting way too heavy. He cracked the window a little. "Uh — how do you get to your school?"

Levi apologized again. Mike noted he seemed to do that a lot.

"Turn right here and head down for a bit."

Mike pulled the car out as they made their way to his school.

Ten minutes later, they parked and walked over toward the track. Neither had spoken on the drive except for Levi's directions.

"Mike, you okay?"

"Huh?" Mike asked. They were walking side by side. It was light out, but overcast — a typical cold November day. No one was out but them.

"Sorry if I said too much back there."

"You say *sorry* a lot." Mike walked a few paces. Levi got quiet. "I don't mind it. Just noticed."

They walked in silence again, Mike feeling like he should change the subject.

"I can't imagine how Eli — he's what? Like twenty-five or something?"

"I think." Levi said it softly.

"He and Kieran look good together, though."

"I was worried about them that night," Levi added.

"Worried?"

"Yeah. I mean, I liked Kieran, but I didn't know him, you know? And then I caught them kissing outside just before you got there."

"That's sweet."

"Yeah, but I didn't know if it was too soon, you know? Like, was Eli bouncing back or —"

"You think he is?"

Mike noticed Levi shake his head. "I don't think so. Kieran really seems to be into him."

"And Eli? He seems to be —"

"I think Eli is actually waiting on Kieran. If that makes any sense."

Mike furrowed his brow. He would've thought the opposite. "If Kieran's really into Eli, then —"

"I don't know. It just feels like Eli now knows what's important. Doesn't want to fuck around — sorry. I meant — wait around not saying stuff just because you're scared. I dunno. I think Eli wants Kieran to just come out and say it already."

"Say what?"

"I guess how he feels, you know?"

Mike thought about that as they made another lap, not talking. His hands were getting cold so he put them in his jacket pockets and stepped up a bit to match Levi's stride.

"So, what did you want to ask me about?" Levi asked as they turned the second curve again.

"Oh — I — well — it's kinda not really that important. Not compared to —"

"What?"

Mike felt like Levi was older than high school somehow. The way he spoke. Direct. He never used *bro* or *sup* like the guys on Mike's floor. Even Michael did that with them sometimes.

"You and Michael were a thing before, right?"

Levi kept walking, not saying a word. Mike wasn't sure how to ask, so he just said it.

"I thought we were." Levi kept looking at the ground as they walked. "Why?"

"Michael has never said anything, but I saw you both at the party. Especially when you were talking outside on the deck."

He noticed Levi nod.

"You know, he never called me his boyfriend until you told him that night."

"Really?" Levi asked, looking over at him.

Mike nodded. "I wanted to be, but he was always so weird. And when he mentioned we needed to stop at that party, that you'd be there — I just put one and one together."

Levi remained quiet as they rounded the third curve.

"I was actually going to tell him if you were together, that it was okay. I didn't want to get in the way. I wouldn't have if I had known."

"You didn't get in the way."

Mike pondered that. "I didn't?"

"I think there was something going on before."

"So you were together?"

Levi stopped and looked over at Mike. "He came out for Spring Break in March and we — were together."

Mike wasn't sure exactly what that meant.

"And then you weren't?"

Levi looked down and then back to him. "I gave myself to him, Mike. And then he went back to Nashville. And he just — quit texting me." Levi kept his eyes locked on Mike's until he understood.

"I'm sorry for prying, Levi. I — I didn't know."

Levi began walking again, their third lap. They walked almost down to the next curve before Levi spoke again.

"I knew he'd found someone else. I mean — I thought so. Saw his Insta pics."

Mike nodded. He'd looked at Michael's Insta that first night they met at Orientation.

"I wasn't stupid. He lived in Nashville. He was going to college. I was still in high school." Levi said it sarcastically. "Like it was going to work out."

Mike kept his mouth shut.

"And you know what? I would've been hurt, but gotten over it if he just had called and said *Sorry Levi, I met someone else,* you know?"

Levi seemed to be upping the pace. Mike increased his stride to match.

"So we talked about Eli and all the bullshit going on. And if he was coming to Portland or not."

"He said he might have gone to Vanderbilt," Mike added, looking ahead as they curved the track again.

"Yeah. I'd wondered why he actually came here, to be honest." Levi half-laughed. "I thought it was because of you."

"Me?" Mike was surprised.

"Well, I didn't know you. I just thought he met someone here. Besides me. And that was the reason he moved up to the dorms."

"I didn't meet him until Orientation."

"Really?"

"Yeah. Didn't know him until the first day."

"Well. Doesn't matter. I was kind of prepared for it anyway."

Mike mulled that as they walked. Neither spoke.

"Why?" Mike finally asked.

"Why what?"

"Why didn't you yell at him? Say *what's wrong with you?*"

Levi stopped. Mike walked a pace ahead and turned around.

"Because I don't think anything is wrong with him."

"You don't?"

"No. He's just — I don't know exactly what happened. But he's just afraid. He doesn't want to hurt my feelings, so he disappeared."

"But that feels worse."

"Oh, it does. But I'd already figured —"

"Why? Was he —"

Levi began walking again, shaking his head. "No, he's fine. Seriously. It's just — I have a hard time trusting anyone anyway."

Mike caught up and resumed his pace next to Levi.

"I do, too. It's why I wanted to talk."

He looked over and saw Levi staring at him.

"I like Michael. I hope that's okay to say."

Levi shrugged, but Mike stopped.

"If he hurt you, I'd walk away from him in a second. I don't want to be with someone who would hurt someone."

"No, you got it all wrong, Mike."

"Then, what?"

Levi took a breath and looked away for a moment. The sun was going down and it was getting colder.

"Listen, Mike. Michael is a really nice guy. He just — he sometimes needs to grow a set of balls, you know?"

Mike smiled slightly.

"Like — he's had it pretty good. You know? His folks seem nice. Big house. Easy life. All of it."

"But —"

"But he never learned how to say things like they are. And because he's a nice guy, he feels like he can't let people down. That's the biggest thing you'll need to work with him on. He'll go out of his way *not to* hurt you."

Mike looked at him, trying to figure out if that meant Michael was good or bad.

"Just make him talk to you. It's easier if you're together — like see each other every day. We — we only could message each other from here to Nashville."

Mike looked around the empty track and back to Levi who was watching him.

"Do you love him still?"

"In my own way. But I also know it'd never be anything."

"Really?"

"Mike, what are you worried about? Has he done something to you?" Levi seemed a little worked up.

"No — I just —" Mike looked around again, uncertain why he was here now. "Ever since that night when you introduced me as his boyfriend, he hasn't said it but a couple of times. I counted."

"Have you confronted him about it?"

Mike looked down. "No. I thought I was being dumb."

"You're not dumb, Mike. Don't put yourself down."

"I just — you said I could DM you and I —"

"I'm glad you did. Let's keep walking. It's getting cold."

"Sorry. I can drop you off if you want."

"No, I like talking. Just helped to keep moving, is all."

They made another lap.

"Can I ask you a question?" Mike asked.

"You just did." Levi smiled slyly as they walked.

"Smart Aleck."

"No, my ass is smart, not my Aleck!" Levi joked, and Mike shook his head.

"Okay, what?"

"Do you find it weird talking to Michael's boyfriend like this?"

Levi smiled. "No, not really."

"I think I'd be all weirded out."

"Why?"

"I dunno. I guess — maybe — I'm a jealous guy. I dunno."

"Jealous? Of me? Seriously?"

Mike nodded. "Maybe." Levi laughed.

"Why? You're like a million times more than me!" Levi teased.

"Am not! I'm just —"

"Hot. And smart. And —"

Mike blushed. "Stop it."

"It's true."

"No — I'm just —"

"Why are you worried about me? You think I'm gonna swoop in and steal your boyfriend?"

Mike shook his head. "I guess — well, I guess I fall in love easily and then worry something will happen and they'll leave. Like —"

"Brandon?" Levi asked.

"Brandon?" Mike questioned. He hadn't put that together. "No — like my —" He stopped.

Levi stopped and turned to look at him. "Like what?"

Mike wasn't sure if he should say anything. He'd already blabbed way too much today.

Levi looked at him.

"Like my mom. She left when I was — like five."

Levi looked at him, but deeper. Mike saw him take a step forward and then stop.

"I'm sorry," he said again, this time quietly. Mike could hear the wind cut through.

"It's okay. I know — I'm a mess." Mike kicked at the asphalt.

"You're not a mess. My dad —" Levi trailed off.

Mike looked around the darkening track, feeling the cold wind slap at his face.

"I guess I always expected the worst, so when Michael quit messaging me — it didn't hurt as much."

"That's bullshit," Mike heard himself say it. Levi looked over, startled.

"You don't deserve to live like that."

"There's lots you don't know about me, Mike. It was hard."

"Same here. But it's not a competition."

Levi stared at him, but Mike held his gaze.

"Maybe you're jealous because you don't want someone to break your heart?" Levi asked.

Mike thought about it. "Probably."

"Michael won't do that. But keep talking to him," Levi reinforced.

Mike nodded. They remained silent, both staring at each other.

"We should probably go," Mike finally said. Levi nodded.

They turned and walked off the track back toward the Corolla.

Once they were in the car, Levi gave Mike directions to his house.

"Thanks for talking with me."

"Of course. I'm always around to talk shit," Levi laughed. Mike did too.

"You know — you're a nice guy, Levi."

"Nah. I'm a dick. You just don't know me yet."

"I think that's bullshit."

"Wow — big words!" Levi teased. Mike blushed.

"I hope we can be friends. Even if I'm dating your ex."

"Hey, Mike —"

He looked over.

"You gonna tell Michael we met?"

He didn't answer right away, keeping his eyes on the road. Then back at Levi.

"I don't want to hide it."

"Me either."

"But —"

"Yeah. I know. He's gonna freak."

"Maybe a little."

Mike nodded. Looked at the wheel.

"I don't want to scare him."

"Me either."

They sat with it.

"Michael's gonna want to know what we talked about."

"That asshole? I hadn't noticed we were." Levi joked, and Mike laughed.

"Seriously. I hope we can be friends," Mike said, pulling into the driveway.

"We already are." Levi leaned over the console and gave Mike a hug.

"Now go kick Michael's ass." He said it as he got out of the car.

The Novice's Chapel

THE MADONNA'S face had been giving him trouble for three days.

Not the form of it — the form had been settled in cartoon and pricked onto the wet plaster a week ago, and the form was simple enough, a young woman's face inclined slightly toward the angel at her left, the eyes lowered, the mouth holding something between a smile and the absence of one. Marco had painted such faces a hundred times. He could paint such a face in his sleep.

The trouble was the color.

The Virgin's face wanted to be colder than her mantle. He had decided this in the first week of the commission, in the way painters decided such things — not by argument but by a kind of internal music that confirmed itself when the brush met the wall. The mantle, ultramarine of the highest quality the cardinal's purse could secure, glowed warm in afternoon light despite its blue. The face, to balance it, wanted the cooler register — flesh tones tempered with a touch of green earth, the smallest amount of black, a thinned wash that would let the underdrawing show through and lend the face the quality of distance, of reverence held back from the viewer.

He had been mixing the wash all week. He had not yet been satisfied.

This morning he had risen before lauds, walked the empty corridor down to the chapel before the priory had stirred, and climbed the scaffolding alone in the gray light to look at what he had laid down yesterday. The face was wrong. The face had been wrong for three days. The wash was too warm, or it was too cool, or it was the right temperature but the proportion of green earth was off, or the proportion was right but he had loaded the brush too full. He could not tell which. He stood on the scaffolding in the gray light with his hands at his sides and looked at the Virgin's face and thought, *I do not know what is wrong with you.*

He climbed down.

He went to the basin and washed his hands, though there was nothing to wash from them.

He came back into the chapel and waited for the day to begin.

Tommaso arrived shortly after the bells, as he always did, with the small leather apron tied at his waist and the muller in one hand. He nodded to Marco. He went to the low table. He began to grind.

They had not spoken of the cardinal.

Three weeks had passed since the morning Marco had returned from the chamber upstairs and climbed the scaffolding with hands he could not steady, and Tommaso had climbed up beside him and put a hand on his hand. They had not referred to that morning. They had returned, the next day, to the rhythm of the chapel — Tommaso grinding, Marco painting, the bread broken at midday, the small cup of watered wine the priory permitted to artisans not seated at the brothers' table — and the morning had become a thing that had happened and that lived now in the silent space between them, neither claimed nor denied.

The letters from Venice had not resumed.

Marco had stopped expecting them. He did not know whether this was acceptance or surrender. He suspected that, at the level on which a man could observe himself, the two were difficult to distinguish.

He climbed the scaffolding for the second time that morning, carrying a fresh dish of the wash he had mixed the previous evening. He set it on the platform. He took up the brush.

"The lapis is thinner today," Tommaso said from below.

Marco looked down.

The novice was at the low table, his head bent over the muller, his face turned toward the stone he was working. He had not looked up.

"Thinner."

"Cooler. You have been mixing it differently for the Madonna's face. Cooler. The mantle was warmer."

Marco was silent. He looked at his brush. He looked at the wash in the dish.

"You noticed."

"I have been grinding it for you. I have been watching what you do with it."

Tommaso said this without ceremony — the way a man names the weather, or the day of the week, or any other small fact that did not need underlining. He continued to grind. Marco continued to look at him.

He had not credited the novice with an eye.

He had credited him with steady hands, and with the patience of his vocation, and with a kind of quiet attention that was useful in a chapel and not commonly useful elsewhere. He had not credited him with the kind of seeing that a painter required of himself. He realized, now, looking down at the bent head and the steady muller, that he had been a fool. The novice had been seeing him for months. The novice had been seeing the pigment and the mantle and the temperature of the wash and the gradual cooling of the Madonna's face. The novice had been holding all of this in his attention while Marco had been laboring under the assumption that he was the only one in the chapel who knew what he was doing.

"I have been," he said carefully, "trying to make her face hold the room. The mantle pulls forward. The face has to stay back."

"Yes."

"You see that."

"I see what you do."

Marco loaded the brush. He moved it toward the wall. His hand was steady this morning. The wash, when it touched the plaster, lay cooler than yesterday. He could not yet tell whether it was correct. He laid down a small stroke at the edge of the cheek, where any wrongness would be easiest to chip out. He stepped back.

He looked at the face.

He could not tell yet. The plaster had to dry. The pigment had to settle. The afternoon light would tell him, or it would not.

"Maestro."

He looked down again.

Tommaso had stopped grinding. He was sitting back from the muller, his hands resting on the edge of the table.

"What will you do when the chapel is finished?"

The question reached Marco the way questions reached him in the chapel — through the slight delay of the room's acoustics, the small echo from the vault above. He heard it, and then he heard it again as it returned to him from the stone. He stood with the brush in his hand and considered the question as it came back to him.

"I have not allowed myself to think of after."

"Why?"

"There has not been an after for me to think of."

The novice said nothing. He did not press. Marco looked down at him and saw that he had returned his hands to the muller and resumed grinding — slowly, evenly, the way he always ground, with the patience of a man who would grind for an hour to produce a thimble's worth of color and would consider the hour well spent.

Marco let himself stand on the scaffolding for a long moment.

"There was — " He stopped. He started again. "Before this commission, there was a future I had been imagining. I do not know how to imagine it now."

"Because of the work."

"Because of the work. And other things."

"Other things."

"Yes."

Tommaso did not lift his head. He continued to grind. Marco understood that the not-lifting was a courtesy. The novice was giving him the privacy of being half-spoken-to, the way a confessor sat behind the screen. The voice without the face. The grace of being heard without being looked at.

"The prior has been asking me," Tommaso said, after a moment, "when I will take vows."

Marco lowered the brush.

"I have been a novice for three years. The prior has been patient. He is not patient indefinitely. The chapel has been my reason for waiting."

"Your reason for waiting."

"Yes."

Marco set the brush across the dish. He sat down on the platform of the scaffolding, his legs dangling over the edge, his back against the upright. He had not done this in weeks. He felt the chapel beneath him as a single space — the apse, the low table, the bent head of the novice working at it. The morning light from the high window was beginning to find its first angles on the stone.

"The chapel will be done by spring," he said.

"Yes."

"And then you will take vows."

"Then I will decide."

Marco sat with this. The not-deciding-yet. The novice had been holding his vocation in suspension because of a chapel that he had no claim on, no obligation to, no reason to wait for except the reason he had not named. Marco felt the weight of this like a small heat in him. He did not know what to do with it. He sat with the brush across the dish and the dish on the platform and looked down at the novice's bent head and could not look anywhere else.

"You have not asked me," Tommaso said, "about the brother."

"What brother?"

"The one I do not have. By blood."

Marco waited.

"I had a brother once. Not by blood. We were raised in the same household. The same priest taught us our letters. He left when we were sixteen. He went to the coast. I do not know where on the coast. I do not know which coast."

"He never wrote."

"He never wrote."

The novice said it without grievance, the way a man names a fact about a country he has lived in for too long to be surprised by it. Marco understood, slowly, that he was being given something. He understood, also, that he was being given it in a particular form — as a fact, not a confession, with the door left open for him to walk through if he chose, but with no pressure for him to do so.

He chose.

"I had — " He stopped. He had not said the name aloud in the chapel before. He had not said the name aloud anywhere in months. "I had a friend in Venice. His name is Alessandro."

"Was."

"Is. I do not know."

Tommaso did not look up. He did not stop grinding. The muller turned. The lapis darkened on the stone.

"He has not written in some time."

"No."

"And you have not written to him."

"Not since — " He stopped again. *Not since the cardinal showed me that everything I wrote had already been read.* He could not say it. The walls might or might not be listening. The novice would understand without the saying. "Not since some weeks."

"Was he kind."

"He was."

"Then he is loved."

The novice said this in the same tone in which he had said that the lapis was thinner today, in which he had said that he had been a novice for three years, in which he had said that his brother had never written. The tone did not invite response. The tone laid the small fact of Alessandro's having-been-loved on the stone of the chapel like a coin set down on an altar — quiet, deliberate, not asking to be picked up.

Marco felt a heat behind his eyes.

He did not weep. He had wept on the scaffolding three weeks ago and Tommaso had been there and he had not wept since. He suspected that some allotment had been used. He suspected, also, that there were other allotments he had not yet drawn against and that today was not the day to spend them.

"Yes," he said. "He is loved."

The chapel was very quiet.

He sat on the platform for a while longer with his legs dangling. He looked down at the novice. The novice was grinding lapis. The novice was working at the same speed at which he had been working when Marco had first looked down. He had not changed his pace. He had not looked up. The conversation had been conducted at the rate of his hands on the muller, which was the rate at which any conversation in this chapel had ever been conducted.

Marco picked up the brush again.

He climbed back to standing.

He looked at the Virgin's face — the small new stroke at the edge of the cheek, drying — and he considered it. He could not tell yet whether it was correct. But he could see, today, what he wanted from it. He wanted the face to be cooler than the mantle, and he wanted the cool to suggest distance, and he wanted the distance to feel earned — not aloof, but composed, the composure of a young woman who has been told a difficult thing and has not yet decided how to carry it.

He understood, looking at the face, that he had been painting himself.

He laid down a second small stroke. He stepped back. He let it be.

When he climbed down at midday for bread, he realized, on the third rung of the ladder, that he had not thought of Alessandro for an hour. The realization came with the small panic he had come to expect on such occasions, and beneath the panic the older guilt, and beneath the guilt — and this was new — a third thing, which he did not name but recognized as a kind of permission. Not permission to forget. Permission to rest.

He stood on the chapel floor and looked at Tommaso, who was setting the muller in the basin and rinsing his hands.

The novice did not look up.

Marco understood that the not-looking-up was, today, a different not-looking-up than it had been at lauds. It was no longer the courtesy of the confessor behind the screen. It was something else. It was the courtesy of a man giving another man room to walk back into the world after having spoken what he had spoken.

Marco walked across the chapel and broke the bread.

In his cell that evening, Tommaso opened the small book of psalms he had been given when he entered the priory. He turned to the seventy-third. He had been turning to it often, lately. He read it slowly. He set the book aside. He did not pray. He sat in the dark with his hands folded, the way he had been taught to fold them, and listened to the building settle around him.

Chapter Sixteen

LEVI SURPRISED ELI when he walked into the kitchen early, poured himself a bowl of Frosted Flakes and milk, grabbed a spoon, and sat down at the circular kitchen table just by Graham's patio door. Eli watched him the entire time, holding his cup to his face, blowing on the steam out of habit. The sun had been up for an hour, but the clock was already pushing eight.

Levi wore a hoodie pulled up over his head, which reminded Eli of the novice in Graham's book he had picked up again last night to read. But he was also wearing just boxers below — and Eli stretched to look down at his feet as he walked toward the table, bowl in hand — furry slippers with googly eyes that shook as he stepped.

His ensemble hadn't surprised him.

When Levi sat, he looked over at Eli without saying a word and quickly signed *Good morning.*

Eli moved his left hand cautiously from the mug and signed it back, curious when Levi had decided to switch to *his* language. Maybe because he wasn't a morning person and didn't like to speak. Or he was playing by Eli's rules at his house. Or Levi had always been this way and he'd never noticed. It was the first time he recalled seeing Levi so early. Of course, Levi had never stayed over at his house before, either.

Eli signed *How did you sleep?* — testing him further. He was curious to know what Levi knew.

He put his spoon down mid-bite and replied *Okay.*

Eli perked up a bit. *Hmmm,* he thought. *Ready to help today?*

Yes, he signed. *Different from last year.*

Impressed, Eli momentarily forgot about Levi's ASL skills and recalled last Thanksgiving. He and Graham had decided to help serve meals at the shelter and had begun their odyssey with Levi, his sister Lucy, and their mom Susan. He remembered that day well, although it had seemed so long ago. Levi, especially, had grown so much since then. And not just physically.

Levi had gone back to his cereal when Graham walked in.

"When's Kieran coming?"

"Anytime."

"Better get a move on then, Levi," Graham said while filling up a water bottle at the sink.

Levi signed to Eli, causing him to giggle a little. Graham noticed and looked to Eli for translation.

"He says he's already dressed."

Graham gave Levi a look up and down and turned to Eli again. "Tell him that while some might enjoy it, Mickey Mouse boxer shorts probably are not the look he's going for at the shelter."

Levi giggled and gave Eli a look that said *Go on. Translate.*

Eli obliged, not holding back on his normal, fluent speed, but Levi signed in return: *I never knew how to do "Mickey Mouse" in sign before.*

"What is this? *Speak in Secret Language About Graham* day?" Graham teased while walking over to the table.

Eli signed to Levi *He's on to us. Look casual,* getting a laugh from him. Levi was waking up now.

"We'll talk later," Eli said aloud for the first time that morning, and winked, causing Levi to laugh before standing and rinsing his bowl in the sink.

As Levi disappeared down the hall, Graham watching, he turned back to Eli. "Did you know he could sign?"

Eli shook his head.

"Hmm. Wonder what else we don't know about him?"

It was more a rhetorical question for Graham, but Eli was thinking the same. Maybe Levi had learned when he spent all that time at the library? Or in school lately? Or — who knew? He wondered why he was only now finding out.

Graham looked back toward something in the living room and began to stand. Eli followed his gaze and saw Kieran walking in with — an almost identical version of himself. Eli's eyes opened as he stood as well.

Kieran came up and paused, like he had forgotten something, and turned around gesturing for his "twin" to step forward.

"Danny wanted to come along," he said.

Eli's mind connected the dots quickly. He'd heard of Danny before. And Sean, Kieran's older brother.

"Welcome, Danny." Graham extended his hand.

"Hi, Mr. Tier —"

"Just Graham, please."

Danny smiled. Eli couldn't help but notice how Danny smiled almost the same way as his older brother, causing a little crease to form just above his eyes, making his freckles look like they were dancing up and down. Red hair. Short. His face was almost that of Kieran's, except he had fewer freckles. They were still there, but just not his signature feature that Eli had found he loved in Kieran.

"Hi, Danny. I'm Eli." He stepped forward, just past Kieran, and shook his hand.

Danny looked to him as if sizing him up, but was smiling, like he already knew. Eli wondered if Kieran had mentioned him before. Or, if Danny knew he was his brother's boyfriend. Probably not, he thought. Not given his household and mother.

Eli instinctively stepped back to Kieran's side, but he could see him subtly take a step away. No hug. No kiss. It felt incomplete. But he saw Danny watching, and once again reminded himself: Kieran was still closeted.

"How did you get here? You both ride over?" Graham asked, knowing Kieran's motorcycle was standard.

"Sean dropped us off."

Graham kept his gaze. Eli hadn't spoken of the Callahan household much to Graham, so Sean was a new name. Eli himself had never met him, but he knew where Sean stood in the line of brothers.

"His older brother," Eli said to Graham. Danny looked over at him, like most everyone who ever met Eli for the first time did when he spoke. He caught Kieran giving Danny a *don't stare* look. Danny suddenly looked away, embarrassed.

Eli stepped over to Danny and asked, "Do you know any deaf people?"

He saw Danny's face flush, just like his brother's when he was embarrassed or felt caught in the act. "No." He shook his head.

"Well, now you do." Eli patted him on the shoulder and laughed warmly.

Eli caught Kieran's eyes. He was getting good at reading them. In the month since the Halloween party, they'd spent time together each day, although it was getting cold and more difficult for Kieran to ride his motorcycle. Many times Eli would stop by and pick him up. Sometimes Pat would drop him off after a shift. Eli asked if she knew, but Kieran said no, and felt ashamed he hadn't told her, he said.

That had begun to be a recurring theme: Eli understood Kieran's desire not to hurt his mother, not to cause any shame or problems for the Callahan family. But he also wanted to see his boyfriend without feeling like he was sneaking around. Kieran was old enough, Eli had told him, that he should live his life in respect of, but not in deference to, his family.

But, he understood. At least for now. Even last night before Kieran had left to return home, like he always did, they'd spoken of it.

Kieran was sharing that his mother had been bringing up his being gone so much, assuming he had some girl he was hiding. Eli had asked gently how he responded.

I almost said it, he had signed to Eli. They were getting better at having conversations that way, occasionally Kieran stopping and asking how to sign something.

What stopped you? Eli had signed back.

I don't know.

I think you do, Eli pressed, but put his hand on Kieran's gently after they finished the words.

Kieran had nodded, ashamed. The red face. His trademark. Just like Danny a moment ago.

"Hope you don't mind. Danny heard I was going to help out and wanted to come too."

Kieran gave Eli a look that indicated there was more to it, but they'd share later when alone.

Eli nodded while Graham said that the shelter would welcome Danny, making him feel included.

"Would you mind if I used the restroom, Graham? Before we go?"

"Sure. Let me show you."

Eli watched Graham take Danny out of the kitchen before turning to Kieran and kissing him quickly.

Kieran sank into it, but then pulled away, looking back to see if anyone was there.

It was just Levi. Standing in his jeans, sneakers, and the same hoodie Eli saw him wearing to breakfast, smiling at the two.

Get a room, he signed.

Eli snickered, but he couldn't decide if Kieran was embarrassed or surprised Levi knew ASL.

Ready? Levi signed just as he turned to see Graham and Danny walking back to join them.

Kieran walked over. "Levi, this is my kid brother Danny. He wanted to come as well."

"I'm almost eighteen. I don't think I'm a kid, Kieran," he said, smiling, before turning to Levi, who seemed surprised, like Kieran had been a moment earlier. Eli wasn't sure, but Levi clammed up quickly, like his brain was still in sign mode.

Danny extended his hand and Levi watched it, like he wasn't sure what to do, before catching himself. Eli looked over at Kieran, then back at the two. Watching Levi gently shake Danny's hand, and mumbling something he couldn't hear, it became apparent.

Levi was struck.

Eli forced Kieran to drive his car. He wanted to chat with Danny and Levi and it'd be easier to turn and look at both sitting in the back. Graham had said he'd meet them there. Had to go pick up Oscar the Grouch.

"Like Sesame Street?" Danny asked, confused, as they stood in the front hallway getting ready to leave.

Kieran had laughed at that one before telling his brother it was Graham's best friend down the street.

"I wouldn't go *that far,*" Graham had said, but smiled for Danny's amusement.

As Kieran drove, Eli turned to the back and asked Danny if he knew much about the shelter.

"Just what Kieran told ma last night when he said he wouldn't be around for dinner."

Eli turned toward Kieran. "You getting into any trouble?"

Danny answered before he could, causing Eli to turn to try to understand what he said.

Eli noticed Levi telling Danny he needed to let Eli see his face to understand, which brought a small "sorry" from Danny before he repeated himself. "Ma was going to give him all sorts of shit, but he said he was helping the homeless people so he was doing what Jesus would do or some bullshit." Danny was grinning, teasing his brother, but Eli noticed Levi turn away when he heard the *homeless* part.

"It's true!" Kieran yelled from the driver's seat as he waited at a stoplight. Eli saw him looking into the mirror back at his brother, and figured they were just as he expected brothers to be.

"So why did you come along then?" Eli asked directly, before realizing that sounded a bit harsh.

Danny didn't pick up the tone, however, because he volunteered that their ma thought it was a lovely idea. If they weren't going to have a traditional Thanksgiving meal together, at least this would be living out Christ's mission, or something like that, he shared. "Besides, I got out of going to church."

He grinned and looked over at Levi, who turned back and gave a small smile.

"First time for you, too?" Danny asked Levi.

Eli watched as Levi replied without looking at him. "No, I was there — last year."

"Oh, cool. Well, you can show me what to do then."

Eli lifted his hands awkwardly since he was twisted in his seat looking back, and signed to Levi *You okay?*

Levi's eyes perked up, like he had forgotten about their secret language, and replied with his fingers. *Yeah. Just remember stuff.*

Eli nodded.

"You know how to sign?" Danny nudged Levi to get his attention. Eli could tell he was curious.

"A little," Levi had replied quietly.

"Levi's my brother from another mother," Eli said, and noticed Levi look up, a smile starting to return to his face.

"Can you show me some signs?" Danny asked Levi. Eli noticed he didn't ask the actual deaf guy, but understood as Levi shrugged and began to show him a few things.

"Who all is coming?" Kieran caught Eli's attention with a tap on his arm.

Turning back into his seat, he responded that Graham and Anthony were coming, of course. And he heard from Donna that she was dragging Brett there, too. "I don't know if Sonya and Angie are," he added, but felt a tap from the back seat on his arm.

Turning, Levi had leaned over to tell him that Angie's kids were coming so his mom and Lucy were going to be with them and Sonya, as well.

Eli nodded and turned back toward the front. "Guess it'll be the eight of us, then."

Kieran nodded and pulled onto the highway before laying his hand down on Eli's knee, like he had done many times over the past couple of weeks. Eli noticed it. Then looked over at Kieran, who didn't understand what he was looking at until he followed Eli's eyes down to his hand and abruptly pulled it away. Eli smiled.

Kieran was cute. But he'd need to get more comfortable doing something perfectly innocent. Besides — Eli glanced to the back seat — Danny had seen, he was sure. And he had resumed learning sign from Levi, seemingly not caring.

Eli saw Brett and Donna's Mercedes in the parking lot, idling, mist coming out of their exhaust. It was still a Benz, but now an SUV, different from the one Niles used to drive. Eli wondered if they'd traded it in specifically because of that. Probably.

"Eli!" Donna stepped out of the car and walked into his arms with her air kisses, but she stopped and turned to Kieran, doing the same. Brett stepped over and shook Kieran's hand before reaching for Eli's, but Eli pulled him into a hug. Brett wasn't getting away without one and, to Eli's surprise, gripped a bit tighter than he had anticipated. Eli wondered if Brett needed it. Probably.

"Levi —" Donna came over and welcomed him before turning to Danny. "My god, you look just like —" She turned toward Kieran, but Danny stated clearly, "I'm the good-looking one," and beamed.

Donna's eyes went up and then settled into her classic gaze, the one Eli knew meant she held respect. Danny was now in her club. Reaching over and putting her arm around him, she looked over at Kieran, who was standing next to Eli smiling. "I *like* this one."

Eli laughed along with everyone, taking the moment to quietly put his arm around Kieran's back while watching Danny's eyes. He noticed. Looked right into them, then over at Kieran, who was busy responding to Donna about something, then back to Eli. He knew there was something between the two of them. Probably.

Inside the shelter, it was already starting to hum along. Eli saw a line of people already forming around the outside, and a few workers were handing out tickets, he assumed, to get in. It wasn't terribly cold today, but he didn't want to stand outside too long himself.

"Well, hello, stranger!" A tall, sturdy older woman, probably pushing seventy, stepped up with a clipboard and glasses on those little chains that hung from them around her neck. She let them dangle across her chest as she welcomed them. "I'm so happy to see you again — Eli, right?"

He remembered her, although he couldn't place the name.

"Marjorie!" she answered without him asking, pointing to the *Hello, My Name is:* badge she was wearing.

Eli thought she understood. Most people who volunteered probably couldn't remember, especially if they were there once or twice a year.

Eli stepped over and gave her a hug. "Graham is coming, too, but I brought friends."

Eli introduced everyone, Marjorie handing them name badges to write on as he went. She stopped at Donna and admired her Christmas tree brooch pinned on her green cashmere sweater.

"It was Grandmother's. I thought it might be festive," Donna had said.

Marjorie seemed enamored with it. "Lovely," she simply said, but her eyes were fixated.

"I remember you!" Marjorie finally got to Levi and paused, looking up and down at him. "You were here last year. You've grown up." She spoke like a grandmother to him. Levi looked down like a grandson would. Eli wondered if Marjorie was going to mention he'd been on the receiving end of the line. But she simply welcomed him, and proceeded to give him an assignment.

"Donna, why don't you and your husband help work the room for me, clear tables, help me keep track of other volunteers to help our patrons find a seat, that sort of thing?" She handed Donna a clipboard and, from what Eli saw, power. Donna smiled, taking Brett's hand in hers.

"Eli — how about you and —"

"Kieran," he shared again.

"Yes — Kieran. Why don't you two help out on the line. Potatoes and corn. One healthy scoop." She walked them over to a supervisor already waiting for them.

Turning to Levi and Danny, she waved Donna over. "Donna, why don't these two help do the cleaning for you. Assign them to wipe tables, throw out trash, that sort of thing. That work?" Donna took charge without needing to be asked. Eli watched as she walked with the two boys to the wash station on the other side of the hall.

"Hold up, you old fool!"

Eli immediately saw Graham walking his way, followed by Anthony, who seemed to be trying to catch up.

"Graham!" Marjorie intercepted, surprising him she remembered his name. "Thank you for joining us again," she said before seeing Anthony step up beside him, a little out of breath.

"You look the spittin' image of Santa, you know that?" She didn't hesitate.

"You're much too kind, which is more than I can say for this lug." He pointed to Graham, who gave his classic smile that Eli knew meant he was enjoying every minute.

Marjorie stopped, as though an idea had just popped into her head. "I'm sorry, what's your name?"

"Anthony Atwood," he stated, trying to look at her clipboard to see if his name was present.

"Would you mind being a greeter? At the door." She pointed over to the main entrance that people had been waiting at. "It would be nice to have someone friendly like you to help direct people, answer questions. Especially for the children."

"Children?" Anthony asked innocently. Eli felt like he knew what that meant. Like Anthony had expected adults looking for a meal, that sort of thing. He had thought the same last year. Until he met Levi and Lucy.

"Well, unfortunately, yes. There'll be families coming. You can pretend to be Santa helping out, something like that. The kids will be scared enough, this big noisy place," Marjorie pointed all around the large warehouse-looking building.

"Oh," Anthony caught on, his demeanor suddenly transforming almost instantly as if he really were Santa Claus. "Yes, of course. Happy to."

"Just point them over to the line, show them where the bathrooms are," she pointed out locations. "If you have anything you don't know, just take this walkie-talkie here and call me, okay?" Anthony took the device and lifted it to his mouth, pretending he understood its usage.

Graham reached over and flipped the switch on for him, causing Anthony to pull it away, like it was his toy, not Graham's. Eli laughed and saw Kieran doing the same.

"Graham, why don't you join the prep crew?" Marjorie directed and began walking. He gave a little salute to Kieran and Eli while Anthony yelled out after him, "Don't burn the rolls!"

Eli loved those two.

"Let's get aprons on." Kieran took Eli's hand to walk toward the crew chief before realizing what he was doing, and let go. Eli shook his head and smiled. He was happy Kieran decided to join today. It felt right. Looking across the hall at Donna and Brett talking with Levi and Danny, he noticed they seemed to be paying attention to her words, her clipboard in hand.

He didn't know a lot about Danny, but he liked him. And he suspected Levi did too.

Probably.

They had taken turns, Eli on mashed potato duty while Kieran scooped out corn. Eli kept trying to show Kieran he needed to shake the juice off the serving spoon before placing the buttery kernels on the plates, but Kieran finally teased, "If you're the corn master, why don't *you* try then?" Eli accepted the challenge and they swapped spots.

Then Kieran began to tease Eli more, giving him a hard time like Eli had given him: "Make sure you shake the spoon more," and "We don't want corn soup on the plate, Eli," he'd say, and laugh. Eli had a mind to show him what else he could do with that spoon, but laughed along.

"Fine. Take your damn spoon back then. I'm on potatoes." He relented as Kieran giggled, swapping spots again.

"Am I going to have to separate you two?" Marjorie appeared, obviously delighted with them both.

"He made me do it!" Kieran joked, pointing to Eli like he was twelve and they'd been caught stealing candy.

Eli was about to land a joke in return when he noticed both Kieran and Marjorie looking over toward the entrance. Eli saw lots of people look their way.

Anthony stood there smiling as two small children practically climbed up him, excited.

"They think he's Santa," Kieran set the spoon down and signed. An older man who was waiting in line in front of them turned to look as well. "Those kids sure do look happy."

Eli saw Anthony full of laughter, the delight in his eyes, and a woman — he guessed the mother — attempted to pull her children back in line. Eli noticed Marjorie walking that direction before Kieran nudged him and nodded toward the man standing in line waiting on his potatoes.

"Sorry," Eli added before handing the plate to Kieran. The man smiled and walked along.

He grabbed the next plate as it came down the line, but looked up to see Donna pointing to a spot off in the back, and Levi rushing over to wipe the table down. Then Marjorie was walking with the little kids and their mother in that direction.

Looking back at the plate, he scooped potatoes on it and slid it over to Kieran before looking back out. This time, he saw Anthony walking in that direction as well. Eli looked over at the entrance, but someone else seemed to have taken his place.

Another plate slid his way, so he scooped another helping of potatoes on it and handed it off to Kieran, who caught his eyes and darted his own toward the hall. Eli noticed Marjorie had set Anthony at the table with the two little kids, their mom taking her coat off and speaking with her, looking exhausted.

Another plate. Another scoop. Another handoff to Kieran. This time Marjorie was gone when he looked up. Danny was over by Anthony now, the two kids on each side, one reaching up to touch Anthony's beard. Others were looking over at them.

Another plate.

"Go light on these next two, Eli." Marjorie appeared. "It's for the kids," she nodded back across the hall.

Eli split his scoop in half and handed it to Kieran, who had obviously been following along, and added a small serving to each. Eli watched her make her way down before moving onto the next plate. Looking up after, he saw Marjorie returning while Anthony seemed to be reading something to them. Someone had surfaced a book, he guessed. Maybe the mom. Maybe Marjorie. Donna was already over at the cleaning station talking with Brett while Danny was walking their way.

Another plate. Another serving.

"You two doing okay?" Danny walked up with a cleaning rag in his hands.

"How's Santa over there?" Kieran asked his brother, who looked over and smiled.

"The kids think he is the real deal."

"Maybe he is?" Kieran added before putting another serving on the plate Eli just passed him.

"I didn't realize little kids would be —"

"It's good you're here, Danny," Eli interjected. He didn't want him to finish that thought for some reason. Maybe because it felt like it shouldn't be that way. But he wasn't here to philosophize. The next plate arrived.

"You're wanted," Kieran told his kid brother, who turned and saw Brett waving for him. Looked like a spill needed cleaning. "See ya," he said, and walked that way.

Eli passed the next plate over and smiled at the man in front of him who looked like he was maybe twenty-five.

Kieran noticed and filled his plate before moving it down the line.

"It's sad," Kieran looked at Eli, speaking softly. Eli understood the gist. All he could do was nod.

They kept at the plates. Kept seeing more people coming down the line. Eli remembered thinking the same thing last year. How many people were actually coming today?

"Kieran, Eli — lunch!" Marjorie had yelled down the line.

Eli had put his spoon down as another volunteer stepped in to take over, but Kieran looked puzzled.

"C'mon, babe. Lunch," Eli said, not realizing how long he'd been on his feet, and how tired he was.

Kieran's eyes widened as Eli realized he had called him *babe* in front of the others. He shrugged. He was *babe,* and he was tired. And hungry, now that he thought of it. Grabbing Kieran's hand, he pulled him back toward the front of the line and took off his apron. He remembered volunteers stood in line right along with the patrons, no distinction.

Kieran followed his lead as they waited for a gap and then joined in front of a young couple who didn't look older than twenty. Eli wondered what their story was, but everyone here had a story, he figured, so he smiled and nodded. The guy nodded back while his girlfriend, sister, or whoever she was stood as if in a daze.

Eli pulled Kieran along behind an elderly man who clearly had trouble hearing. Eli saw him turn and wondered if he was deaf, or if his hearing loss was just due to aging. The volunteer had been asking what dressing he wanted for his salad, prepared Dixie cups with different types and was placing them on his tray, but he kept rotating his head and pointing to his ears.

Can I help? Eli signed, to see if he could understand.

The elderly man's eyes came alive, and he raised his shaky hands — dirt under the nails, frayed coat and too-short sleeves — and signed back. *You know how to speak?*

Eli smiled politely and signed *what dressing he'd like,* pointing down at the colored cups.

The man asked for ranch if they had it, and Eli followed along, translating for him while Kieran stood close behind, taking care of Eli's tray for him.

When they reached the end of the line, by the desserts, Eli reached over and grabbed both options for him before turning to see Danny standing right there, waiting to help with the tray. Eli turned to look at Kieran, guessing he'd called his brother over.

They followed him and sat down close, giving the older man space, but presence beside him if he wanted. He went about eating, not signing anything, only occasionally looking over at them.

Kieran kept looking over at the man, but Eli pointed to his plate and nodded, suggesting he eat. The man would chat if he wanted. Eli thought hard about that. Sometimes, it was nice to just be around.

"How's the turkey?" Eli asked Kieran. He had taken a slice of ham and was scooping up some potatoes to go along with it.

"Good, but I'm gonna be sleepy soon," Kieran smiled, still sneaking glances over at the older man just down the way.

Eli poked his hand lightly with his fork to get his attention and smiled. "You work tomorrow?"

"Off. But I'm on Saturday again."

"Want to stay tonight? It'll be late before we get out."

Kieran looked like he would melt, the warmth coming up from his eyes as he took another bite before answering.

"Danny's here, and —" his demeanor had changed, back into what Eli felt like was protective mode. Or closet mode.

"We can give him a lift home."

"Ma might see."

"We can drop him off. I don't have to come in."

"But then she'll ask where I'm going, and —"

"And what?"

Kieran set his fork down, looking slightly panicked. "Danny might say something. He doesn't *know*."

Eli gave him a *really?* look before seeing Danny cleaning a table two rows over. Eli locked eyes momentarily and nodded his head toward Kieran as if communicating *Your brother is something else.* Danny straightened up and walked their way.

"Slacking off?" Danny surprised Kieran, who almost jumped. Eli grinned, catching Danny sharing in the same delight.

"Aren't you supposed to be working?"

"I am. Taking the trash out. C'mon." He pulled at his brother's sleeve, but Kieran slapped him off. Eli had to laugh. They were funny together, just like he imagined a brother would be.

"We can give you a lift home tonight, if you want, Danny," Eli boldly stated.

"I thought Sean was picking us up," Danny asked Kieran, who latched onto that forgotten fact and presented it back to Eli.

"Yeah, Sean said he'd pick us up when we're done. Just call."

"Well, don't call. We can drop Danny off and you can stay tonight." Eli fixed that little problem and did so right in front of Danny. Kieran looked like he was about to throw up.

"You okay?" Danny sat down next to him and put the cleaning rag on the table to pull his brother his way.

"I'm fine," Kieran pushed him off, but Danny looked over at Eli, confused.

"I was just suggesting Kieran could —" Eli was sharing the truth with Danny, but Kieran interrupted him.

"It's fine, Eli. Maybe next time," he pleaded almost, and nodded slightly toward Danny.

"I don't mind," Danny offered. "I mean, if you want to hang out with Eli tonight. That's cool with me."

Kieran whipped his head toward his brother, surprised.

"Ma would ask all sorts of questions, and —"

"I'll tell her for ya," Danny offered.

"It's okay."

"It's no big deal, Kier —"

"Some other time, Danny!" Kieran shot him down quickly, and then apologized, quietly. "Sorry."

Danny gave Eli a look, and then held his hands up like pleading for truce. "I'm gonna get back to work." He grabbed his cleaning rag and left, giving Eli an *I'm on your side* look.

Eli reached over and tapped Kieran's hand lightly, making him jitter. "I don't mean to push, but — I kinda do, too, babe."

Kieran nodded and looked around, as if to scout for anyone watching. No one was, everyone consumed in their own meals, stories, lives.

"I'm sorry, Eli. I really want to stay. I'm just —"

Eli was tempted to tell him it was okay. Don't worry. But he'd learned not to interrupt people, even when they were silently asking you to. Sometimes, it helped to let them resolve the thought on their own.

"I'm just scared, is all."

Eli nodded, pushing aside the plate.

Kieran looked around, and then reached over and grabbed his hand and squeezed. "I promise. I won't keep you waiting on me. I just — need to figure this out."

"I'm not going anywhere, babe."

Eli saw Kieran's lips pinch up as if he were holding something back, but something distracted his peripheral vision.

Looking over, he saw the older man signing to him. *I'm finished.*

Eli smiled. *Good?*

Good.

Eli waved for Levi, who was standing next to Donna, to come up and clean. Kieran helped the older man up, but he waved him off. Kieran signed *Nice to meet you.* But the old man was already walking out.

Eli touched Kieran's back to get his attention and signed *You made a difference.*

Kieran simply nodded.

Marjorie appeared just as Eli and Kieran were standing, asking Kieran to take over for his brother while Eli went back to mashed potato duty. Eli gave Kieran a quick squeeze on his arm and resumed his earlier post next to a woman who could've been his own grandma, but spent more time talking with the lady next to her than him, which was fine. He was busy watching Danny and Levi sitting together for their meal, not so ironically taking over the same spots he and Kieran just had. They appeared to be laughing about something, both looking over at Kieran and teasing him.

Eli smiled as he scooped potatoes on plates and continued watching.

They were fitting in. Such a different sight from last year, when Levi was so quiet, almost scared.

He remembered walking with Lucy that day. She had wanted pie, he recalled, and glanced down at the same location where desserts stood now, remembering how full of energy she was. He was already *Uncle Eli* to her even then. But Levi, he remembered, had been enamored with Graham and his stories. Eli hadn't put together at that point that Graham was *the author* who made such an impact on him.

Eli looked back over his shoulder toward the kitchen, where Graham was laughing with someone over rolls he'd just taken out of the oven. He wondered if they knew Graham was a famous author. Probably not. Graham didn't work that way.

He scooped more potatoes onto a tray and saw Kieran wiping down a table just over the way, giving him a look with that sly smile of his that seemed to steal his heart without trying. Last year volunteering, he felt, was special. He'd met and been touched by so many people, just in this place alone. And now he couldn't help but feel the same.

More potatoes. More people coming through the line. More of Anthony with other kids who arrived delighted to see Santa. More hope for someone he knew he was falling in love with in a completely different way than Niles.

He looked over at Donna, who had stood next to Brett and rested her hand on his arm briefly, Brett smiling for the first time since — since he could remember.

He stole another glance at Levi and Danny, who had gone from laughter into a quieter conversation, but endearing. Like they were sharing something important.

Perhaps they were.

Chapter Seventeen

KIERAN LAY in his bed staring up at the ceiling, at the faded glow-in-the-dark stickers of stars and planets he had placed there back when he was fourteen and thought it'd be cool. His ma was off to church and then some *window shopping* with two of her church friends, she had said last night when he got home. Black Friday was amusing to her — she just enjoyed people-watching. But he knew she got in there to bargain with the rest of them. He'd explained he'd probably be gone when she got home, but had been evasive when she pressed where he was going.

He hated lying to her. So he tried to convince himself that not telling her the truth wasn't the same as lying. It still felt like it, though. But she didn't press. Just gave him a look he knew too well. The same look she gave him when he tried to convince her he didn't know what she was talking about, when she'd asked why he was suddenly interested in doing his own laundry at age thirteen. She knew. She always knew.

"You going to El's today?"

Kieran looked over at Danny, who had opened his door and stood in a pair of sweatpants and a tank, like he just got out of bed.

"You ever knock?"

"No. So, are you?"

"Maybe. Why?"

"Just checking if I had the house today."

"Throwing a party?"

Danny gave his brother an *uh, sure* gaze.

"Probably. I gotta text him."

Danny came in and sat on his bed, Kieran still lying under his blanket.

"I like Eli. He's funny."

Kieran didn't respond. Wasn't sure what to say.

"How come you didn't stay there last night?"

Kieran looked up at Danny like he'd gone mad.

"What?"

"You know — I could've told ma somethin'," Danny pressed.

"Why are you —" Kieran began, but Danny pushed.

"I noticed you get a stick up your ass whenever someone mentions anything about —"

"Do not!" Kieran sat up, the blanket falling down from his chest.

"Fine. Jeez. I was just tryin' to help." Danny stood and left his room.

Kieran watched him go and felt guilty. He always got along well with Danny. They'd team up against Sean sometimes, Danny always taking his side on things, but there was never any bad blood. And he never yelled at him, even if Danny was being stupid about something. Danny was the more daredevil of the two, but Kieran knew he had to look out for him. He was the responsible one.

This sudden interest in Eli, though, scared him. It was like Danny was on to him. Knew. And was teasing him, or pushing to see if he'd spill.

Kieran got out of bed and pulled on a pair of shorts and a t-shirt, but changed into flannel pajama bottoms after feeling the chill of the house.

Danny was sitting at the kitchen table eating a Pop-Tart and staring at nothing. He didn't look up when Kieran walked in and grabbed one of his own, before pouring a glass of milk and sitting next to him. For a while, they both sat eating the pastry, Danny looking at nothing, Kieran looking at his brother.

"What?" Danny finally looked over and asked, seemingly perturbed.

Kieran felt himself push back in the kitchen chair. Danny seemed — angry.

"Nothing — sorry."

"You know, you piss me off sometimes, Kieran." Danny set his Pop-Tart down on the kitchen tablecloth.

Kieran wondered where this was coming from. How? What had he done?

"And the thing is, you don't even realize, do you?"

It was like Danny knew exactly what was going on in Kieran's mind.

"I see things, Kieran. I'm not stupid."

Kieran sat still, looking over at Danny.

"I know Eli is your —" He paused, taking a huff of air like he was priming for an explosion.

"Danny, he's just —"

"Don't, Kieran. Don't tell me he's just a friend. That's bullshit and you know it. *I* know it."

His stomach dropped. His heart began to pump like he was running up a mountain.

"And you know what? I don't care. *I like Eli.* He's nice and he *obviously* likes you. So — what's the problem, Kieran? Why are you lying to me?"

Kieran went still. A million thoughts flew in and out of his brain in milliseconds, and all he could do was flail around inside, trying to catch any one of them — something to tell Danny.

"I'm your brother. I tell you *everything*, Kieran."

Kieran's lip began to quiver and he felt like he was falling off the cliff, desperately trying to grab on to something to keep from going over.

"You're gay? So what? Who gives a shit? Because I don't. Never have."

Never have? Kieran thought. Did Danny always know?

"And the thing is, Kieran, it's your business, so I never pushed. But I *saw* you two yesterday. And I hate that someone who obviously loves you — you're treating like shit."

Loves?

A fire ignited inside him. That Callahan Irish temper Kieran usually controlled had jumped the fence.

"Bullshit. I saw how you kept pulling away from him. I saw you hold hands and then freak out when you thought I noticed."

"I was —"

"Being a pussy. That's what you were."

"You don't know what —"

"Levi and I both watched. Talked about it yesterday even. *He knows.*"

"You talked with Levi?" Kieran couldn't believe his world was crumbling.

"What do you think I am? Some dumb little kid? Levi's like his little brother. 'Course he knows."

"What — what did he say?" Kieran's anger was being put out, fear taking its place.

"Not much, other than you seemed like some scared little kid whenever I'm around. He saw it too."

Kieran looked down at the table, unsure what to do.

"You're not gonna tell ma, are you?"

"You really think I would? C'mon. You know me better than that. God, it's like you're all stupid 'cause you like some guy —"

"Eli isn't just *some guy*, Danny."

"Sorry." He stopped and then looked back at Kieran. "You're right. Eli *isn't* just some guy. And you need to treat him better."

"I don't treat him bad. I love him, for Christ's sake!" He screamed it out and then cried, holding his eyes like he would as a child.

Danny got quiet.

Kieran felt his hand rest on his shoulder and looked up, trying to wipe his eyes, fully embarrassed.

"Have you told him?"

Kieran shook his head.

"Why?" Danny seemed to be calmer, concerned.

"Because I'm fucking scared, Danny. I don't want to fuck this up. And ma'd kill me if she knew, and —" He rested his head back into his hands and sobbed.

Kieran felt Danny's arms around him. He must have gotten up and held onto him standing behind the kitchen chair.

"It's okay, Kieran. Ma's not gonna kill you."

"Yes she will, Danny. She'd think I'm going to hell, and — that'd kill her, Danny." He couldn't stop shaking.

"No it won't, Kieran."

He stayed that way, sobbing, until finally he calmed down. He had been trying to figure out a way he could do this, love Eli, but keep his ma happy. And he kept drawing blanks. Now Danny knew. And he still was no closer to figuring this shit out, he realized. All he'd done was made a fool of himself sobbing in front of his little brother.

Danny sat back in his spot and looked at Kieran, but it was hard to look back. It was like Danny had x-ray vision. He knew everything.

"Kieran?" Danny's softer voice returned, the one he normally used. Kieran didn't say anything, just stared across the table at his ma's mending pile she worked on during the day.

"I think you should tell Eli."

Kieran listened. Mulled his words. Felt sick to his stomach that he was unable to respond to all this.

"I have."

He noticed Danny's eyes lighting up. "He knows you love him?"

"No — I mean — maybe — I haven't —"

"I'm confused."

"I told him about ma and all —"

"No, I meant tell him you love him."

"Why?"

"Why? What do you mean, why?" Danny's voice elevated slightly. Kieran seemed to sink down again.

"If I do, it's not like I can bring him home and say, *Hey, ma! I want you to meet my boyfriend!*" he spat out.

"You don't have to. But — wait. Is he your boyfriend? Like for real?"

Kieran nodded.

"Then *tell him you love him,*" he said, pushing at Kieran's arm. "You *do* love him, right?"

Kieran nodded, but added, "You don't understand —"

"I understand more than you realize, Kieran," Danny interjected, and Kieran looked fully at his brother. Danny's eyes were showing more than before. Like he had more to share.

"He won't wait forever, you know."

Kieran began to tear up again. He knew. That's what he worried about.

"Forget ma, I think Eli deserves to know."

"You're right. He does. But — ma will —"

"Forget *her*, Kieran. You can deal with her later."

"I can't just leave the family, Danny."

"No, but I know — and am cool with it."

"What about Sean? Huh? And — well — ma?"

"Sean probably already knows. Besides, his girlfriend's brother is gay. *You know that.* He doesn't give two shits about who you fuck."

"Danny!"

"What? It's true." Danny pushed, but began to smile. Kieran hated when he made him smile while he was trying to be serious.

"I'll help!" Danny sat upright and offered.

"Help? How?"

"I dunno. I'll — uh — I'll tell ma I'm gay, so when you do she'll be over the shock already."

"Danny! Quit being stupid." Kieran pushed back and looked back at the table trying to think this through.

"I'm serious, Kierp. We'll figure it out, okay? Quit worrying so much."

The old nickname caught him sideways. Kieran just looked at him and then resumed trying to sort his thoughts.

"I'm gonna go shower."

"Going somewhere?"

"I dunno. Maybe."

"Where?"

"Told Levi I'd DM him, maybe do something. Don't have school."

Kieran nodded, not really thinking about that.

Danny got up and began to walk out of the kitchen. "Kieran?"

"Hmm?"

"I think you should go over to Eli's and tell him."

Kieran looked down. He wanted to. Maybe he could.

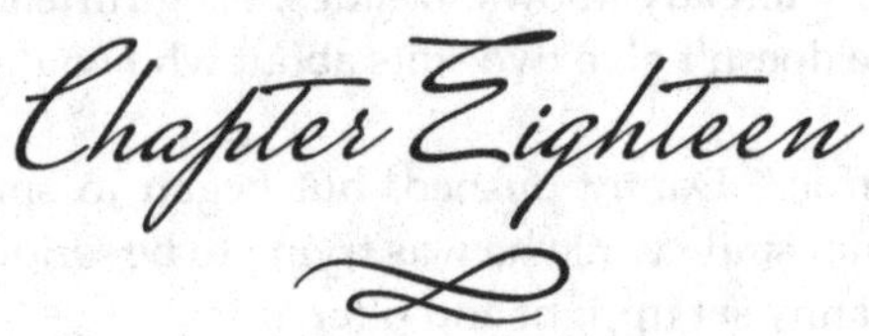

Chapter Eighteen

You awake?

DANNY TEXTED Levi before he got out of bed. He'd been learning a lot about Levi over the past three weeks since they met. Like Levi loved Twizzlers. So did Danny. Levi hated math. Danny did, too. Oh, and Levi sucked at Super Mario Odyssey when they'd played in Danny's room last week. Danny could whoop his ass any day, but he understood why now.

They'd gotten into a long discussion two nights ago after everyone went to bed. Kieran still hadn't gotten home from Eli's, he was sure, and he sat up in his bed messaging Levi, not wanting to stop even though they both had school in the morning. He didn't care, because Levi was finally telling him about living in a car, not knowing much about his dad, heavy shit.

He remembered saying something stupid about homeless people when he first met him on their way to that Thanksgiving dinner thing. God, he felt like a dumb fuck. No wonder Levi was all weird.

least ur cool now right???

LEVI

I guess

I mean ur not like gonna b like that again

Never thought wed be like that b4

Danny felt like someone slapped the shit outta him. *Guess not,* he thought. He'd always just assumed he'd have his room. They were poor, he knew, and he really hated that, especially in seventh grade when he didn't have whatever bullshit shoes everyone else was wearing. But he decided then it didn't matter anyway. He'd fuck someone up if they gave him shit. No one did. Not to his face, at least.

But Levi? Living in a car. Goddamn.

im sorry

dont be I dont like when ppl say that

Danny nodded. He could see that in him. Guessed he'd be the same way, too.

wanna come over again?

Danny changed the subject because he wasn't sure what else to say. He just felt like he wanted to say something.

I guess or you could come here if you want u dont have to tho

no thats gas.

really???

Now it was Saturday morning and he was sure Levi would still be asleep, but he tried anyway.

hey

just wake up?

LEVI

still asleep

ur cappin

Levi sent a smile emoji.

up for me comin' over?

bet

Danny watched as Levi was messaging something else.

u driving?

They had talked that first week about Levi finally getting his license. Eli had helped. He even used Eli's car to take the test. But he didn't have a car of his own and insurance was too much for him to pay to drive his mom's car.

Danny was in the same boat. He'd been driving for over a year now, but Sean wasn't gonna let him take out his truck. He'd be gone anyway. And Kieran only had his bike. Besides, it was freezing outside.

ll catch d bus

uber

$$$

imma jump in d shower

u don't have to jump Skip is fine

Danny smiled.

ur so funny Im ded

Levi sent a tongue sticking out emoji, but Danny quickly followed with an eggplant.

big yikes

Levi added a wide-eyes emoji that made Danny laugh aloud.

cya

Danny got himself ready and told his mom he was heading up to Levi's. She remembered him from last week. Said she liked him. Seemed very polite. Asked if he was Catholic, her usual spiel. Levi played it cool, Danny thought. His mom even invited him to come along to church with Danny sometime, if he'd like. Danny laughed afterwards when they were in his room. *She's super churchy sometimes,* he apologized, but Levi was cool. Said she was nice. He liked her.

"Remember to invite him to Midnight Mass next week, Danny," she'd said.

"Mom!"

"What? He doesn't have to convert. And it's a *nice mass,* Danny. He might enjoy it."

"He probably has stuff going on with his mom."

"Is something troubling his home?" She became concerned.

"No — I meant — Jeez, mom. It's gonna be Christmas. He's probably got like — I dunno — Santa and stuff, you know?"

"Does his father live with them?" she asked, lowering her voice, like she always did when referring to his own father.

"No," he replied, and then added before she asked, "and I don't know the details. He said it's just his mom and little sister."

"I know what that's like," she muttered, but Danny heard it.

"Can I go now?"

"Don't be fussin', young man. You may be almost eighteen, but I'm still your mother."

"Yes, ma."

She gave him a peck on his head and called after him as he put on his coat. "Here, take this," handing him a $10 bill. "For the bus. And you text me when you get there. It's cold out."

Danny thought about his mom on the way. He had to transfer, so it took a little longer than he expected, but he didn't care. They had all day. He couldn't remember if Kieran had to work today. He was gone already when Danny left. Maybe he went over to Eli's?

He hadn't said a lot about him since Thanksgiving. Danny sorta felt bad; every time he saw him come home at night, he'd go over to his room and ask about Eli. But he didn't push too hard. He knew that it was probably terrifying thinking about telling their ma he was gay. Kieran was always the worrier compared to him. Danny worried sometimes, but usually if he was going to pass a pop quiz, shit like that. His ma? Not really. He loved her, of course. And he'd never pull some shit to get her going. But his gut didn't think she'd care too much. Well, maybe she wouldn't care if Eli were Catholic. He laughed a little. He didn't know. Never asked. But his gut told him Eli wasn't.

Sometimes, he just wanted to tell her, *Ma, Kieran is afraid to say it, but he has a boyfriend and is terrified you're gonna hate him.* He'd imagined her, alone at the kitchen table while he ate lunch and she watched, saying something like that to her. And she'd ask all sorts of questions and get herself worried because her precious baby Kieran was all freaked out. Danny giggled to himself. *He* was the baby of the three brothers, but she treated Kieran like he was. Maybe she always knew Kieran was the more — what'd they call it? Sensitive?

Not Danny. Not really. He'd just tell her. *Ma, I'***m gay. And here***'s my boyfriend...* He stopped in his mini-charade because he almost said *Levi.*

Huh.

"Hey!"

Danny stepped off the bus down the block to find Levi waiting. He'd messaged him when he was almost there, but didn't expect to see him standing right there in the cold.

"Took you long enough," Levi nudged him while keeping his hands in his coat pockets, shivering. Danny nudged back and smiled, following Levi as he walked back up the street.

"We had like fifteen million stops," Danny explained, but Levi cut him off — "blah blah blah" — and giggled, his breath freezing in the air around them.

"I'm gonna get you!" Danny reached over to grab Levi, but he took off running ahead, Danny following, laughing. He felt like a boy playing tag, Levi giggling as he turned the corner by some shrubs and got a lead on Danny, but he didn't let up.

Finally, Levi ran past a cottage home and around the side to a barn-like house where he stopped, out of breath. Danny followed him up the stairs, breathing heavy and feeling the cold.

"Mom, he's here," Levi yelled out as he entered the warm house, Danny behind.

He hadn't thought about Levi's mom being home. Just then a little girl came running up to him, jumping. "Are you Levi's friend?"

"Lucy — go away!" Levi yelled at her while unbuttoning his coat.

"Yep. I'm Danny," he said, standing still, his coat, hat, and gloves still on, his face still cold from outside. But his glasses fogged so he suddenly couldn't see.

"You look funny!" Lucy giggled.

"Lucy, mind your manners." Danny heard from someone as he took off his glasses to see Levi's mom walking his way.

"Hi, Levi. Cold outside?"

Danny was amused. She was like most adults — stating the obvious in the form of a question. But he was gonna be on his best behavior. This was the first time meeting her.

"It's freezing!" He hugged himself and danced a little, causing Lucy to laugh. Levi had already stripped his coat and gloves off and was starting to reach for his hat when his mom admonished him for not helping Danny.

"Mom, he's almost eighteen. I think he can take off his own coat."

Danny smiled. He was just like him with his own mother.

"I'm so glad I didn't have twins," she rolled her eyes and extended her hand to Danny. "I'll hang your coat up. Want some hot chocolate or something warm? Do you drink coffee?"

"I'm okay, Mrs. —"

"Susan. We're not fancy around here," she smiled and reached for his hat as he removed it.

"Thanks," he said, and looked over at Levi who looked like he was ready to move out of this little family gathering.

"Are you and Levi gonna play with each other?" Lucy asked innocently.

Danny nearly coughed, looking over at Levi whose eyes bulged.

"Lucy, leave them be. Let's get ready to head to Mrs. Claus'. We got to make the gingerbread house for next week, remember?"

Mrs. Claus? Danny asked himself and gave Levi a confused look.

"I'll tell you later," Levi said aloud.

"Very nice to meet you, Danny. Make yourself at home."

"Thanks, Mrs. — uh — Susan. Bye, Lucy."

"Bye, Danny!" She ran up and hugged his legs before Levi took Danny's hand to drag him away down the hall. Danny looked back as Susan was starting to help put on Lucy's coat when he heard Lucy say *I like Danny.*

Me too, Lucy Bell, Levi's mom replied.

Inside Levi's room, he stood by his small bed and pointed out the few things he had to decorate. It wasn't as done up as Danny's, but then again, Danny thought, he had lived in his room for years.

"What's this?" Danny walked to Levi's desk and picked up a library book with a clear plastic cover over it.

"Just a book I'm re-reading."

Danny read aloud: "The Oltrarno Series: The Hours of San Frediano. By Graham Tierney."

He looked over at Levi. "Re-reading?"

"Yeah. I wanted to go back and — well — it's a long story."

"Hey wait. Isn't uh —" Danny flipped to the title page inside, pointing to Graham's name. "Didn't someone say Eli's roommate Graham writes, too?" He looked over at Levi.

"That's him."

"No shit?"

Levi smiled. "No shit."

"Damn. I didn't know he was — that's bussin'."

"You're funny," Levi sat on his bed and leaned against the wall. Danny sat down as well, still holding the book.

"Why?"

Levi shrugged.

Danny flipped to the back and saw Graham's picture. "I had no idea he was famous. That's like so extra."

Levi giggled again.

Danny set the book back and leaned over toward Levi. "You're like the giggly monster," he teased, smiling.

"You just make me laugh."

Danny looked down. He liked making Levi laugh. He thought he was too serious, too often.

"So, whatcha wanna do?" Danny laid back on Levi's bed looking up at the ceiling, taking in his room.

"Dunno. We could play cards or something."

"Ehhh."

"Or maybe, uh —"

"I should've brought my Switch. Didn't think of it."

"Why? So you could beat my ass at Mario?" Levi teased and kicked Danny gently with his socks from the head of his bed where he was sitting upright.

Danny reached over and grabbed them and began to tickle, causing Levi to squirm and laugh. Danny loved it, but let go.

"I'm gonna get you!" Levi blasted out mid-laugh-recovery, but Danny just smiled before sitting upright and turning to sit cross-legged facing him.

"Let's play 2 Truths and a Lie."

"What's that?" Levi asked.

"I say two things about me that are true and one lie, and you have to guess which one I'm lying about. If you're right, you get a point. We go back and forth until someone gets like — I dunno — five or something."

"Okay," Levi sat upright and crossed his legs to match Danny's, leaning slightly forward.

"I'll start."

"What if I want to start?" Levi teased.

"Well, then you start."

"I just said *what if?* Not that I wanted to."

"I'm gonna tickle you again," Danny leaned over with his hands outstretched, but Levi leaned back already giggling.

"Fine — I'll go," Danny began. "Uh, I am a senior in high school. I own a boat. And I know how to whistle."

"That's easy. You're lying about the boat."

Danny let out a buzzing noise and quickly said, "Wrong! I have a rowboat up at my grandpa's. I can't whistle worth shit." He puckered his lips and blew, but a waft of air was the only thing that came out. Levi laughed.

"One point for me," Danny gleamed. "Your turn."

"Okay. Uh —" Levi thought for a moment before starting. "I'm a junior. I love dancing. And I write stories."

"Oh, this is too easy," Danny's eyes went wide, Levi's smile brightened daring him to guess. "You don't dance."

This time Levi let out the buzzing noise and laughed.

"You actually dance?" Danny was incredulous.

Levi jumped up laughing, did a little shake with his butt and a few movements Danny was sure he'd learned off a TikTok video, then resumed his position back on the bed.

Danny loved it. Levi was so cute doing that.

"So, you don't write stories?"

"Nope. I just read them."

"Huh. I could've sworn you did."

"Nope. Maybe someday. Dunno."

"I think you'd be good. You should talk to Graham, since he is one, ya know?"

Levi shrugged. "Your turn."

"Okay — uh —" Danny thought of another lie. "Okay, I've got one. I love Twizzlers —"

"I *already know that*."

"Fine," Danny laughed. "Okay — how about — uhm — I'm single, never kissed anyone, and I'm gay."

Levi's eyes went wide. Danny smiled. He wanted to push a little.

"What's your guess?" Danny asked.

Levi looked down at his socks and picked at the lint rubbing off one before answering.

"Uh — I — I don't know."

Danny leaned over and touched his hand, causing him to look up.

"Guess."

Levi took a breath. "Okay, but — I might get it wrong, so don't like hate me or anything, okay?"

"Then I'll get a point, no problem."

Levi bit his lip for a moment and then answered: "You're — uh — gay?" He spoke the last word so softly, Danny had to strain to hear him.

Danny leaned back and, once again, gave the buzzing sound. "Wrong."

Levi looked up.

"You're not gay?"

"No, dingus. I AM. *That*'s my lie."

Levi's eyes widened, a small smile forming like he was finally getting it. Danny honestly didn't care. He hadn't even come out to himself until just now, but it seemed like a *who gives a shit* moment to him. He was waiting for what came next.

"Uh — that's uh — cool — I — uh —" Levi was acting like it wasn't a big deal.

Danny watched.

"You never kissed anyone?"

"That's true. Never made out." Danny made little kissing sounds and puckered his lips.

Levi laughed and threw a pillow at him, making Danny laugh alongside him.

"Wait up. That means —" Danny watched Levi piece his lie together, anticipating his reaction, like he was opening a Christmas present.

"You're not single?" Levi suddenly looked stunned. "I — I thought —"

Danny noticed him looking almost devastated. He quickly leaned over and reached for Levi's hand, switching gears.

"Levi. Levi, I meant — I meant I was single until today."

Levi looked up at him still on the verge of being upset, but now confused.

"I mean —" Danny took a breath. He thought this would be fun, but now he felt like he was trying to steer a car without brakes.

"Listen, Levi — I was just trying to say — uh — I — well — I thought maybe we could — you know — be — *a thing*."

Danny looked up slowly to read Levi's eyes.

They morphed right before him. From upset, to shock, to understanding. Danny felt his hands soften from squeezing too hard, and then Levi's thumbs began rubbing gently against his finger.

"Really?" Levi asked.

Danny nodded.

Levi bit at his lip, Danny noticing his eyes water a bit.

"You're not playing with me?"

"No, Levi. I'm not."

"Cause — someone — well — I wanted to be — with someone before — but — he —"

"I'm not him."

Danny didn't know all of Levi's story. He had been cagey about it. Danny had been asking over the past few weeks if Levi had someone. He pegged him for being gay from the first day they met, but didn't care. Made him realize it about himself. But he never got the whole *it's a thing* business with coming out. You just were who you were, is all.

But he felt there was more to it with Levi. Like, he should be a little more careful. Pay attention.

Danny looked over at Levi who looked like he wanted to laugh and smile, but cry at the same time. He reached up his right hand and cupped Levi's face gently. Leaned in and kissed him. Lightly. But a kiss. His first.

Levi gave a half laugh, half breath like he'd been holding it, causing Danny to smile. "You're really cute when your lip curls up like that."

"Does not," Levi turned away embarrassed, but looked back and wiped his eyes. Danny just beamed at him, still holding his hand.

After a moment, Levi looked back at him and asked, "So — like — are we —"

Danny nodded. "If you want to be."

Levi nodded looking down a little shy.

"So, we're a thing," Danny announced.

"A thing," Levi repeated and smiled.

Danny leaned back, his legs cramping from leaning over on them too long, but Levi refused to let go of his hands, grinning as he pulled him back like a rocking horse and into his lips.

Levi kissed him quickly as Danny fell backwards again, this time Levi giving him a little push so he rolled onto his back. Levi laughed, but Danny leaned over, grabbed his hands, and pulled him on top of him, both giggling until they settled, Danny laying flat, Levi resting on top, his head falling down onto Danny's chest.

"This is like fucked up," Levi said. Danny's ears perked. He said the word *fuck* a billion times. Well, not around his ma, but between Sean, Kieran, and him, he was the grand master of the f-word. But he couldn't really remember hearing Levi cuss much beyond *shit* or stupid words he didn't even pay attention to.

"What's fucked up?" He rubbed little circles around Levi's back while staring up at his bedroom ceiling.

"Us. Like — is this real?"

Danny grinned. "Hope so."

Levi leaned up and looked at him. "Really? You're not like gonna bail on me or anything, right?"

Danny noticed Levi wasn't playing. "No!" He almost asked why he'd even say that, but remembered him earlier and thought one of Levi's stories probably explained it. He'd maybe get to hear it one day. But he wasn't gonna push.

"Levi?" He looked up at him towering over, his hair hanging around his head. They couldn't have been more opposite with hair styles, Danny's short just like Kieran's, while Levi's was longer, almost like — like Eli's, he now realized, and let out a little laugh.

"What?"

"Just thinking — your hair is like Eli's, and mine is like my brother's." Danny let in on his thoughts. Levi grinned.

"You're cuter."

Danny lit up, rolling Levi to the side, who fell over laughing while Danny switched spots, looking down on top of him. "I'mma tell him you said that," he laughed while holding his arms. Levi began play-struggling, but Danny was holding on tight.

"No! I'll deny it in court."

"Levi?" Danny got serious, Levi followed suit.

"Mmm?"

"I don't know what the fuck I'm doing. I just realized I like you a lot not thirty minutes ago. I mean — I knew before — but — you know?"

Levi looked at him. If he did know, Danny couldn't tell.

"I never really thought about liking another guy, you know. I mean — I didn't care or anything. Just never came up. But — there's just something about you that — I dunno — makes me —"

"Hard?" Levi laughed at his own joke.

Danny was stunned for a second before recovering. He'd misjudged him. "I thought you were like the shyest guy who never said anything when I first met you." He looked back at Levi who was smiling, staring a hole in him.

"But that was obviously bullshit," Danny teased, and Levi laughed. "*You*'re worse than me!"

"Am not!"

"Are too." Danny leaned down and pressed his lips to Levi's to settle it once and for all. This time, he let them stay for a while. Testing it out. He'd not really known how to do this, but he was figuring it out. Levi's hands came up to his short hair and began pulling his head closer, like he was seeing how long they'd go.

Eventually, he let go and Danny pushed himself back up, looking down at Levi. His lips seemed plumper, red. Wet. And his eyes — they were so relaxed. He'd never seen Levi look like that before. Like he was truly happy. For real.

"I'm happy I met you," Levi whispered.

"Me too," Danny said.

A moment passed and Levi said, "You're happy you met yourself?" Then his smile curled up and he began laughing at his own stupid joke.

"That's it!" Danny began to tickle Levi who squirmed and kicked until he got out from under him and fell off the bed, landing on his butt on the floor laughing. Danny plopped down to join him, both sitting with their backs to his bed looking at the underside of Levi's desk. Danny's hand found Levi's as they sat there listening to nothing but each other breathe.

"You gonna tell your brother?" Levi finally asked, relaxing his head on Danny's shoulder.

"Guess so. Is that cool?"

"Yeah, I don't care. I'm out."

"You are?"

"Duh." Levi lifted his head and turned to say, like it was that obvious.

"I knew, but I didn't know — if you know what I mean," Danny laughed and Levi returned his head to Danny's shoulder.

"Eli helped me a lot."

"Yeah?"

"Mmhmm. I really feel for him, especially after —"

"After what?"

Levi sat up and looked at Danny. "You didn't know?"

"Know what?"

Danny listened for the next few minutes as Levi gave him the lowdown on everything that happened with him and Niles. He mentioned Michael not being able to come to the funeral. How everything played out.

"Oh my god, I didn't know," he kept saying, and "I can't imagine what he —" without being able to finish. But it really hit when he put everything together. "Wait. Kieran was the paramedic who —" Danny couldn't bring himself to finish the thought. Levi nodded.

"I think so. I never asked Eli, but some things he said, I guess that's how it happened. He was at the funeral."

"He was?" Danny looked over at Levi, unsure if he had known somehow and forgotten. If Kieran had said it. Maybe he had, like he sometimes talked about work, but Danny hadn't put two and two together. Or maybe he hadn't. But now, all the puzzle pieces clicked into place.

"Jesus Christ. I never realized how —" Danny kept thinking about his brother holding all that in. Only to fall in love with Eli. He wondered if Kieran finally got the balls to tell him. Jesus. No wonder he'd been all fucking weird with this.

"I tried to help, but —" Levi continued, unaware of Danny's conversation with his brother about Eli. "I sometimes don't know what to do." Danny looked over at him. He had his own shit and he was still trying to help Eli? Wow. Danny felt like his own stupid problems were nothing.

He thought about *Kierp.* Hadn't called his brother that in months. He could feel it sitting there now, wanting out.

"I remember back when I was two, I couldn't say my brother's name. Kieran. Came out as Kierp, which sounds stupid, but it stuck."

Levi looked over.

"Don't say it much. Just — when shit's bad."

"Like now?"

"Yeah. Today's a Kierp day." Danny gave a small smile. "He calls me DanDan. Same deal."

Levi nodded, like he'd been handed something he understood was small and rare.

"It's why when I caught them on Halloween making out, I —"

"What?" Danny stopped him. He was learning all sorts of stuff about his brother he never thought of. He couldn't imagine his sweet, little, nice, kind, gonna-be-a-priest-maybe-one-day Kieran, ma's favorite, making out with Eli. Oh, this was too much. "You saw them?" he asked, more incredulous, but happy for some weird reason. Like maybe he had his brother all wrong. He wasn't the saint he always mocked him for being, and he loved the idea.

Levi looked down again, embarrassed. "I wasn't trying to. I just —"

"Uh huh. So you were jerkin' it watching my brother and Eli," Danny teased, laughing, but Levi punched him in the arm and laughed along. "WAS NOT! Perv!" Danny loved seeing Levi like this.

"No! We were at a party and —"

"You went to a party with Kieran and Eli?" Danny imagined some rave at a warehouse.

"Not *like that.* God! You're my boyfriend for like five seconds and then —"

"Hold up." Danny put his hand up, stopping Levi mid-sentence. "*Boyfriend?*"

Levi looked at him as if second-guessing something. "Well, we *are.*" He looked right into Danny's eyes. "*Aren*'t we?"

Danny's grin came up, making his eyes squint, nodding.

That earned another arm punch from Levi before he laughed.

"Damn. You're strong."

"And you're cute."

"So, we're perfect together," Danny laughed and nudged Levi who settled back into resting his head on Danny's shoulder.

"I feel for Eli," Danny spoke quietly.

"Me too," Levi agreed. "But I think he really is doing a lot better with Kieran now."

Danny imagined his older brother right now at work. Wondering if he was texting Eli between runs. Wondering what Eli was thinking about him. Wondering if he could do something to get his brother over the hump. And he got an idea.

Without moving, Danny began to tell Levi about his ma. Levi had met her. Already knew she was uber-Catholic and all that, but Levi said he liked her. She was nice to him.

"She wants me to invite you to Midnight Mass."

"When?"

Danny almost made a joke, but realized that Levi probably didn't know much about the being Catholic. They'd never spoken of it, but something told him Levi wasn't into the whole religious thing.

"Christmas Eve — late. Like midnight."

"Oh — duh," Levi made the joke at his own expense. Danny smiled.

"Do you want me to go with you?" Levi asked, still resting his head.

"If you want. I *have* to go, but don't feel like I'm trying to convert you or something. If it were up to me I —"

"Sure, I'll go. If your mom doesn't care."

"You will?"

"Sure. It's like all Christmas-y and stuff, right?"

"Well, uh — yeah, I guess. The star and wise men and all that. But —"

"Then I'll go. Just gotta ask mom."

Danny paused, rolling that around. "Do you all do anything special on Christmas Eve?"

Levi didn't speak for a while. Danny realized he'd forgotten the whole *homeless* thing and didn't know what to say next.

"Not really. When —" Levi stopped for a moment, but reached over and held onto Danny before speaking again, his head still resting, both looking off into the darkness under Levi's desk. "When we didn't have a place, I remember going down to the Dollar General to get Lucy something. I got one of those little bags 'cause I didn't know how to wrap it up." He stopped and Danny just held on to him, not pushing.

"I hid it in my coat. Lucy was asking mom that night if Santa was gonna find us." Danny felt Levi shake a little like he was cold, and pulled a little tighter. "I told her he would, but only if she was asleep. He doesn't come if you're awake."

Danny felt Levi pull his hand free and wipe at his eye before returning it under his arm, safe on Danny's side.

"She kept asking how Santa would know where —"

Levi stopped. His voice broke and he started to cry. Danny's own eyes welled up. He imagined the scene. And hated hearing it.

"Santa wouldn't know where we parked that night. But — but I wanted her to know he would."

Danny rubbed Levi's arm tucked under his, holding him close and feeling the warmth of his body. He leaned his head against Levi's and listened.

"She was so happy when she got that fucking stupid doll," Levi got out between tears. "Mom didn't see me, but she — she couldn't look. Lucy was — Lucy kept saying —" Levi wiped at his eyes again and grabbed Danny's side once more, holding on tight. *"Santa came! Santa came!"*

Danny reached up and held Levi's hands. He had no idea. No words. Nothing, but heartache for him. For his family. But he kept a hold of Levi. He didn't know what else to do.

A few minutes went by and Levi calmed down. Lay quiet holding Danny. He wondered if he'd fallen asleep, but he saw him looking out into space.

Danny rested his head back against Levi's and held on, warm against him.

"Listen, Levi — you don't have to go to Mass with me —"

"No, I want to."

"But — I want you to be with your family, you know?"

Levi didn't respond. Didn't move. Danny waited.

"I will be."

Danny didn't understand. How would he, if he was at Mass with him? Unless he was going to ask them to come along too. But — well, never say never, he thought, but it seemed weird: *Hi, Susan. I'm taking your son to Midnight Mass. Would you and Lucy like to come, too?* God, his ma would like that, but *come on.*

It took a couple more minutes, Danny thinking it through. Then it hit.

He would be.

Holy shit.

Danny found himself being pulled along the pathway toward the cottage sitting in front of Levi's home, cold because they'd run without their coats thinking it was only a few steps away. Cold was still cold, Danny thought, but kept hold of Levi's hand.

He had decided to go ask his mom then and there. Like *right now,* when they got to talking about Christmas Eve plans. Danny wasn't sure how he'd be able to come get Levi, but maybe he could ask Kieran to help, since neither he nor Levi had wheels.

"No, that won't work. Your brother doesn't either," Levi threw out that idea.

"I could take the bus up and we could —"

"Mom'd never go for that. Besides, it'd be like late on Christmas Eve. Would the bus still be running?"

Danny didn't know. It was starting to feel like this might not work.

"You could take an Uber?"

Levi shook his head. "It'd probably cost like a ton and I don't have —"

"Me neither," Danny finished for him. "We're both poor," Danny added.

"Together," Levi said, and grabbed his hand. Danny smiled and looked over at him. Levi smiled back, like something clicked.

"What about Eli? Think he'd give you a lift?" Danny asked. "I could ask Kieran if —"

"Maybe. I can text him."

Danny watched. Levi didn't wait. He was getting the idea that once Levi made a decision, he ran with it. No fucking around. He liked that about him. Get shit done. He smiled watching Levi text back and forth.

"He thinks it's weird I'm going to church, but he said he would," Levi shared his screen with Danny to read. Eli was hilarious in his messages, he saw. He could just imagine Kieran and him going back and forth like that.

"Tell him we're only initiating in the cult on Tuesdays so you're safe," Danny laughed.

But Levi did.

"No, you didn't tell him that!" Danny was mortified after Levi showed him the message sent. He was only joking. But Eli replied:

ELI

Oh, well, I might come then too. Cult initiations are so tiring, tho. If I had a dollar for every…

Danny laughed reading over Levi's shoulder, but noticed that he could feel Levi's — presence? Energy? Scent? — *something* — being so close. It was — more than nice.

"Tell Eli I'm gonna tell Kieran to ask him out."

Levi complied, Eli responding:

We're already going steady, but he's working his courage up to ask me to the snowball dance out at the high school.

Danny laughed and slapped Levi's knee, who was grinning wider than before, happy to be the messenger.

Now he was being pulled along over to ask Levi's mom for permission and he wasn't sure exactly what to say.

"Hey, boys!" Susan looked up with —

Danny's eyes grew wide. *Was that Mrs. Santa Claus?* Levi looked at him and began to laugh, knowing exactly what he was thinking. Levi quickly grabbed Danny's hand and walked him right up to — Mrs. Claus? — who somehow knew what was coming.

"Mrs. Claus, I want to introduce you to Danny Callahan," Levi said, trying not to laugh. Danny noticed Lucy was beaming sitting next to her at a fold-out table making a gingerbread house, icing all over the place.

Mrs. Claus stood and shook his hand, smelling exactly like warm cookies and milk. All around was Christmas — everything. He'd not paid too much attention, but realized that the outside of the house was decorated too. Like *really* decorated.

Okay, he thought, *I know the whole Santa thing is bullshit. But this is — she's like the CEO of Christmas.*

"Welcome to our little workshop, Danny."

Levi leaned in and whispered, "It's our neighbor, Angie. Lucy thinks she's the real deal."

Danny's eyes relaxed. He wasn't high after all. He settled into the white lie. "Thanks, Mrs. Claus. I didn't know I took the bus all the way to the North Pole."

Angie giggled and looked over at Susan who was helping Lucy.

"We are pretty far north," she practically sang before asking if they'd like some cookies.

"Thanks, Mrs. Santa," Levi said and winked, whispering in Danny's ear that Angie made the best.

"Danny, wanna help us?" Lucy asked, holding the evidence of her icy glue all over her hands.

"Uh —"

"We will later, Lucy. We needed to talk to mom first though," Levi told his sister.

Susan looked up just as Angie returned from somewhere with a couple of warm cookies in napkins for each. "I'll help, Susan, if you need to go talk," she sat down next to her young protégé, who was concentrating on trying to put together a piece of the roof that apparently kept slipping.

Susan walked into the kitchen, Levi following. Danny turned and followed as well.

"What's wrong?" Susan asked as she turned on the tap to wash the icing from her hands, looking over at her son who leaned his back against Angie's counters. Danny stood at the doorway leading back out to the dining room.

"Danny asked if I could go to Midnight Mass with him on Christmas Eve."

Susan looked over at Levi as she turned off the tap and pulled a dish-towel to dry her hands.

"Midnight Mass?" She leaned back onto the counter looking over at him. Danny watched, unsure what to do.

Levi nodded.

"On Christmas Eve?"

He nodded again.

"What time?"

Levi tilted his head like she'd asked the stupidest question in the world.

"Uh, *midnight*."

Susan looked over at Danny with an *Are you like this with your mother?* look.

"Mom asked me to invite him," Danny offered. He wasn't sure what to say, so he told her the truth. She had asked.

Susan looked at him.

"It's not like that," Danny nervously chuckled a little. "Not recruiting or anything," he tried to pass it off as a laugh.

Susan turned to Levi. "Do you *want* to go?"

Danny suspected she was asking if he was being pressured.

"Church? No. But I want to go because my boyfriend asked me."

The world stopped spinning.

Susan looked right at him, then to Danny who couldn't breathe, let alone know what to say. Then back at Levi.

"Can I?" Levi persisted, like he'd planned it. Maybe he had, Danny wondered. He'd surprised him several times today already.

"I had a boyfriend who took me to Midnight Mass once, before you were born," she said to Levi. "Called it *Date Mass*," she chuckled.

Levi looked at her, but something was off. Just a little. Levi seemed curious, Danny thought, listening carefully.

"It was pretty. All the candles and choir and greenery. Sweet smoke coming from a contraption they swung around."

"Incense," Danny heard himself say, and then shut up. Susan and Levi both looked over.

"That's it. Incense. Smelled like we were going to meet the king or something." She smiled, remembering, before turning back to Levi.

"Was that —" Levi began to ask, but Susan shook her head. Not whoever or whatever he was thinking, Danny guessed.

Susan looked down. So did Levi.

"We don't have to. I was just asking if —" Danny heard himself trying to make things easier. But Susan cut him off and apologized for doing so.

"Sorry, Danny," she said, after starting to ask if his mother knew.

"Not yet, but —" Danny began to reply.

"Will she be okay?"

Danny looked down now, his turn. "I — I hope so."

"Maybe I should talk to her," Susan said, and looked between Danny and her son.

"I don't want to cause any trouble, Mrs. — uh — Susan." Danny wondered if maybe this wasn't going to be as easy as it seemed.

She didn't answer. Levi looked at her and then at Danny before walking over and putting his hand in Danny's. He wondered if he did that specifically for his mom to see, or because he wanted to. Maybe both.

She saw. And smiled before walking over and fussing with her son's longer hair. "You need a haircut, Mister, if you're going to Date Mass with your boyfriend. See how his hair is short and clean. Good lookin' fellow like that." Danny felt his face flush; he knew his freckles would pop.

"Aww, he's so cute when he blushes," Susan teased and stepped back to look at both of them. Levi squeezed his hand, but looked scared shitless.

"Levi, baby — it's okay. I'm letting you go. Relax. You're scaring Danny," she consoled him.

Levi turned to look at Danny as if he hadn't been aware his grip was a vice. He took a breath, and Danny let out a small laugh.

"You're okay with — us?" Levi asked her.

"Levi, honey — I couldn't be more okay. I just want you two to be careful, is all. Okay? Promise me that."

They both nodded.

"And I don't mean sex, although you're old enough to know about that stuff."

Danny smiled, but saw Levi's face turn redder than his had been. *Now he* looked cute. Susan laughed.

"Danny, I'd like to call your mom and talk to her. But if you are not out to her, then —"

"I'm gonna tell her."

Susan stopped and looked at him.

"She needs to know," Danny added.

"Aren't you scared?" Levi asked.

"Shitless." It just came out. He quickly followed with a "Sorry, Mrs. — uh — Susan."

She laughed. "I'd be scared shitless, too. But, I'm happy to talk to her, if that will help."

"Thanks."

"Either way, I want to talk about logistics. I can take you, but I don't want to keep Lucy awake because —" Susan nodded toward the other room where Mrs. Santa was *helping*.

"We're gonna see if Eli will take me," Levi offered.

"Eli? Church?" she said, like the two didn't mix. Danny laughed. "I'm gonna recruit my brother."

"Ahhhh. Play the *gang up on Eli* game?" She smiled.

"Something like that."

Susan stepped forward and paused in front of them. "Let me know once you've squared away the details. And I still want to talk to your mother, Danny. But I'll wait to call. Lots going on that night and I'd like to know where my son is going to be out late."

"He'll be in good hands, Mrs. — uh — Susan."

She snickered and looked down at their hands, gripped tight around each other.

"That's what I'm worried about," she laughed and walked out of the kitchen.

Vespers

THE CARDINAL HAD COME at midmorning.

He had been in the chapel for nearly an hour. He had stood before the apse and looked at the Madonna's face, and then at the angel's, and then at the mantle, and then at the floor where the patterned tile had been reset by the priory's mason in a herringbone Marco had not asked for and had decided, the day it appeared, to like. The Cardinal had said very little. He had walked the length of the chapel twice. He had come back to the apse a third time and stood there longer than the first two times combined.

When he had turned to leave, he had stopped at the door and looked back across the chapel — not at Marco, who had been on the platform of the scaffolding the whole time, but at the painted face of the Virgin. He had stood there for what Marco, looking down, had measured at perhaps ten breaths.

Then he had nodded once, to no one in particular, and walked out.

He had not spoken to Marco. He had not spoken to Tommaso. He had not given any instruction. The captain of his household had left a small purse on the muller's table on his way out, which Marco assumed was the next installment of his payment, and which Tommaso, when Marco descended an hour later, had set carefully against the wall without opening.

The other visitors had come in the afternoon. Two priests of the Cardinal's curia. A patron Marco recognized from a Florentine commission years before, who had wept briefly and then apologized for weeping. A novice from a neighboring house who had stood at the back of the chapel for a long time and crossed himself three times before leaving. A widow in black whose name Marco never learned.

By vespers, the chapel was empty.

The light had moved across the apse in the slow late way of Roman afternoons. The Madonna's face — cooler than the mantle, composed in the way Marco had wanted — had been lit obliquely by the high window for an hour, and then had dimmed, and then had been lit again briefly by the candles Tommaso had set in the iron stands at either side of the altar.

Marco had not climbed the scaffolding all afternoon.

He had been sitting on the lowest cross-board, his feet on the stone floor, his hands folded between his knees. He had been looking at the work without thinking. He had been waiting for the day to end.

Tommaso came in from the corridor at vespers carrying a small loaf and a wooden cup. He set them on the muller's table. He set his apron beside them. He came across the chapel and sat down on the cross-board next to Marco — not against him, not far — and for a while neither of them spoke.

Then Tommaso said, "He came back twice."

"The Cardinal."

"Yes."

"I saw the first time."

"The second time was after vespers. While you were at the bath. He was alone."

Marco was silent.

"He stayed perhaps a quarter of an hour. He did not call for me. He stood where he had stood in the morning. I watched him from the corridor. He did not know I was there."

"What was he doing."

"He was looking. He did not pray. He did not cross himself. He looked. Then he left."

Marco sat with this. The Cardinal Rospigliosi who had read his letters, who had named what was in them, who had stood in the chamber upstairs and broken him open — that Cardinal had returned to the chapel alone and looked at the Virgin's face for a quarter of an hour without praying.

"Maestro."

"Yes."

"You do not understand yet what you have done."

Marco turned his head slightly. He did not look at Tommaso fully. The chapel's light was at the angle that flattered the Madonna and showed Tommaso's face only in part.

"He came to inspect his property," Marco said. "He found it adequate."

"He came to inspect his property and found it had ceased to be his property. The work is no longer his. The work is its own. He cannot harm you now, Maestro. He cannot afford to. The chapel has his name on it. If you were tarnished, the chapel would be tarnished. He will protect you the way he would protect any of his commissions, because the commission has become a thing he is admired for. The admiration is now part of him. He has no choice but to keep you above reproach, since reproach for you is reproach for him."

Marco was very still.

"He does not know this consciously yet. But his body knew it today. He stood for a quarter of an hour and did not pray. He was understanding."

"Tommaso."

"Yes."

"How do you know this."

"I have been watching him for months. I have been watching what he does when he is not performing. He came here twice today. He has been admired by his own commission. He has been corrected by it. I think it has taken something from him that he did not expect to lose, and given him something he did not expect to find. It will take him weeks to know what."

Marco looked down at his hands.

"You have put him in your pocket, Maestro. You did not know you were doing it. You did it by being who you are. The Virgin and the angel have become greater than the man who paid for them. He will keep them, and to keep them, he must keep you."

Marco said nothing.

"In a month this chapel will be known in Florence. By summer it will be known in France. The Cardinal's name and yours will be on every cleric's tongue from here to the channel ports. He cannot afford for those tongues to find anything in your name they could turn against him. The fame that is coming has already protected you, although you do not yet feel it. He will not even attempt what he attempted before. He cannot. Too many people will be watching."

The light shifted again. Tommaso's face came partway into shadow. Marco found he could look at him now without the shadow becoming an obstacle — found, in fact, that the shadow helped.

"You are leaving in the morning," Tommaso said.

"At first light."

"To Florence."

"Toward Florence. I do not yet know if I will arrive there."

"You will be looking for him."

"Yes."

Tommaso did not answer for a moment. The chapel was nearly dark now. The candles at the altar were the only sustained light.

"Maestro. There are things I have not said to you."

Marco waited.

"I have lain awake. I tell you this because tonight I will not lie to you. I have wished for the comfort of your hand. There have been nights I have not slept for wishing. You will know what I am saying because you have wished it also, in your own way. We have been together in the chapel for nearly seven months. Some of that has been the work. Some of it has not."

Marco closed his eyes.

"I tell you this not so that you will respond. I tell you this so that you will know I am not a man who chose easily. I have wanted what I am not going to have. I have been awake with the wanting."

"Tommaso —"

"Let me finish. I have been thinking, lately, of Simon of Cyrene. The Roman conscripted him. He carried the cross for a stretch of the road. The Gospels do not say how far. The Gospels do not say what passed between him and our Lord. He carried, and then he did not carry, and our Lord continued to Calvary."

Marco said nothing.

"I have been Simon, Maestro. I have carried for a stretch. I have wanted to be more. I am not meant to be more. I have known this longer than I have wanted to know it. The chapel has been my reason for waiting only insofar as the chapel has been you. The waiting is finished. You must continue. I must remain."

The candles guttered briefly in some draft from the corridor. Marco watched them right themselves.

"I will take vows. I have decided. I will speak to the prior at lauds tomorrow. He will be glad. He has been patient with me longer than he should have been."

"Tommaso."

"Yes."

"Will you be at peace."

The novice was quiet for a long moment.

"I will not be at peace as I have understood the word until tonight. I will be at a different peace. The peace that is the peace of having known what one is for. I have not been certain what I was for, Maestro, until I watched you climb the scaffolding for the first time. Some men know early. I know late. But I know."

Marco's hands were trembling now in his lap. He folded them tighter.

"Christ loved the world enough to walk to Calvary. There is no more pure thing than that. I have been thinking — and I tell you this carefully — that the love that walks beside the beloved for a stretch and then releases him is not a lesser love. It is the love that knows itself. It does not require the destination. It is fulfilled in the carrying."

Marco did not trust himself to speak.

"You will go to Alessandro. I do not know if you will find him. I do not know if he is alive. But the going is now possible because I have helped you carry. That is what I have been for. I am not telling you to take comfort in this. I am telling you because it is true."

The chapel was silent.

Marco sat with what Tommaso had given him. His chest ached in a way that was not grief and was not relief and was not anything he had a name for. It was the ache of being seen exactly as one is and being released exactly as one is. He had not known the body could feel such a thing.

He turned to face Tommaso fully.

The novice was looking at him calmly. There were no tears. There was no asking. The face Marco had been painting for weeks — the composure of a young woman who had been told a difficult thing and had not yet decided how to carry it — was on the wall behind them, and was, also, on Tommaso's face in this moment, except that Tommaso had decided. The composure of a young man who had been told a difficult thing and had decided exactly how he would carry it.

Marco rose slightly from the cross-board.

He leaned across the small distance between them.

He pressed his lips to Tommaso's cheek, just below the bone, briefly. The kiss was firm. It was not hesitant. It was not long. It was the kiss a man gives a brother who has just spoken to him truthfully about something difficult. It was also more than that, and both of them knew it, and neither needed to name what the more was.

Marco drew back.

Tommaso closed his eyes for the duration of one breath. He brought his right hand to his cheek, where the kiss had been, and held it there. He did not weep. His mouth moved very slightly, in the shape of a word Marco could not hear and was not meant to hear.

The novice opened his eyes.

"Maestro."

"Tommaso."

They looked at each other for another moment. Then Tommaso lowered his hand. Marco rose. He went to the muller's table. The brush he had used for the Madonna's face — the sable he had favored above the others, the one Tommaso had steadied with his hand on the scaffolding the morning Marco's hands would not stop shaking — was lying across the rim of the lapis dish. Marco picked it up. He turned. He came back to the cross-board. He laid the brush in Tommaso's lap without speaking, and rested his hand on Tommaso's hand for the count of three breaths.

Then he straightened, and crossed the chapel to the door, and walked out into the corridor without looking back.

He left at first light.

The Cardinal's window had been lit later than usual the night before. Marco had seen it across the courtyard from the corridor outside his quarters when he had returned from the chapel. He had not known what it meant. He had not, he discovered, needed to know. The window had been lit. The Cardinal had been awake at an hour when most of the household was asleep. Whether he had seen anything, whether he had been told anything, whether he had been only at his correspondence — Marco could not know and did not, finally, ask.

In the morning the courtyard was empty. Marco's small bag was on his shoulder. He had paid the priory's gatekeeper the last of his silver. The mule he had rented from a stableman near the Lateran was waiting at the gate, breathing white into the cold.

He looked up once at the Cardinal's window. The shutters were closed. Whatever was behind them was beyond Marco's reach.

He passed under the gate. He turned north.

The road to Florence ran through hills that would be greening in two months. Today they were brown and the sky was a pale washed blue and the air smelled of woodsmoke from the bakeries beginning their morning fires. Marco rode slowly. He had nowhere to be by any specific hour. He had the rest of the day, and the next day, and the day after that.

He did not know where Alessandro was.

He knew, more clearly than he had known anything since Venice fell silent, that he was riding toward him. He knew this not because he had received any letter, not because he had any information, not because anything had changed in the world's facts. He knew it because Tommaso had named it for him last night. *You will be looking for him.* The naming had been the unlocking. The thing Marco had been unable to do for himself, Tommaso had done for him with a sentence in a darkened chapel.

The road climbed slightly. The mule's breath was steady. Marco rode.

He understood, somewhere between the third and fourth hour of riding, that he loved Alessandro more clearly today than he had loved him a year ago. The love had been refined by absence and by the chapel and by the Cardinal's surveillance and by Tommaso's hand and by Tommaso's speech and by Tommaso's kiss received without being asked for. He did not yet know what *more clearly* would mean when it arrived at its destination. He only knew that the loving had been purified.

He thought of Tommaso once, around midday, when the sun broke the cloud cover and the road was warm for a stretch. He thought of the brush in Tommaso's lap. He thought of Tommaso's hand on his cheek. He did not stop. He did not turn back. He continued north.

In the chapel that morning, the priory's brothers had already begun the work of dismantling the scaffolding when Tommaso came in from the corridor. Two laborers from the Cardinal's household had arrived at first light. They were taking the cross-boards down one at a time, working from the top. The platform Marco had stood on for seven months would be timber for some other commission by evening.

Tommaso stood in the door of the chapel and watched.

He had taken his apron off the night before, as he always did. It was folded on the small shelf above his bed, beside the book of psalms and beside the brush Marco had left him. He understood — not all at once, but in the slow way of understanding when the body had known for some time and the mind was only catching up — that the apron would stay folded now. The chapel was finished. There would be no working day to put it on for. It would wait there, on the shelf, until the prior gave him some new task that called for it. Or, more likely, until the prior gave him an entirely different life, in which an apron would not be the right garment.

The muller's table was carried out by two of the priory's lay brothers as Tommaso watched. The dish that had held the lapis for the Madonna's face went out in a basket with the other dishes, packed in straw. The pigment jars went out separately. The small horsehair brushes — Marco's — would, Tommaso understood, be sent on to whichever of the master's apprentices in Florence had been designated to receive them.

He stood in the doorway until the chapel was bare.

The Madonna's face was still on the wall. Her composure unchanged. The chapel was now the chapel. It was no longer the place where Marco had worked.

Tommaso turned and went to his cell.

He sat on the edge of the small bed. He looked at the brush on the shelf. He looked at the book of psalms beside it. He sat for what may have been a quarter of an hour, or may have been longer; the chapel's bell would ring for terce and he would know.

The bell rang.

He went to terce.

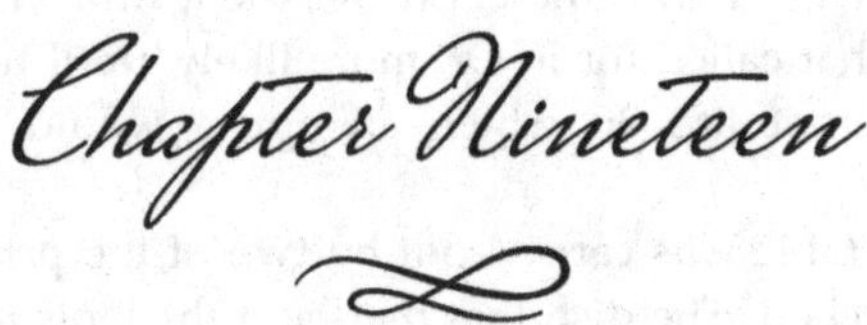

DANNY LAY in bed as the sliver of sunlight began peeking through the shade he always kept closed on his window. He grabbed his phone and saw Levi had sent a message last night after he'd fallen asleep.

LEVI 🤍

gud morning bae still on for tnite? mom still wants to tlk to urs

Followed by a bunch of heart, kissing, and hug emojis.

Danny smiled. Levi had seemed so excited last night when they were talking. Danny guessed he couldn't sleep. He rolled over and texted back.

il tell her ina bit

Danny was right. Levi said he'd been up since 5. Felt like a kid again waiting for Santa, but this time he'd already got his present. Danny smiled. Levi really was falling hard. Danny had never been in love before. Didn't know exactly what meant you were in love, but guessed something like always thinking about them or can't get enough of them, but felt like there was probably more. Either way, ever since he and Levi became a thing, it was like his whole life changed, only no one knew it.

Well, Levi's mom did. And his mom would. Just as soon as he got his ass outta bed and told her.

It was already Christmas Eve. He'd been trying to think of a way to bring it up. He wasn't scared. Well, that wasn't true, he thought as he rolled back and kicked the covers over. It was freezing so he pulled the blanket back across his legs. His phone said 21 degrees, chance of snow tonight. For the moment, he forgot about his mom and worked out a plan on how to grab his long underwear from his drawer and change into them as quickly as possible.

Fully clothed and teeth brushed, he walked out to the kitchen — the only room in the house with any heat. Probably because his ma was cooking already. She had turned on the lights of their little Christmas tree out in the living room and had the radio on — but not her usual station, the one Danny hated competing against when he tried to talk to her. It was some old Christmas song station. She was humming while wearing an apron making —

Oh yes. Cinnamon rolls. His taste buds came alive.

She only made them at Christmas. He'd almost forgotten.

"Well, Mister sleeps-til-noon is awake at — what?" she teased in her own motherly way, looking up at her owl clock on the kitchen wall. "Sakes, it's not even 7. You got a fever?" She smiled and returned to kneading on the table, flour scattered and her hands full of the sticky dough.

Danny sat at the chair that flanked the doorway, an extra for whenever they pulled the table out far enough to actually seat more than three in its normal pushed-against-the-wall state.

"Levi wants to come to Mass with us tonight."

"Well, that'd be lovely," she replied, not looking up from her rolling pin.

Danny watched as she began to divide the dough.

"There's something else, ma."

"What's that, Danny boy?" She was using the metal yardstick to measure out squares, concentrating on her dough.

Danny felt safe. He'd seen enough TV shows to know that he should be scared. Or worried about what she'd say. That he should keep his mouth shut. Tell him to act straight. Keep it cool. But that wasn't who he was. And this wasn't just him bullshitting with his ma. He was doing something that felt like she'd now see him.

"Levi and I are together."

"That's nice. What else were you going to say?" She continued working on the rolls.

"No ma, we're *together*. He's my boyfriend."

Danny sat watching her finish cutting the square with the same knife she used for everything when she cooked. Watched her trim off the edges and put them back in the mixing bowl. Gently peel up the prepared square and lay it down for trimming slices to roll. All of it, Danny had seen her do every Christmas.

He didn't say anything. He knew she heard him. But he kept his mouth shut. His ma worked on her own time, he had learned over the years. When pressed against the wall, she'd fight. But let her control her own conversation, that came out much better.

Maureen walked over to the sink and washed her hands. Danny watched her use some dish soap and her nail brush, cleaning out the dried dough bits around her fingertips before reaching down to the kitchen towel hanging from the tie around her apron. He watched her look at her hands as the threadbare towel — the one with Santa Claus' face on it that he had loved seeing when he was little — dried them.

Watched her turn and walk over to him, stopping right in front to look into his eyes. Danny tried to read them, admitting he was a little nervous.

"I like Levi. He is a nice boy."

Danny was going to reply, but he saw her face lift slightly, his cue to remain still. He looked down, but then brought his eyes back to hers.

"I expected this from your brother," she said. "Not so much from you."

Danny registered what she just said. She *already knew* about Kieran. Kierp would shit himself when Danny told him.

"You sure about this, Danny boy?"

He nodded.

"Does Levi's mother know?"

He nodded again. She followed, looking away slightly, thinking.

Maureen placed her hand on Danny's right shoulder and stepped just a smidge closer. "I want to talk to his mother."

Danny nodded.

She stayed where she was, looking right at him. He couldn't read her. Was she upset? Accepting? He knew nothing.

"She wanted to talk to you, too," he said, keeping eye contact. He knew to stay with her. If he looked away — well, he knew not to look away.

She kept her gaze, then nodded and patted his shoulder before turning around and resuming her work on the rolls.

"Danny, get me the cinnamon tin out of the cupboard, please, and then have some oats. They're on the stove."

"Okay, ma."

Danny sat in the same chair watching his mom work with a hot bowl of oatmeal in his hand. He'd sprinkled some of the cinnamon in for flavor, but handed the tin to his ma before resuming his post. The Christmas music played low while she proceeded to butter up the planks and sprinkle on healthy amounts of sugar and cinnamon. His mouth could taste it all the way from there, watching and waiting.

He washed his bowl and put it in the sink rack before turning to his ma, still working on greasing up the brown trays that were older than him, giving her a peck on the cheek, and heading back to his room.

she knows

im comin tnite?

bout us

Danny watched the dots appear and reappear before Levi finally sent his message.

she ok?

she wants 2 talk to ur mom

shit

no she is ok

really

yea

ok ill tell her

Danny sent a heart emoji to Levi's kiss and set his phone on his nightstand.

In practically a Christmas miracle, he thought, he rolled open the shades to his room, and snickered to himself. Everything looked different lit up even if it was just 8 in the morning.

The phone on the wall in the kitchen rang and he turned to look down the hall, but stopped at his doorway. His ma didn't have an iPhone or anything "fancy like that," she'd say. Just the pushbutton wall phone that was black with a big long spiral cord hanging on the wall right above where Danny had sat earlier. That was good enough for her, she'd told Sean once when he tried to buy her a phone. The phone company was threatening to cancel the service because they were the only ones left on the block who had one. But she persisted. Now, it rang and Danny could hear her pick it up on the third try.

"Callahans," he heard his mom's voice. It sounded polite with a bit of *Who's calling on Christmas Eve morning when I've got rolls to bake?*

"Oh, yes. Nice to hear from you. I was just speaking with Danny. That was quick."

Susan. Danny was sure of it. Levi must have told her and she wasted no time.

"Yes, he's very welcome to attend. Are you Catholic, dear?"

Danny smirked, wondering what Levi's mom would say.

"Of course. Why, yes." He heard his ma laugh. "Yes, I met Danny's father at Midnight Mass, actually."

What? he thought to himself. He didn't know that.

"Yes," she laughed again, "lots of young people take their dates."

Danny held his breath.

"Mmhmm. Yes. He did. Mhmmm."

He wondered if they were getting into the *real* reason for the call.

"Well, what do *you* think?"

Danny listened as his ma was quiet, the sound of the light Christmas music still playing on her old radio spilling down the hall.

"Well, I tell you, Susan —"

Danny heard her name. They were already on a first-name basis.

"— back in my day —"

She paused. He wondered what happened. But then she laughed.

"Oh, I'm much too old for that."

For what? he wondered.

"Well, that's very kind of you," she said, followed by more *mmhmms* and *reallys*.

What the hell were they talking about? Danny was practically rocking on the balls of his feet, but he didn't dare walk down the hall to look at his ma. He could imagine her talking on the phone, sitting down at that same kitchen chair where he had told her about Levi, curling the phone cord between her fingers.

"Well, I have to tell you, Susan, I'm worried for him, but perhaps not the way —" She stopped.

"So you understand my concern."

"Of course. I just want him to be happy."

"True. That's true."

Danny heard his ma let out a loud cackle of laughter. "Well, when you put it *that way* —"

What in the hell were they doing? Telling jokes? Danny was biting at his nail, literally, and caught himself. He did that sometimes when he was nervous.

"Mmm —" Her voice lowered before speaking up. "Well, then, as long as *you're* okay with it, I don't have any objections other than I don't want them sneaking around. His older brother moved his girlfriend in after I told him that I'd rather know they're here together than out there in who knows what dirty place getting themselves into trouble, if you know what I mean!"

Danny's mind flashed back to that conversation. Sean looked so embarrassed. But his girlfriend stood right next to him holding his hand, getting *that lecture* from their ma. Then she kissed him on his cheek and pronounced that he was no longer her little baby boy. Danny and Kieran had both retreated down the hall but were listening, just like he was doing now.

"Good! I'm glad you had that talk with Levi. I need to sit Danny down and —"

Danny rolled his eyes. He'd *already* had to suffer through the sex talk with her four years ago. What else was she going to say?

His mother laughed. "Well, Susan — I'm a good Catholic. Raised to be. And the Church is very important to me. But I also realize there are — shall we say — *things* — that sometimes we need to be realistic about."

Danny's eyes shot open. Really? His ma said *that*?

"Well, you're a good mother then. I would rather those two be here under my supervision than out there doing who knows what to each other with — drugs and that marijuana and —"

Drugs? Why was she even bringing that up? Danny thought. He'd never even tried a cigarette.

"Yes — yes — I know. They're both good boys." She quieted as Danny continued eavesdropping.

"Well, I agree. They are growing into young men. Just — it's hard to see them that way."

Danny wondered if he ever would be a parent. If he would think the same.

"Hmmm? Oh — I suspect around 1:30 or 2. Father O'Brien runs a clean mass."

Danny imagined the priest being the judge at a boxing match, running a *clean fight*, and snickered.

"You're welcome to come, if you'd like, dear."

Of course, ma always tried to get people to show up at Holy Cross.

"Oh — well, yes. Especially if she's only six! She must be excited for Santa Claus."

Levi's sister. Now they had moved on to his sister. Danny shifted his weight and leaned against the door, but it began to push back so he corrected himself and shifted to the door frame, stepping a foot into the hallway.

"No, me too. I always had such a struggle to provide Christmas for the boys, what with Patrick always gone and all."

His dad? Danny stood up, leaning out. What about his dad?

"Oh, you poor dear. Sounds like you and me both had a dickens — huh? — Oh, of course, some nights, it was — well — *you know how it is.*"

Danny wondered how *what* was.

Then he heard her sniffle once.

"Well, yes — we should. Maybe after Christmas is over. I — I'd like that. I'd be hap — what's that? Oh, I don't want you to go to any trouble."

Now this conversation seemed to have ceased being about Danny and Levi and into — something about *them*. He felt like maybe now he needed to let them be, this wasn't his to hear.

Danny walked back into his room and sat on his bed, picking up his phone by habit.

still talkin 2 ur mom

Levi texted back almost immediately.

i kno tryin 2 hear but ther talkin bout comin here or sumthn cant tell

moms out in d kitchen

ma is 2

jst hung up txt bck

Danny looked up as his ma walked into his room and sat on the side of his bed.

"I just spoke with Levi's mother. She's a lovely woman."

Danny noticed her good mood.

She leaned in and spoke again as if no one should hear. "Did you know Levi's father left her to manage two kids all on her own? Shame, that is."

Danny knew, but he didn't tell her.

"Anyway, she and I agreed to your and Levi's special friendship and —"

"He's my boyfriend, ma," Danny interjected and then apologized for interrupting. "Sorry, ma."

She had paused and looked at him before resuming. "Uh — boyfriend. Corrected. Anyway, we have some ground rules. Susan is telling Levi now. We agreed."

Danny imagined Susan sitting on his bed giving the same spiel.

"No sneaking around, Mister Danny. I mean it. No Callahan is going to be caught in some trash motel with hooligans. We may be poor, but we have dignity, and I won't have any of that nonsense with either of you!" Her thick Irish mother eyes were speaking harsher words than Jesus would allow her to say outwardly.

Danny quickly nodded. Of course. He wouldn't dare.

"Good." She relaxed a little. "Number two. Just like I told Sean, you're old enough now to behave like a man. No disrespectin' Levi, no two-timing, or none of those shenanigans, hear me?"

Danny nodded fiercely again.

"I don't know exactly how boys work like this, but I do know if you make a commitment to a lady, you keep it. And Levi may be a boy, it don't matter a hill of beans to me. You respect that young man. I don't want to hear no cryin' cause of you, Danny boy!"

She'd worked herself up again, but Danny kept nodding. He was amazed she was worried about Levi more than him fucking around behind her back.

"Which brings me to Number three. I may not know how all this works, but I know just because you can't get him pregnant doesn't mean you've got free license to go scooting around each other like a pair of dogs in heat! When you play, Danny, you pay. So, keep your loins in control. You're from Irish men who had trouble with that one and I knows how to prove it, just lookin' at ya!"

And there it is, Danny thought. *The sex talk.*

His ma looked down and then back over, reached up and fussed with his hair. "Danny boy," she seemed to melt back into the ma he always knew as a boy, the one who made him feel better after he bruised himself, or messed up on a test, the one who pulled him up in her arms when he was little and scared of the thunderstorms that came through sometimes. "I want you to be happy."

"I am, ma."

She smiled. "Levi is a nice boy, isn't he?"

"Yeah, he is."

"Just be careful, promise me."

"I promise I will, ma."

She looked at him for a moment before saying, "That's all I ask for," rising and heading back towards the kitchen. "You can help me with the next batch of rolls," he heard her say as she disappeared down the hall.

on d way

ok knock bell dont wrk

Levi gave a thumbs up and Danny pocketed his phone. It was already 9:15 and his ma was fussing at him about Kieran. She liked to get to church early and he still hadn't shown up to get himself washed up and presentable.

"He's coming with Levi," Danny tried to explain for the third time this evening.

"I thought you said he was with that friend of his."

"He is — was —" he tried to get through to her. "All I know, ma, is that —" he almost said Eli's name, but didn't want to get into it with her — that was for Kieran to deal with. "His friend is giving them both a lift here. Levi just messaged that they left."

"How far —"

"20 or 30 minutes, I guess."

"Lands sakes. He won't get back until nearly 10 and I want to be at Holy Cross by 10:30. You know how busy it'll be."

"It'll be okay, ma."

"But your brother has to —"

"Kieran will be okay. I think he changed over at Eli's."

Damnit, he yelled at himself. *Now she's gonna want to —*

"Who's Eli?"

God, I'm so stupid, he practically slapped himself.

"That's Kieran's friend. Eli. No matter, he said he took his sweater and stuff so he'll be ready."

"I can call Sean. He's supposed to meet us there anyway and —"

"It'll be fine, ma. Promise."

Danny noticed her walk into the living room and adjust her hat, the one she always wore to Christmas Midnight Mass. He noticed the small sprig of greenery she tucked into her coat. He remembered her doing that every year since back when he still thought Santa was a thing.

His mind drifted over to Anthony, the old man who helped at Thanksgiving with him and Levi. He wondered if he played Santa at the malls and stuff. He'd be perfect for it.

"Danny, get your shoes on. You're not ready," his ma scolded him.

"Okay, ma." He grabbed the only pair of good shoes he owned, brown penny loafers he got on his last birthday from Sean and his girlfriend. To go with the suit Kieran got him for his upcoming graduation. He'd never worn them before, but took them out of their tissue wrap in the box he had put in his closet. He hoped they'd hold up to the snow that had started falling a couple of hours ago.

They'd walk over to Holy Cross. Just a couple of blocks. But the snow was already starting to pile up; he didn't want to get his new shoes all messed up.

"Here, let me look at you," his ma came into his room and stood in front of him. "You sharpen up nicely, Danny boy."

"Thanks, ma." He blushed.

"Aww, you got that Callahan red to your cheeks." She grabbed at them, but he pushed her hands away, shy, which she adored. "You're a handsome man, Danny. And not just because I'm your mother."

Danny looked down, bashful. His ma still made him feel like he was a kid sometimes.

"You make that Levi be good to you, you hear?"

Danny looked up and nodded. "He is, ma."

She nodded, like she had more to say, but some other time.

The door flew open and Danny and Maureen heard voices coming from down the hall. She walked ahead of him into the hall and stopped in her tracks, Danny behind her.

There was Kieran standing nervously in the front door, Levi standing next to him, and —

Eli walked through and made his way towards Maureen.

"Merry Christmas, Mrs. Callahan! I'm Eli."

Danny watched as Eli took a few steps towards his ma in the living room and extended his hand, that smile Danny remembered seeing before.

Danny looked up at his ma and then over to Levi, who was focused on Eli, then to Kieran who was staring right at Danny, as if to ask for help. Danny remembered what his ma said about Kieran earlier that morning and wondered when Kieran would finally give up the act. She knew. He knew she knew. Danny had half a mind to walk over and tell him, just so he could relax. He looked like he was about to shit diamonds.

"Oh! Well, it's very nice to meet you, uh — Eli." She raised her hand and Eli took it lightly, shaking before placing his other hand over it and beginning to speak.

"Kieran has told me about how much you mean to him. I can see why."

His mom's eyes shifted from Kieran — whose own eyes seemed to be trying to register what was happening — to the black leather gloves Eli was still wearing, then back to his eyes.

Then Danny saw something he didn't think he had before: his ma blushed. Her cheeks turned red, just like his did when he was embarrassed or someone paid him a compliment. Kieran's did it worse. Maybe that wasn't a Callahan thing. Maybe they got it from her.

Danny noticed Eli was dressed up. Dark charcoal long coat, wool trousers with black shoes that looked polished. Suit coat and tie with a fancy scarf folded just so. He looked like he was going to an upscale dinner more than mass.

"I love your hat," he complimented ma again and she blushed all over.

Danny looked across at Levi and realized he hadn't noticed. Levi was dressed up, too. Like, he looked really good. Like — *really good.*

"Ma, this is —"

"Yes, Kieran. Eli." His mother stopped Kieran in his tracks and turned back to Eli who still cupped her hands in his.

"Welcome to our home, Eli. You're very kind."

Eli released her hands and gave a small bow.

Kieran looked like he didn't know who this man was.

"If you don't mind me asking, Eli —"

Danny's gaze shot back over to his ma. He knew she didn't have much time for diddle daddle, as she called it. He saw her gesturing towards her ears.

"— are you —"

"Deaf. Yes. Well — I can hear some things, but these —" He took his right glove off and pointed to his hearing aids. "— help some. But I can usually understand if I see your face as well."

Danny noticed his mom reach over and almost touch his right ear. Eli looked like he didn't mind.

"That's so fascinating. I always heard of people who could do that, but —"

"Ma!" Kieran stepped forward, embarrassed.

"It's okay, Kieran," Eli turned and signed.

Maureen watched as Kieran replied in sign. She looked amazed.

"Well, I'll be —" she put her hand to her heart, surprised at her son.

Eli turned and grinned. "He was just apologizing, but I told him he worried too much."

She turned to look at Kieran who now had the red embarrassed face and looked down.

"Kieran Patrick Callahan! What has gotten into you?"

Levi walked around the trio and came up next to Danny, gently putting his arm around his back.

"He's just nervous I'm here. I was supposed to give them a ride, but I hope you don't mind if I invite myself to join you to mass."

Danny noticed his ma beam, like she just won a scratch-off from down at the liquor store. "Of course I wouldn't mind, Eli! We'd love to have you!" she shared and pulled him into a small hug.

Eli leaned in and gave Danny and Levi a quick wink before stepping back, smiling.

Danny looked over and saw Kieran staring at him. Actually, at both him and Levi, together. Eli followed. Then his ma, who wondered what they were looking at.

She stepped back and saw him and Levi standing together, Levi's arm around Danny, both dressed up — probably for the first time ever, Danny thought.

Danny looked over at Levi and smiled. Shrugged as if to say *let 'em look,* and then turned back.

"Oh, don't you two look so handsome! All dressed up! Here, I want to get a picture!" She walked down the hall.

Kieran stepped over. "What the hell is going on? Does ma even know about you two?"

"Yeah, Kieran. She does. Told her this morning," Danny said and didn't give a shit.

Eli raised his hand for a high five and Danny slapped it, like *mission accomplished*.

"And she didn't kick you out or call Father O'Brien to exorcise you or something?" Kieran panicked.

"Nope. Even spoke with Levi's mom."

"You're shitting me. MA? Our ma?"

Kieran looked over at Levi who was smiling, but nodding that she had.

Eli stepped up and touched Kieran's arm, causing him to jump a little.

"Here, I want to get a picture," their ma reappeared from her bedroom with one of those disposable cameras. Danny wasn't even sure where she got it, but it didn't matter.

"Here, you two stand in front of the Christmas tree." She positioned Danny and Levi together and took a photo.

"Hold on. I want a picture, too," she said, and turned to Eli. "Would you mind?"

Eli took the camera as she stepped between the two boys, both putting their hands around her and smiled. Eli took the photo, handing the camera back saying he'd like a copy if she wouldn't mind.

"Now, you two," she gestured for Eli and Kieran.

Kieran looked over at Eli and began to protest, but she stopped and looked right at him.

"Kieran, son. It's Christmas. I'm no fool. I know."

Danny grabbed Levi's hand as they stood off to the side watching. He noticed Eli stayed right by Kieran.

"You do?"

"Yes, Kieran. I know." She looked back at Danny and Levi and smiled before turning to her son. "When Danny told me about Levi this morning, that surprised me a little. It shouldn't have but it did."

She looked over at Levi who was watching, all eyes on him, and leaned a little into Danny.

Danny noticed his ma smile a little before looking over at Eli, then back to Kieran.

"I actually had been waiting for you."

"You — what?"

"Kieran."

His older brother began to tear up. Levi grabbed Danny's hand tighter.

Their ma nodded and looked into his eyes.

"You — you don't hate me?" he choked out. Danny saw Eli reach around and hold onto Kieran, but his ma pulled him into her arms and let him cry on her shoulder.

Danny looked away, unsure how to give them privacy, feeling like maybe this should be just between them. Levi turned to look at the tree while Danny snuck a glimpse of Eli as he slowly stepped over by them.

Eli put his hand on Danny's shoulder and pointed out an ornament hanging that Kieran had made in fifth grade. A photo of him with his name in glitter across the top. Danny was going to tell him about it, but decided not to speak. He didn't want to disrupt anything. Instead, he nodded and turned it around for Eli to see. *5th Grade* in glitter. Eli smiled.

Levi pointed to another ornament hanging slightly higher, this one of Danny. It didn't have his photo, but he remembered making it, using all different color glitters and glue to spell his name. Levi made a little gesture to his own heart, and Danny smiled. There were lots of their stories hanging on this tree.

"Eli," Danny heard his ma say his name, and tapped his arm, pointing their way. Eli turned and saw her waving him over.

Danny and Levi turned to watch as his ma pulled him over and stood with Kieran who seemed to be calming down. He noticed she made a point of looking up at him directly.

"I explained to Kieran that I'm happy you two can be here. And I expect to see you here more often, okay?"

She emphasized the last part as if to ensure he understood.

"I'd love that. And you are always welcome at my home. Maybe we can have a dinner there sometime?"

"Oh, that would be lovely. But let's get through Christmas first, shall we?"

Eli nodded and smiled. He had placed his hand lightly on her upper back; they both turned towards Kieran.

Danny let go of Levi's hand, walked over, and pulled Kieran into a hug.

He didn't know why. Didn't care that his ma and Eli were standing right there. Didn't worry that Levi was watching. He just knew the feeling and wanted his brother to know he loved him. He felt Kieran pull him in tight before giving him a squeeze and letting go.

"Kieran, why don't you go freshen up your face and then we'll head to Holy Cross, okay?"

Kieran looked over at Eli, then disappeared down the hall.

"It's cold out, so I think I should drive us," Eli said to Danny's ma.

"Oh, it's only a few blocks," she seemed to think he was making a fuss.

"I insist. I want you to arrive in one piece," he pushed and she smiled.

"Well, that's very kind of you, Eli."

Kieran returned, straightening his tie under the sweater their ma gave him last year for Christmas, when she pulled him in front of the tree. "I still want that photo of you two," she'd said and took two. Then asked Danny to take a picture with her in between.

Danny looked through the viewfinder and saw his ma smiling like she was at a wedding. Eli handsome, holding on to her, his brother on the other side smiling, but he knew he was still wrapping his head around everything.

"Eli, can you teach me how to sign?" Danny heard his ma ask as she put her arm around his, walking out into the cold.

"I'd love to."

"I want to be able to talk with you."

Chapter Twenty

KIERAN PULLED the Volvo up to the front of Holy Cross to drop off Danny and Levi so they could save the pew. Eli stayed in the back. He had insisted Maureen take the front.

She'd told Eli to call her Maureen on the way over. She kept marveling at the car, but more at Kieran driving it. Eli had handed him the keys earlier, walking out of the house.

Kieran didn't need to be told what Eli was doing. Eli was letting his mother see them. Not announcing anything. Just letting the car say it. Her son was driving. His car. At his insistence. Maureen had not missed a beat of it.

He pulled around and wedged the Volvo between a pickup and a minivan. Eli was already out, opening Maureen's door. Kieran wasn't sure what Danny had told her that morning, or what she'd worked out on her own. But Eli wasn't being polite. Eli didn't do polite.

He walked alongside them. His mother was telling Eli something about Kieran as a kid. Eli probably couldn't follow her in the cold and the dark, but he was nodding. Kieran caught his eye. Eli smiled over Maureen's hat.

They came in through the side door of the vestibule. Eli stopped to look inside. Everything dimly lit. Candles at the altar. Red and gold cloth draped along the rail. A Nativity set up beneath with real evergreens around it, the manger waiting. People already standing along the back, scanning for empty pews. Maureen reached for the holy water font and blessed herself. Eli watched, then followed her without dipping his hand. Kieran dipped quickly, made the sign of the cross, and caught up. She genuflected and scooted into their pew.

Levi was already sitting on the far side of Danny. Both of them looked up. Maureen paused and gestured for Eli to go around her. Eli looked back at Kieran, then wedged himself in next to Danny. Maureen sat, pulled the kneeler down, and tapped Eli's knee, pointing so it wouldn't catch his shin on the way down.

Kieran knelt beside her. Down the row, Danny did the same. He whispered something to Levi, then turned back, folding his hands the way they'd been taught.

Kieran reached up and signed *You can sit. It's ok.* Eli nodded and looked around again.

Kieran closed his eyes and listened, his hands folded, leaning on the back of the pew ahead. He wasn't sure what he believed. Never had been. But he'd always followed what his ma told him, and at Mass that meant kneeling when she knelt. He'd never prayed for anything. Never thought it mattered. He'd just think. Listen to people whisper. An occasional cough that'd echo off the rafters.

Now he felt Eli looking at him. Felt his presence. Felt warm. Tonight it wasn't just his life to wonder about.

Maureen sat back. Kieran reached down to flip the kneeler up. She was trying to say something to Eli, who pointed to his ear — the small gesture Kieran had come to know meant *I can't follow you.* Kieran touched her arm and whispered that Eli couldn't hear her well from there.

"Tell him I'm happy he's here." She gave a little shake with her hands to indicate he should sign it.

Kieran's eyes opened slightly. He raised his hands and signed.

Eli smiled and signed back.

Kieran leaned to his ma. "He said he's happy you invited him."

"I didn't know to invite him." She kept her voice low, but she looked up at her son.

"I told him you probably would if you met him."

"You're right. I would've. Maybe God heard and passed it along." She nodded toward Eli, who smiled back, not knowing why.

Eli signed *I like your mom. You look like her.*

"What did he say?" she leaned in. The delight on her face — like she was a little girl, like he was letting her into his secret.

"He says I look like you."

She beamed and patted his hand. He squeezed hers.

He was still looking at her when he caught it, just down the pew: Danny and Levi, sitting still and looking forward, their hands joined, just out of view of anyone around them. He looked back at his mother. She had caught it too.

Levi noticed her looking and pulled back, embarrassed, but Danny glanced over at him and reached for the hand again, placing it back where it had been.

Kieran looked at his mother. She smiled, looked over at Eli, and turned her eyes forward.

Someone patted his shoulder.

Turning, Kieran saw his older brother Sean leaning over between him and their mother.

"Almost didn't get here. Nowhere to park." He spoke too loud.

"Lower your voice." Maureen turned toward Caitlin, standing directly behind Sean. "Merry Christmas, dear."

"Merry Christmas, Mrs. Callahan," Caitlin whispered.

Kieran felt Sean nudge him, his chin tipping toward the other side of the pew. Turning, he saw Eli smile and nod.

"Who's —" Sean started, but the lights dimmed, and Maureen leaned past Kieran to cut him off. "They're getting ready to start."

"Just wondering who —"

"There'll be time for that later. Find your seat."

"But ma —"

"Sean Michael."

Kieran watched his brother's eyes narrow as he took the pew behind them, not coming off Eli. Caitlin gave Kieran a small wave. He returned it and turned forward.

He could still feel his brother's stare from behind.

Down the row, Danny had not let go of Levi's hand.

The lector rose to the lectern and began to read.

"Translate for Eli, Kieran," his ma whispered, but Kieran shook his head and pointed. A woman stood just to the side of the altar, signing the whole thing.

"Don't have to," he whispered back.

His ma saw, looked back at him, pleased.

The church was at capacity. Whole families, old-timers, lots of couples, all of them looking up at Father O'Brien. Kieran had grown up with these rituals and never thought much about them. Eli was watching them like they were new. Kieran watched Eli watch the incense move around the altar, watch a server carry the porcelain Christ child up and lay him in the manger, watch the candles being lit one by one.

Eli looked over at him sometimes. Like he was trying to understand something. Kieran's ma would point to her place in the missalette and Eli would nod, and she'd smile and look back to the altar.

When it came time for communion, Kieran leaned back from his kneeler and signed to Eli that he'd be right back, miming a small loop with one hand. Probably not the right sign. Eli nodded and gave him a wink.

He stood and let his mother go ahead of him. Danny took the spot behind him. Kieran turned into the aisle and glanced back. Eli and Levi had already leaned together, signing something between them. He didn't know what. He didn't need to.

Walking back through the pew, Kieran followed his mother past Eli. He went to take his old spot past her — but she stopped at it and knelt down to pray. Kieran took the empty seat right next to his boyfriend.

Eli looked up at him and smiled, and gestured for him to sit.

Kieran knelt down instead. Eli now directly on his left. The choir began to sing *What Child Is This,* and the church lights dimmed.

He closed his eyes and listened. Wondering.

Eli coughed. A baby was crying somewhere in the back. The couple sitting behind them settled into their pew. Then his ma tapped his arm. He opened his eyes. She was pressing one of her strawberry candies into his hand, nodding toward Eli.

Kieran leaned back on the kneeler and handed it over. Eli looked puzzled until Maureen smiled and gestured toward her own mouth. He smiled back, nodded, unwrapped it, popped it in.

Kieran looked around the church. Everything was finished except the closing. It was quiet. Peaceful. Growing up, this was when he'd start to get sleepy, waiting to get home. Presents and his ma's cinnamon rolls, the movies Sean would put on the TV during the day, the card games they'd play. That had been the stuff he wanted, not church.

But this was new.

Maureen sat back. He and Danny did the same. Kieran reached down and flipped the kneeler up. He leaned back. Eli's hand was already there, sliding into his and holding it tight.

His mother looked over and saw. She looked up at Kieran and leaned in.

"Date Mass," she whispered.

She smiled, and turned her eyes back to Father O'Brien.

Kieran sat with the words. He felt the heat come up the side of his neck. Down the pew, Danny was holding Levi's hand the same way. Eli was looking forward, but his thumb moved on Kieran's knuckle.

They stood for the closing prayer, and the choir started *Joy to the World,* and the lights came up bright. Kieran turned and signed to Eli about driving home — dropping Levi, dropping Danny, the route. Sign was sometimes easier than speaking.

Eli took Maureen's arm as they came into the vestibule, where Father O'Brien stood in his vestments shaking hands and wishing everyone a Merry Christmas.

"That was so lovely, Father."

"Thank you, Maureen. Glad to see the boys. And —" He turned toward Eli.

"Father, this is Eli —" His mother started, and stopped. She didn't know his last name. No one had told her yet. Kieran leaned in.

"Pelletier."

She looked over at him and back at the priest. "Yes. Eli Pelletier." She leaned in and lowered her voice. "He's deaf."

Kieran caught Eli's eye. Eli looked amused at the whole production. Kieran watched as Father O'Brien smiled, handed Maureen the missalette he'd been holding so his hands were free, and signed *Welcome*.

Eli brightened, gave Kieran a quick smile, took his hand from Maureen's arm, and signed back *Thank you*.

"I didn't know you knew how to sign, Father," she said, handing the missalette back.

"Just a few. But it's important to meet people where they are, don't you think?"

He smiled and shook Eli's hand, then turned to greet Danny and Levi behind them, who looked shy but stepped up.

Kieran shuffled them out the side door so the crowd could keep flowing when he felt a hand clamp on his shoulder. Looking back, Sean was at his ear.

"Who's the guy?"

Kieran stepped just outside the door to let others pass and turned to Eli, who was with their ma.

"Eli, this is my brother Sean."

Eli extended his hand. Sean reached across Kieran to meet it.

"Nice to meet you, Sean," Eli said.

Kieran saw Sean look his way before returning to Eli. He knew what his brother was thinking, hearing his boyfriend's voice for the first time. Eli beat him to it.

"I'm deaf mostly. But I can do okay if you take it slow."

Kieran locked eyes with Eli for a moment before realizing Sean was looking between the two of them.

"Sean. Aren't you going to introduce Caitlin?" their ma asked.

Sean was still looking between him and Eli, like he was looking for something.

"Hi, Eli. I'm Caitlin." She reached across and shook his hand.

"Lands sakes, boy. What's gotten into you?" Maureen reached for Caitlin's arm and started toward the parking lot, where Danny and Levi were waiting by the edge.

Kieran reached for Eli's hand and followed, knowing Sean was just behind.

They stopped under a streetlamp. Snow was falling slow and steady.

"That was such a beautiful Mass," his ma was saying to Danny and Levi as they approached. Light snow had started, the flakes illuminating like a snow globe under the lamp. Danny and Levi seemed to be dancing on their toes trying to keep warm.

"What did you think, Eli?" His ma turned to look directly at him, still holding Caitlin's arm.

Sean pulled Kieran back a step just outside the streetlamp's beam. "Who's this guy?"

Kieran wasn't sure he wanted to get into it right here. "Eli."

"I *know that,*" his brother said, trying to keep his voice down. Kieran could see everyone talking under the streetlight, but Danny kept looking their way.

"He's my — my boyfriend."

Kieran watched his brother's face, dimly lit from the snow falling in the yellow light. He looked over at Danny, who immediately walked around the group toward them.

Sean leaned forward and stage-whispered. "Wait. You're — *a fag*?"

Kieran stepped back. Sean was too close.

"What's your problem, Sean?"

Danny stood between them, getting into his older brother's face. Sean took a step back, but Danny stood firm.

Sean glanced over at his ma — standing with Caitlin and Levi — then leaned around Danny toward Kieran. "What the fuck, Kieran? Does ma know?"

He began to nod, but Danny took over.

"What's the matter, Sean? Never seen a *fag* before, huh?"

"You know?"

Sean seemed to back down. Danny stood firm.

"I'm a fag, too, Sean."

Kieran's eyes went wide. He had never seen Danny stand up to his brother like this.

"What?" Sean shook his head like he'd misheard.

"Levi's my boyfriend." Danny tipped his head toward the small group, who were all looking their way now.

"You're fuckin' kidding — "

"Sean Michael Callahan. Watch your language. We're still at the house of the Lord, ya hear!"

His ma boxed his ear, quick. Danny stepped back and turned to look at Levi.

"You know about — them?" Sean pointed through the snowflakes toward Kieran, then over at Danny.

His ma turned and looked, then back to Sean. "What are you spouting on about?"

"Kieran and —"

Kieran felt someone take his hand and turned to see Eli stepping next to him. It felt reassuring.

"I think Eli is sweet." Caitlin came up beside her fiancé and gave Kieran and Eli a small smile.

"Has the world lost its mind?" Sean looked at her, then scanned everyone looking back at him, the snow falling harder now, collecting on their coats.

"I've a right mind to ask Father O'Brien over there to come —"

"Let's go, Caitlin." Sean cut her off and turned to walk away.

"Don't you turn away from me when I'm speaking to you, young man."

"*Ma* —"

"Don't you *ma* me, either. You may be older, but I'm still your mother, and the good Lord put me on this earth to raise my children right. Now, if you have a problem with your brothers, you sit down and talk it over like a *man*. Don't you go running off like your father, you hear."

Kieran saw Sean's eyes. Stunned. He looked over and caught Danny's. His ma stood firm. For a moment, no one said a word. The night breeze moved the snow across their faces, frozen breath misting around them.

"Kieran."

"Yes, ma."

"You go on home with Eli."

"You sure, ma?"

"You ask Eli if that's alright."

Kieran turned and tried to speak to him, but it was too dark. He pulled Eli's hand and walked him over toward the streetlamp before signing what just happened. Eli nodded immediately. *Of course.*

"He said *of course,* ma."

"Danny, you go with your brother for now. We'll figure out everything in the morning."

Sean looked over at their younger brother, confused.

"Kieran, ask Eli if he's all right with Danny tonight, too."

He did. *Of course,* Eli signed back.

"It's fine, ma."

Levi looked over at Danny, nervous.

"Sean Michael. You, Caitlin, and me are gonna go home and have some words. You hear?"

Sean looked down, mumbling something Kieran couldn't catch.

His ma walked over to Danny and kissed him on the temple, pulled Levi into a brief hug, and stepped over toward Eli. She stood right under the lamp, where he could see her.

"You're a good soul, Eli. Thank you for helping this old woman."

"I'm happy to do whatever you need, Maureen."

She patted his lapel and nodded. Then turned her head slightly toward Kieran.

"Kieran. You let me talk tonight. Okay?"

"Yes, ma."

"Good boy."

She turned back to Eli and pulled him into a hug.

"Merry Christmas, son."

Kieran wiped a stray snowflake from his cheek.

A snowflake.

Chapter Twenty-One

KIERAN WOKE.

The room was dark. Not like his room at home, where light from the streetlamp outside always bled through. And it was quiet. Too quiet. No fridge motor purring down the hall. No radiator gurgling.

He turned his head, looking for his clock radio. Wasn't there.

Then he remembered.

Eli was breathing beside him, slow and steady, his arm draped warm across Kieran's chest. Kieran lay still, letting himself wake the rest of the way.

The shape of the room came in slowly as his eyes adjusted. The dresser. The desk against the wall. The frames arranged on it in a pattern — him and Eli in the center, Eli and Niles in the gold frame off to the right, angled. The chair in the corner where they'd dumped their clothes on the way to bed. Eli's teddy bear sitting beneath them, half-covered.

This was the first time he'd slept in the same bed with Eli. He'd dreamt of it since their first kiss last Halloween, but —

Kieran felt embarrassed, thinking about how long it took him to come out to his ma. So much time wasted. He could've been sleeping next to Eli's warm body, held in his chest, his back pulled close, Eli's legs intertwined. But he couldn't stay, not without his ma starting to ask questions about why he hadn't come home.

He exhaled a small laugh. Ironic that his ma was the one who'd told him to stay with Eli last night.

Last night.

He'd forgotten. It was Christmas. He smiled, thinking how cliché it might sound, but he'd already gotten his present. He nudged his butt back into Eli, feeling a little naughty. Eli groaned softly. Kieran stopped. He didn't want to wake him. Lying here was something he knew he'd always remember — more than their first kiss.

Or maybe second-most. The first he'd hold onto was from last night, after they got home.

Home?

Kieran closed his eyes, but stayed awake, thinking. This really felt like home.

His mind wandered, the way it always did when he didn't have to get out of bed but was already awake. Thinking of this and that.

Home. It was too early to let his mind go down *that road* just yet. But it felt nice to think about.

He'd need to get back to his house, though. He hadn't brought a change of clothes. That had been his excuse, actually — last night. He giggled, remembering. Told Eli he needed to sleep naked because he didn't have a change of underwear for the morning. Joking. Teasing him. But Eli had shrugged and said he slept naked anyway, then stripped. Kieran's face had gone red, but he'd followed suit. Eli flipped off the lights. It wasn't until nearly three that they got to sleep.

Kieran opened his eyes and let them wander around the room again. The teddy bear, sleepy and resigned on the chair. The clothes piled over it. They hadn't gotten home until a little after two.

They'd had to drop Levi off back at his house. He'd wanted to stay with Danny, but Eli had gone into dad mode and told him no. Susan would be awake waiting. Besides, it was Christmas. She'd want him home. Levi had tried to protest, then switched up to ask if Danny could stay with him instead, but Eli had been right. They didn't have time to explain what had happened. Levi had given Danny a kiss goodnight and they'd left.

Kieran smiled, remembering Eli yelling over to them on the porch steps to get a room, and Danny sassing back, *We're trying to!*

Graham hadn't been awake when they walked in, but Kieran figured he wouldn't mind Danny staying down the hall in the guest bedroom. He was pretty sure Danny didn't mind it either.

Kieran rolled onto his back. Eli nudged closer and laid his head on Kieran's chest, then started a low snore. He'd never had this before. He was the short skinny guy. It felt a little out of place, having his boyfriend lying on his chest. He'd always thought it would be the other way around.

He felt Eli's breath roll across his bare skin, felt his dark hair, and began to run his fingers through the short waves while staring up at the ceiling.

He wondered if his ma had made Sean talk last night, or if they were going to this morning. He and Danny had always been closer, but he'd never thought Sean would call him a *fag*. He didn't know why. He'd thought, if anyone, it would be his ma who had a problem.

He didn't hate Sean. He kinda felt sorry for him. Maybe he should've told him earlier — eased him into it. Instead of springing it on him at Mass. Maybe Sean was just startled. Caitlin had seemed cool with it. She'd even seemed to really like Eli. She'd help Sean, he figured.

But he didn't want to go home. At least not today. Everything felt awkward. And he'd never been able to yell back at Sean. Danny would, though. Just like last night.

Kieran imagined Danny and Sean rolling around on the living room floor, his ma trying to break it up. Danny was out for blood when he thought you'd done him wrong. Kieran wondered if he'd be even worse now that he was dating Levi. He always seemed to be the protector. He wondered what Levi must think of their family.

"Mmmerry Christmas, babe." Eli stretched and spoke at the same time, then leaned up on his side, propping his head on his hand and looking right into Kieran's eyes.

Kieran lifted up to kiss him softly, then lay back, his smile a mile wide.

"Merry Christmas, baby."

"*Baby?* I'm a *man*. Uggg." Eli teased, making caveman grunts. Kieran laughed, lifted the sheets, looked down, lowered them, and nodded. "Yes. Yes you are."

It was the first time he'd seen Eli blush. He ducked his head and tried to cover himself with the comforter.

Kieran reached over to play tug-of-war, trying to pull the covers off, before Eli won — ripping everything off Kieran and exposing his entire body to the cold room.

"Hubba hubba!" Eli teased, looking him up and down. Kieran grabbed at the sheet to cover himself, his face redder than Eli's had been a moment ago.

"Stop it!"

"Never!" Eli jumped on top of Kieran's chest, pinning him down, and blew raspberries against his neck. Kieran squirmed.

"Uncle! Uncle!"

Eli kept going, then reached his lips and settled into a longer kiss. Sweet. Kieran melted.

Eli lifted his head and smiled down at him.

"I —" Kieran caught himself.

"What?"

Kieran looked away. Eli reached up and turned his face back, gently.

"I want to try something." His cheeks went red again. "If that's okay."

Eli sat back. The covers slipped — and Kieran's eyes followed.

"Eyes up here." Eli laughed and pointed at his own face.

Kieran went redder. Sat up. Raised his hands.

He looked nervous. He started to sign.

He pointed to himself. He closed both hands into fists and crossed them over his chest. He pointed at Eli.

Eli watched, taking it in — Kieran, looking hopeful, saying it the way he had hoped he might. Eli raised his hands.

He pointed to himself. He closed both hands into fists and crossed them over his chest. He pointed at Kieran.

I love you.

The Oltrarno Passages

The Far Bank is the second book in **The Oltrarno Passages**, a series following the lives of Levi, Danny, Eli, Kieran, Anthony, Graham, and the family they've found in one another — set alongside the continuing tales of Marco and Alessandro that Graham and Simon first brought to life together.

Their stories are far from over.

About the Author

Michael Manosca first pursued a career in the arts, studying in Chicago, but storytelling has always been at the heart of his creative expression. His travels across the world have shaped his perspective, infusing his writing with the depth and nuance of the people and cultures he has encountered.

Michael writes in a deeply personal format, inspired by the relationships and experiences that shaped his upbringing. He explores the intricacies of friendship, the search for identity, and the quiet moments that define us. Through vivid characters and emotional depth, he hopes to craft stories that linger in readers' minds long after the final page.

When not writing, he can be found wandering the northern woods, exploring new cities, or enjoying a lively conversation in a tucked-away café. He currently resides along the western coast of the United States and is already working on his next story.

Also by Michael Manosca

Beyond Ties that Bind

Treffen

Bloodlines

Prism

Almost Always

Reflections at the Window

By Lantern Light

Flickering

A Language of Water

Static & Signals

The Oltrarno Passages: Across the Arno

www.ingramcontent.com/pod-product-compliance
Lightning Source LLC
La Vergne TN
LVHW030917080826
845145LV00013B/2934

* 9 7 8 1 9 6 9 9 1 5 1 7 8 *